Praise for PUPPET CHILD
(Talia Carner's previously published novel)

- TOP 10 FAVORITE FIRST NOVELS 2002
  …a stunning book, gripping and thought provoking. Carner and Puppet Child deserve a huge audience….
  —Book Browse (www.BookBrowse.com)
- OUTSTANDING AUTHOR AWARD 2003
  …a fantastic book. It made me cry and feel for these characters. Talia Carner's writing style is phenomenal… next best-seller!
  —Book Review Cafe (www.BookReviewCafe.com)
- …engrossing, carefully researched novel…compelling popular tale of intrigue, suspense, and romance… harrowing in detail and psychologically astute….
  —The Independent (East Hampton & Southampton)
- …a masterful storyteller has crafted a riveting plot…rich character development and constant surprises …a suspense-packed story!
  —Big Apple Parent (www.ParentsKnow.com)
- "A passionate book that is hard to put down….The book lends itself to provoking discussion…."
  —The Times-Beacon-Record (Feature article)
- …a socially issues narrative …an emotionally compelling drama.
  —Midwest Book Review
- An author with the power to make a difference in society. …Excellent narrative blends with compelling dialog…. a must read.
  —BookLore, (www.BookLore.co.uk)
- …this is a gripping and plausible page-turner that is very highly recommended.
  —Dead Trees Reviews (www.DeadTreeReview.com)
- …action-packed, fast-paced, breath-holding novel kept me turning the pages long after bedtime…This dynamic book will not be finished, put down and forgotten.
  —Book Loons Book Reviews (www.BookLoons.com)
- A powerful modern day social tale that pulls no punches as Talia Carner wastes no words...
  —The Best Reviews (www.TheBestReviews.com)
- …Carner has woven an intricate story from a sensitive subject...From the amazing opening until the very last page, I was hooked!…
  —Huntress Book Reviews (www.HuntressReviews.com)

- …provides enthralling, "thinking" reading for courtroom buffs and legal thriller lovers. …solid, well-researched commentary provides poignant and topnotch suspense….

  —Rebecca's Reads Book Reviews [India]
  (www.rebeccasreads.com)

- A Silver Award! …Talia Carner wastes no words….This book is a powerhouse….

  —Blether [Scotland] (www.blether.com)

- …a page turner filled with action, surprise and suspense…

  —Anton News, "Boulevard" (www.Antonnews.com)

- …The final chapters mount the suspense, bringing the work to a dramatic conclusion…

  —Timeless Tales (www.timelesstales.net)

- The story is compelling… exciting and realistic, making it a book we recommend.

  —SA Report (By Joan Zorza)

- …a story fraught with tension…. grips you and dares you to read further. …tension grows with each turning of the page.

  —Books n' Bytes (www.booksnbytes.com)

- …The story unfolds with many twists and turns…difficult to put down…. The author has succeeded admirably.

  —ReviewsOfBooks (www.ReviewsOfBooks.com)

- …a novel of almost pure suspense … a well-written, gut-wrenching, heart-breaking novel that is impossible to put down.

  —Curled Up With A Good Book (www.CurledUp.com)

- Carner skillfully depicts the myriad laws and politics that shape our courts….Puppet Child is a heart wrenching tale… expertly woven to its dramatic conclusion.

  —Women On Writing (www.WomenOnWriting.com)

- …A gripping and plausible page-turner…highly recommended.

  —ViewReviews (www.ViewReviews.com)

- Prepare to be stunned by a master storyteller who writes with passion and power in an arena none dared enter before…..

  —Nancy Robinson Masters, author, "All My Downs Have Been Ups."

- Beware: It is one very difficult book to put down…. Kudos to Carner for the courage to write so compellingly about judicial injustice…

  —Susan O'Neill, Author," Don't Mean Nothing: Short Stories of Viet Nam."

- …a sensitively crafted, solidly researched novel that carries the cold ring of truth and impels the reader to hang on to find out who will win....

    —Annie Blachley, Correspondent, The New York Times/The Los Angeles Times & Author, "Good Medicine."

...Talia Carner has brilliantly exposed a sensitive subject without exploitation or treacly sentiment. ...a novel that sparkles with intelligence and is as momentous as today's news.

    —Judith Richards, author, "Summer Lightning" and "Too Blue To Fly."

A Must Read. Both compelling and entertaining, Puppet Child will leave you breathless...

    —Kay Allenbaugh, author, "Chocolate for a Woman's Soul series."

A gut wrenching story of injustice, rescue and responsibility that grips you from Chapter One and never lets go. ...delivers a gutsy heroine and suspense to the last page.

    —Chris Gilson, author, "Crazy for Cornelia"

Taut, suspenseful and enlightening! ...Carner's novel is relevant ...beautifully told, a simultaneously heartbreaking and life-affirming page-turner you won't soon forget.

    —Ruth Knafo Setton, author, "The Road To Fez."

China Doll

A novel

Talia Carner

Talia Carner

Dec. 2007

MECOX HUDSON

Published by Mecox Hudson, New York, NY and Windsprint Press, Kansas City, MO.
www.MecoxHudson.com
PO Box 230174, Ansonia Station, NY 10023

Library of Congress Cataloging in Publication Data
Carner, Talia Y.
China Doll: a novel / Talia Carner
p. cm.
1. Intercountry adoption-Fiction. 2. Americans China
-Fiction. 3. Orphanages-China. 4. Adoption-Fiction I. Title

813'.54-dc21   2006922098

ISBN: 978-0-9773821-2-5

Cover design by Nili Glazer, www.NiliStudio.com
Author's photo by Robbie, www.PhotosByRobbie.com
Interior design by Robert Aulicino, www.aulicinodesign.com

To my father, Yitzhak Yoffe (1917-1991), who taught me that a parent's love is not biology.

To the voiceless abandoned babies of China. This is my song for you.

Full many a flower is born to blush unseen
And waste its sweetness on the desert air.

—Thomas Gray, *Elegy Written in a Country Churchyard*

PART ONE

The Butterfly Kite

One joy scatters a hundred griefs.
—A Chinese proverb

Chapter 1

October 2000

The stage lights were dazzling, the drumbeats victorious, the cheering intoxicating. They exploded as though they had lain in wait throughout the years it had taken Nola to get here. She clutched the microphone, and her voice lifted above the ceremonial courtyard of the Supreme Harmony Palace, above the audience of thousands with rapture in their eyes. Yesss. These people were hers, and she was theirs. Here in the Forbidden City, she stood on the very spot where emperors of the Ming and Qing dynasties had exhorted, decreed and ordained. But while the emperors' words had instilled fear, her songs released joy.

"We are tall, we are short, we're black, we're white,
We are blessed or are cursed by fate or birthright.
But the whole world over,
Peace is the color of a dove,
And we all share,
The feeling of love."

Yes! Nola tapped her feet and flipped her head from side to side, hair swinging. The crowd was on its feet, blurry through the tangle of her rust-colored curls. She repeated the refrain in French, Spanish, and then Chinese to a field of swaying arms as thousands sang along. Their voices carried beyond the southern wall of the Forbidden City into Tiananmen Square. Eleven years after the massacre, she was the lucky one to honor the dead—and the living.

"And we all share,
The feeling of love. Love. Love."

The breeze caressed her hot skin. She held the last note until a new round of applause exploded. "Thank you," she called, her body resonating with the beat of the music, eager to go on. "Thank you all so very much!"

Wade, her husband, stepped out of the left wing with a glass of water. "A Divine Songbird," he mouthed. It was the title *People* magazine had given her fifteen years before, when she had burst on the scene as a teenager. She gulped down the water and turned back toward the crowd.

Her gown felt light and fluid as it streamed over her body and its sequined glitter captured the rosy glow of the stage lights. She raised her arm high to unfurl the train of her dress, attached to her wrist. Like a butterfly's wing, it flashed from pink to orange to a fiery red.

The crowd roared, demanding another encore. The hooded-eyed Chinese prime minister, seated in his cordoned box, rose to his feet and clapped. His lips read, "Bravo! Bravo!" and Nola lifted her eyes to the inky sky where her song lingered, where her mother was surely watching, still disbelieving that Nola could ever make it.

The fragrance of honeysuckle and orange blossoms wafted through the night air. Nola's fingers brushed the cords in her neck, taut, ready for more. Behind her, the band broke into "A String of Magical Moments," and she was back with the thousands of upturned faces, singing to them and wishing this magical moment would never end. What else was there? Her offstage life, just several feet away, loomed colorless and stifling.

But Wade's hand signaled a T from behind the silk-embroidered curtain. Her time was up. If he didn't monitor the instant the audience's fervor for her peaked, she would linger like a guest overstaying her welcome.

Single flowers wrapped in fine rice paper and bouquets tied with silk ribbons flew up and landed at her feet. Stealing time, she gathered a few flowers, selected an orchid and presented it to Jean-Claude, her musical director. He tossed his shaggy dark hair off his shoulders, and his eyes held hers in a shared moment of victory. Reluctantly, she broke the contact, blew a kiss to her musicians and waved again to the crowd. "I love you so very much," she said into the microphone.

With rehearsed grace she glided off the stage, her head turned back to the light as though it were oxygen. HBO's overhead camera zoomed away on its cable across the plaza to take in the mass of people, while the crane camera, hanging on its jib, coasted just above Nola's head. It followed her until she rounded the curtain. In the sudden darkness, hands caught her as she groped her way backstage. The video crew Wade had hired in hopes of selling footage to the smaller networks made room for her to pass. Her eyes strained to adjust. Perspiration collected in the hollows of her collarbones and trickled down between her breasts. She gathered up her hair with both hands and someone dabbed her face, neck and back with a cold sponge. She shut her eyes, listening to the audience out there. In the rising collective murmurs of the dispersing crowd there was a resignation to the fact that there would be no more music tonight. Her best show ever was over, and she had triumphed.

An arm wrapped around her sticky skin. Nola recognized it before she heard Wade's voice.

"I'm so proud of you!," he said. "Lucky the audience missed that B flat—"

Her eyes still shut, her chest heaving, she cut him off. "Not even Yanni got this many encores here." She wiped her face with a small towel, surreptitiously dabbing her eyes before opening them fully. She let out a spent smile. In her high heels, she looked directly at Wade's newly laminated teeth. Wade Dalton, her husband, her manager. Seldom her lover.

"Tonight you've conquered China," she heard a man say.

Her glance took in the tall Eurasian in a black suit, who stood a step away, his body so still he seemed unaffected by the activity around them.

Wade slapped the man's shoulder. "Daniel Chen, the U.S. Cultural Attaché to China."

A reserved smile played on the planes of the man's cheeks and in the eyes that hinted at his Chinese genes. His gaze was direct—not curious, but possessing knowledge. With a nod, Daniel Chen handed Nola a small brocade box tied with gold string. His fingers were long and tapered, like those of a pianist.

"Nola's the best goodwill ambassador the U.S. ever had here," Wade said. When the man did not reply, he added, "It was a fortunate turn of events that the Chinese rejected Madonna. Too racy for them."

Untying the string, Nola shot Wade a look that said to ease up. This dignified man must have heard the criticism Wade had leveled at her. And Daniel Chen must have known that several other almost-at-the-top singers like her had vied for the spot Wade had somehow managed to win for her.

Daniel Chen did not even glance in Wade's direction, but regarded Nola like a man trying to read her, not a fan in the presence of a star. She wondered why, given his job title, he had made himself scarce in the few days she'd been in China.

Her stylist draped a shawl over her shoulders. She winked at him in a gesture of thanks.

"Fifteen minutes to change before your grand backstage exit." Wade's teeth shone like those of an animal in the presence of a rival. He patted Nola's bottom, and, responding to a signal from the producer, walked away, taking the assistants with him.

Nola released the lid of the box. On a bed of ruffled satin lay a small, disk-shaped bottle. She held it up to the light to study the miniature image of a firebird, its tail feathers curling downward through the cage bars.

"It's not painted on the bottle's exterior, but underneath the glass!" she exclaimed and examined the dainty, exact brushstrokes. "How exquisite."

Daniel Chen finally spoke again. "It's the ancient Chinese art of reverse painting. The last details are drawn first, inside the bottle." His voice was unassuming, yet wrapped around something solid. "The artist figures out where to place the wisps of feathers before there's a wing."

The snuff bottle's opening was tiny, the details smaller than she thought possible. What was the subtle Chinese meaning of this gift? Nola's nail traced the fine lines of magenta and mint and aqua in the curling tail. "This is the finest piece of art I've ever seen," she whispered.

"Like your art," Daniel said. "Few historical figures have imprinted words on people's hearts the way you did tonight. Your songs unite people with universal emotions."

Some admirers' words thrilled her more than others'. A surge of her earlier euphoria swelled up in her. "Thanks." She smiled at him and was surprised at the glimmer of green in his eyes.

Her stomach rumbled. The only food in her dressing room would be a banana for her potassium fix, but it would have to do. She started walking toward the area below the stage, fearing reaching her dressing room, her reentry to her empty off-stage world. Daniel matched his steps to hers while her bodyguard hung back at a respectable distance.

"You have more power than you may know," Daniel said.

She laughed softly. "The only 'power' a singer has is to make people happy for the moment, for the hour, maybe for the day."

"Ms. Sands, there's a place you should see."

"You must be the one who prepared my itinerary. Isn't it full?"

His gaze penetrated her, cutting through glamour and fame. "It's an orphanage that's not on your official schedule."

She tightened the shawl about her. We are blessed or are cursed by fate or birthright.

Daniel could not know how narrowly she had escaped being one of those institutionalized children herself, nor could he know that her foundation supported such homes; Wade had hidden certain facts of her life.

"I'm sure your cause is worthy," she said, her tone tender. "But I can't risk offending my hosts." Or Wade. Or the orchestrated plan that, at long last, had taken her to the top.

"Sorry. I don't mean to impose on you."

Her finger found a sharp corner of the small gift box. The edge pressed the soft tissue. "We each give what we can," she said, and resumed walking.

The sucking sound of a hydraulic lift, the banging of hammers and the shouts of stagehands calling orders grew louder. A couple of assistants peeked at her and disappeared, but their presence hung in the air like an order to prepare for her next obligation.

She tossed her hair back. "What does a cultural attaché do? China doesn't get enough visiting American artists to keep one busy."

"I'm on a human rights watch for the United States."

"Oh. My goodwill concert tour is merely a distraction, I guess."

Across the crescent crease of his smile she noticed the fine slash of a scar. "Judging by tonight's performance, a welcome break," he said.

At a narrow hallway of straw mats and canvas sheets nailed over two-by-fours, bare light bulbs threw shadows down more arteries that criss-crossed under the stage and were teeming with people. Four of her American musicians huddled together, and the sweet smell of marijua-na reached Nola. She would ignore it; the musicians had worked hard for her tonight.

Wade would have raised hell, for the Chinese authorities had warned they'd cancel the entire tour if anyone were caught with illegal drugs.

She caught Daniel glancing at three security men as they beamed their flashlights behind partitions. "Deranged fans can pull off demented stunts," she said by way of explanation, "and Wade's not one to leave anything to chance."

"Neither would the Chinese," he said. "Dissidents are under house arrest in each of the six cities of your tour."

A string tugged in her heart. "I'm so sorry," she said. "Is there anything I can do for them?"

"You are bringing a taste of democracy. Their confinement is the small price they're willing to pay."

She stopped in front of her door, her hand on the bamboo latch, hesitating to undo it. From the next room over rolled the laughter of her stylist and his staffers. Two roadies, wearing the tour's black Double Happiness shirts that sported the Chinese four-loop calligraphy in gold, squeezed a dolly down the narrow passage. She waved at them to pass while Daniel flattened himself against the wall.

She cracked the door open, wishing to linger, even if she wasn't up to Daniel's challenge. "Thanks for the gift," she said. "I'll cherish it."

"Thank you for your gift of music." Again that hint of a smile played in the corner of his lips.

Nola shut the door behind her, dropped into an armchair upholstered in brocade, and kicked off her shoes. The room, although temporary, was filled with mahogany furniture, brocade draperies, silk rugs, lamps, *objets d'art*. Wade had spared no expense in creating for her a scene of unbridled excess. A beautiful interview setting. A dungeon of loneliness.

She wiggled her toes on the rug with its lone pink lily floating on blue water and dropped her face into her hands. She heard Wade outside keeping journalists and assistants at bay until she "freshened up." She would rather he let them all in—the reporters, musicians, staffers and stylists. Anything to put the stagnant air in motion. Even have Wade come in and, for once, love her for who she was—not the performer, but the person. In her head, a bass chord gathered force. Surrounded by people, she had no one. How different would she have felt had her parents and sister been here, or anywhere. She started to cry.

The words of Janis Joplin, who had been a friend of her parents, echoed through her mind. "Tonight I made love to thousands of people, but I went home alone."

A flock of stylists and assistants were tending to her hair and face, massaging her feet, and fluffing her ice-blue dress. Wade strode in, muttering into his cell phone. His solid figure looked tapered in his Italian-cut tux. He covered the mouthpiece, examined Nola's gown, and one of his pale blue eyes winked. "You're beautiful, Honey. Ready for the big exit scene?" He gave her bottom a pat, and she felt her nostrils flare in annoyance. She would speak to him about this gesture, even if it meant opening the gate to an argument.

Jean-Claude, a small-framed man with big nose and ears and motorized by nervous energy, drained a glass of champagne. "One concert down, five more to go, and you'll be the star on top of every Christmas tree. Ten million more records sold! Didn't I promise?" Jean-Claude asked in his French accent, an affectation, no doubt. He had too good an ear not to have perfected his pronunciation after nine years in New York. He blew Nola a kiss and dipped into a floor-sweeping bow that reset her mood. "And now I must breast-feed my musicians. *A bientôt.* See you soon at the hotel party, my Ginger Goddess."

She laughed at the name he had coined for her reddish hair. "*A bientôt,*" she mimicked him. "I love you, but you're crazy."

He jumped and kicked his heels. "Cute-crazy. Good-crazy, yes?"

"The best there is." Wade made a play of punching Jean-Claude's shoulder and let out a rolling laugh. Nola smiled. A long time ago, when Wade had discovered her singing the national anthem at her high school football game, she had adored his carefree laughter.

"Nola!" called out thousands of fans. "Nola!"

She stepped out the Gate of Heavenly Purity and onto a marble bridge. Wade kept half a step behind, but his gentle touch on her left elbow instructed her to pause for the cameras. Nola squeezed her arm against the feel of his hand to draw from his strength. Her other hand skimmed along the marble dragon head carved into the banister, rich and sensuous to her touch. For a wild instant she thought of jumping onto the sleek banister and sliding down, her arms and legs stretched out in abandon. "Whoopee!" she'd call out and slide right into the loving arms of these people—

"Nola! Nola!"

Around her, marble balustrades glistened in the moonlike glow that poured from concealed light panels, also a part of the set. Smiling at the popping flashbulbs and the miniature green tally lights of the live TV cameras, she adjusted the chiffon shawl of her dress so its blue-beaded edges would sparkle. She savored the excited faces and clapping hands. This was where she belonged, what she had worked for, for so long.

The bridge curved onto a red-carpeted path through the crowd. Policemen formed human chains to keep people back. There had never been this many. Nola flinched at the sight of her own security men shoving admirers and reporters away, but like gushing water, people rushed back to close in behind her as soon as her staff moved on. This, too, was orchestrated. The limousine could have whisked her away through the back gate instead of parking seventy feet away, but Wade knew to exploit every photo op, and she was grateful for it.

The small young woman moved so fast that Nola had no chance to comprehend what was going on. The woman with cropped black hair burst from the crowd, ferreted under the arms of the policemen, and thrust a bundle against Nola's chest. Someone yelled, "A bomb!" but instinctively, even before Nola's mind could register what her arms did, she grabbed it.

She was still absorbing the impact when the wriggling confirmed what some part of her already knew: It was a baby.

By then, the woman had sprinted away and disappeared into the crowd. The two security men chasing her halted in their tracks to scrutinize the sea of people. Network producers frantically gestured "Keep rolling!" Nola heard Wade's "God Almighty!" mingled with the shouts of the paparazzi as their flashbulbs exploded in her face.

A tiny foot in a red sock kicked and freed itself from the package in her arms until an ankle rested on her forearm. Was this some publicity stunt she hadn't been told about? Dazed, Nola lifted the blanket off the tiny head. A smile bloomed on the round face with its dark, almond-shaped eyes, and an arm rose up to touch Nola's nose.

She smiled down. "Hello to you, too." The little body was light, but solid. How old was this baby? Was this some bizarre prop?

Reporters thrust their microphones toward her. "Who was that woman?" "Did you stage this?" "How much did you pay for the baby?" "Is that a girl?"

In an instant, all sights and sounds around Nola receded, leaving behind this incredible surprise. The moment was incomprehensible, yet there was an order to the chaos, as though this event were written in a script she hadn't yet read. She gazed down at the little face, at the eyes so wide and trusting, and the word that ran through her head—illogical, implausible, capricious—was "mine."

Photographers pushed closer to Nola, their cameras closing in on her. Excited clucking rose from the crowd. Shouts from network reporters drowned out one another. Nola scanned the crowd as the security staff shoved them away. In the chaos, no one seemed eager to reclaim the infant. Policemen yelled. Some ran after the woman.

It all seemed so far away. The bubble of calm that enveloped her and the baby shimmered with bliss, pushing away her ache over Wade, her parents and her sister.

She bent her head and brushed her lips against the baby's crown. "Mine," she whispered, telling herself that she must be nuts to be so happy.

Chapter 2

"We've had our share of crazies, but never anything like this," Wade said. Still leading Nola on the red carpet toward to the limousine, he reached out to take the baby from her arms, but she pressed it closer to her chest. The baby's soft fist clutched her finger.

"Not yet," Nola mumbled, a part of her mind still hanging back in disbelief.

"Smile for the cameras," Wade whispered, his lips unmoving.

Leslie, her choreographer and stylist, walked backward like a crab and bobbed his shaved head in astonishment. He snapped his fingers. "Hocus pocus. It saves me calling the bellboy to order one."

Five police officers broke through the circle of Nola's security men and motioned that they would take the baby. She straightened and shook her head. Her feet carried her toward her double-stretch limousine. Wade flanked her on one side while her bodyguard helped her into the car.

"Send people to comb the place for the woman," Wade ordered him. "Go."

"All eight hundred temples and palaces?" replied the bodyguard.

The car doors closed on the world outside and the cacophony subsided. The air in the steel-and-glass cocoon was still. In Nola's lap, the baby stuck its fist in its mouth. Nola stroked the soft cheek and was rewarded with a big smile. The features were wonderfully delicate, like those of a painted porcelain doll.

"This was magic." Nola examined the fine eyebrows, the cupid mouth's lips, the feathery eyelashes, the rounded chin. The tip of her finger traced the contour of the cheek toward a tiny, perfectly formed ear. Who was the mother? Nola tried to bring back her brief sighting of the childlike woman who had been the giver of this extraordinary gift, but the image was blurry. *Thank you*, Nola said in her head. *You have no idea. Thank you a million times.*

Leslie slid closer. His smile drew creases around his mouth. "Isn't a baby proof of God's optimism?"

"This baby's people could be dangerous," Wade muttered. "God only knows whom we're dealing with. We can't get involved."

The infant let out a quick lolling of her tongue: "Lulululululululululu."

Nola burst out laughing. "You should teach me how to do that." She tried imitating the sound. "Lulu-lulu."

Her limousine swerved away toward the Gate of Heavenly Peace at the northern end of Tiananmen Square, shaking loose the last reporter. High on the red wall, a twenty-by-ten foot silk banner with Nola's picture flapped in the breeze. The billboard artist had made her seem taller than her five-foot-three and emphasized every Caucasian feature that was different from the average Chinese woman's. Her hazel eyes blazed in a cat-like green, her otherwise straight nose pointed up impertinently, her cheeks were carved hollow, and her hair flamed curlier and redder. The artist offered a peek into a cleavage more generous than Nola's already enhanced one. As the wind caught the silk banner, it bucked and flexed the muscles in the thigh gleaming through the slit of her dress and in the bicep of the arm holding the microphone.

Nola glanced at Wade for his reaction; he wasn't one to permit artistic freedom with his promotion plans. But Wade's gaze darted from her to Leslie, and back again. "You may be tickled, but you understand that this baby is not our problem. Right? For publicity, though, in front of all those cameras, you did well not dropping it before you knew what it was."

"This is China; 'it' must be a 'she,'" Leslie said.

Her finger clutched in the little fist, Nola gave herself to the sense of contentment. The baby's weight in her lap radiated happiness into the whole of her. Wade would never understand what a perfect ending the baby's appearance was to an exhilarating performance, just as he failed to comprehend the depth of her loneliness at other times.

The baby turned her head, searching for Nola's breast.

Nola smiled. "You won't find anything of interest there." She tapped on the driver's partition. "Please find a drugstore." She shifted the baby's position and chanted, "I'm sure you need diapers, and bottles, and formula—"

"Don't get carried away." Wade scratched his palm. "The Chinese will demand it back within the hour, I'm sure."

"Speaking of diapers," Leslie said as he took his hairdresser's cape out of his bag and tucked it under the baby, "your dress is too precious to serve as one."

The baby squirmed in Nola's arms, then, grabbing the diamond necklace, tried to pull herself up. Her arm was thin, yet strong.

"Take it easy." Wade reached to unclench the baby's fingers. "This is expensive stuff."

The infant's mouth, twin ruby cushions, curved down in the onset of a cry.

A wave of protectiveness washed over Nola. She flicked an angry look at Wade. "He didn't mean to hurt your feelings," she told the baby, and rocked her against her shoulder. The soft, yet solid body contoured right into hers. "Little Dumpling, I'll take good care of you."

The baby rolled her tongue as though trying to speak: "Lululululululululu."

"Lulu? Is that your name? It's a pretty one. Lulu."

The limousine drove on through the Forbidden City. At night, the majestic temples and secret-filled gardens lay dormant, as they had since the ousting of the last emperor, even though once taboo for common people, they were now open to all. As the car passed marble palaces, red-roofed pagodas, and moss-covered rocks, Nola felt more than saw the timeless beauty of the place. She rested her cheek on the silky crown, her breathing in rhythm with the baby's.

After a minute, Lulu began to whimper. The limousine slowed at an intersection. Nola stared into the depths of an ancient willow drooping over a pond and caught the shimmer of twinkling starlight. What now?

"How far is that drugstore?" she called out.

"This is not New York. This baby needs a wet nurse, and hundreds of people are waiting for you at the hotel ballroom. We're not going to stop." Wade flipped open his cell phone cover. "We'll find a discreet way to get rid of it."

"Her," Nola corrected. "Look how cute she is." Nola jiggled one of her gold-and-diamond drop earrings in front of Lulu and chanted, "Your mommy wanted me to make you happy. What kind of food do you eat? Do you need a diaper changed? A pacifier? Are you colicky?"

"Colicky! How come you know so much about babies?" Leslie asked.

Nola's emotions ricocheted off invisible walls of old doubts. She avoided meeting Wade's eyes, but felt him searching her face. "My innate resourcefulness," she told Leslie. Only Wade should be able to understand why she pulled the baby closer and rubbed her nose against the soft cheek.

Wade glanced at his watch and drummed his fingers on his teeth. Then he punched numbers on his phone. "Roberta? This is the damndest, weirdest thing. Another crazy fan," he said to Roberta Fisher, his publicity guru. "Get someone to take it off our hands. I'm sure the authorities will show up for it."

Lulu resumed crying.

"Shshshshhh. No one's taking you away." Nola flashed her beaded handbag in front of Lulu. Distracted, the baby tried to stuff its corner into her mouth.

By the time they reached the hotel and re-entered the clamor of popping flashbulbs and shouting reporters, Roberta had taken charge, and Lulu was crying.

"This is a *fabulous story.*" Roberta's voice could be heard on the other side of the street. A big-boned woman in her late forties with a poodle-like mop of brass-colored hair, "Big Mouth" Roberta had been a radio-show host on CNB's popular "Saturday All-Night Party." She had been forced to leave the station when listeners, offended by her faked on-air orgasms, boycotted the sponsors.

"This is not a 'story,' " Nola told her over the baby's cries.

"Sure it is. It happened right in front of the paparazzi. TV networks from a zillion countries have original footage. We might as well cook something delicious out of this."

"This is some bizarre conspiracy. We're being set up," Wade said.

"Elvis, maybe?" Roberta asked.

Nola stomped her foot. "You saw what happened. A young, desperate mother wanted to give her baby girl a better life." She stabilized her voice. "No evil intentions."

"That was no Easter bunny dropping an egg in your basket. A 'gotcha' is sure to come." Roberta pursed her fleshy lips. "We need a pre-emptive spin. I vote to offer a discreet, moderate sum if a family shows up. But until then, we milk this for all it's worth."

Every scheme Roberta came up with was exaggerated, a reflection of the woman herself. Refusing to be shaken out of her euphoria, Nola kept her attention on Lulu, but the baby was bawling, and the urgency of her needs vibrated in Nola's head.

"Don't cry, Dumpling. I'm going to feed you," she cooed. "Very soon."

"Nola, what does your husband say about this?" shouted a reporter. Others followed: "Are you planning to keep it?" "Is it deformed?" "What made the mother get rid of her child?"

"That's enough." Roberta raised her hand toward the reporters. Holding on to Nola, she barreled by the uniformed doormen. "You're not going to speculate about the who and why, Nola-pooh. You're a goodwill ambassador and you're going to stay away from the subject of why women in China abandon their baby girls. *Capeesh?*"

Behind Nola, Leslie lifted the short train of her dress. Lulu twisted in her arms and pitched herself forward, crying. Nola gathered in the flailing limbs. "I know you're hungry," she whispered while entering the hotel. "Do you want milk? Tofu?"

They reached the elevator to the penthouse suite. Yoram, her body-guard, hung behind, scanning their surroundings. A former Israeli commando officer, he had been hired by the insurance company that had issued the half-a-billion-dollar policy on Nola for this trip. He jumped into the elevator just before the doors closed.

"Hand it to one of the maids," Wade told Leslie. He snapped his fingers.

"Chop chop. We've got to go down to the ballroom in ten minutes."

Nola wished they would all just disappear so she could be alone with the baby. She rocked and sang to the infant, calming her, while Roberta bombarded the air.

"I'll grant an exclusive photo session to *People* magazine and reserve the personal interview with Nola for *Good Morning America*. What do you think, Wade? It will be broadcast live by satellite, right here from Beijing. And that *Vanity Fair* story we've been working on? Wow. We can still make the editorial deadline even if it's been put to bed. As we speak, they're processing tonight's photograph of Nola on stage for the cover. Nola, it was a good idea to make a national secret of your dress design. Right? Right. What time is it in New York? Twelve hours' difference? Right now, Eddie at People is watching CNN and salivating at her desk. Come to think of it, I should call Oprah. It's time she brought Nola on her show. You've been too much of a Little Red Riding Hood, but minus the wolf waiting for you on your way to Grandma's. No drama. Refusing to spill any childhood trauma. Now we've got a twist! What do you think of the headline 'Woman Unexpectedly Thrust Into Motherhood?' Nah. Something shorter. How about 'The Accidental Mother?' "

"This is hardly a case of 'motherhood,' " Wade grunted. "More like keeping a puppy when a friend's away, and it will be over very—very— soon, when the Chinese take it back."

"Uh-uh. Motherhood is in. At thirty-one, Nola's the right age. The perfect New-Age thing." Almost the girth of both Nola and Wade put together, Roberta grinned down at them and started panting. "I'm having an orgasm. We can get into *Good Housekeeping*. Let's give it a couple of months so Nola can decorate the nursery, concoct some baby-food recipes, what have you, then we'll schedule the cover story. Let's see, their lead time is three months." Her breathing grew harder. "Fab-uu-lous. That'll take us to late spring. Renewal, sunshine. Perfect timing."

Within the elevator's confines, Nola pressed against the wall, trying to envelope herself again in the bubble of happiness. *Shut up!* she wanted to shout. "Please let me concentrate," she said.

"I'm coming!" Roberta emitted a series of escalating groans. "Oh, it's so good—"

The Chinese elevator operator kept his face to the panel. In the mirror, Nola saw crimson climb up his cheeks, but Yoram, a young, dark string-bean, grinned at Roberta, and she winked at him in response.

"We get your point, girl." Wade rapped Roberta's back as though he was dislodging a fish bone stuck in her throat. "Let's stick to your specialty, which ain't sex."

"Big girls have twice the appetite but only half the opportunities." Roberta's booming laughter followed Nola as she hurried through the foyer. Wade crooked a finger at Yoram. The fighter who had beaten terrorists on the Lebanese border was in for a scolding.

In the dining room, Roberta screamed into the phone.

"That linebacker has no unexpressed thoughts," Nola said as she and Leslie retreated to the bedroom. "But did you hear? Her scheme includes keeping the baby," she added with delight. Whatever Roberta's reason was, it fit as though a spot had been ready within Nola.

She lay Lulu on the king-size bed, and the baby's wail resumed. Nola called the hotel kitchen and located an English-speaking order-taker who said she was a mother.

"What do you feed a baby?" Nola asked.

"How old?"

"—Uh—not a newborn." Nola pressed down Lulu's drooling lower lip and peeked at the twin white dots pushing the skin. A toothless gum closed on her finger. "Almost teeth, but not yet. And she tries to sit by herself," she added.

"Six-seven months old? I boil half-milk and half-water, and add rice flour to thicken it. Some sugar, too. Maybe scrambled egg?"

How was she to feed the baby an egg? With chopsticks? A spoon? Her sister Jenna had loved applesauce. Or perhaps it was one of the few foods her mouth could manage after the accident.

"What are you doing?" Leslie asked. "Wade told me to give her to a maid."

"The milk with rice flour sounds good. Thanks," Nola said into the phone and hung up. "I'm getting her a Coke."

She walked with Lulu to the small kitchenette and returned with a can. Seeing Leslie's raised brow, she said, "It was originally concocted by a pharmacist for tummy aches." When her mother was too stoned to go out for milk, nine-year-old Nola had often given baby Jenna Coke.

"You'll ruin your dress."

She turned her back to him. "Take it off until we go downstairs."

"We need to get going!" But he unzipped the dress, unhooked the built-in bra, and helped her step out. He held up an embroidered silk kimono sent over by the Chinese prime minister, and after she slipped into it, tied the robe's belt and adjusted the floppy sleeves. "Even the percussionists are packed by now and on their way to the party," Leslie murmured as he arranged the gown over a padded hanger on a wall hook.

"May I have some fruit juice?" Nola asked, stalling for time alone, and Leslie left through the door to the adjoining bedroom, now converted into a giant walk-in closet. In the room beyond, a staircase led down to a suite crowded with Leslie's and Wade's staffs in addition to local interpreters.

Hoping that Coke still contained its medicinal qualities, Nola soaked a rolled washcloth corner in the soda and gave it to Lulu. While Lulu sucked with vigor, Nola removed the cutout plastic bag that had been tied with a string over a sodden printed rag serving as a diaper. Before removing the cotton pants and frayed jacket that must have serviced generations of babies, Nola checked for a note. There was none.

Still sucking on the washcloth, Lulu pulled her foot up. Nola sponged the thin little buttocks, then fashioned one of her smallest T-shirts into a diaper and secured it with a hotel laundry plastic bag and Band-Aids. "Let's get your cute head in this other T-shirt," she told Lulu. "Where are your hands? Here they are! One, two … Tomorrow we'll get you clothes."

A maid brought in the diluted milk in a glass bottle and a used pacifier.

"Thanks." Nola cradled Lulu, surprised that the baby's fingers closed on the bottle as she sucked. Her brown eyes never left Nola's face. Their gaze was alert and intelligent.

In the silence that ensued, Nola stroked the soft skin of the baby's legs. It was warm and dry and so velvety to the touch that she wanted to let her fingers linger on it forever. She had forgotten the feel of Jenna's skin, so many years ago. "You're smart and beautiful," she murmured to Lulu, amazed anew at the rush of tenderness. In the ballroom on the mezzanine floor, a party was coming to life, and here she was alone, yet the bass note in her head was gone.

If only she could believe in herself.

After a while, Lulu let the rubber nipple pop out. Nola rose to pace the room, holding the compact body against her shoulder. Lulu laid her head in the crook of Nola's neck, utterly trusting and relaxed. *Mine.*

Just as Leslie returned, Nola heard the baby's burp and smelled the scent of milk.

"Did you hear that?" she whispered with a sense of achievement, as though she had passed a test. "I never thought it possible, but I'm in love with this little creature as much as if I'd given birth to her an hour ago."

"Where did you come from baby dear? Out of the everywhere, into the here," Leslie said, "George MacDonald, who died in 1905."

Nola laughed. "You're impossible. Get housekeeping to send up a crib."

"Keeping the puppy? Won't Wade be surprised."

"He'll indulge me." The Wade she had known until three years ago before they shifted the balance of their agent-artist relationship and married had never refused her. She stroked the baby's back. "He wants to keep me productive."

"But focused. No distractions." Leslie brought the tall glass with vitamin-fortified juice to Nola's mouth. He raised his watch to her eye level. "We'd better get going."

She glanced at him. Starting as her choreographer, Leslie had removed, one by one, the stylist, chef, hair-dresser and the theatrical makeup artist who stood in the way of his artistic vision. "I'd hate to start bickering with you. I hope you'll get over your shock and take my side," she said.

"When it comes to your fighting with Wade, I'm from the UN."

"We don't fight—"

Leslie's diamond studs sparkled as he looked toward the ceiling, addressing a divine entity. "I thought making the Olympic gymnastics team was exciting enough." He addressed Nola again. "The maid's waiting for the baby."

There was a knock on the door. Leslie opened it, and when Jean-Claude burst in, the emotional high of the evening blew back in. Nola's body remembered being the instrument that had absorbed and synthesized all her musicians' sounds.

"I want to tell you again how fantastic you were tonight." Jean-Claude kissed both her cheeks. "You make people homesick for something they have never had." His eyes traveled down her robe and stopped at her bare feet. "You're not dressed? Ginger, we're all waiting for you!"

She bounced Lulu as she replied, "Hold your horses, Uncle Jean-Claude. Have you met Lulu yet?"

A smirk plastered his narrow, angular face. "Who cares? They're a dime a million here. Let's go."

Lulu's bray was like the bleat of a wounded lamb. Nola shot Jean-Claude a warning look and cooed comforting sounds to the baby. "I need to settle her down—"

"I'm getting bad crazy." Jean-Claude's bony face grew taut and white. "You have dozens of people working for you, plus a whole hotel staff! Tonight's the biggest night not only of your career, but the careers of the musicians I've nurtured so that you could have the best band in the world—"

"Chill out. I'll be down in a minute—"

His large ears, sticking out through his unkempt hair, turned crimson. "It's our night, and you're ruining it! Our families are having block parties, with second cousins and neighbors' grandmas watching us on TV, jumping out of their skins with pride. And you wipe-ass for some orphan?"

Nola's fury tore through her voice. "What have you been snorting?"

"Since when have you become one of those chicks with runaway hormones?" He yanked Nola's gown off the wall hook and shook a finger near the baby's face. "Send it to the pound."

"Get out!" she yelled, as her hand covered Lulu's head.

Jean-Claude turned to Leslie, "What about your staff? Are you going to let her ruin everything for them, too?"

"Out!" Nola shouted.

His French curse was a string of undecipherable "f"s just before he slammed the door.

Nola's breathing came in short gasps.

"Don't let him upset you. It will show in the cameras," Leslie said.

"The cameras. Yes." She felt her nostrils flare. "After fifteen years in the music world, you'd think I'd be immune to all the loonies."

The mock flick of Leslie's wrist was incongruous with his G.I. Joe physique. "That's the other side of our genius."

Her heart still pounding, Nola bent her head toward Lulu. How quickly the bliss was punctured. "The trick is to ignore them all and just do what I want to do," she told Lulu, then halted. This was the first lie she'd told her baby.

"Jean-Claude's nuts, but you'd better be prepared to get some versions of his reaction with a baby around," Leslie said. He held up her dress to step into it.

Nola touched her burning forehead. "Don't remind me that I'm an industry, not a person," she mumbled. "Everyone has an agenda."

And Wade, her hero, she now suspected, might top the list.

Chapter 3

A tawny light crawled from the bathroom door onto the pillow they shared, and Wade's eyes shone tiger-yellow. Even after his flossing and brushing, Nola detected the faint smell of the rare martini he had fixed himself to celebrate their success.

He stroked her arm. "I live vicariously through you."

"Live vicariously? You make music happen because you make it possible for the world to hear." How grateful she had been to be the one taken under his wings. In the semi-darkness, she tried to resurrect that old awe of him, but it was like evoking the exhilaration of youth. She could remember how it felt, yet was unable to wrap herself in that rich texture of the experience.

Against the whining of the bar refrigerator, of an elevator creaking to a stop somewhere, and of the whirring of the air-conditioning, small, sweet squeaks, a cross between sucking and moaning, came from the crib in the far end of the room. Wonder filled Nola like the billowing of a curtain. She stretched her arms on the headboard and rotated her ankles, bringing to mind Lulu's adorable smile and wise, dark eyes. If only the baby were awake, she could again lift her up in the air and listen to that gurgling laughter.

There had been a moment of anxiety at the party. "I saw the look on those officials' faces when they came to take the baby," Nola said to Wade. She paused, still uncertain what had made him defuse their request.

"I made them drink instead." He laughed. "Partying must be against their commie law."

"Thanks for not insisting that the baby must leave," she said, pulled up the blanket and snuggled in it. A sweet smell hung in the room. There was magic in the air Lulu inhabited. No wonder adoptive parents forged an instant bond with their new infant. Wade was accepting Lulu's presence. Soon he'd come to love her.

He broke into her reveries. "We haven't yet talked about that B flat—"

"Can't you, for once, stop working? It can wait for rehearsal."

"I'm a perfectionist. As you are," he replied.

She turned her back toward him. "Good night."

"How about something to help you fall asleep?" He pressed against her, kissed her neck, and his finger toyed with the loose strap of her nightgown.

She looked at the thin reddish city light slashing a line between the curtains. "It's late."

"Sure." The note of sarcasm was unmistaken.

"I'm sorry—" she said.

He turned her shoulders toward him and planted a hard kiss on her lips. "Why can't you be happy with me? You're my life."

"I want you to sometimes forget that I am a singer."

His hand ran along her body, searching. "Which is what I'm doing this very moment."

As he proceeded, his hands and mouth demanding a response, she summoned fantasies of lovers she'd had before she married him, or the celebrities whose agents had arranged their dates for publicity purposes. She was surprised when Daniel Chen wandered along the paths of her untapped passion. At the party, they had talked for a couple of minutes, he oblivious to the noise and hilarity in the room, she pulsating with the beat of the drums. She had wanted to dance with him, to lay her hand on his back, to feel his body heat.

She did now, with Wade's warm breath panting in her ear.

She had barely slept when Lulu's cries woke her.

"Jesus." Wade tossed a pillow over his head.

Nola rose and picked up the baby. From the pile of toys and toiletries a staff member had purchased, she took out a disposable diaper and put one on the wriggling body. The Velcro tabs stuck at odd angles and the diaper was crooked. As the baby continued to fuss, Nola carried her to the kitchenette and warmed up the milk.

Lulu refused it. She broke into a wail that turned into a shriek. Her body stretched and struggled to escape Nola's grasp as though wishing to flee her own skin.

"That's it!" Wade yelled from behind Nola. She heard him jab at the phone. "Send in a maid to take the baby," he barked at someone.

Nola's tongue tasted metallic with the sense of failure. "No, no," she told him over Lulu's wail. Holding her tightly, Nola nudged the bathroom door wider. The little light left on changed the hue of the room the way a drop of milk lightened coffee. She prattled on, "You see? You're here, and it's me."

Lulu's wail continued uninterrupted.

"On the double," Wade said to whomever was on the other end.

Nola spoke in hushed tones. "Please let me handle her." Cooing, shushing, whispering words of comfort, she tried putting the pacifier in Lulu's mouth, but the baby flipped her head from side to side with more vigor than Nola had believed that little body could possess.

"You need your sleep." Wade punched his pillow into a neck roll.

In Nola's arms, Lulu pushed her away, screaming, then batting her short hands against her own head. For a moment, Nola's resolve wavered. Someone else would have known what to do. "Shhh-Shhhhhh." She bounced Lulu with a mixture of helplessness and despair. She might fail as she had with Jenna. "Why don't you go sleep in the other room?" she asked Wade.

"Do you have any idea what's awaiting you tomorrow—today!—with interviews and then the video shoot in the market and a dozen film crews driving us all nuts?"

The green light on the digital clock showed it was five-thirty. They had gone to bed at close to two. Nola clicked on the remote control of the CD player, adjusted the volume to low, and resumed her pacing. Maria Callas singing a love aria came on, and Nola joined in, humming. She tried the pacifier again.

This time, Lulu accepted it. The crying subsided, and Lulu sucked on, her eyes regarding Nola like a wise old man's. Tears still glistened on her eyelashes, and Nola had the urge to lick them.

The long-buried defeat echoed in her head, then receded. "Are you feeling better?" she whispered.

Lulu's head turned toward the source of the music, and she gave her pacifier a series of strong sucks.

A tap on the front door brought Nola to the foyer. She sent the maid away and re-entered the room, forcing herself not to glance at Wade. Her hand caressed Lulu's hair, damp with perspiration, and gently pressed the little head onto her shoulder. Lulu took a breath that filled her whole body, then let it all out.

Nola continued to stroll around the large dark room, the quiet tune in the background. A little bubble of pride percolated inside her, as though calming this baby had been an accomplishment greater than a triple encore. Lulu's breathing was slow and even, and Nola wished this moment of bliss would never end. *Mine.*

After putting the baby down in her crib, she lay on her back, listening to Lulu's occasional lip smacking. She gazed at the dark ceiling stretching away into a limitless expanse. The rhythms of this land were perplexing. Nothing was familiar, not even human relationships. What unfathomable pressures drove Lulu's mother to such desperation? Nola conjured an image of a teenage peasant, illiterate, starving, forced by her in-laws to give up a baby girl in favor of trying for a boy; maybe Lulu wasn't even this woman's first. *I'll take care of her for both of us. I promise.*

Nola fell back to sleep, sinking to the bottom of the ocean, yet still aware of one open frequency, her newly assigned radio station, tuned to Lulu.

She was unprepared to hear Leslie's voice cutting through her sleep. "Rise and shine," he intoned as he pulled open the shades. He set a glass of orange juice on her bedside table. "Workout time."

"Please, God," she groaned.

"An honest mistake, but it's only me, Leslie." His shirt was unbuttoned down to his navel, yet the starch kept it stiff and almost closed, allowing a calculated glimpse of the muscular chest of the former dancer.

Nola got her bearings. A tectonic shift had rearranged her life. Groggily, she dragged her legs off the bed and approached the crib. The scent hovering about it was the sweetest she had ever smelled. She inhaled once, twice, trying to capture the fragrance as she did a piece of inspiring music. Lulu lay still, her eyes riveted to the swaying of a colorful mobile.

When Nola appeared in her line of vision, a wide smile broadened her face. She grabbed the bars and tried to sit up. "Lulululululululu," she said, and a quickening went through Nola.

"Lulululululululu to you," Nola imitated, rolling her tongue.

"Practice your voice first," Leslie told her.

"Ha-ha-ha-ha-ha—ha—" she belted. In and out. In and out. She watched to see if Lulu became frightened by her loud voice, but Lulu just babbled back. Nola moved up the full range of her vocal cords, climbing over four octaves. "Do-re-me-fa-sol-la-ti-do. Do-ti-la-sol-fa-me-re-do-o-o-o-o."

"O—o—o—o—o," Lulu said. "O—o—o—o—o." A smile snapped onto her face. It was so jubilant, it took all of Nola's self-control not to squeeze her.

Leslie wrapped Nola in her robe. "Aren't babies a wonderful way to start people?"

"Certainly a wonderful way to start a day."

A maid appeared in the doorway of the wardrobe room. Her felt-soled shoes made no sound as she stepped to the silver teacart, where she filled a bowl with yogurt and sprinkled granola on top.

"I can get my own cereal," Nola said to Leslie. "Given a chance, you and Wade will top Celine Dion's entourage of a hundred and twenty."

"You're up?" Wade came in and kissed her head. His bouncing step showed no sign of sleep deficiency.

Nola yawned, walking to her bathroom. She sat on the toilet. "Do-re-me-fa-sol-la-ti-do—do—do—" Her voice bounced off the marble walls of the stall. "Do-ti-la-sol-fa-me-re-do—o—o—o—"

Wade stepped in, tore off some toilet paper, folded it and handed it to her.

She did not reach for it. "I can get my own toilet paper," she said.

He offered no reply, but moved away to check himself in front of the full-length mirror. Last year, as a present for his fortieth birthday, he had treated himself to a liposuction of his stubborn love handles. Nola averted her gaze. He demanded as much of himself as he did of her; perhaps he wanted to look more attractive to her. She just wished his efforts weren't so over the top.

"Leslie says I should get into martial arts," Wade said. "It's graceful, but it also teaches complete control over body and soul."

Yes, Nola thought. Daniel's quiet inner strength was probably the result of years of such training. She picked up the toothbrush and discovered that Wade had already put a dollop of green toothpaste on it. She brushed her teeth, her eyes fixed on the small snuff bottle Daniel had given her and which she had placed on a silver tray. The glorious bird with the generous colorful tail, she realized, was the Phoenix, the traditional symbol of China's dowager empress. A woman of power. What irony! Right now, the woman that stared back at her from the mirror had bags under her eyes. The tip of her nose blazed in red, a sign of stress. Since the formerly bulbous cartilage had been snipped and shaved as part of the resculpturing of her face at the onset of her career, the blood vessels in her nose had become the barometer of her agitation level.

At the other end of the ten-foot marble counter, Wade was tracing his finger over the brass filigree of a peony on the magnificent cloisonné vase. He was still in awe of the little details he had toiled so hard to own, yet this very awe ensured that they were never fully his—even though his private collections were of museum quality, the kind Nola had always desired to surround herself with.

He turned away from the vase and collected his watch and money clip. He looked straight at her nose. "We'll need a more permanent solution to sleepless nights."

She retrieved her Dead Sea sponge and scrubbing salt for her shower. Yes, they needed to sort out this monumental change and its ramifications. "I need you to talk to the ambassador about keeping the baby," she said.

His reflection in the mirror was a bit off center. "The timing is lousy. I wish you'd gotten a goldfish. Doesn't cry at night." He lifted her chin. "I'll be talking to Ashford about a few other things anyway."

Her broad smile was cut short as a beep sounded from Wade's Palm Pilot in the next room. He stepped out to get it, glancing at the sky outside. "We'll have a full seven hours of good light for the shooting."

"Last night's production went off like a military campaign. You were incredible," she said. The myriad details Wade handled never ceased to baffle and amaze her. "I trust that today's will be the same." He had hired an award-winning former NBC executive producer to document the entire China tour and to coordinate all the independent network directors. He was shooting footage to sell to TNN, PBS, foreign affiliates and for her own music video, which Wade would distribute through record stores, Internet music retailers and her website. And even if separate crews for HBO, VH1 and MTV were a royal pain with their shooting of disjointed parts of various songs, the presence of them all affirmed her recent move to the top.

Wade tapped the end of an imaginary cigar. "You ain't seen nothing yet. Five more cities to go." He checked his Rolex and told Leslie, "Have her ready at ten for the media interviews here. *Extra, Entertainment Tonight, Access Hollywood* and several others Roberta has lined up." He punched some keys on his organizer. "I have to make some phone calls."

"The first of which is the ambassador," Nola said.

"Is that your idea of a souvenir from China?" He laughed. The first time she had heard that carefree laugh, it sounded like a pot full of coins tossed up in the air. Only someone who had grown up with loving parents could laugh like that, she had thought. She had loved those parents even before they took her, a teenage orphan, into their bosom.

And she still liked his laughter. She should try harder to make their marriage work. Everyone made adjustments. She kissed Wade's cheek. "Thanks for understanding."

When he closed the door behind him, she jumped up in delight, her arms up in a V. "He's recovering from the shock," she told Leslie.

"He's flummoxed. It's like you stopped taking the pill and didn't consult him. The poor guy didn't even have nine months to get used to the idea."

Nola swooped Lulu up in her arms and danced with her around the room. "It's time. Wade's been consumed with work all his life." Deanna, his first wife, had wanted to start a family. Wade, always on the road and obsessed with Nola's career—on which his own depended—had objected. Things were different now, and she, who had been the one scared of a mother role, was taking the risk. She trumpeted into Lulu's belly, "Yesss!"

Leslie finished mixing wax-based foundation for her nose, strong enough to hold through repeated makeup applications. "How will the Italian Didonatos react when their lapsed-Jewish daughter-in-law presents them with a Chinese bambino their pretend—WASP son doesn't yet acknowledge?" he asked.

Nola laughed. But as Leslie approached her with a small sponge, she felt the question mark that curled in the darkness of her guts. She stared into space. Wade's avoiding a confrontation notwithstanding, he had no room for Lulu in his life.

Chapter 4

(1977 - 1980)

"Nola, sing for us," Mom said, and Nola was happy for the attention even though that evening, yet another sandaled, scruffy-looking couple with rolled sleeping bags had appeared at their door, colorful stickers from Istanbul, Berkeley and Tibet covering their backpacks. The visitors stretched out their smelly feet and complained that Smithtown was two hours out on Long Island—nowhere near New York City—and hitchhiking further up to Nissequogue was a bitch in a suburb full of stuck-up middle-class capitalists.

Nola sang "Knowing Me, Knowing You," even though she wished these friends of friends would stop dropping in like this. It wasn't a generous thought, because Mom always said they should all love one another, and if everybody was full of love for their fellow humans, the world would be a better place. Nola didn't know who the "fellow humans" were, so how was she supposed to love them?

She said nothing. She had already ruined Mom's singing career seven years before by "being born when no one was looking." Nola never dared ask where had someone finally seen her? In the woods? On the beach? Or in the middle of a concert, like that one in Woodstock where Mom had met Dad when he played guitar with Bob Dylan?

Feeling special for the moment, Nola sang "Love Child," and then she didn't want to stop, so she sang "Big Girls Don't Cry." She knew lots of other songs from practicing with Mom, except that Mom rarely went on gigs anymore. Sometimes Mom ironed her hair and got a ride to a local bar, where she sang for tips, but most of the time she just relaxed on pillows of many colors and spoke about world peace and people loving one another. She smoked Kent cigarettes in a gold stick, which she held in her long, pale fingers. She'd also let Nola roll her cigarettes with the pot Dad brought home, and Nola would watch Mom suck in the smoke long and hard, her eyelids heavy, her eyelashes dark and curled like a movie star's. Tonight's visitors said Nola had the same green-colored eyes as Mom's, but they didn't say she was as beautiful. The cigarettes' sweet smell gave Nola dreams although she wasn't sleeping, and she wondered why the dreams had jumped the line instead of waiting their turn.

In the morning, she brushed Mom's long wavy hair from its middle part and fanned it out on the Indians pillows, where light from a fringed lampshade was reflected in the hundreds of dime-size mirrors sewn onto the pillows. Mom also had a tie-dyed skirt decorated with these mini-mirrors, each stitched on with a different-colored thread, and Nola would wear it when she danced.

There was plenty of room to dance in their small cottage. Instead of real furniture, there were mattresses on the floor, two huge beanbag chairs, a bookshelf made of wood planks laid on cinder blocks, and stacks of fruit crates that held a large record collection and the stereo system. And lots of pillows all over the place.

Their house was the caretaker's cottage on the estate of the big house, which Mom called a "mansion." So it wasn't really like poor people's homes, except that nothing ever got fixed. Nola wished her parents would make it look nice so the other girls would be allowed to come and play, but when she had asked for living room furniture for her birthday like in other homes, Mom said that "Materialism is so bourgeois."

Nola didn't understand those big words that meant something not nice about the other girls' parents, unlike her parents' friends, who were "anti-establishment," Mom said.

In a day or two, the visitors would go out to buy food, like cheese and cold cuts or canned peas and ravioli, because Mom never went shopping. But the guests didn't know it yet, so Nola went to the big house, where plates were always ready in the refrigerator with sliced tomatoes or sprigs of parsley on top.

The big house had beautiful furniture and carpets and framed mirrors. The spooky old man with his scary wheezing sat by the window and gawked at the Long Island Sound, and when Nola opened the back door, he crooked his already crooked finger and tried to smile, except that only half his face moved, and then saliva drooled out. The cat that always wrapped around his neck pawed at the string of saliva until it detached.

Nola helped herself to the food and brought over a plate to the old man, placing it on the small table in front of him. She gave him a fork and a spoon, but not a knife, because he could only use one hand, and that one shook. She didn't sit with him, because with his mouth always drooling and food smeared all over his chin, he was too gross to look at.

Dad, who was the old man's grandnephew, would later sit with him. So would the woman who lived on the third floor and who didn't mind his being gross. She now came down, her face sour, like she had just bitten into a lemon, but said nothing when Nola used the phone to call for oil delivery since the furnace had run out and she borrowed a blanket because Mom had given hers to the guests.

Dad was home when Nola returned and said that he was proud of her because she was a precocious girl, "the smartest second grader there is."

Nola got her notebook, where she collected new or long words, and wrote "precocious." Some words were beautiful, like colored glass beads, each with its own tint and transparency. One day she would string them into songs. Elvis, who had just died—Mom cried about it—had written songs all by himself.

Nola asked Dad if people could make money from writing songs, and he asked why did she need to make money? They weren't poor; they were rich with love. Nola didn't say that she wanted money to have their house fixed. In the big house, people always came to fix things that didn't even look broken, or to paint walls that weren't chipped, or to plant gardens where no one but she ever walked. Even the huge lawn around the big house was bright green, not like the scraggly yard near their cottage, which was on the other side of a horse barn that no longer had any horses. Mom said that was a blessing because she hated the odor of manure. But Dad was saving up to buy a horse and dreamed of moving the family to a ranch in Colorado where they would work the land. Nola didn't understand why, he couldn't work the land right around their house, but she didn't ask, because he was home now between gigs and taught her how to drum, until Mom told them to stop and for Nola to go outside because she was noisy.

The Nissequogue estate sat at the edge of a high cliff overlooking the Sound. Long Island, Nola had learned in school, was shaped like a giant whale. It was separated from a state called Connecticut by the Sound. On clear days, she could see Connecticut from the cliff and wondered whether another girl just like her was standing there right now and looking back at her.

Getting down to the beach was tricky, because the wooden staircase, which had been built before the old man had become old, had many missing steps. Nola clung to the jagged cliff and stepped in gaps in the rock, even though Dad had warned her that she could kill herself and shouldn't even think of going down to the beach.

How could she not think of something after being told not to think about it? Besides, at the beach, where the sand squooshed between her toes, she had discovered a cave made of a large overhang rock, with driftwood on the floor and a carpet of pretty shells. There was a hush in the cave, and when she sang, her voice echoed, so it sounded like there were two of her singing, not quite in harmony, more like one Nola chasing another Nola. Could the girl in Connecticut hear her? She sang louder and louder. Maybe that girl really did hear her, and that echo wasn't one Nola chasing another, but that other girl singing back to her.

Nothing in her life had been as exciting as when she was eight and
Jenna was born. Mom, who, for weeks after stayed in bed instead of on
her floor pillows, said Jenna was another accident.

Dad was home a lot to feed the baby and even buy food for Nola and
Mom. He made Nola get up every day and not miss the school bus to
Smithtown Elementary. Nola loved school, but she never knew when the
school bus would arrive at the estate gate because Mom was against
clocks, just as she was against a TV and a phone. The year before, there
had been some business about a case-worker, and Nola knew that if that
woman ever knocked on the door again, she must wake Mom up real
quick and make her wash her face and comb her hair before she let the
woman in.

When Dad went on tour, Mom got irritated with this baby who wouldn't
stop crying even though Mom yelled at her to stop. Nola felt bad for
Jenna, whose little fingers and nose and eyes were one big miracle.
Sometimes, when Mom became upset, Nola would take Jenna for a walk
even though it was winter and the baby had the sniffles. She would first
pinch a stub of cigarette with a roach clip and light it to make Mom feel
better and then she and Jenna wouldn't have to stay outside for too long.

The best part of it was that when Nola returned, Mom would hug her,
tell her what a responsible, good daughter Nola was, and then she would
kiss Jenna, too. Mom said this baby would be beautiful, which made
Nola happy, because in case Jenna wouldn't be able to sing, she should
be beautiful.

By summer, Mom felt better because she spoke about "No-Nukes"
and explained that in the Cold War, the government kept inventing new
ways to endanger our small planet and its inhabitants. Now it was
nuclear weapons and submarines.

One day, Mom and Dad left baby Jenna home with a visiting friend
and took Nola on a long bus ride to Washington, D.C. Thousands of people gathered in a rally against the dangerous weapons the U.S. was pointing at Russia because the Russians had their missiles directed at
America's shores. Nola hadn't seen any cannons or missiles from across
the Sound, but liked the thrill of the protest. Everybody camped around,
carried signs and sang songs. Once, a man streaked naked across the
stage, and everybody cheered. Nola was terribly embarrassed to see that
penis flapping as he ran, but she couldn't take her eyes off it. It looked
like the head of a dead turtle and probably felt like one to the touch.

Carly Simon was there, and Bruce Springsteen, and Bonnie Raitt, and
James Taylor, and the Doobie Brothers. Dad performed, then Mom sang

solo, while Nola stood in front of the stage with their friends, jumping and dancing along. She couldn't imagine feeling more a part of something big and important until Dad invited her on stage and Mom handed her the microphone.

Nola sang "Teach Your Children," and when she finished, the crowd cheered and wouldn't stop. Bono kissed her cheek and asked her to sing more, so she sang "Hot Child In The City" and danced as if she were alone at home, while her lungs pumped out the music. When she was done, her head felt light in a weird way. She stood there, looking down at all these people who loved her, and she felt grown up, not just ten, and very special, like a goddess; she had given them something that made them happy. She now understood what it meant to love "her fellow human beings," because she loved every one of them. Mom had been right all along. Love made the world a wonderful place.

Nola stayed up late, then fell asleep in a sleeping bag on the soggy ground with a boy younger than she who kept pulling on his penis. She decided that at home she would talk her parents into sleeping one night on the beach so the three of them could sing and then gaze at the stars. Love was close to home, too, she thought. She should write it as a song.

Jenna was a year and a half old when she had another cold and couldn't breathe. She cried, then choked, and, frightened, she cried even harder and wouldn't stop no matter what Nola did.

"Just shut her up," Mom sobbed. "I can't take it anymore!"

So Nola thought of the treatment the woman who watched the old man gave him when he wheezed real bad. Nola boiled water in a large pot, put a chair next to the counter so Jenna could reach it, placed Jenna's face right above the hot water, and covered her head with a towel to keep the steam in.

"Breathe," she ordered Jenna, and demonstrated. "In and out."

But stupid Jenna dropped her face into the hot water.

Chapter 5

Nola's workout over, she gulped down juice and, still dripping sweat, stood by the window with Lulu in her arms.

From the height of the fourteenth-floor penthouse suite, an unobstructed view of the city stretched out for miles below her. Cranes filled the skyline. Every other building going up was a steel-and-glass skyscraper. The scaffoldings, though, were made of bamboo intricately tied together and seemed dangerously precarious. Straw mats were stretched between the bamboo poles to catch falling debris.

"Look, Lulu, this is Beijing, your city."

"Ta-ta-ti."

Nola continued to chatter and point out the sights to the baby. Details presented themselves, clearer, sharper than in previous days, as if imprinting themselves on her memory for Lulu's benefit. The baby, though, was more interested in grabbing Nola's lips, nose and hair. Nola laughed at her antics and went on talking. When Lulu was ready to speak, it would be English. Maybe in time Nola would hire a Chinese tutor for both of them.

At the intersection below, hundreds of bicyclists stopped at the traffic light, allowing a crossing army of more cyclists to pass. Handlebars touching, wheels aligned like in a giant sardine can, they filled each side of the road, with motorized vehicles in the minority. In the midst of traffic, farmers pushed handcarts or rode tricycles with supported flatbeds heaped with fruits and vegetables.

Leslie finished laying out the ultra-pale pink silk shantung suit for Nola to wear for her interviews and added a short, belly-revealing lace camisole.

When she did not move from her spot at the window, he joined her. "Look at all that food. Remember Russia? It was pitiful the way people were reduced to becoming gatherers."

"China feeds its people. Daniel Chen says that with twenty-two percent of the planet's population and only seven percent of the arable land, this is quite a feat."

"'Daniel says,'" Leslie repeated. "The silent intellectual with a soft spot for all wretched humanity. A martial-arts expert, a writer, and drop-dead gorgeous. How very romantic."

Nola's mind quivered with forbidden imagery. She pushed it away; she had promised herself to give Wade more of her attention. "You're a yenta twice over," she said to Leslie.

"The sexually downtrodden can't be a yenta." He grinned. "And then there's this secret job of his."

"What's that?"

"That 'cultural attaché' title is a hoax. Daniel's probably a spy."

She giggled. "That would be too obvious."

"Have you noticed the scar on his cheek? Spy, for sure. In case you're interested, I'll pick up some gossip, find out about his love life—"

"There's no need to intrude on his privacy," she replied. Whatever Daniel wanted to reveal he would do at his own pace. As in poetry, there was as much meaning to the white spaces around this man's words as in the words themselves.

It was early afternoon when, in her fourth costume change—a multi-layered sheer jersey dress in varying shades of pale blue—Nola twirled and bumped and grinded her way through the market. The wide center aisle was lined with thousands of people held back by her civil security. The uniformed police had to be kept out of the cameras' sight.

Under the clear October sky, the air was warm and zesty with the aroma of ripe fruit and baked sugary desserts. On cue, smiling at the crowd, occasionally reaching a hand to touch an infant, Nola sang. She summoned all her emotions, aware of the cameras that recorded every expression on her face. Her sound tracks, though, would be redubbed with studio-quality recordings, while selected background noises would be inserted for effect.

Straw mat awnings shaded tables with large, flat baskets of red chili, passion fruit, leeks, berries, watercress, cherry tomatoes, litchi nuts, beans and asparagus. Huge burlap sacks stood on the ground, their tops folded back to reveal spices, roots, nuts and herbs. The displays of eggplant, broccoli, oranges, curly lettuce and pineapple were piled so high that the grocers had to climb onto stools to reach the top. Shoppers wended their way through, carrying plastic bags or balancing on bicycles with wire baskets filled with purchases wrapped in newspaper.

Across from the twelve-piece band at a corner of the intersection, Lulu sat in her new stroller under Leslie's watch, her fist occupying her mouth, her curious eyes taking everything in. Leslie's assistant chased away the flies.

The Chinese crew members pushed the spectators away to create a wider passage. Her mouth moving, Nola cut a series of dance steps diagonally across an intersection and pirouetted toward the battery of cameras. The excited crowd, with its clucking chatter, pushed forward again.

She loved it all. As with last night's concert, the joy of belonging to these people returned. She was enriched by them the same way they were taking something important out of this surprise event that had broken the routine of their day. They would speak about it with wonder to their relatives and neighbors. They would tell of the rusty curls, disbelieving that people could have hair so different from theirs. She would remember their delighted faces, the simplicity of their anonymous existence, and would want to write more songs to warm their hearts.

Wade dashed about in his blue pressed-crease jeans, a starched denim shirt and cowboy boots that had never been marred by cow dung. At breaks, he slapped the shoulders of whichever two men were closest. "Great job, troops."

The director instructed the crew to get a shot of an old woman holding a monkey on a leash and negotiating the sale of her pet. The monkey grabbed a cluster of bananas from an adjacent stall, bringing a torrent of shouts from the farmer's wife. She emphasized her protest by pelting the monkey's owner with rotten tomatoes. The argument escalated and the crowd cheered.

A troupe of eight young men joined Nola with their staged dance. As they moved in unison, a fly circled her head, but she kept her smile, never twitching a muscle. She concentrated on hitting her invisible marks while not losing a single beat. The cameras were on her, too many people were involved, and she owed it to all to be her best. The fly would be edited out of the film as long as it didn't land on her nose or get into her mouth. But she longed for another costume-change break. Refreshed, she would bring Lulu to her trailer, play with her, and kiss her sweet face.

The hours stretched on. Nola's hair reeked of spices and her skin was sticky from perspiration and insect repellent. Again and again she shucked costumes and changed, then reshot scenes to give each crew different footage. The smallest detail had been choreographed; nothing had been left to chance, yet the texture of life pulsated with its own rhythm and its unpredictability added the exotic touch that would be incorporated into the recording.

An old chicken merchant with a thin pigtail under a peaked coolie hat inched his bicycle through the intersection, oblivious to the scene he was entering. Cages made of woven twigs were mounted on the front and back of his bike, and heads of chickens clucking helplessly poked out. On the director's cue the man was allowed to proceed. Continuing to spin and prance around him, Nola ignored the rankness of the terrified fowl and focused on her song and the steps.

The cameras were rolling when one of the guitarists cut off his playing with a shout. "No! Another Chink spits his gob!" The Chinese people's habit of hawking phlegm and spitting it on the ground regardless of who was standing there had become a joke among the staff. Now the musician went for the man's throat.

In the chaos that ensued, Wade calmed the musician and, with the help of an interpreter, apologized to the stunned Chinese man.

Just as the shooting restarted, Nola heard Lulu wail. Her voice halted and she looked away.

"Cut!" yelled the director.

Nola dashed over to the baby and picked her up. "I'm here," she cooed. "Dumpling, I'm here."

"Will the talent please get back in place?" the director called.

Lulu bawled. Ignoring Yoram and two of his security men trailing her, Nola rounded the corner into a quieter side street, where vertical lines of Chinese calligraphy decorated the stores. Each door, painted red for good luck, led to a tiny food establishment that sold hot noodles or sticky, doughy cakes. The proprietors stood outside and stirred chest-high steamy pots that gave off a fishy odor. Here and there, a customer sat on a chair on the sidewalk, a bowl near his chin, his chopsticks shoving noodles into his mouth.

Bouncing in Nola's arms, Lulu stopped crying. A thought sprouted in Nola's head. Was Lulu's mother in the crowd, too, watching, checking to see that her crying baby was cared for?

Wade approached with Jean-Claude and Leslie's assistant. "Ready?" he asked Nola and nodded toward the aide. "The baby's a distraction. She'll keep it inside the trailer."

"This place is an overload of sights, smells and sounds for Lulu," Nola replied. "Just give me a half-hour break, and I'll take her upstairs to our suite where it's quiet."

"Run off in the middle of the shoot?" Jean-Claude glared at her, his bony fingers dancing at his sides on invisible keyboards.

Wade's eyebrows shot up. "Do you know how much half an hour costs?" he asked Nola. He turned to the aide, "Take it."

"'Her,' not 'it,'" Nola said with indignation. "She's a girl, not a turtle, and her personality shines through like a lantern."

"I can certainly *hear* this personality," Wade said. For the first time in years, the old port wine birthmark on his neck became visible. It had long ago been laser-treated.

Perspiration dripped down Nola's neck and temples. "We'll have to leave her when we go to the embassy tonight, but the rest of the time I should be the one to calm her."

Jean-Claude smacked his hands on his thighs. "This is unbelievable. Are you forgetting you have a job to do?"

"That's enough!" Wade cut him off. He sent Nola a meaningful look, grabbed her elbow, and pulled her to the side.

"I've been going along with this lunacy. You can't expect it—this—to get in the way of your work. We're going to finish this shoot. Now."

Just then, a mouse scrambled between her feet and made to the edge of the gutter. She let out a yelp, and the startled mouse stopped and raised its head.

Wade stomped his cowboy boot. A squeak was followed by the crackling of tiny bones. Something gooey spread under Wade's sole.

"Take the baby," he ordered the young woman. His eyes shot darts of anger at Nola.

Nola's morning orange juice climbed up and turned to acid in her throat. She handed Lulu to the aide and walked back.

An assistant director sprayed her with insecticide to repel the multiplying flies. Decomposed vegetables filled the curb, and the stench lined Nola's nostrils. She stood still. Cold sweat trickled down her spine as she turned her gaze away from Wade and the Chinese valet cleaning his boot.

Chapter 6

At the American Embassy foyer, Nola eyed the guest book made out of the pages of *Town and Country* magazine that featured the U.S. ambassador to China with his wife at their Beijing mansion. It was a PR coup, no doubt the product of the dual-fronts public-relations by the publicity section of the State Department supplemented by the PR firm Wade kept on a yearly retainer. It emphasized the significance of Nola's six-city tour in the context of U.S.-China relations.

The ambassador, Mr. Hartley Ashford, greeted Wade and kissed Nola's hand while his wife twitted next to him. In her thin voice, Margot Ashford read aloud from the guest book's inside cover: "Goodwill Ambassador Nola Brings to the Middle Kingdom A Message of Friendship and Peace!"

Until now, Nola's press coverage had been only in the context of her entertainment work. Now, as she added her signature under her own photograph, she suppressed her thrill as she said, "How kind of you."

Wade lifted a fallen gardenia and tucked it into the lapel of his tuxedo. "Madam?" He offered her his curved arm, and she looped her hand around his elbow. His outburst at the market still lingered under her skin, but being back in his good graces smoothed things out, the way lapping waves erased footprints from the sand. She needed warmth. Battle-weary after a day of fighting over Lulu, she could use any friendly gesture.

As she and Wade entered the ballroom, her eyes searched for Daniel; he might be the kind of person to offer an oasis of understanding.

The quartet launched into a rendition of Nola's "Let It Be. Make It Happen," and Ambassador Ashford hummed the melody.

Laughing, Nola said, "It was just released!"

"Your songs catch on fast," he replied. He was a big man with a large-lipped mouth and a fleshy nose. He lifted two champagne flutes from a passing tray and handed one to Nola and one to Margot. Wade refrained.

"The room looks sensational," Nola said, scanning the details, and Margot beamed.

Snaked around the gold chains of each of the two huge crystal chandeliers were long-tailed red paper dragons. Giant paper butterflies, their wings reinforced with metal loops, hung over the row of arched windows that opened to the garden, while Chinese red lanterns flanked the gold molding of each window. Scattered around the room were Chinese-style lacquered rosewood settees and cocktail tables with fretwork or openwork geometric designs, and hexagonal mahogany tables with matching straight-back chairs with armrests carved in motifs of clouds, sunbursts and ocean waves. Rich brocade fabric depicting fishermen and weeping willows drooping over ponds upholstered the Western-style sofas. American paintings and bronze sculptures complemented the decor.

As the Ashfords greeted new guests, Wade's gaze caressed Nola's mint-green chiffon gown. Halston had been chosen as the official American designer for this tour, and the Mandarin jacket that went with the dress was embroidered with Chinese-style flowers and leaves in silver and gold. The pattern was repeated on her satin shoes and evening purse.

"You look beautiful." Wade held her hand and twirled her around.

In a minute swell of contentment, she pirouetted. Nuances of a marriage, she thought, were little stage directions subconsciously understood—until one partner altered a line and threw things off balance.

"I'm sorry if I was short with you today."

"We both need to make adjustments," she said. "When we get home, maybe we should seek counseling."

"I don't need a shrink to tell me that music is your experience; it is fed by your passion. If this baby is your new passion, so be it."

Geez, thanks, she wanted to say, but didn't.

He pulled her closer. "Whatever works. Your music makes you an immortal."

The smell of the gardenia in his lapel was suddenly overwhelming. "I'm not talking music, but marriage," she murmured. "I may be your creation, but does that make you my Master?"

"We are what we are." He disengaged his hold on her. "A party in your honor is awaiting you."

An image of the crushed mouse flashed in her head. She pasted a smile on her face. What had possessed her, three years ago, to respond to Wade's first-ever romantic overture, thus ruining the great thing they had going for them?

With the ambassador at their side, Wade and she worked the crowd of foreign diplomats, high-ranking Chinese officials, a dozen American Fortune 500 CEOs, and African and Asian diplomats in dazzling national costumes. Their wives, bedecked and bejeweled for the highlight event of Beijing's social season, dotted the crowd. Nola basked in the attention and responded with small talk to words of praise and adoring stares. She was back in her element, but the physical nearness with the movers and shakers of the political and business worlds left her perplexed. These people had accomplished a lot more than she had, yet they looked up to her.

The ambassador was called to attend to other duties, and Wade became engaged in conversation with the CEO of Motorola. In the lull of introductions, Nola craned her neck toward the patio and spotted Daniel. He was chatting with a mustached man wearing a red turban and with the Chinese Minister of Culture, whom Nola had met when she arrived. She watched Daniel's smooth cheeks and the line of his jaw, so well-defined. He must be in his mid-thirties, just a few years older than she, yet the ease with which he straddled two worlds revealed a self-assurance rarely found in men this young. He appeared comfortable anywhere, secure in his own skin.

He caught Nola's eye, gave a twitch of a smile, and excused himself to approach her. She took in the whiff of his cinnamon aftershave. "I missed the scene last night," he said.

"I didn't get a chance to tell you about it at the party." She would have, had he asked her to dance.

"The embassy's TVs are tuned to CNN. The baby's surprise arrival was replayed several times today."

She laughed. "Stay tuned. I've already given a series of interviews." Roberta's babbling about the PR blitz she would brew materialized into ten six-minute interviews squeezed into the one-hour window in Nola's schedule. In each, Nola had voiced her intentions to give the baby a home. More interviews were planned for tomorrow. A *Vanity Fair* writer who had been given permission to shadow Nola for the tour had taken notes while Nola played with Lulu, and the magazine photographer shot several rolls.

"The Xinhua News Agency has made no mention of it," Daniel said. "That's the state-run news organization."

"Babies may not be newsworthy items here. But this baby's the sweetest, brightest and friendliest creature I've ever met." Nola started toward the large patio. Lanterns of varying sizes gave the place an aura of enchantment. With a wry laugh, she added, "My staff's having a hard time accepting the new competition for my attention."

"What's their problem?"

She looked at him. Wisps of straight black hair fell on his forehead. He really had no idea what her life was like, or how many people—families—depended upon her for their livelihood. She helped herself to an endive leaf and licked the dollop of caviar from the top, relishing the salty, smooth texture. "Don't you need to introduce me to some important guests?"

"Do you want me to?"

"I'm here on a job." She raised an eyebrow and added with a note of sarcasm, "I do whatever's expected of me."

He smiled. "I don't."

"I envy you."

The lantern-dotted path leading into the depth of the garden was inviting. She made toward it, ready to absorb the sensual radiance of the stars, to reflect back the opaque glow of the moon, to dance naked if the time and place permitted. For once, Yoram and his team had to stay in the front sentry house with the small army of musclemen of the other dignitaries.

"I take it you mean to keep her." Daniel tweaked a leaf off a low shrub and brought it to his nose.

"I'm in love. Totally. Wade spoke with Ambassador Ashford today about taking care of the paperwork."

Daniel bent down again and picked the seeds of another plant. He pressed them between his fingers and brought them close to her nose. She inhaled the biting, sweet scent. "Anise," he said. He picked a cluster of leaves, sniffed and handed it to her. "Thyme."

Far behind them, an arrangement of Chinese music with the distinct, quavering, high half-notes played by stringed instruments filled the garden with its mysterious sound, utterly foreign, yet pleasing with its naked soulfulness. The hundreds of multicolored lanterns scattered around the grounds cast muted glow. Nola held on to the thyme twig, inhaled its scent again and placed it in her purse.

The path ended at a large pond, where four-foot tall paper swans, lit from the inside, bobbed on the surface. Their lights broke in tiny ripples of inky water. Nola stopped under a tree whose branches were laden with teardrop-shaped magenta flowers.

Daniel scraped off a cluster of tiny petals that together formed one flower and tossed them onto the raised wing of the nearest swan. "Make a wish. I'll see that it comes true."

She laughed at his surprising jocularity. "Do I cross my fingers?"

"That's what the swan is here for. Just wish with all your might."

He placed more petals in her hands. They felt velvety, like Lulu's skin, and Nola squeezed her eyes shut and prayed to be a wonderful mom to this amazing baby. Then she opened her eyes and dropped the petals onto the paper swan's other wing. Daniel crouched and gave the swan a gentle nudge. The graceful creation glided away, awash with its own glow, its body cutting through the lights that twinkled on the inky surface. What would be this man's wish? World peace?

He nudged away a second paper swan.

"Why another?" Nola asked, as she picked another flower.

"Swans mate for life. I wouldn't want to mess with the order of nature."

The light of a blue lantern made Daniel's scar visible, like a fine line of glaze. Nola poked the stem into Daniel's lapel. "May I?" she asked, then, as his body heat reached her, she stepped back.

For a few moments, the only sounds were the gentle lapping of the water, the distant exotic music, and the jumbled soft concert of crickets and night fowl.

"This is an awesome country," Nola finally said. "I wish I had time to study its art and architecture."

"Most are products of past glory. Modern times have not produced anything half as enchanting. In fact, a lot of good stuff was destroyed."

She giggled. "And you're the one in charge of my program here? You're supposed to extol China's virtues." Leslie might have been right; maybe Daniel was a spy.

"I can only give you a well-rounded view of this land, so you can take with you more than a saccharine-coated picture of a system that would never admit to going wrong."

A bird let out an odd, keening cry. "Like the orphanage you mentioned?" Nola asked.

"Like many social experiments gone awry. The Cultural Revolution subjected a whole generation of educated people to untold suffering."

"Margot Ashford and I visited a nice orphanage the day of my arrival," Nola said. "The children were well-dressed and they sang in a room full of toys." She didn't say how, looking at them, she had felt numb with the pain of their loneliness. No toys, she knew, could wipe away the fear of never belonging to anyone.

"That's a showcase institution, one of several built here after the International Women's Conference in '95 and a '96 report from Human Rights Watch made the government aware that their practices were frowned upon. Until then, the Chinese government maintained that natural selection should do its work without human interference. Out-of-quota and abandoned babies were 'surplus population' to be disposed of. The Chinese were shocked to discover that the West didn't take kindly to this view."

She thought of Lulu, of Jenna, of herself. "I lost both my parents at twelve."

"I'm sorry. I didn't know."

She bit her lip. "It's not in my press releases."

"So much for a star's life being an open book?"

She felt the tip of her nose flushing. "If reporters ask, I don't answer. They're sympathetic."

For a while, neither spoke. The soft light from the nearest green lantern shimmered in his eyes. Nola's gaze tried to pierce the depth of the garden. "How far is that orphanage?"

"Within walking distance."

"Can we go now? If there's a back gate, I'd love to make an end-run around the press." Her bodyguards in the front would never know.

A few hundred feet to the right of the embassy ran the main alley of the Silk Market. During Nola's sight-seeing on her first day in Beijing, the shops had been open to the street, and their merchandise had hung from ceilings and spilled onto tables on the sidewalk. Now the stores were shuttered with rolled-down iron grills. The click of Nola's heels on the cobblestones echoed in the deserted alley. Her satin shoes weren't made to tread on terrain rougher than red carpet. They would soon be destroyed.

Daniel walked beside her, his nearness like a thousand promises that made her feel guilty about Wade. There was a spring to Daniel's step, yet also an economy in the controlled movement.

"Most abandoned babies are not orphans. They have parents who aren't allowed to keep them," he said. "The girls are victims of both the one-child policy and the peasant preference for boys. In rural areas, baby girls are called 'maggots in the rice.' " There was anger in his voice. "In addition, an in-quota child must be born within the year assigned by the local bureaucrats. And a second child can't be kept. Ever."

"What if it is?"

"The penalties are huge: bone-breaking beatings, the destruction of homes, the loss of jobs and social benefits. Couples end up getting rid of a first-born girl to try for a boy, and then keep him only if he's healthy."

In the distance, two old women swept the empty street of debris and collected it into plastic vats. "Daniel," Nola asked, "How did you get into this? Where did you grow up?"

"In Maryland."

"Maryland! How normal."

"My parents are both professors at Johns Hopkins. I stayed close by, in Washington, D.C.—when I'm not on sabbatical from Georgetown University, like now."

"I still don't understand your job at the embassy."

He shrugged. "Acting as our government's human-rights watcher is the only way for me to have access to local resources. The Chinese government is very picky about who it lets close enough to take a look. My published political articles have denied me the entry the Chinese reserve for those who write favorably about their government's practices."

"Which of your parents is Chinese?"

"My father. His family invested all its hopes and savings when they sent him to America to medical school. He met my mother when she interviewed him for her sociology term paper." He glanced at her. "Don't look for a childhood trauma to explain my compassion. I had an uneventful upbringing among people in academia who made tolerance their religion."

How conventional he made it all sound. Her curiosity to know intimately what it was like to grow up among ordinary people would never be satisfied. Nola brought her fingers to her nose and sniffed the traces of anise and thyme. "Is there a woman in your life?"

His Adam's apple bobbed. "In a way."

If he were gay, Leslie would have detected it. "Where is she?" Nola asked.

"It's a long story; I'll tell you when we have time."

How long could a story be? On the other hand, if he asked her to explain her relationship with Wade, she'd describe a marriage made of gray layers of admiration, mutual interest, ambition and gratitude. If only she could also list the absolute premise of passionate love.

Daniel turned left off the market's main alley onto a narrower one and stopped in front of a three-story structure with the large industrial windows of a sweatshop. A single light bulb burned in a fringed paper lantern hung over the double metal door.

Nola pointed to a small plaque written in Chinese. "What does it say?"

"'Large, happy door,'" he read. "Human-rights watchers call it, more appropriately, 'the Dying Rooms.'" He pressed down on the handle, and the door opened with a squeak.

In the foyer, Nola's eyes adjusted to the darkness while her nostrils contracted against the onslaught of urine, disinfectant and mildew. Somewhere, a baby's cry was answered by a chorus of others. The canned laughter of a TV audience echoed down the stairwell.

"Anyone can walk right in," she said, surprised. "No one steals unwanted babies."

"It's part of the tragedy. They are sold for their organs, or kept alive to become beggars and prostitutes."

"Prostitutes? I thought this was a babies' orphanage."

"Many Asians infected with venereal diseases, including HIV, believe that having intercourse with a child cleanses them, that a child's virgin body soaks up all the impurities. The age of that 'child' has become younger and younger."

Disposable babies. Good for one-time use. Nausea churned Nola's stomach and sent a clammy sensation through her body. She peeked through the glass of a door on their right. Lit by an occasional dimmed electric lantern, a huge room stretched out. About twenty cribs were lined up against each wall, while dozens more made a double center row, leaving two wide aisles on either side.

She pushed open the door and stepped in. Cries and moans assaulted her. Here and there she caught a repetitive movement as babies rocked themselves. "Where is everybody?" Nola went to the first row and found two and three babies to a crib. In spite of the chill, no blankets were visible. "There must be some night care-takers."

She stopped next to a crib where one of the babies was standing, following her movements. Catching Nola's eye, a pathetic smile stretched on the face that was split by a harelip. Little arms reached up for her. Nola bent and picked up the baby, but its loose cotton pants were sodden; there was no way she could hug the baby without soaking her silk dress. From her outstretched arms, the baby tried to grab her hair. Just as Lulu had done.

"A recent arrival. She's not drugged with sleeping medication." Daniel smiled at the infant. "And she still communicates. She probably hasn't been tortured because of her deformity."

"Tortured?"

"By relatives, kids, neighbors."

"Someone loved and protected this baby girl until she was old enough to stand. Someone's heart must have broken giving her away," Nola mumbled, thinking of Lulu's mother. She surveyed the crib for identification. "How do we find out her name?"

"Even in functional families, children are often numbered rather than given names, especially girls. Girl one, girl two."

"My foundation underwrites craniofacial surgeries for kids, but we haven't reached China," Nola said. Careful to keep the baby away from her dress, she carried her and crossed the vast room toward a table. Beside it was a playpen filled with a tangled heap of skin and bones swathed in colorful fabrics and twisted into unnatural positions. It took Nola a moment to distinguish six babies with disabled limbs contorted into odd angles.

The Dying Rooms. Now she understood.

She put the baby down on the dressing table. On the shelf below was a stack of large cloth squares of all colors, probably donations from the neighborhood sweatshops.

"Let me change her. You'll need your dress clean for the LeRoy Neiman presentation." Daniel struggled to free the baby of her sopping rags. His chin pointed toward a narrow metal cabinet. "Look in the closet for some shirts."

Nola tried the cabinet. It was locked. "The clothes they lock. The babies they leave unsupervised," she muttered. She looked for a sink. There was none. She took a premoistened towelette out of her handbag and handed it to Daniel. She watched him wipe the baby with expert, tender hands, and was struck by a sudden urge to be back at the hotel with Lulu.

A creaking sound at the door made her turn her head. A tiny old woman, carrying a mop and a pail, pushed the door open with her posterior, turned around, and eyed the visitors. She cleared her throat and spit on the floor.

On the other side of the room a baby broke into a wail. Several others joined in. Daniel, clucking Chinese sounds to the girl he was holding, tied the ends of the folded diaper around the protruding little belly, then left her with Nola and went to speak to the cleaning woman. Nola fashioned another cloth into a top, crossing it around the baby's chest, and carried her back to the crib. The body, larger than Lulu's, was warm as she held her close. If only she could fly this baby to America, one of her foundation's doctors could fix her. For now, all she could offer was a fleeting hug.

The moment she placed the girl in the crib, the large, slanted eyes showed the hurt of disappointment, the misshapen mouth contorted, and she began to cry. The babies on the other side of the room continued their concert of wails. Nola looked around, powerless against the urgency of the need tearing at her from all directions. At the door, Daniel handed the old woman some yuan.

"She's confirmed that the night staff has left. They must have paid off the city supervisor," he said when he caught up with Nola.

"This is hard to believe."

He glanced at his watch. "Wade must be looking for my ransom note."

As Nola turned to walk out, short gasps like quick whistles made her stop and look down.

The exposed ribs of an almost naked baby fluttered like those of a frightened chick that had fallen out of its nest. The face was of an aging ape. The cloth diaper, soaked in brown liquid, had come loose. The swishing breathing bubbled its way through fluid. Nola overcame her revulsion at the stench of excrement and touched the child's chest. The skin felt hot and dry.

"This one should be in a hospital," Nola said, indignation consuming her. "She still has enough lung power to push air. She can be saved."

"By whom?" Daniel asked.

Nola was afraid to pick up this fragile creature, but asked Daniel to tell the woman to bring water.

The water the woman brought over in a wooden bowl was ice cold.

Nola raised her head toward the ceiling. "There must be two more floors like this one. No heat, no blankets, no warm water—" she stopped.

Daniel moved on from crib to crib, touching the babies, separating those who were tangled, or rubbing a baby's back. Nola hesitated for a split second, then gathered the flouncing hem of her gown and tucked it into the back of her panty hose. She removed the soiled diaper. Careful not to move the baby, she wiped the skin. The bed, too, was soiled. Nola stripped one side of the sheet, wiped off the vinyl mattress cover, fashioned new bedding, and slowly pulled the baby to the clean part before she cleaned the other side.

The baby never opened her eyes. Her breathing turned to a continuous gurgle. The body would lose the battle very soon. Nola covered her with a few silk squares. There was nothing else to do. Another wasted life.

She straightened up to see Daniel watching her. Self-consciously, she untangled her dress and let it drop back down to her ankles.

Her head swimming, she walked to the cluster of crying babies and located the infant who was screaming the loudest. Half naked, he had a badly twisted leg with an atrophied foot. But he was healthy enough to demand what was due him. She gave him her hand, and he clutched. Just like Lulu did. Another baby pulled herself up to a standing position, but when holding out her arms to be picked up, she lost her balance and fell with a thud on her bedmate's head, who, startled from sleep, let out a weakened shriek.

Nola bent over their crib to comfort them. She must get back to the party. Her party, which she had so looked forward to. "I want to take all these babies with me; who would even know they're gone?" But there were too many needing her attention. And what if she carried lice or disease back to Lulu? In her softest voice, she began to sing the song she'd written, "The Road to a Better Day."

The crying subsided while Nola sang and moved about. She caressed a cheek, stroked a head, rubbed a stomach, or let her finger be grasped in an infant's fist. She circled the aisles again as some babies fell asleep, sucking their thumbs.

Her song ended. "I'll be back," she whispered to the babies. "I promise." The building was a hundred yards from the Silk Market; she could find it again on her own.

She stopped again at the dying baby's crib. Something dark was moving next to her head. Chomping on the face!

"Oh, my God!" Nola yelled, and flung her handbag at the creature. "There's a rat!"

The rat shot out of the crib and scrambled away.

Nola's body shook. Blood trickled out of a gash in the cheek.

"It was eating her alive!" Nola cried out.

"Maybe it smelled death." Daniel halted. "The official death rate in these orphanages is eighty percent."

Nola's scalp contracted. "How is something like this possible?"

"About the same as in Nazi concentration camps. There are forty thousand welfare institutions in China—often warehousing young, old and disabled together—and most look more like this one than the one on your official itinerary." He handed her a tissue.

She accepted it and blew her nose. "The Dying Rooms," she whispered. "Warehouses of discarded lives. No one would ever believe the horror of it."

"Not unless they were told."

Chapter 7

Back on the patio, Nola's heart raced with the enormity of what she had seen. Yoram, all six-foot-five inches of him, stationed himself so close she could smell his heady sweat and count the hairs between his knuckles. Glowering at her, he muttered into his sleeve. The insurance company would pay him a bonus if it didn't have to cough up any of its policy. Nola selected a fig stuffed with an almond from a passing platter. A moment later, she spit it into a napkin. The Dying Rooms. How could the human mind comprehend the existence of such a place? Daniel's words kept screaming in her mind. Eighty percent. A new-age Nazi-style elimination of the unwanted. How was it possible in these times? God. Wasn't there someone to stop it?

A disoriented bird shrieked above, its sound darting about the garden. For a split second everything in front of Nola spun—the food stations, the people in exotic outfits, the kaleidoscopic décor. If she didn't eat something, she might faint. But when she tried a crab-stuffed shrimp, it turned to glue in her mouth.

"Wade's coming," Yoram said in a flat tone.

Dinner's spicy aroma steamed the air and clashed with the stench that clung to Nola's nostrils and was probably fermenting on her skin. Wade would smell it. She stepped back under the branches of a nearby maple tree and scrutinized the party for Kong Ruiji, the Chinese prime minister who had accepted the American gesture of friendship in the form of her Double Happiness concert tour. She must speak with him.

She spotted Leslie, looking sensational in a white evening jacket, pinstriped satin pants and a red bow tie, conferring with an American general. He was probably getting boot-camp training tips, which he would put to good use, torturing her into better and better shape.

Jean-Claude, catching Nola's eye, pulled his oversized penguin-print bow tie as far as its elastic would allow and, grinning like a jack-o'-lantern, snapped it back. Roberta scurried toward her, her eyebrows pinched together under her mop of bangs. Ambassador Ashford, accompanied by several dignitaries, passed by the patio and yodeled, "The queen of the party." His small entourage raised their glasses. A camera flashed, and its brightness blazed into Nola's head. It hung, pulsating like strobe lights.

She sent a weak smile without making eye contact. Beads of perspiration erupted on her upper lip. She dabbed at them with her napkin, then picked something cheesy from a passing tray and forced it down. Eat. Get your blood sugar up.

From the open lawn behind her, a chorus of frogs broke into a concert. It amplified in her ears with its disharmony. Wade neared, his face trapping something wild trying to break out, but Leslie cut in front of him and tugged on Nola's arm. "Let's visit the little girls' room." When she started following him, he whispered, "Oh, my, my. Whatever happened to your dress?"

In the vast powder room, upholstered stools lined the wall-to-wall vanity below gilt-framed mirrors. Nola dropped onto a stool and shut her eyes. "I caused Wade to worry," she murmured as Leslie took out cleaning fluid from a case he kept for all eventualities and rubbed off what he referred to as "Not chocolate éclair" from the heels of her shoes and her dress.

For the next half hour, she felt like a zombie as the Ambassador and Margot Ashford, with Wade trailing behind them, guided her around the ballroom, introducing her. She smiled and tried to make small talk, but more than once she began a sentence only to forget what she had meant to say. After a while, she plastered an apologetic smile on her face and pointed to her throat, and Wade explained that she must preserve her voice. Although it was against protocol for guests to ask for her autograph, she complied with those who did. Anything to fulfill her duty and be left to think.

The Dying Rooms. Lulu. When was the exact moment within these past twenty-four hours when her former world of music and adulation began to feel like fraud? All she wanted to do was hold Lulu and bury her face in the infant's belly, generating squeals of delight. She wanted to smell Lulu's scent. To play peek-a-boo. To promise Lulu that she would never, ever, see the Dying Rooms. How was it possible to love so fast, so completely?

Kong Ruiji showed up in Nola's line of vision. He greeted her with an effervescence that forced her to clear her head. She needed to speak with him about Lulu.

"Our favorite diva! My people love your singing," he called out and held her hand in his. Even though he was slight, his hand was square and his grip strong, an incongruity that banged at the gate of her consciousness.

"Thank you for choosing me to sing for them." She tilted her head in a gesture of respect. She posed for a photograph with him, then another, while he flashed a brilliant smile to the camera. Behind her, she felt more than saw Wade gloating.

As soon as the flashbulbs stopped and the photographers moved away, Nola opened her mouth to talk about Lulu, but at that instant thought better of it. It would insult Ambassador Ashford, whose help in the matter Wade had already sought. Her interference might also undermine Wade's efforts while she tried to appease him.

Her smile was thin. "I'm amazed by your perfect English," she told the prime minister.

"I bet you can't recite the second and third stanzas of 'The Star-Spangled Banner,'" he said. Her own reflection glimmered back at her in the lenses of his glasses.

She forced a laugh. "Did you, too, sing it at football games?"

He began to recite,

On the shore dimly seen through the mists of the deep,
Where the foe's haughty host in dread silence reposes...,
He reached,
Praise the Power that hath made and preserved us a nation.
Then conquer we must,
When our cause it is just,
And this be our motto, 'In God is our trust!'

Nola felt dizzy again. This gregarious man, who seemed to embrace Western culture, was the one responsible for the Dying Rooms. Eighty percent. *Then conquer we must, When our cause it is just.* That was the Chinese policy. She wanted to leave, to be back at the hotel, where she could protect Lulu.

She excused herself for taking too much of his time and touched Wade's arm. "Let's leave," she whispered.

"Are you OK?"

She shook her head. "Let's go. Now."

"What's the matter with you tonight? You disappeared with Daniel for almost an hour. You know better than to flaunt a love affair."

"Love affair?" She had expected a possible insurance premium-hike argument. Barely keeping her voice down, she said, "Daniel is not my lover."

"The reporters don't know that."

Blood thumped in the veins of her temples. "But do you?"

His eyes narrowed. "Have some respect for my intelligence."

She bit her lip. In spite of her promise to herself, she was causing Wade pain, escalating their problems. "I'm sorry to make you jump to the wrong conclusion," she murmured, her voice tight and small. "Can we leave now? Please?"

He held both her shoulders, his fingers hard on her flesh. "Honey. Are you noticing that you are intent on fucking everything up?"

Behind her, someone dropped a glass, and amid the shattering of crystal came a mumble of apology. On a love seat to her left, a gray-haired man reclined toward a young woman with cropped blonde hair, blocking her chance of escape. He said something soft in French.

Wade's eyes darted away as he spotted someone behind her, and his face brightened. Nola followed his gaze for the source of his instant transformation. Astonishment filled her when she recognized the slicked-back salt-and-pepper hair and tanned face of the CEO of BRW Entertainment approaching the prime minister.

"What's George Mauriello doing here?" she asked, feeling the same distrust she had felt since meeting the new CEO a little over a year ago.

"You're one of Phonomania Records' biggest-selling singers. With this tour, you're probably the biggest. Another reason not to fuck it all up."

BurgerRanch World, or as its new umbrella conglomerate had renamed itself, BRW Entertainment, had been the largest fast-food chain in the world when it purchased hundreds of radio stations, a thousand movie theaters and StarVision, the second largest movie studio in Hollywood. Fourteen months ago, it acquired Phonomania Records, a cozy home that had nurtured Nola through the vicissitudes of her career. Mauriello ousted Keith Schwartz, the affable president who had gambled on her success the first time he heard her fifteen years before. BRW's brisk expansion into the entertainment industry had been making a splash.

She watched Mauriello and the prime minister conversing like two old friends. Although Nola owned the copyrights to most of her music, Phonomania Records held both the licensing and distribution rights. "For a communist premier, Kong Ruiji knows every American honcho," she said. "Maybe Mauriello is bending his ear about the counterfeiting of music and films. BRW must be losing millions of dollars in royalties."

"It would be impolite to criticize one's hosts," Wade replied. "And Mauriello has his priorities. He's got a fat contract to open BurgerRanch restaurants here."

The conversation was so normal that Nola breathed a little lighter. If only she could find a way to stop pushing Wade's buttons. "Burger and rice?" she asked.

"No messing up with branding." He laughed, his anger seemingly forgotten. "The first phase is six hundred restaurants. They'll name them 'Bao-Ji-La' to make them easier for the Chinese to pronounce." Wade spoke while his eyes roved around the room. "Mauriello is a lobbyist, not a businessman. As a former U.S. senator, he's the ideal front man with connections."

"I liked the family environment of Phonomania," Nola said. "Are we still cool with Mauriello? We've only had dinner with him once since he's entered the picture." They had missed his New Year's bash in Bali because of her concert tour in Brazil and Argentina.

"The synergy among the various businesses—all catering to the same audience—benefits us. You now have the largest entertainment conglomerate in the world behind you."

She glanced at Mauriello. Perhaps he could use his political power to influence the closing of the Dying Rooms. Perhaps Bao-Ji-La could sponsor the opening of decent establishments instead.

Ambassador Ashford waddled over, his arms outstretched. "Ready for the unveiling?"

"What? Oh." She had totally forgotten about the painting.

With his arm on her back, Ashford steered her indoors. One of his aides handed him a microphone, and he flicked it as a test. On that cue, the crowd of three hundred parted, creating a passage to an easel on which sat a large canvas, covered by a white sheet.

Hundreds of lithographs and thousands of prints of LeRoy Neiman's collage depicting Nola's goodwill China tour had already been sold around the world. But the original painting would be seen for the first time tonight.

She sipped her champagne, letting the bubbles tickle the roof of her mouth, and surveyed the crowd. These were not ordinary people. Most had reached high levels of political or economic success. And they adored her, she reminded herself. This was what she had wanted, and she must savor this moment of recognition and of her making artistic history with a Neiman painting. A recollection of the high she had felt when he did sketches of her months ago in New York came back. She hadn't been able to resist peeking at his work and loving it.

She tried to listen to Ambassador Ashford speaking about the painting, but his words echoed against images of the Dying Rooms that occupied all the spaces in her head. No wonder Lulu's desperate mother had devised a creative way to give her baby the best chance she could think of.

Applause accompanied the burst of primary colors on the magnificent montage of images. Against a background of the Great Wall, snaking its way over mountain peaks and the Forbidden City with its temples and hidden courtyards, Nola stood holding a microphone. Showered by gold records like falling stars, she was wearing a pink dress, its wing-like train raised. Only she knew that the upward tilt of her head that had become her signature silhouette was a tribute to her dead parents.

Ambassador Ashford pointed to details on the canvas. "LeRoy Neiman has cleverly inserted themes that appear in Nola's albums. Our Nola's unpretentious choice of music—from classic pop to hip-hop—has given her audience everything they love. In an environment in which performers outdo one another with gimmicks and quirks—none too clean or moral—our girl-next-door Nola is our national treasure."

"The girl next door," who had been the village orphan, Nola thought, as a staffer revealed U.S. President Corwith's dedication on the back of the painting, and Ambassador Ashford offered it to the Chinese prime minister. Kong Ruiji responded with a short but flowery speech about China's friendship with America, then presented Nola with a jade sculpture of a willowy Chinese maiden holding a lotus blossom.

After more congratulatory comments, the guests dispersed to their dancing and eating. Her eyes unblinking, Nola kept staring at the maiden. Unlike millions of other disposable babies, Lulu would grow up to be a maiden like this one only because she had been given a second chance on life.

"You look pale. Don't drop it." With the reverence Wade saved for precious antiques, he took the jade from her and placed it in its padded box.

Nola let out a tired smile. "We need to talk." She would tell him that Lulu had already changed her in ways she hadn't believed possible; she would say how much she wanted them to be a happy family, a whole one. "Let's leave," she added just as Ambassador Ashford planted another glass in her hand.

"By the way, what's the deal with that Chinese baby?" he asked.

"Wade spoke to you about her this morning, right? She's a beautiful, intelligent baby," Nola replied. "I'm sure there's some red tape to be cut so we can take her to the States—"

Wade interrupted. "We haven't had a chance to talk about it."

She felt her forehead crinkle. Synapses clicked in her head, going nowhere. Wade had had all day to tell her he had been unable to contact the ambassador. Had he knowingly kept this information from her?

"If the Chinese allow this precedent, soon every visiting foreigner will have babies chucked at them, like flying golf balls," Ashford said.

"I'm planning to adopt her," Nola said.

"Play it down until things are sorted out." The ambassador pulled a pipe out of his pocket and waved it at someone behind Nola.

A quiver went through her. "Roberta Fisher is handling the press—"

"My point exactly." Ashford turned to Wade. "Big-Mouth Roberta is the last person we want working on this. I strongly suggest Nola refrain from giving any interviews or making any statements about this matter."

"I've already taken care of it, Mr. Ambassador," Wade said.

Nola tossed a glance at her husband. What did he call all the interviews she had already given? "Is there a problem with our keeping the baby?" she asked the ambassador. "After all, it's amply clear that her mother didn't—couldn't—care for her."

Ambassador Ashford rocked on his feet. His hands spread over his midsection. "Oh, the Chinese want that baby in an orphanage, where she belongs."

Nola's heart flipped. "An orphanage? It's out of the question!"

"This creates very bad publicity for China's abandoned babies crisis," he replied.

Words swirled around Nola. "This baby wasn't abandoned," she responded, her voice shrill. "She was placed in my arms."

"Hon, you've visited an orphanage here." Wade spoke with exaggerated patience. "The baby will be fine there."

"That was the official tour." Nola narrowed her eyes at him in a cue he should get. "It was a showcase institution the Chinese wanted me to see. And even there, you're talking about a life of hopelessness and loneliness."

As Ashford accepted a Scotch from a waiter, Nola caught a look he exchanged with his wife.

"Yes. We went together," Margot said in a breathless rush. "There were toys and murals and attentive caretakers. The children staged a performance for us. Weren't they adorable, with their black shiny hair and those cute little bangs and button noses and mouths?"

The ice cubes in Ambassador Ashford's glass clinked.

"Does anyone here stop to think that we are talking about a life—the life of a baby?" Nola cried out. "No! She'll die there—"

"Take it easy. It won't be as bad as you think." Wade's arm around her shoulder felt like a giant leech. To the Ashfords he said, "A great party. Thank you for everything. We've had an extremely busy day today. She's exhausted." He put his mouth to her ear. "Get a grip on yourself. And show some respect."

Nearby, three men dressed in U.S. Navy whites burst out laughing at a joke.

An orphanage. This was a huge misunderstanding. The champagne soured in Nola's stomach. Blood thudded in her temples. She scanned the room for Kong Ruiji's dark-framed glasses. She must speak to him.

The prime minister was nowhere in sight, and Ambassador Ashford's words came as though from a distance. "Let's see how things pan out. You're our representative, their guest. Together we'll take care of you." He took the last gulp of his drink, then extended his hand toward Nola. "May I have this last dance?"

Chapter 8

(1980 - 1981)

Jenna's shrieks woke their mother, who became lucid enough to yell that Nola should do something. Nola flew out of the cottage and ran through the woods without shoes or jacket. She kept slipping on the snow, but made it to the big house, where she babbled and cried so much that the caretaker couldn't at first get out of her what had happened. Then the woman called an ambulance. It took a long time for the paramedics to find the estate, longer than it had ever taken to deliver a pizza. Nola waited in the cold at the gate to show them the way to the cottage. She was more scared than she had ever been in her life, but was sure that once the doctors took care of Jenna everything would be all right. A few weeks later, when Nola was finally allowed to visit her baby sister in the hospital, nothing was better. They had grafted skin from Jenna's stomach onto her face, yet it looked worse than the old man's face did. Even in horror movies Nola hadn't seen such a face. She sat frozen by the crib, shock and guilt filling her throat. The medicinal smells of the hospital made her bones cold.

It was her fault, even though Dad told her it wasn't really, that she wasn't a trained nanny. Dad and Mom fought a lot, and Mom, who was in bed all the time, cried, and didn't say much when Nola curled up on the floor by the radiator to take away the chill. The cold had not left Nola's limbs since the time she had run in the snow. The sharp lines of the radiator cut through her sweater into her back, and it felt right, like a cage, where she should be put.

When Jenna was well enough to leave the hospital, the caseworker placed her with Miss Helga, a German-born nurse who lived near Nola's school. It was close enough for the family to visit, but while Nola went over every day after school to play with Jenna and teach her songs, and Dad sometimes went too, Mom never did. "Taking care of you is hard enough," she told Nola.

Nola wished she wasn't so hard to take care of, but didn't know what to do. Especially after Dad stopped coming home.

All summer she didn't want to fall asleep, in case he returned from his gigs and she'd miss him, but ended up falling asleep. Mom said Dad had a girlfriend with a little girl. Nola wanted to know whether it was that girl from Connecticut, who like her, made up songs and sang them. Were that girl's songs better? If only Mom weren't against a phone, maybe Dad would call. He had once said that if she wanted something very hard it would finally happen. So she prayed very hard for Jenna to be better and for him to come home.

Suddenly, just as school started, Mom went away to a hospital and Nola couldn't visit her as she had visited Jenna. But Dad returned.

He told Nola that he had missed her and would never again live away from her. No, he hadn't been to Connecticut. Where did she get that idea? He had been to California, where a lot was happening, and to New Jersey of all places, which Bruce Springsteen was putting on the map. Dad brought new records: Air Supply. Blondie. New stuff from Fleetwood Mac. Kiss Unmasked. Nola stared at the faces with white-and-black makeup and tried to comprehend the music they produced. Dad had her listen to rap, which was new, but he didn't believe it would catch on because white people were bigots.

Dad bought a motorcycle to get to his gigs, and now that Nola slept, she'd wake up before dawn to hear the roar as he veered around the house and into the horse barn before he killed the engine. In the silence that followed, she would fall back to sleep, happy that he was home.

Together, they bought Jenna new clothes and toys and brought it over to Miss Helga's. Mom was away for months, and Nola thought about how she could never have all the people she loved at the same time. It was terrible gaining one and losing another. "Trade-off" was a new word she had written in her notebook.

Trade-off wasn't fair. Down in her cave in late fall, when the waves were so high and noisy that she could hardly hear herself, let alone the girl from Connecticut, Nola decided that if she had to trade the most important thing for Jenna to get better, she would trade her singing no matter how it hurt to give it up. At three, Jenna colored beautifully and made up silly little stories to go with her paintings. The pictures and stories came to her as easily as songs came to Nola, and the two of them performed them when Dad came.

No unexpected guests appeared at the door to stay, and when Mom finally returned, she no longer smoked cigarettes, not even the rolled ones. Mom said they had ruined her voice and she wanted to start singing professionally again. She ironed her hair again, and the two of them had what Mom called a "search and destroy party," in which they found all the cigarettes in the house and drowned them in the toilet. Afterward, they gobbled down a whole Sara Lee cheesecake and Nola drank coffee for the first time. It was like being friends, not a mother and a daughter. If only Mom would agree to have a TV, they'd watch it together; the kids at school said that "The Love Boat" and "Diff'rent Strokes" were cool.

That afternoon, having the best time with Mom, Nola forgot about Jenna living elsewhere, but then felt guilty and promised God she'd never ever forget her sister again, especially since Jenna loved her so. She could now read the hands on the clock and would wait by the front door for Nola's visit when school was over and then cling to her all afternoon. Nola knew she didn't deserve Jenna's love, but it was she who talked Jenna into cooperating with whatever surgeries the doctors recommended. The nurses at Smithtown Hospital even allowed Nola to hang around past visiting hours, because Jenna was the only kid whose mother never came.

With every surgery, until the bandages were off and the bruising and swelling went down, Nola prayed very hard, and little by little, it happened. The tightened skin around the left eye relaxed, and the red patch across the nose and cheeks paled and smoothed. Jenna got better and Nola didn't even have to give up her voice. Like Dad had said, it helped to want something very much. Now Nola wanted very much to be a famous singer. When Nola was small, Mom said, people used music to convince the government to stop killing innocent people in Vietnam and sacrificing tens of thousands of American soldiers. Music could change people's opinions, Mom said. Songs like "Where Have All the Flowers Gone" and "Bridge Over Troubled Water" had moved governments. The power of music hadn't stopped with the Vietnam War, Mom explained. There were new causes for music to take on. Now it was about giving women equal rights, which was an amazing thing not to have if Nola just thought about it, Mom said.

One winter afternoon, when the sky was getting dark at four, the belly stove was sending its heat into the room, and Nola's parents were talking about the Equal Rights Amendment, Nola rested her head in her Mom's lap. Mom hadn't cried once since her return from the hospital the year before. Nola looked up at the pale cheeks, at the smile playing on her mouth. "Can Jenna move back home?" she asked.

Mom jerked and shoved Nola's head off her lap. "Jenna's fine where she is."

"But you don't even know her!"

Dad touched Nola's shoulder, and when she turned, she saw his eyes blinking fast, telling her to shut up.

"She's adorable and she's all better. No hospitals or anything," Nola gushed.

"We'll talk about it another time." Dad pulled Nola toward him.

It was so unfair. Even the social worker who came to talk to Dad said that Jenna was better off with Miss Helga. How could that be? Miss Helga was a witch. Secretly, Nola called her "Mini-Nazi." The woman had eyebrows that zigzagged when she spoke, and she never ever smiled.

Mom collected any old shoes and began working on a collage. She painted them in metallic copper and bronze, and after they were dry, placed paper flowers or river-polished pebbles or stuffed condoms in each. Dad said this was great art. Mom said it was self-expression. Nola didn't understand how anyone could express anything but her own self, but didn't say it because, with so many shoes to work on, Mom would be busy and smiling for a long time.

Dad signed up for gigs closer to home, sometimes not even as lead guitar. He checked Nola's homework. He was proud of her good grades. He told her which books to take out of the library and then quizzed her on them. He composed music for her poems, and the two of them sang together and Mom clapped and said they made a very good team. Nola was just sorry that Jenna couldn't be there.

That year, Ms. Beverly Cutter invited Nola to join the drama club, and gave her the part of the lion in *Aesop's Fables*, and then of Dorothy in *The Wizard of Oz*. Nola also got to sing the national anthem at school games and Christmas carols over the PA system. Even though the kids thought she was weird, with clothes that weren't right, they played with her, although the girls told her she couldn't come to their homes after school because her parents were "hippies," which meant refusing to buy living room furniture and a TV and a telephone. It hurt, but with things so much better at home, Nola dared not mention it to her parents—or speak again about bringing Jenna home, even for a visit.

When Mom began to smoke again, Nola knew this was "drugs." Sometimes when the three of them sat together on the Indian pillows and made music, Dad smoked too. Once, after they all fell asleep, a cigarette started a fire. Nola woke up to see a pillow burning. She screamed and pulled Mom away. Then she poured the water from the teakettle and kept screaming while she filled the lobster pot in the sink, but then she couldn't lift it. Dad just sat next to the burning pillow and laughed and laughed at her efforts to pick up the heavy pot. Nola's nose ran as she cried and scooped the water out of the large pot with a smaller pot, and finally put out the fire.

The next day, both Mom and Dad apologized and said it had been a lousy thing for them to have done and swore they'd be much more careful in the future. They kissed her and told her that she was a terrific kid. Also, she must promise never to tell that nosy social worker who might then decide to take her away like she had taken Jenna. If that happened, Nola figured, Mom would first be sad, but then she would forget all about her, too.

Afterwards, Nola always worried. What if something terrible happened to her parents, like that fire, but she was too small to save them?

One day, while playing hopscotch with some girls, she saw the social worker at school talking to Ms. Cutter. Yellow mushrooms grew in front of Nola's eyes. She felt herself get wet. She dashed to the bathroom and hid there until long after the bell rang, when Ms. Cutter came looking for her. She hugged Nola and told her not to worry, she was a good student, which showed that everything was fine at home. Nola walked around in her wet underwear and jeans until school was over.

The only thing left was to grow up fast and become a famous singer. She'd fill up their cottage with couches, and chairs, and lamps. Then Jenna would live at home, and they would be like any other family.

Chapter 9

Another day with this baby, more time to wrap herself in her sweetness. Nola sat with Lulu on the carpet, the baby babbling happily and banging on the keys of a plastic pop-up toy. Nola pressed on the blue key, and a door popped open. Dingggg. The head of a dog jumped up. "Look," she said and guided Lulu's hand. "Dog," but Lulu's attention was diverted to the red, green and yellow keys producing a cat, a fox and a cow.

To Nola's surprise, Lulu returned to the blue key and hit it. "Do-o?"

Something sweet spilled into every fiber of Nola's being. "Is she trying to say 'dog?' " she asked Leslie.

"Do-o," Lulu said and hit the blue key again. She looked up and her almond-shaped eyes twinkled.

"She's just making baby talk." Leslie laughed. The tan of his chiseled face emphasized the gray in his eyes. "But one day she'll make a fine stand-up comedienne."

Nola kissed the bridge of Lulu's nose. "We need to give you a bath," she said, but the idea of the slippery body in the water terrified her.

She called the maid in, and after the woman demonstrated how to wrap her forearm around the baby's back and grip the far arm, Nola felt that another milestone had been conquered.

But there was so much ahead of her. Thoughts of the orphanage right off the Silk Market mixed with her lingering unease over Wade's equivocation on the subject of Lulu's adoption. Earlier, when she had asked him why he hadn't talked with Ambassador Ashford as he had promised, he just stood at the window, gazing outside, seemingly preoccupied. She had seen him examining other people from the corner of his eye, calculating, measuring landmarks and positions he could use in a battle. Until now, that person had never been her.

Leslie fished in his bag for combs and arranged them on the vanity table. He lit an incense stick.

"It may be bad for the baby," Nola said, and he put it out, but some of the spicy aroma lingered.

Nola submitted to Leslie's ministrations. As he massaged her scalp, the only sounds in the room were Vivaldi's "Winter" turned low and Lulu's babbles. Her mind on Ashford's words, hanging onto his final statement that he and the Chinese would take care of their important guest, she flipped through a folder Wade had left behind. There were Internet printouts of Billboard, MTV and foreign press reviews. Unlike the collection of blurbs sent weekly by the clipping service in an album, these photocopies were full-length articles. She picked a loose page and scanned it.

"*...with the U.S. and China's mutual enemy—the Soviet regime—out of the race, these two leading global powers are jostling for supremacy, a struggle in which there can only be one winner.... Chinese leaders use unabashed xenophobia, portraying both the West and their neighbors as bloodthirsty and imperialistic.... This new century will see China becoming the most powerful military force on earth, with economic power to match.... The Chinese are exploiting U.S. naiveté by acquiring as much American scientific and military technology as they can through open channels, and then proceeding to obtain more through clandestine, illegal means.*"

On the carpet, Lulu plopped on her back, rolled on her stomach, and, with a grunt, raised herself on all fours. She lifted and placed one hand forward, then another, and then collapsed. She laughed and rose again. How could Wade not see how enthralling this baby was?

Nola waved at the newspaper clipping. "Leslie, listen to this. We can learn something." She began to read aloud.

"You're giving me an idea for a new dance number inspired by Chinese costumes." Leslie's feet moved in staccato steps, and he broke into a short choreographed jig. "This is good stuff. Conflict. A great dance number with theatrical visuals. The world going up in smoke...."

Nola raised her voice. "*The White House should wake up from its euphoric ignorance to smell the tea. Instead, it has mustered its most formidable weapon: a cultural dose of pop music! Send Nola Sands and let this China doll reset the buttons on the control boards of history.*

"*The Chinese, chuckling behind their bamboo screens, act too polite to refuse the gesture, which they regard as an asinine, disingenuous Western notion of friendship....*"

If it weren't for Leslie's fingers tangled in her hair, Nola would have jumped up. "Gosh! What an insult to me, to my role here—"

"Nasty people—Brrrrr." Leslie faked a shiver. "You're supposed to read only good reviews." He took the page out of her hands and jammed it back into the folder. "It's politics. Of the worst kind. Now relax." He rubbed gel into his palms and pinched the ends of her hair.

Snatches of good-byes came from the living room as Wade's breakfast meeting broke up. Nola's back straightened. She would take him to see the Dying Rooms and then talk about Lulu's adoption. After all, he had supported her in sponsoring orphanages in Ireland and Mexico. He had helped her establish the home for children at the estate where the old man had lived. Wade had been her mentor, protector, friend, soul mate.

Wade, wearing a white turtleneck, was on the phone, his back relaxed on the couch, his legs in grayish gabardine pants crossed at the ankles. He twirled the carved stamp of his name in Chinese at the end of a three-inch stick. Upon their arrival, each crew member had ordered such a "chop" made of soft stone, and Wade had since been peppering his documents with red stamps.

He was discussing with the chief engineer some unforeseen problems in dismantling the Forbidden City stage set and transporting it to Shanghai for the next concert. Something about getting the government to provide enough eighteen-wheelers, otherwise unavailable for rent.

Nola leaned on the doorframe. "Hi," she said.

He tossed her a somber look and went on twirling and talking on the phone. No sooner had he hung up than the phone rang again. It was their Manhattan office, where a team of secretaries did Wade's bidding while they also answered fan mail, autographed Nola's photos, and fielded letters requesting donations of either her money or her eggs. Two webmasters updated her site, responded to fans' e-mails, led music chats, and surfed the Internet to squelch rumors.

Nola waited a few minutes, then gestured that she wished to speak to him.

"I'll call you back in a few," Wade said into the receiver and punched the disconnect button. He looked up at her, but did not rise. "Yes?" His tone was cold.

"Wade, I'm—I'm sorry. I know you were worried about me."

He scratched his palm with the clean end of the chop. "That's one thing. But you've offended others. You have a responsibility to those who put themselves out for you. Important guests came to salute you—from the Chinese prime minister to George Mauriello—and you blew them off." His voice gathered anger. "In all the years I've known you, you've never acted like such a primadonna. And now, of all times?"

"Very important things are happening in my life—"

"You bet! After fifteen years you're close to being number one!"

"I mean—"

His hand checked his thinning hair although it was sprayed solid. He got up. "Look, we have a crew call for the filming at the Great Wall tomorrow at dawn, which makes today a hell of a short and busy day. I'm still battling with the Ministry of Tourism to restrict public access where we're filming in order to keep tourists out. We're dealing with the stage set, the most expensive the world has ever seen. I have a dozen TV crews running all over the place, fighting with my director, while Roberta—of all times!—is negotiating a comeback to CNB Radio. We're in the middle of a concert tour, the media is climbing up my ass about this baby, and I have a rash that's driving me nuts. All I ask is that you be a good girl and cooperate with me until I can breathe."

"What about what I need from you?"

The sweep of his hand encompassed the world outside. "Who is all this for? Cleopatra?"

"You've been incredible," she said. "Now please understand that I have to keep Lulu. Help me find a way to work it out—"

His voice rose. "Didn't you hear what I was just telling you?"

She felt herself shrink as if a corrosive substance ate her bones. "Please talk to me. I can't handle shouting."

Wade's eyes, those pale blue orbs, honed in on her. His features softened. He circled the coffee table and put his arms around her. "Sorry. I love you," he said, and put her head against his shoulder.

For a short moment she leaned against him. He was her refuge; there was no one else to call family. "I need your strength, your loyalty," she murmured.

"You've been the center of my existence," he said, his voice quiet. "Even when I was married to Deanna."

She nodded against his shoulder. There had been no change in his devotion between their first twelve years as artist and manager and the past three years as wife and husband. All marriage had done was to put them in the same bedroom for whatever hours were left of their late nights. "Maybe slipping into marriage like a wheel into its groove is part of the problem," she said.

"Our problem is that you seem to forget that we're partners."

"I don't want us to be merely partners who sometimes have sex," she said with sadness in her voice. "Am I being unrealistic to want more?"

"*You* want more? Remember that next time you so impetuously jump into the sack with a lover in the middle of an important party—"

She jerked herself away from his hold. "Wade! Daniel's not my lover."

"Excuse me. He reads you poetry under the Beijing sky."

Her hand clamped at the base of her throat. "How can you think I'd cheat on you?"

He lifted his palms to stop her from saying any more. "Hey, I've told you before. Your music is fed by your passions. If you don't live, life won't come out in your voice. A new lover will keep your energy fresh."

She bristled. "Is that all you care about?"

The phone rang again. "Don't answer," she said, but he had already picked it up.

He covered the mouthpiece with his hand and spoke to her. "Listen. Tomorrow, you'll have a brutal day. Take it easy today, exercise, go shopping…. But whatever you do, don't let the media bait you into making any more statements."

Outside the room, Nola kept her hand on the doorknob, lingering. How was a gravy train supposed to feel?

"How did the Yankees do?" She heard Wade asking whomever he was speaking to on the phone. At the answer, he gave a hearty laugh. "Get me tickets for the World Series, will you?"

Leslie peeked out of the room, Lulu in his arms. "Well?"

Nola shook her head as if to rid it from the cobweb of bewilderment. "I must get Lulu adopted. Today. I can't do it alone. I don't want to—and I don't know how."

Lulu pitched forward, her arms outstretched. Nola took her and cradled the compact body, rubbing her cheek against the crown of Lulu's head. After her bath, the baby smelled of powder, the color in her cheeks was high, and her tuft of clean hair fanned out like a black dandelion.

From behind her, she heard Wade speak into the phone. "Yes. One million shares of Motorola. You can't beat a billion-three market of Chinese for beepers and cell phones. And while you're at it, I want a complete due diligence on military technology our government has cleared to move into the commercial and export market." He listened for a moment. "Fine. Buy me another two of BRW. Yes. That's two million shares. BRW Entertainment. *Capeesh?*"

"Wade's buying a nice chunk in the company that holds your contract," Leslie said. "He puts a lot of eggs in one basket."

"If you want a financial chat, you're talking to the wrong person."

On the crown of Lulu's scalp, in a spot where the bones had yet to fuse, the skin throbbed with a pulse. The utter vulnerability of her head sparked a fire inside Nola. She handed the baby back to Leslie, swiveled on her heel, and stormed back into the living room.

She slammed the door behind her. "If you have time to speak to your broker, you have time to speak to me. Please tell the operator to hold all calls for ten minutes."

The look of astonishment on Wade's face quickly changed into amusement. "What is it now?"

Her heart banged against her ribcage. She settled in the armchair set perpendicular to the couch. "How much money is there in my foundation?"

"Lots. Why?"

"More than a million?"

He laughed. "Yup. A lot more than several millions. Why?"

She had allowed him to patronize her, she knew. That, too, must change. "There's this orphanage here I want closed, moved and reestablished. Come see it with me—"

"The foundation is doing plenty in the orphan department. You can't start taking over all the orphanages in China."

"Just one at a time. You should see how horrible this one is. Eighty percent die—"

"I've told you before: we must pick more visible causes. It does you no good to spend so much money on a cause and then keep the kids' privacy. It has no PR value."

Inserting more courage into her voice than she felt, she said, "I want this done. I'm not asking for your approval—only your help."

He rose to his feet. "In that case, I'd better scoot off to my next meeting where my contribution will be appreciated—"

She could kick herself for handling this matter so awkwardly. "Please sit down," she said, more softly. "We must talk this over."

He looked at his watch. "I asked you to wait a couple of days."

"You have time to chat about the World Series, but not to talk to me about a baby? I know we've never dreamed of raising one—" She wet her lips. "Female singers have babies. Madonna is blossoming as a mother. Diana Ross had five pregnancies with two sets of kids years apart. Faith Hill travels with three young ones—"

"Sure. And when was the last time either one cut a platinum eight times over? And have you seen them going on the road for months at a stretch? Celine is nesting in her pad in Las Vegas!"

"I'm finally ready to give it a try." Nola's voice was quiet, filled with the gravity of this revelation, but tears pinpricked her eyes.

"And how do I fit into this family planning? Am I supposed to be the father?"

"Why not? You were terrific with Jenna—"

His hand gesture was dismissive. "What a waste of time that was. And did you think I enjoyed it? I had to relieve you so you could sing!" He shook his head. "It would never work."

"Why not?"

"Why not?" He addressed an imaginary audience. "'Why not?' she's asking." He looked back at her. The teasing smile did not leave his eyes. It irked her almost as much as his anger did. "For all the very obvious reasons."

"Whatever these reasons are, they aren't obvious to me."

He ticked off his fingers. "You're just breaking into the number-one spot. You've been pissing off Jean-Claude and the musicians. And if you think Leslie will just let you compromise your artistic commitment, think again."

"Why is the whole world against my keeping Lulu?" she cried out.

"The 'world' wants you as you've always been. Theirs. You don't belong to yourself. You belong to the more than two hundred people who depend on you for their livelihood—from the roadies and costume designers to your website techs and tour personnel. And you belong to the record industry—the TV hosts, BRW shareholders, the stores' sales staff and even the factory workers who manufacture your CDs. You are a big business. And you want to walk out from it all to play dolls?"

"I'm opening up to the most incredible experience of my life. To have a child is to believe in everything all over again."

He gathered some papers and flipped through the bills in his money clip, counting. "We are our work. The factory worker is no less chained to his machine than the president of the United States is chained to the Oval Office. No one has the freedom to walk away. Not Jean-Claude, not Mauriello—not even me."

"I'm not walking away from my work—"

"There are three million castaway babies in China. Yesterday, a cameraman found a live one peeking from a garbage bag when he was trying to take a discreet leak in the market. I saw a dead one under a bush in the Forbidden City. Are you going to adopt them all?"

The truth hit her. The gap that yawned between them had opened the moment Lulu was thrust into her arms. "From the start, you had no intention of adopting Lulu!" she called out. "You just humored me, dragged me along with false hopes!" She scrambled to her feet. "Lulu is a fact in my life—she's no longer an option to deliberate about. She's my daughter."

A vein bulged in his brow. "You're pushing me into reminding you what happened the last time you cared for a baby—"

The room turned hollow, airless, the floor dropping from under her feet. Suddenly she saw the two of them in new roles. She was in the audience, watching him on stage with a clear vision of who he was, who she was. Then their life together was like a magnificent stage floor being dismantled, exposing the roughly hewn lumber, nails, ropes, then collapsing.

"I will adopt her. With or without your consent." Nola walked backwards as she spoke. "And if I am so important to so many people, let it be for a reason beyond selling more CDs. I can be the voice for these other babies. I am going to make sure someone stops their dying."

Chapter 10

Stepping outside the hotel doors, Nola stopped. She registered the paparazzi, a wriggling mess, like a beached school of jellyfish.

The sky was still overcast, low clouds connecting it to the earth. The air was moist with the smell of rotten roots and fried food. "No comment," she mumbled again and again to their questions. "No comment."

The ground swayed under her feet. With Wade's outright refusal to have Lulu in his life, the hope of stabilizing her marriage had evaporated. What now? Until she could arrive at answers, she had none to give to the media. The irony of it! Normally, she and the press had coexisted in a neat symbiosis. She needed them to grow her into a star, they needed her to nourish their survival. Over time, many of the reporters had become acquaintances. "Next time get me out through the garage," she muttered to Roberta.

"The reporters are multiplying like falling autumn leaves the longer you're silent about the baby," Roberta said. "That's good. Keep them guessing—and hot."

Carrying Lulu and flanked by Leslie and Yoram, Nola half ran to the limousine, leaving Roberta to bask in her battles with the media.

The limousine sailed past wide blocks of ten- and twelve-story concrete structures punctured by hundreds of windows and decorated with laundry hanging from balconies. The mammoth buildings tapered into dilapidated four-story houses with exposed cinder block walls, galvanized roofs and crumbling verandas.

At the commercial district, the limousine slowed to inch its way through thousands of people and bicycles moving every which way. Nola's misery would not desert her. Lulu had chased away the loneliness, but now both of them were dependent on Wade. Without his support, Nola was anchorless. In her head, questions spun like a compass out of control. What would it take to adopt? How could she handle whatever paperwork would be required? Would the Chinese allow it without her husband's consent? How would she go about getting for Lulu a Chinese exit permit and a U.S. entry visa?

Traffic became organized in the main thoroughfare, where the center lane for motorized vehicles was flanked on either side by much wider bicycle lanes. The metal railings kept the multitude of pedestrians from spilling into the road. Nola craned her neck to scan the row of small shops, each marked with Chinese characters. The store windows were dusty and cluttered with electric appliances, work tools, sewing supplies, kitchenware, herbs and furniture—all strewn or hung about. No touch of modern merchandising and display concepts was visible.

Against the creaking of farmers' wooden pushcarts, ringing bicycles and blowing horns, Leslie kept silent as he toyed with his huge necklace, a Pueblo silver and turquoise piece. Nola was certain he was under Wade's orders to keep her to her routine, by whatever means. Was he paid a bonus at the end of the year for all the rehearsals or recording sessions she didn't miss?

Since no car seat could be found in the stores, Nola held Lulu in her lap. The closeness of the trusting little head resting between her breasts filled up the empty spots inside her. She brushed her lips over the fuzzy head. "I love you," she whispered.

"Lulululululululu."

For Lulu's sake, whose wide eyes savored the goings-on in the street, she had to carry on. "Look," Nola said, with a cheerfulness she didn't feel, as she pointed out the window. "Look. These are your people."

Of the thousands of pedestrians, only a few wore the traditional gray Mao suits with mandarin collars. Most were dressed in plain European-style clothes, the women in shapeless shirts and straight-leg cotton pants in faded blue. Sometimes, a short jacket was thrown on top. Only the occasional coolie hat tied under a wrinkled chin, or the rare thin pigtail dangling down a stooped old man's back hinted at an exotic past.

A makeshift stall displayed a blurred photo reproduction of her latest album, and Nola recognized the Chinese characters that translated her name as "Bashful Fire," more of a publicity ploy than a direct translation, she had been told. A young man stood beside a table piled high with cassettes.

Leslie straightened in his seat. "Pirates! Wade and Mauriello should see this."

"It gets my music around." Nola said, and averted her eyes to the sun's rays breaking through the clouds, which scrambled away from the heat.

The limousine was about to cross an intersection when the music of cymbals, small drums, wooden clackers, flutes, gongs and woodwinds stopped all traffic. Rows of women moved in a dance. They were dressed in matching red silk pajamas with wide green scarves tied over waists broadened by age. Each woman's hair was twisted in elaborate loops from which cherry blossoms or tiny bells dangled and swung in rhythm with her feet. Holding long-stemmed pipes, fans, or colorful batons, the dancers' arms swayed, painting delicate calligraphy in the air.

Lulu turned her head toward the sounds.

"The Golden Girls," Nola called out. "Look, Lulu." A similar mission of older retired female factory workers had welcomed her at a reception upon her arrival. Now Nola watched these smiling women, whose stage makeup failed to pop open eyelids drooping with years, or to lift cheeks gathered in pouches at the jaws. The high-pitched half-notes of their singing were haunting in their strangeness. The voices, clear, yet girlish, were filled with delight.

"What guileless dignity," Leslie, a perpetual student of dance, said.

It was the joy on the performers' faces that arrested Nola's attention. She had known this emotion ever since her childhood performance at Woodstock. The street was their stage. Nola searched the simple dance for stories of these women's lives, but found none. No hint that many of them had to desert a baby or risk a job and housing and starve—or even suffer beatings—as Daniel had described. No hint that they had endured the hunger, forced migration and persecutions of the Cultural Revolution. Just like her, music helped make order of their lives' chaos.

And just like them, she should go on living.

At the Seven Whispers Garden, the air was filled with the resinous aroma of pines. Inside the gate, in a large pebbled bed, half a dozen trees stood far apart, each in the meditative state of a live sculpture. Coerced over years into dance positions, their branches formed a serene composition only a gardener with the soul of an artist could have created.

Leslie walked ahead with raised arms to contemplate divine intentions. Yoram followed at a distance as Nola pushed the stroller down mud-packed hidden paths. Light waltzed on the gravel around clusters of tall reeds and broke through manicured branches, casting bewitching shadows on the ground. Every new turn unveiled a new imaginative arrangement of plants, rocks and light, each a perfect picture framed by a trained pine or a gap in the sculptured rock.

Lulu fell asleep pressing a cloth diaper to her cheek. The yellow blanket accented her black hair and high-lighted the pink of her cheeks. Nola crouched and listened to her breathing, even and worry-free. This was music she could listen to forever.

At the far end of the garden, about twenty men and women, young and old, practiced Tai Chi. Their fluid, harmonious movements flowed into one another like the gentle coursing of water. Nola was mildly surprised to spot Daniel in the group. With balletic grace, his hands traced the air, moving as though he held a tall porcelain vase, turning to hand it to an invisible maiden on his other side.

If Daniel saw her, he gave no indication, but his face glowed with an internal peace.

"He's the most self-contained man I've ever seen," Leslie said.

Nola turned away. She was intruding on something personal.

Leslie went on speaking in a hushed voice. "Martial arts steel the body and soul like no other discipline." He paused. "Have you read any of his books?"

"About U.S.-China relations? They're probably full of academic lingo." She glanced at Daniel again. The man's depths eluded her, yet attracted her, too.

"Ask for his poetry book. I'm sure he'll sign it with a kiss."

"What poetry book?"

"Chinese. He's translated some into English all by his lonely self." Leslie's hands imitated the swelling of ocean waves, or a galloping Arabian horse, beautiful all the same. His silver and turquoise necklace never moved as his back remained erect. "How he could have missed the chance to dazzle you with his poetry I don't know."

Nola stroked Lulu's velvety hair. "I'm only a side assignment. All he wants is to get me out of the country with as little to do as possible so he can go back to passing clandestine messages in fortune cookies to dissidents."

"No man could resist your charms, which, as I could see last night at the embassy garden, you showered on Daniel. No straight man, anyway." Leslie raised his hands as though cupping clouds and then gently lowered them down to earth.

"He has a secret code I couldn't begin to crack, even if I wanted to." She felt a light blush rise in her cheeks. "He's impervious to looks, fame, or money."

"He's smart enough to know that each of your platinum records is equivalent to a Ph.D."

"He's smart enough to remember that I'm married."

"Anyway, he's flat-footed. You wouldn't be interested."

She burst out laughing. "Flat-footed? Otherwise he's perfect?"

"Oh, yes, that scar of his." Leslie's eyes took on a dreamy glaze. "Too bad he isn't gay. I could go for him myself."

She regarded Leslie. His silhouette was exquisite. Softly, she said, "Must be tough being alone. All this traveling can't be helping any."

Leslie's lower jaw, strong and square, slacked in a rare show of emotion. "It's fun looking for love in all the wrong places." He touched her arm. "Time to meditate and think positive thoughts." In imitation of the Tai Chi group, his hands extended outward, the fingers bunched up as though milking life's potion from the air.

Yoram twirled a straw between his teeth and hummed something for-eign. She indicated to him to keep his distance, then turned the stroller with the sleeping baby and followed the gurgling sounds of a small waterfall. It cascaded into a pond tucked behind an imposing jagged rock formation. Pierced with water holes, the rock looked as though it had been dropped there at Creation.

There was symbolism in many things Chinese. That was the mystery, the allure of this hidden pond. Beauty was better enjoyed when stum-bled upon. Nola settled down on a flat rock at the edge of the water, curled her legs into a lotus position, and placed her index finger in Lulu's palm. The little fist closed on her finger, warm, innocent, so flawlessly waiting for life to happen. Even the miniature nails were a miracle of existence. Her baby.

But as in her childhood, there was a trade-off.

The wind rustled through the cluster of cattails. Nola sat still, breath-ing in the chalky smell of drying stones and the green fragrance of fresh-ly clipped shrubs, and wished she could transport herself into a medita-tive state like Daniel and Leslie could do. Years before, during the months when she had sought Judaism, the spiritual end wasn't medita-tion as it was a connection all the way back to the traditions and histo-ry of the Jews.

The rabbi had said that God was everywhere: in the sky and the earth and the sea. Staring at the waterfall, Nola tried to empty her mind of all thoughts, to become one with nature and perhaps to discover God. But as the water bubbles popped at the surface of the pond, they burst with images from the Dying Rooms: the hare-lipped baby who had clutched at her; the sick infant being eaten alive by a rat; the cold loft stuffed with shivering babies who lingered in vomit and excrement. How many had died in the fourteen hours since she had been there?

In the greenish water, lilies floated on the surface, their delicate pink flowers swaying in the soft breeze. A frog burped and jumped onto a leaf. A dragonfly buzzed, its translucent wings catching the sun's rays and breaking them into rainbow-colored prisms. The wind rustled through the cluster of cattails.

When Daniel had said she had more power than she gave herself cred-it for, he had no knowledge of the times she had faced almost-empty venues, or her grueling sixteen-hour days, or that she was still only as good as her last album. Yet, in her anger, she had told Wade that she would become the voice of these babies. How unrealistic. It was one thing to fight for Lulu's adoption and quite another to fight for the fate of millions of abandoned babies. How presumptuous to think she had the power to move a government! But then again, her parents' friends—those scruffy hippies of her childhood—had done just that. With demonstrations and music, they had forced the ending of the Vietnam War.

Lulu's cupid mouth stretched into a smile as she slept, and she emitted a tiny satisfied sigh. Unlike the Dying Rooms babies. The words blasted in Nola's head. Eighty percent. How could she not act?

A pink petal fell into the water and lolled a bit before slowly sinking. The green depth hid it, never again to be seen by a human eye. Lost forever. So was the flash of orange caught in the wing of a monarch butterfly. So were those starved, neglected babies.

Like a time-lapsed photograph of a flower opening, a song began to build in Nola. The babies who died were like flowers blooming unseen and doomed to die unenjoyed, their beauty never admired, their sweet scent never savored.

The words, inspired by Thomas Gray's "Elegy Written in a Country Churchyard," and the music, shorthand for emotions, emerged. Nola began to hum. *Flower babies bloom unseen, Flower babies die unloved.* The music presented itself, as though it had merely been hibernating in her and was lazily waking out of its slumber.

She stood up and sounded the words, tasting them, feeling their flavor in her stomach and throat. Her diaphragm expanded as the music rose within her, starting, erasing itself, starting again.

There is a place where babies live,/ With no hope for tomorrow.// A place where flower babies die,/ Filled with only grief and sorrow.

The concept was right; its execution needed work. Nola played with the lyrics, searching for the right verse, the catchy rhyme.

Flower babies, petals plucked,/ The color's gone,/ Morning dew dries up/ Before the day has begun—

She should try for the images. The crowded cribs, the twisted limbs, the rats…. Her voice rose, lamenting. *Lost in the cold of the night,/ In a place with no heat or light. /*

Lulu woke up and regarded her seriously, half-dazed from her sleep. Nola sang, collecting the disjointed notes and words. It finally all came together. Nola's hands gestured in the air as she conducted the orchestra within herself.

The song ended. Nola's breathing came hard but her head felt light. The trance that had transported her to the magical realm of music snapped, like Cinderella's spell at midnight. She heard Leslie clapping and turned around. Lulu, imitating him, brought her pudgy hands together and gurgled.

Daniel rounded the tall reeds. He stopped and smiled. The light shimmered in his dark hair, breaking in earthy tones.

"Were you here the whole time?" she asked.

"Long enough."

Leslie's gesture encompassed the garden. "The artist in her milieu."

"The best things in life are free: truth, kindness and imagination." Daniel's gaze hooked onto Nola's. "And they are all experienced in the soul."

Nola's skin buzzed with the whir of the magnetic field between them. Daniel knew the song for what it was. Last night's visit to the Dying Rooms had been their shared experience alone.

"The best things in life are free," Leslie repeated. "Sounds like a fortune cookie."

A faint motion in the water made Nola lower her gaze. Two goldfish swam by, a big fish followed by a smaller one. A mother and a baby.

Daniel stepped over to the stroller and spoke Chinese to Lulu, with a quick intake of air like the slurping of noodles, alternating with short clucks. Lulu clucked back, and her feet kicked with delight.

"Glad to finally meet you," he said in English. "I've heard a lot about you." He tickled her toes in their socks. Giggling, she raised her arms toward him.

He unsnapped the stroller straps and brought her to his chest. He held her, his eyes closed. His face contorted, and Nola was startled to read pain.

Behind him, over the top of the cattails, a cuckoo hopped and tried to settle. It flapped, swooped down, then flew away.

Chapter II

(1982 - 1983)

On her way through the woods to the big house, Nola liked to fool the birds. "Trrrrrrrrrlllll, trrrrrrrrrrrrrrrrrrrllll," she would sing, or "Kewkewkew-eweeeeee-eweee," and they answered her. She'd switch to "Tzwitz, tzwitz, tzwitz," and soon the woods would be filled with a choir of her conducting, like Snow White. Sometimes Nola spotted a squirrel, a rabbit, or a doe with her Bambi, and although none ever clustered around her to listen, she imitated Snow White's trilling.

One day, when she went to the big house for a plate of food, the old man raised a weak arm toward the next room. It was like a huge living room, but with even bigger windows on three sides, and Mom called it "the orangerie." Nola stepped in, and at the sight of a shining black piano something tightened down between her legs, at the place she sometimes touched.

After that, two evenings a week, Ms. Beverly Cutter from school came over to give her lessons on what she referred to as "the Steinway." Nola went over to practice whenever she felt like it. She left the windows open for the birds to hear. The old man also listened, but she didn't mind him at all. Since Jenna's accident, she had become friendlier toward him, because she could tell that he was a nice man beneath the disgusting face. Sometimes, he would point a trembling finger at a composition in the music books, and Nola would play it. She was only sorry that Jenna wasn't around to hear, especially when their father came with his guitar and the two of them jammed. That's what he called their playing together.

Nola liked Ms. Cutter, who always said nice things about her being a great kid and musically talented. Ms. Cutter was a perky woman whose dark curls were in perpetual motion. She had a big smile and many large teeth that on her looked friendly. She was slight, but had a protruding stomach, like a shelf on which she leaned her folded arms. Nola tried to imitate that posture but could never manage it. When Ms. Cutter was around, there was always something interesting on which to rest the eyes, because summer and winter, her long black skirts and black sweaters created a backdrop for a collection of jewelry made of silver, ceramic, feathers, stones or glass.

For Mom's birthday, Nola used her savings to buy the biggest, most beautiful "I Love You, Mom" card she had ever seen. It was as big as the world atlas, had pictures of brilliant flowers and exotic birds, and it was so special that the manufacturer wrapped it in cellophane. The card was also like a promise to protect her parents from any bad things that were sure to come, worse than the fire.

Something wonderful would surely happen when Mom got the card, Nola was certain. Maybe Mom would remember sweet Jenna, who had to live with Mini-Nazi that never smiled because, she said, no one paid her to smile. But after Nola had given her Mom the card and got her out of the house for a walk by the cliff, Nola's hopes were over because Mom didn't even want the Sara Lee cheesecake. There was no difference in the air, except that the anticipation that had been so exciting, was spent.

And then Dad came home and told them that the deposit he had put on a ranch in Colorado had been stolen. Mom said it was his fault because he was too naive to be a businessman or even a rancher. Nola didn't mind losing the money too much. Just a little. She was sad about the furniture they could have bought instead, but was glad not to move away from Jenna and school, so things evened out, except that other dads who weren't musicians knew how to take care of things, and their children didn't have to worry about them. Something thin but strong, like a fishnet, lay about Nola, and sometimes she feared her feet might get tangled in it and she'd trip and fall.

When Ms. Cutter asked who knew of a special place to stage an Easter egg hunt, Nola suggested the lawn on the big estate even before she had asked the old man's permission; she knew he wouldn't mind. And sure enough, when she told him, half of his face smiled, so she dabbed with his napkin at his drool before the cat got to it, and he touched her fingers in thanks. His skin was dry and cold, like the belly of a dead puppy, and it sent shivers up Nola's arm. How could anyone be so old for so long? Still, she brought him a bowl of red Jell-O with two spoons, because now she didn't mind sharing with him.

Since it was spring, Nola went to check on the stairs leading down to the beach. More steps were missing. She had to hold on to a jagged rock, and she cut her hands and scraped her thighs. For a second she lost her footing and thought that maybe, as Dad had warned, she might break her head. Her next thought was, who would then be good to Jenna? But by the time the thought flashed through her mind, she had balanced herself.

Tucked into a crevice in her cave was an old issue of *Rolling Stone*. Nola sat on driftwood and leafed through damp, curled pages. There was one story about the Captain and Tennille and one about the Bee Gees, who bought their parents homes and cars. That's what she was going to do. She couldn't wait to grow up. Just as it was awful to be old for so long, so it was awful to be little for so long.

The day the kids came to set up the Easter egg hunt around the estate, Nola's parents were out on gigs in New Jersey. That was better than being embarrassed by Mom in her weird long dresses, with her talk about loving the world, and her showing off her stupid stuffed shoes.

Happy at having something to give that no one else could—the gardens, the woods, the view from the cliff—Nola had a million ideas. The best was to create a maze for the egg hunt. The old man's gardeners had brought to the mansion many new shrubs but hadn't yet planted them, so she instructed the two biggest boys in the class to move shrubs and block the regular driveway. It would be more fun if people had to take the trail leading to the cliff, then cut back through the woods where they could hear the birds. Nola painted large arrows to direct the hunters.

This was going to be quite a different egg hunt, said Ms. Cutter, and Nola felt she would burst with excitement. And tomorrow, Mini-Nazi would bring Jenna over, and there would be awe in her four-year-old eyes. The old man had his caretaker buy goodies for all the kids. It would be Nola's special day, better than her twelfth birthday three weeks before that no one remembered because Dad wasn't home.

Hours after Nola had fallen asleep alone in the cottage, she heard the roar of Dad's approaching motorcycle. She heard Mom's laughter, bell-like and raspy at the same time. There was a hesitation, probably when they noticed the blocked driveway. Nola giggled as she saw in her mind's eye Dad lifting the front wheel of the motorcycle and taking the detour. She heard the roar gathering power, and then receding. Then there was silence; probably they were cutting through the woods. Happier than she had been in a long time, Nola fell back to sleep.

Her parents' bodies were found on the beach the next morning. The motorcycle had flown off the cliff, the cops told Nola when they came to the cottage, and at first she was sure it was a mistake, because the sun was shining and it was a going to be a beautiful day, her day. At the same moment she also knew it wasn't a mistake. She had always expected something awful to happen.

The police did something called an autopsy, which was really cutting up her parents to see what had killed them, as if Nola didn't know it had been her fault. It made no difference that later, the nosy caseworker told her that her parents' blood had contained alcohol and marijuana.

In the coming hours, days, weeks and months, loss and guilt overtook all sensation and thought. Nola was no longer hungry or tired. Words no longer shaped themselves into sentences. Instead, visions of the boys moving the shrubs and the arrows she had painted stalked the dark paths of her brain. The pain was so intense, so unrelenting, that Nola wanted to jump out of her skin and run away. She'd leave her skin for Jenna, so that Jenna wouldn't know she was gone.

Chapter 12

Nola returned from the Seven Whispers Garden to find Big-Mouth Roberta waiting in front of the hotel. Wearing a loose magenta suit, with huge brass earrings dangling on both sides of her face, Roberta poked her head into the limousine. She reeked of cigarette smoke, a sign of a broken promise. Wade did not permit smoking; he hated its lingering smell.

Roberta handed Leslie a cell phone. "Don't leave home without it. We're on spin control here."

As soon as Nola stepped out of the limousine, the horde of paparazzi, three times its earlier size, descended, shouting questions. "Are you planning to adopt her?" "How does your husband feel about it?" "Were you contacted by the Chinese government?" Uniformed hotel security men shoved them back to make room for Yoram and three of his men to shield Nola. In her arms, startled by the noise, Lulu broke into a whimper.

"You're scaring the baby," Nola told the reporters, keeping her voice low so as not to further frighten Lulu. "And please cut those flashbulbs."

But they kept popping in Lulu's face, and she screamed at the onslaught. The shouts continued.

With Roberta grabbing her elbow, Nola made for the hotel entrance. Nola reached the huge revolving door, large enough to accommodate both guests and luggage. "After this morning, I thought we'd use the garage to avoid all this," Nola muttered.

"You can only hide so much. There's a media frenzy over this baby all over the world. We must give the sharks little nibbles or they'll become too hungry to control."

Nola stopped. She'd give them something to nibble, all right. "You're wasting your time on me," she called out. "It's the orphanages you should be looking into. And take pictures so the world can see the Dying Rooms."

"That's enough!" Roberta hollered.

Lulu cried louder. Nola spoke into the battery of microphones. "By the Chinese government's own statistics, the death rate is the same as it was in Nazi concentration camps."

"What's the matter with you?" Roberta's earrings jangled with her grumble.

"Are you determined not to give this baby back?" a reporter shouted.

"I will not send her to die." Pushing the revolving door with her shoulder, Nola went in. She felt an enormous sense of accomplishment; she had never before taken a public stance about a controversial issue. Unlike her orphanages or craniofacial foundation, where the residents or patients required discretion, saving the Dying Rooms' babies would demand public exposure. And the first to be saved would be Lulu.

"I can't believe the stunt you just pulled," Roberta hissed. "I told you to shut up!"

"Don't you speak to me that way." Nola shot her an angry look and stormed inside. Hopefully, CNB Radio would soon seal its comeback offer. She'd be glad to see Roberta's back.

Twenty minutes later, calmed and propped up in her crib, Lulu was sucking her bottle hungrily. The single tear that glistened on her black eyelashes filled Nola with renewed awe at the miracle of this creature that had come into her life. She wiped away the tear, then put the wet finger in her mouth. The devotion she felt was stronger than anything she had ever felt toward Jenna.

"I'm going to be a good mommy," she whispered. "You just wait. I'll talk with Mr. Hatley Ashford. He'll be on our side. He must be. Right, Dumpling? Right?"

"Aat-taat-tat," Lulu said.

"Right." Nola laughed. She took a notepad and a pencil, stood in the middle of the room, and hummed her new "Flower Babies" song. *There's a place where babies are left to die.*

With Lulu's babbling echoing her notes, Nola kept on, scribbling down new lines. She made corrections, edited it some more, then sang it again. It would be great, she knew. The lyrics would still need perfecting, but the song was there. Although she dreaded facing Jean-Claude and his growing idiosyncrasies, they had a rehearsal scheduled. Might as well; she needed him to infuse her new song with his sorcery.

Wade was out—or avoiding her—which was a relief. Nola rummaged in her CD collection, found Chopin, and turned on the stereo system. The soothing notes of the "Impromptu" poured into the room. "You like music? You'll have a life filled with it," she told Lulu. "And love. Lots of love."

Nola shed her clothes and went into the shower, leaving the bathroom door open to hear Lulu's chattering and rattling of toys.

When she came out of the shower, Lulu was grabbing the bars of her crib, and, her face reddening, tried to sit up. Nola helped her, then called the embassy and spoke with Ashford's secretary, asking him for an immediate appointment.

Instead of calling up a makeup artist, she dabbed a sponge into a small compact, added some blush, and mascaraed her eyelashes. She examined the results, liking the face in the mirror. After so many years with this face, she couldn't imagine what she would have looked like now had she been unwilling to fashion a new face out of the homely raw material she had once been. She wouldn't be here now, of that she was certain.

Packaging. That was how celebrities were created, Wade had explained. Anyone who failed to understand it had no business being in show business. She regretted none of it.

In the wardrobe room she passed on the buckskin pants and knit shirts she liked and selected instead a chartreuse Calvin Klein mini skirt suit, not too short for her meeting with Ambassador Ashford. If only she had the knowledge to make things happen. Damn Wade for making her fend for herself at such a crucial moment.

She picked up the phone again and asked for Mr. Chen at the American embassy. In her mind's eye she saw him standing by the gurgling pond, his gaze soft, his magnificent body full of secret, ancient knowledge she craved to explore. For now, he had given her the gift of understanding her new song. And then there was the way he had held Lulu. Nola had seen love, but also ache.

"Daniel," she said when he came on the line. "Can you find out what I must do to kick the adoption process into gear?"

"You're in for a lot of paperwork. The Chinese government requires more than a dozen documents, and each of those requires authentication beyond anything you can imagine."

"Such as?"

"Take your birth certificate. It was probably issued by a hospital in a certain county—"

"Suffolk, New York."

"Well, then. A top administrator at the hospital must confirm, in front of a notary, that they were the ones to issue this birth certificate thirty-some years ago. Then Suffolk County's notarization is needed to confirm not only that such a hospital existed at the time, but also that the notary's seal is authentic and such a professional is certified to practice in the county. This is followed by a New York state government document, obtained in Albany, which confirms—in another notarized, red-sealed document—that the certification issued by Suffolk County is an official Suffolk County document. Then, the state department in Washington, D.C., must confirm that this is indeed New York state's authentic document. That document is taken to the Chinese consulate in New York, which issues a final document stating that indeed, the U.S. State

Department document is an authentic one. It takes weeks and months."

"Lulu will be ready for college!"

"That's just your birth certificate. You must go through this process for a dozen more papers, from health check-ups for both you and Wade, to home visits by social workers to investigate your living conditions and lifestyle, and ending with police criminal records—or the lack thereof."

This was worse than her battling for custody of Jenna from social services years ago. Even then, with a shrewd attorney, she had failed.

"I must get Lulu out of China a week from Tuesday," she said.

Daniel did not reply. She was learning to read these silences of his. Dignified. Not withholding information, but rather providing her time to reflect. Any decision was up to her.

"Ashford must circumvent the bureaucratic process, then," she said. "Thank you."

"Call any time, any hour," came his soft reply.

Her hand remained on the receiver for a moment longer. Daniel's treatment of her was not the adulation of an admirer privileged to get close enough, as with many men. He seemed to never have noticed a barrier between them.

Nola looked in the mirror above the dresser. Her breasts under the camisole were rounded and full, and the nipples erect against the silk. An image of Daniel doing Tai Chi flickered in her mind, sending erotic sensations to the bottom of her stomach. Beyond the lean-muscled strength of an athlete, there was the way he moved with effortless grace, the energy coiled into his back and shoulders flowing like water through the tips of his fingers. She could almost sense his touch on her skin.

The soft steps of the maid startled her. Nola hadn't locked the door to the wardrobe room after selecting her clothes. The woman shuffled to the low table in the sitting area and picked an orange out of a fruit bowl. With a silver knife, she began to peel it.

"I can peel my own orange, thank you," Nola said, louder than was necessary, as though the woman could understand. "But I need you to help with the baby. Later." She tapped on her watch and lifted two fingers.

The maid covered her mouth and giggled. Nola still found it hard to get used to the giggle that never seemed appropriate to the mood or circumstances.

"What's your name?" Nola pointed to herself. "I'm Nola. Nola."

The maid looked at the tips of her felt shoes.

"Would you teach me a Chinese song?" Nola asked, and went on to demonstrate, "La-la-la-lalalala-la. For babies?"

Bowing her head, the maid shuffled backward and left the room. Nola sighed and locked the door.

With a sensuous feeling, she brought the orange to her nose and sniffed its tangy fragrance. She dug the edge of the knife into the peel and burrowed her finger in the whitish sponge. She opened the fruit and separated a section, then placed it in her mouth. Its juice spurted onto her tongue in a sweet taste different from its smell. She separated another section and bit into it, then took a third.

Everyday delights could be so simple. Nola stared out the window, confounded by a new insight. Peeling an orange on her own. That was what ordinary people did. Since Lulu's arrival, she too, was learning to enjoy these moments of solitude she had once dreaded.

Lulu was asleep when Nola lifted her out of the crib and lowered her into the stroller. "Sorry, Dumpling," she said softly. "I told you I'm a working mother who keeps odd hours."

She stood at the entrance to the huge ballroom Jean-Claude had commandeered. In addition to flying in her core American band, he had assembled local musicians. Chairs and music stands for the forty-piece band were grouped in a loose arch formation. Today, only the dozen American musicians gathered to fine-tune her program for the Great Wall filming the next day. At the far end of the stage, Leslie straddled a gilded chair and observed one of his instructors leading the troupe of male dancers. Jean-Claude stood with his back to Nola, speaking in his singsong French accent to the musicians and the four vocalists.

"—and who knows if she's coming. She might be playing Mommy again today."

Fury rushed through Nola's veins. She stepped in. "How dare you speak about me this way?"

His narrow face went crimson. "We had a deal about what I'm supposed to do, and what you're supposed to do. It's like with my wife. She raises babies but doesn't sing. You sing and don't raise babies. Oui? It's very simple."

"You can go to hell."

Leslie vaulted over the edge of the stage to the ballroom floor. The dancers, all in black, continued to stretch, bend, arch their arms, and practice their pirouettes.

"You're overstepping your boundaries, Dude," Leslie told Jean-Claude. "Without the aid of the Divine, a man cannot walk even an inch, and you—yes, you, you prick—can't compose a single note."

"All I care about is the music," Jean-Claude said. "Live or die for the music, *Oui?*"

"And you need me to flaunt your talent," Nola called out. "So chill out."

"He feels insecure with Lulu around," Leslie whispered in her ear and steered her away. "You should be used to his eccentricities."

"He's never targeted them against me. When do I get to act crazy and get away with it?"

"You already have, Love. Ask Wade. He thinks you've gone off the deep end."

She sucked in her breath. *Leslie, what about you?* she wanted to ask, but she didn't wish to know. "It's called 'evolving,' " she said, and gestured for him to go back to his dancers.

"Okay, okay. I'm sorry. Kiss-kiss?" Jean-Claude leaned forward and kissed the air around her cheeks. "My Ginger Goddess, I'm bad."

They had to prepare for the concert in Shanghai the day after next, plus four more. And in addition to the video shoot at the Great Wall, there would be a dozen others at sites across China. And she needed him to do the arrangement for "Flower Babies", assigning music parts to the various instruments.

She could barely look him in the eyes. "I'm cool. Let's get to work. I've written a new song."

"Friends again?" Whipping the imaginary tails of a tuxedo behind him, he sat at the grand piano. His long fingers flexed and released in the air like a pair of graceful cranes in flight. "Take ten!" he announced to his musicians, who rose and dispersed. He took a gulp from a Coke, wiped his mouth with the back of his hand, and said to Nola, "Let's hear."

Her right hand tapped the piano keys in search of the notes she heard in her head. *Flower babies bloom unseen, Flower babies die unloved,* she sang the repeat line. "I want it melodious, rolling, rising high to a plateau where it plays itself out, trailing into a whisper."

He beamed at her, and his thin, sharp nostrils quivered. "Marvelous." He offered a rendition, adding a few musical ringlets.

"Very slowly, kind of crying for love, mercy and hope," she said. "*Lamentoso?*"

"A prayer. *Sostenuto*, sustained."

"Give me a high key in half-notes, like the voices at the Chinese opera."

"I love it. Love it. Love it," he said. "How deliciously haunting."

It was the way it had always been. The two of them tried out several possibilities. With Jean-Claude's artful facilitation, even a mediocre song could become a hit. And this one had to be as big as "Share The Feeling of Love" if she were to accomplish her new mission.

He played some more. "Got it? *Lamentoso, doloroso, affetuoso.* Very slowly, sorrowful, with warmth."

"Move to allargando, slow but louder. Always ascending," she said, relaxed again, delighting in their creative partnership. "Keep your flourishes."

"My special smoke puffs." His wide grin exposed gums. "Musically, I mean."

She laughed. Jean-Claude's genius made up for his quirks. "I want to perform this in Shanghai."

He stopped playing. "Are you nuts?"

"We've already established that you were the one smoking something."

"You'd be out of your mind to sing this in China." He tossed his dark curls away from his face and his chicken-like neck showed bulging veins. "They'll cart your ass off the stage in a straightjacket. And they'll chop off my fingers. They have those miniature guillotines for musical directors who are disobedient."

"I want to do this," she said in a quiet voice. "I have to."

"Not when I'm around. I've got a wife, kids and a girlfriend to go back to. And the MTV Awards in December, the American Music Awards in January, and the Grammys in February. Don't fuck it up for me."

It was three o'clock by the time Nola was shown into the anteroom of Ambassador Ashford's office, anticipation and dread at war within her.

His male secretary, a bespectacled, clean-cut generation-Xer with private-school diction, was quiet as Nola sat down on the couch and flipped through a copy of Newsweek.

"Do you have any of Daniel Chen's books?" she asked.

"I have his *Washington Post* op-ed piece from last month." He rummaged through files, then photocopied it for her. Crimson spread up his cheeks as he handed her the pages. "You're one of my favorite singers. Whenever I need to give a present, I buy one of your albums."

"Thanks." She flashed him a smile and asked for his name and address. She glanced at the note he handed her. "Christopher, I'll have my next CD sent to you." "Flower Babies" would be the first song on the album. She could see the cover photograph: a baby's cheek being nibbled by a rat.

The door to Ashford's office opened. He shook hands with two Chinese men, then turned to Nola, a wide grin on his face. "Nola, you look lovely. As always." With his hand on her shoulders, he led her into his office.

The spacious room with picture windows had built-in mahogany bookcases and a carved Chinese-style, sumptuous desk, its hefty size in proportion to its owner. The blue in the Chinese rug was repeated in the gathered curtains and reminded Nola of the Oval Office. The American flag hung limply from its pole behind the desk. The smell of tobacco, faux masculinity, dulled the elegance.

"Thank you again for the party last night," she said.

"Where's Wade?" Ashford asked. In daylight, his fleshy cheeks showed a miniature road map of red veins. He walked toward the seating area, where magnificent yellow lilies with no scent had been set in the fireplace.

"He's busy moving the set to Shanghai," she said, and sat down. From above the mantel, President John Corwith's eyes followed her. They were kind, sympathetic.

"You've met the president, of course," Ashford commented. He picked up a pipe from the coffee table but did not put it in his mouth. "Sorry I missed your White House going-away party. I wasn't in the neighborhood."

"Luckily, you're in this neighborhood where I need your help." She smiled sweetly. "I'd like to discuss the baby—"

Ashford emitted a guttural croak she couldn't interpret. "I'd like to put things in context." He leaned forward, but his girth forced him to straighten up again. He used the unlit pipe to punctuate each word as he spoke. "We are in a country where twenty-two percent of the human race is packed into seven percent of the planet's arable land. Got it? For all its historical mistakes, misguided idealism and subsequent chaos and human suffering, the communist regime has built a prospering, self-governing and self-sufficient China. It has been feeding its people, which is no minor feat—"

She fidgeted in her seat. "I'm sorry to interrupt; I don't want a history lesson. I want to adopt this baby."

"Hear me out." He removed a tobacco pouch from his inside breast pocket, opened it, pinched some tobacco, and placed it in the pipe. The biting, fresh aroma was not unpleasant. "They also built an industrial base where none had existed and an infrastructure of transport, communications and housing—all of which has lifted the nation out of the grinding poverty and literal starvation of the pre-Revolutionary years."

"You can go back to the Ming Dynasty. It has nothing to do with me. It has nothing to do with my baby."

"It sure has. You are a goodwill ambassador from the United States to the People's Republic of China, and a guest of its government. The first order of the day is for you to respect this nation for its accomplishments."

She sensed danger rushing toward her like a train through a dark tunnel. "Please. Get to the point.".

He retrieved a metal gadget out of another pocket and tamped the pipe bowl. Then he took a ten-inch-long match from a red jeweled box on the table and sent her a questioning look. She shook her head and pointed toward her throat. With a benevolent expression he put down the match, but grabbed the unlit pipe between his ample lips.

"A billion men and women are studying you, just as they do every foreigner they encounter on the street. But while the citizens of Beijing, Shanghai and Guangzhou have seen many Westerners, there are sixty more cities in China with over one million in population each—sixty cities!—plus thousands of other villages whose people have never met a foreigner." His words came out crooked, like the side of his lower lip that bounced with the pipe. "Through TV and through your music—even if it's pirated—you are reaching these people in a way no other Westerner ever has. While we can't deliver to them a political message of democracy, we can bring to them the feel of personal freedom and individual choice with the image you project, with the songs you sing—with the spreading of American culture in whichever form—so the masses will not see us as the imperialistic villains their government sometimes still portrays. You are being studied and emulated."

She wanted to yank the stupid pipe out of his mouth and hurl it into the useless fireplace. "I'm a singer, not a political animal. And none of this has anything to do with Lulu, the baby I need your help to adopt."

"You're not a 'political animal'? What do you think your job was when you agreed to be our goodwill ambassador?" He rose to his feet and paced by the coffee table. His large frame loomed above Nola, blocking her view of the room.

"You must understand that the Chinese have accomplished their nation's prosperity and stability by instituting national discipline and a code of individual and group responsibility. Yes, the government controls every niche in society, and at times it seems to us a social experiment gone awry. That is because we forget that communism here was grafted onto traditions of obedience going back thousands of years. So when we barge in with our Judeo-Christian mores, judge this country by our values, and meddle in their affairs, we look no different than the Portuguese or the British who humiliated them for centuries. We are just another imperialistic, Western aggressor. Their resentment is understandable."

She was on safe ground again. "They won't resent my adopting this baby. Thousands of American couples have adopted here and were welcomed."

He broadened the circle of his pacing and strode behind the couches. "You are a public figure. The incident with that baby literally thrust upon you was captured by dozens of cameras. The hoopla around it— with commentary by reporters in the U.S., Europe, Africa, Australia and Asia—happens to be extremely uncomplimentary to your hosts. Every entertainment TV show is outdoing the next with talk about the one-child policy, piling on criticism of the Chinese government without even trying to understand the context or to present the circumstances. It is this crisis we are trying to contain."

The gears in Nola's head engaged. Lulu had become an international incident. A *cause célèbre*. The magnitude of the publicity wasn't hard for Nola to fathom; she had been a guest on scores of TV and radio shows, from Argentina to Zimbabwe. There were thousands of such broadcast programs around the globe.

"I'm on your side." Ashford's voice returned to its normal level. "We'll help you with an adoption through official channels, but the process may take up to one year, and the baby you'll receive will be their choice, not yours."

Nola struggled to restrain the quiver of her lips and chin. "I don't want just any baby. I want Lulu. If I'm this big, important goodwill ambassador, why can't the Chinese humor me?"

"They must save face." He waved his pipe in a gesture that nicked her heart. "The only way they know how is to dig their heels in, in what's tried and true for them."

The walls were closing in, concentrating the smell of his tobacco in the room. She needed fresh air. Lots of it, or she would die. "Don't you have all kinds of informal channels of communication with your Chinese counterparts?" she asked. "Can't we cut a deal in which it will look as if I don't get to adopt Lulu, when in fact I will?"

"That's a possibility—if perhaps you hand her over to an orphanage with fanfare, wait a while, and in a year or so, maybe get her back."

"A year? Maybe get her back? And maybe not! Ambassador Ashford, do you have children?"

He shook his head. "Margot and I weren't so blessed."

"I don't see how I could hand her over for one day, let alone a year, to those butchers."

"Don't take it to the extreme. I'm sure they'll put her in a good institution. You've seen an orphanage; it's not bad—"

"Sure. I saw the token one on the official tour. Even there, they believe in tying down toddlers to potty chairs for hours. And they indicated that even adoptive parents aren't allowed to visit the institutions in which their kids are raised." She sucked in her breath. "And I've seen the Dying Rooms."

"The name itself is a demagoguery of the most dangerous sort. Anyway, those places are only for hopeless medical cases. Euthanasia is practiced in many cultures, although I, as a Catholic, won't make any excuses for it." He pointed his pipe at her. "This is a generous offer and I suggest you take it now, because they might rescind it."

"An offer? Who made it? And why might they rescind it?"

He wriggled out of the chair, went to his desk, and picked up a computer printout. "The news wire. Let's see." He put on his glasses as though reading the printout for the first time, then glared at her over the rim. "Eleven a.m. today. Did you make some public derogatory statement against the Chinese government? Hmmm." He read slowly. "Did you say to the press, 'It's the orphanages you should be looking into. And take pictures—?' "

PART TWO

The Phoenix Bird

Do not thrust your finger through your own paper lantern.
—A Chinese proverb

Chapter 13

The embassy doors closed behind Nola. She stood on the large marble steps. The old dread that had roped her ribcage when she was a child, fearing the catastrophe that was sure to befall her parents, now barreled down upon her again. Ashford's words, "…in a year or so, maybe get her back," and "…public derogatory statement against the Chinese government," pulsated in her head.

She forced one foot down, then another, and halted next to one of the giant twin temple lions guarding the mansion. Bees buzzed in and out of the flowers in the front garden with a metronomic busyness. In full daylight, the exotic flowers looked carnivorous and conceited, their tangy aroma ferocious. Nola clenched her fists. For a moment, she forgot where she was or that she was supposed to walk. She unclenched her fists and looked at them as though they belonged to someone else. Her nails had imprinted white crescents in her palms.

There was no way she could face Yoram and his deputy, waiting in the security booth, or the driver in the limousine outside, or Wade at the hotel. She skulked around the building to the small back gate Daniel had led her through. Two American guards were at the sentry post, and after verifying with Ashford's secretary that she had had legitimate business there, they let her leave. She found herself in the alley. There was no sign of either the limousine or Yoram.

Raw and numb at the same time, she wandered through wide, tree-lined streets until she was lost. All the foreign embassies seemed clustered in one district, occupying mansions surrounded by lush gardens, brass plaques on their gates announcing their nationalities. Nola was unaware of the tears that rolled down her cheeks until she was no longer able to read the names.

After the silence of pain, the nearest she could come to expressing the inexpressible was music. "Flower Babies" stirred inside her. She stopped in the quiet street and mumbled the lyrics, testing new words as the music built up in her. She raised her head, letting the melody shape itself around her refusal to lose Lulu. "Flower babies bloom unseen, *Flower babies die unloved…*"

Lulu. Doomed, like a flower that had bloomed hidden from human eyes and died unnoticed. Even if Lulu survived the orphanage physically, she would wilt there without love to nurture her sunny personality.

"Hey, lady!" a guard poked his head out of a booth. He had an Australian or South African accent. "Move on."

Startled, she turned. Behind him towered a pagoda-inspired roof with three monkeys carved into corners that tilted upward.

"Oh, my God," he gasped. "Nola. Right? You're Nola? I'm so sorry— Uh, I was at your concert—I love your songs. Would you like some water? I didn't know it was yo—"

Sniffling, she shook her head and resumed her walk. No cars passed by. She was in a vacuum in the middle of bustling Beijing, like the vacuum inside her that stretched as far back as she could remember.

On one corner, under a tree, three old men sat on a bench, smoking long-stemmed pipes. Above their heads hung half a dozen birdcages in which canaries chirped in a symphony of sound. *Tzwits, tzwits. Kew— kew—kew—Chooooorup, chooooorup-uup-uup-uup, tzwits, tzwits. Kew—kew—kew—us—kew—us*—Everyday life streamed on, flowed over the pebbles, she thought, and people found little pools of bliss, enough perhaps to keep them content. *Kew—kew—kew—us—kew—us. Rescue—us, rescue—us, rescue us—*. Damn Wade for turning his back on her when she needed him more than ever.

Her mind broke out of its stupor. Why was she dawdling, while every minute with her baby was precious? She had left Ambassador Ashford's office with no specific date for Lulu's return, but time was running out. She must tap into the forgotten resourcefulness of the girl who had taken care of her family.

As she flagged a taxi, Nola heard Yoram's voice. "Nola?"

She turned. "How did you know where I was?"

He pointed toward her shoes. "We get signals."

She had forgotten about the security measures installed against possible kidnapping. Yoram had been following her all this time, watching her from a distance. The insurance company took no chance on its half-billion-dollar liability.

Nola wanted to scream.

Later at the hotel suite, the city lights below flickered even before the rosy strip of sun had completely disappeared. Nola's stretch of delight playing with Lulu was broken by another bout of despair.

At one point, Wade had entered the room and indicated to Leslie to leave and close the door. He was furious at Nola for disappearing from Yoram's watch. The insurance company was on the Israeli's ass, he said.

"Yoram has threatened to resign if you ever as much as *think* of going off on your own ever again, detection devices or not."

Anger was an expensive commodity she couldn't afford. Her arms tight around Lulu in her lap, Nola said, "Don't you see how cute this baby is?"

"So is a baby alligator. You don't see me changing my life for one." Wade's teeth shone, but his eyes darkened. "Your behavior only shows how damaging this baby business is. You came to China to do a job, and I will not give you a hand in jeopardizing it." He turned on his heel and left the room.

She clutched Lulu. How she missed Beverly and her guidance and Gabby, her friend from jazz school who had accompanied her in her earlier years on the road as part of the dance troupe. Gabby now lived at Nola's Colorado ranch, nursing her fourth baby. She no longer understood nor cared about the entertainment world. Nola wished she had faith to guide her; it had been years since she had spoken to the rabbi in the Manhattan synagogue. Then he had helped her reclaim her Jewishness in order to ease her admission into Eddie's reluctant family. But her too-short induction into Judaism had failed to confer upon her an identity that would withstand the pressure of time and travel.

"Why don't you call President Corwith?" Leslie asked, holding a steamy washcloth for Nola's face. "He chose you to represent America here. Call him."

"It's five in the morning in D.C. Besides, he'd have to accept his ambassador's assessment of the situation." She shook her head. "I've thought of everything and everyone. Mauriello. He has clout. He may not mind doing me this favor. He could talk to Kong Ruiji. But I know the premier, too; I don't need Mauriello for an introduction. I can go directly to the number-one man in all of China and plead with him. But he must already know every detail of this saga. Don't you see? He's probably the one pulling the strings. No one would take a baby from a celebrity while she's Kong Ruiji's guest without his knowledge—or orders."

"Attatt—paa—eeeggg—" Lulu answered.

"That about sums it up, Dumpling." Nola lowered herself on the carpet and kissed the bridge of the tiny nose.

"There's Daniel. And Keith Schwartz," Leslie said, thinking of Phonomania's first president.

"You're going down the chain of command. Daniel is a staffer from academia. Keith? He's out sailing for many months in Lord-knows-where. Since he's sold Phonomania Records, there's no secretary, no office where I could contact him. If he has e-mail access, I don't know his address." Nola stacked a tower of colorful plastic rings and let Lulu undo it. "I've even thought of sidestepping them all and calling Barbara Walters."

"Well?"

"It's sure to create backlash. That's where the problem begins. The Chinese are upset about the media exposure." She shook her head. "More of it would only make matters worse."

"Well, then," Leslie said. "If Corwith and Kong Ruiji won't help, you must appeal to a higher authority." He donned a white cap, lit an incense stick, and summoned his divine entities.

With Lulu prattling in her lap, Nola watched his ritual. She envied his religious convictions. Even if he created a potpourri of beliefs, plucking practices from every religion that blew along his path, he had a spiritual life that eluded her. All she had was herself.

"I don't want to be away from you all day tomorrow," she told Lulu. "You'll come along to the Great Wall and take naps in the trailer. Okay?" Shipped from a rental company in Japan for the Double Happiness tour, the trailer was a reduced version of the one Nola owned in the States. At fifty feet long, with its split-level space divided into sleeping and living quarters, it was plush and comfortable enough.

"You're up for another tantrum from Jean-Claude," Leslie said. "It's not a bad idea to minimize conflicts with Wade, too."

"If he weren't married to me, he wouldn't have dared oppose me."

Leslie gazed back at her. "You'll have to wake Lulu up before dawn to drag her out. And with my staff coming and going in the trailer, it would be difficult for her. She wasn't a happy camper at the market video shoot."

So Lulu was in Leslie's way, too. At least he was diplomatic about it. For now. Nola sighed. "I guess she shouldn't be the one to make the sacrifices for my schedules. How does Faith Hill do it with three babies?"

"Nannies," he replied. "The maid will watch her tomorrow."

Wade appeared at the door at seven-thirty, dressed in his paisley silk robe. She stiffened. His face was masked by a pleasant expression as he reminded Nola that she would have only a few hours of sleep before the Great Wall shoot. "Honey, dinner is ready for you," he added.

She stepped to the dining room and sat down. The light from the alabaster chandelier did not illuminate the corners of the room, and the silver bowls and gold-plated flatware seemed like a charade. Nola ignored the sleeping pill by her plate. After a few bites, she pushed herself away from the table and, pulled by invisible strings, went back to Lulu, now nestled in the room past the wardrobe. They were running out of time.

Lulu was intent on learning to sit up. She twisted on all fours and dropped her body sideways. Time and again, she pushed herself up, but her body tilted too far, or her foot flailed in the air, knocking her off balance. Finally exhausted, she lay back and held a clean cloth diaper next to her face while sucking on her pacifier. She listened to Nola sing a lullaby and her eyelids became heavy, then they closed. There was a smile on her twin-cherry lips.

Nola returned to her bedroom. From the living room she heard the television in English, probably CNN or the British Sky News. She stood looking at the phone, longing to hear a friendly voice. She thought of calling Gabby even though it was the middle of the night in Colorado. If only Keith were within phone range. Daniel. She dialed the embassy. Some clicks later, they were connected.

In the background she heard the soft notes of Berlioz' *King Lear* overture. "I hope I didn't get you at a bad time," she said. How little she knew about his likes and dislikes. Or who kept him company.

"I've been reading," he said. "I'm ready for a friendly chat."

"Are you home?" she asked.

"Yes," he replied, and she wondered what kind of an apartment he occupied for the year. Must be filled with books. Maybe a flowering plant. Where was the woman who was in his life "in a way?"

Nola slid down the carpet by the bed and hugged her knees. "They have so many unwanted babies!" she burst out. "Why are they so immovable?"

There was a rustle of sheets at the other end. He was in bed. Hopefully alone. Embarrassed by her outburst, she said, "Forget it. I'm sorry to intrude—"

"Don't be," he said softly. "It's tough, I know. You're grieving."

She sniffled. "No one understands it…"

"I'm in mourning, too."

"Over Lulu?" she asked with incredulity.

"My own loss."

She let a moment pass. "The woman who's in your life 'in a way?'"

"Yes." His voice was so low she had to strain to hear. "And our baby."

The skin around Nola's mouth felt taut. "God. I'm so sorry."

"This week it's been eighteen months. I tell myself it's time to get over it."

"But you can't." She clutched the phone to her ear. "I know. It takes longer to heal." If ever.

He began to speak. "Three years ago, I was living in Washington, D.C., with a woman I had met at Human Rights Watch. Kate. Her parents were upset over her choosing me. The notion of having grandchildren who were one-quarter Chinese rattled them. She loved her parents and felt torn. To give herself emotional space, she volunteered for the Peace Corps. They sent her to Uzbekistan. That's in Central Asia, bordering Afghanistan."

Nola's back pressed against the nightstand.

She heard an air intake as he continued, "It was tough on me. Little did I know that it would get worse. After a while, Kate asked me to visit her during my winter break. We became engaged, and I returned home to teach for the rest of the school year. A couple of months later, on Easter, she disappeared. Her body was found a week later." His voice broke.

"Daniel, I'm so sorry," Nola whispered. "How it must hurt."

"She had been gang-raped and murdered. An autopsy showed she was two months pregnant."

"Oh, my God." Nola's fingers shook. She wanted to say that his telling her this was a gift more meaningful than his painted snuff bottle. He had shared himself. She whispered, "Nothing I could say would come out right."

"I wanted you to know." His voice returned to its normal tone. She thought she heard a minute chuckle. "There's a Chinese proverb that says, 'If you have happiness, don't use it all up.' I've been using up all the grief."

The corner between the night table and the bed was a cocoon shrouded in shadows. "I read somewhere that we're made of losses and separations," she said. "Those are the forces that shape us the most."

"How true. For all of us." He let the crackling of the line take over for a minute. "Now that we got this piece out of the way, would you like to talk about something more cheerful?"

"I'm so wrapped up in my fear of losing Lulu, I'm afraid I don't make fun company." Nola moaned. "Not what you'd expect from an entertainer."

"Which is why you called. You can be no-fun company with me any time."

She let out a soft laugh. "Actually, I was thinking of picking your professorial brain." When he didn't reply, she added, "I'll ask again the question I posed so gracelessly at the start of this conversation: Why are the Chinese so immovable?"

"In Taoist philosophy, which is deeply ingrained here, no single person can change the world. A person is like a drop of water, insignificant, a soft substance with no natural shape of its own. From the government's perspective, people—like water—will take the shape that surrounds them."

"My Western mind has a hard time accepting this callous approach to humanity."

"Within traditional Chinese thinking, the government perceives itself as merely abiding by the natural order of things," he replied.

She climbed on the bed and propped up her feet on a pillow. "If no one counts, how does anyone ever accomplish anything here?"

"Many drops of water become a river, and the flow of water over many years may wear down even the hardest of rocks. Harry Wu, the dissident who spent more years in jail than out, has put up an extraordinary fight. He believes that to bow the body is easy; to bow the will is hard."

"Much good it did him."

"He broke the boundaries of silence and made the world take notice."

"What got me into this mess in the first place was the public spectacle of Lulu handed to me." She paused. "Are you saying that to get Lulu back I must do jail time?"

"As a foreigner, you can raise issues that ordinary Chinese can't."

She sighed. "I've tried public criticism. It backfired. The rest is history."

Neither of them spoke for some moments. She broke the silence. "I must get up at three-thirty. Thanks for being there."

"Thanks for listening." Softly, he added, "Good night."

Nola hugged a pillow to her chest. She remained in that position until the maid came in to turn down the bed.

Chapter 14

At pre-dawn, Wade caressed Nola's exposed arm, waking her for hair and makeup. "We'll leave for location at five." His skin glistened from his shower. She burrowed under the covers again. She couldn't face another day. Or him.

"Hon, I have breakfast ready," he said. "You hardly ate last night."

The pleading in his tone was so uncharacteristic that she peeked out from under the covers. Fatigue was etched in the lines by his mouth. His professional and personal lives had long ago melded into one, and she had shaken his central core. She felt a bubble of satisfaction. Let him suffer the consequences of his own doing.

He wheeled over the cart. She forced some cereal with fruit down her throat. A moment later, she jumped to her feet, rushed to the bathroom, shut the door and vomited into the toilet.

At five, before leaving, she stood by the crib, imprinting in her memory the delicate lines of Lulu's mouth, chin, eyebrows. They were the most beautiful she had ever seen; she could stare at this face for hours and never have enough. She breathed in baby scent. *Rescue us.*

With a convoy of vans and trucks behind them, Nola and Wade rode in the limousine on the thirty-minute drive to the section of the Great Wall closest to Beijing. Nola wished Leslie didn't have to ride in her trailer. Wade's efforts to draw her back into the circle of their interests was too taxing on her brain. A line of demarcation etched by Lulu's appearance and disappearance blazed through their life. The before and the after. This was the after. Forever. If only they weren't doomed to be stuck together for another week.

As if nothing had happened, Wade continued his chitchat. He hoped the day's weather would be as good as was predicted, but this was typhoon season, and they had been lucky the Forbidden City concert hadn't been rained out.

Wade's talk—about reading scripts for movies in which she could star—stopped short in her head at the door of the Silk Market orphanage. Would Lulu be sent to such an institution? Nola looked out the window as though the rice fields that stretched to the horizon held an answer to her plight. She thought of the determination with which Lulu had tried to sit up. At what point would this optimism stop?

Without parental love, Jenna had given up long before starting school.

The day of filming was exhausting and stretched Nola's ability to remain attentive to everyone's demands. The *Vanity Fair* reporter, a woman with monochromatic brown hair, skin and clothes, followed her. Nola had been able to ignore the woman's note-scribbling for the magazine cover story all week, but today it annoyed her. She demanded that the tailing stop.

For hours after sunrise, Nola swayed, kicked and twirled up and down the stone-paved section of the twenty-foot-wide wall until her leg and back muscles screamed. She focused on keeping her smile broad, looking for her marked spots as she danced, never lowering her gaze. She swung the silk robes and gauze dresses so the cameras could not see how limp they had become in the raw, dewy air of dawn and humid heat of midday. Without sunglasses, her facial muscles hurt from the effort of not squinting at the bright sun.

The musicians were moved about and set up time and again, but since studio-quality music would be dubbed in later, they didn't need to concentrate as much as Nola did. While the dancers and backup singers also had costume changes, neither group appeared in every scene. Soon, the magnificent undulating wall hugging the curves of the mountains lost its enchantment. A headache drummed in the back of Nola's head and in her temples. She missed Lulu and worry gnawed at her.

At mid-morning, Nola took a break to lie down in her trailer. While Leslie's hair, makeup and clothing stylists went in and out of the living room area, she flipped through a book about China's glorious past. How little it had in common with the horrific realities of the modernday country she was seeing. Where was the solution? She needed a stroke of insight to get her and Lulu out of their hopeless situation. Overwhelmed, Nola burst into sobs.

"You've always been such a trouper, never had any difficulty being 'on' for hours," Wade said as he crouched in front of her, looking up into her face. "This baby is getting you down; you're exhausted."

Nola wanted to kick his face. "I'm working as hard as ever. The baby is not getting me down. It's your refusal to help—"

"I rest my case."

Leslie sent him and everyone else away and closed the door. He handed Nola a cup of fragrant green tea and massaged her neck. At her request, he summoned an interpreter to call the hotel and check with the maid on how Lulu was doing.

"Everything is fine," the interpreter reported. "Lulu just had a mashed banana. The maid will take her for a walk in the hotel garden."

"How normal," Nola mumbled, "except that it's all wrong. I should be the one to feed her bananas; I should be the one to take her for a walk."

"Right now you're here, and your eyes are a sight." Gently, Leslie pressed her lids. "Realign your solar plexus. That's where fear and anger reside. Healthy emotions, but they must be channeled." He watched her readjust her posture. "Seek the center of your being."

"That's Lulu."

He dabbed Preparation H around her eyes. He often used this secret weapon for filming at the ungodly hour of dawn. "Think of the time before Lulu. Way back. The first moment you were conscious of who you were. Not in words. In a picture."

Memories were exhumed. She saw herself as a three-year-old, hungry, crossing the woods alone to get food from the big house. She had taken care of herself in the face of neglect. She had survived. Why couldn't she do it now?

A thought struck her. "How fortunate! We're going to the opera tonight."

Leslie looked toward the ceiling. "Have I missed some voices?"

Nola straightened up in her chair, holding a tissue against her nose to block the odor of the ointment. "Kong Ruiji is hosting the evening for me, right? He's trying to look as friendly as a sticky cake. He's a smart politician who knows a photo opportunity when he sees one. This is my chance to talk to him. Could he refuse me to my face?"

"He may seem friendly," Leslie said, "but you were the one to notice that it's not for nothing that he runs China."

As the last rays of sun painted the sky mauve and orange, the thirteen-hour workday was finally over. In the small plaza accessing the Great Wall, TV and video crew members, musicians and stylists loaded their equipment into the vans. Nola waved at them and, with Wade right behind her, slid into her limousine. She was startled to find Roberta Fisher in the seat facing her. Lounging like a queen on her throne, her flowered tunic fanning around her, Roberta held a cut-glass tumbler filled with Scotch. The limousine reeked of her cigarette smoke that clung to her hair and clothes, and of the too-strong Youth Dew perfume with which she had tried to mask the smell.

"Don't you have some rumors to nip someplace?" Nola asked.

"Soon it will no longer be my business. You'll be on your own to throw sand at your PR machine as your little heart desires." Roberta flicked her finger at the driver, who pulled away while Yoram, sitting beside him in the front seat, spoke into his sleeve. The car swerved onto the two-lane road leading back to Beijing. Roberta glanced at Nola and Wade, swished the drink too close to the rim, and gulped it. "Yummy."

Wade must have had some idea what Roberta was up to, because other than a twitch at the side of his mouth, he showed no reaction. Nola leaned her head back on the headrest, composing sentences for her talk tonight with Kong Ruiji. Outside, the rectangular pools of rice shimmered in a darkening pink. She was tired and had no spare brain cells for Roberta. In thirty minutes she would be holding Lulu, and nothing else mattered.

When she asked no questions, Roberta went on. "CNB wants my fat ass back, and they're willing to pay for it—big time."

"Howard Stern and Imus have desensitized the audience and network management to vulgarities," Wade commented.

"Muck is in," Roberta said, "and I'm it, female-style. Howard Stern talks about his bowel movements? I have more orifices to discuss."

"I'm sure you'll bring up the ratings," Nola murmured.

Wade shot her a look of warning. The second car with more security men passed them to take the lead. Nola waved, even though they could not see her through the tinted glass.

"A new management team at CNB Radio is offering me the morning rush hour to do whatever I goddamn please," Roberta went on. "What do you think of 'The Big Mouth Hour?' I like the sound of it. 'Mouth. Th. Th.' Cute, huh?"

She motioned with her head toward Yoram, whose five-o'clock shadow had appeared at noontime. "I'll miss your hunky bodyguards," she told Wade. "What do you do, measure how low they hang?"

Nola closed her eyes. Soon, very soon, she would be with Lulu. For whatever time was left for them.

Arriving at the hotel, Roberta struggled to pull herself out as if her body was fighting a tidal wave that seemed to pin her down. She sniffed the air like a hound catching the scent of blood, and her ringlets trembled in anticipation.

"Here you are, all my best friends!" she greeted the paparazzi and raised her arms with mock enthusiasm. "Why don't you get lost?" In spite of her previous assertion that this was no longer her job, she took charge, picking out her favorites while Yoram's newly promoted deputy, a well-groomed, robust black man, summoned additional hotel staff to unclog the way for Nola's passage.

Wade waited with Nola in the limousine until it was safe to emerge. He tried to take her hand, but she pulled it away. He spoke with a touch of sorrow, "Say what you will. Roberta is a professional through and through."

"It took the patience of Job to tolerate her for two years, eleven months and three weeks. But who's counting?"

"You'd better be nice to her until the end of this tour. She's promised to stay the week. But once she's back on the air, everyone is fair game. The celebrity she has the most material on is you. Three years' worth of stuff."

"Then it's certainly too late to get into her good graces." Nola surveyed the scene outside, ready to sprint. To be with Lulu. "Didn't you put that gag clause in the contract?"

"The clause isn't half as bad as the negative publicity we'd get if we sued her for breaking it. Trying to shut up Roberta would only give her more material to chew on the air."

Nola couldn't stay alone with him one more second. She flung the limousine door open, rushed past the line of reporters and photographers and into the open elevator. She wanted to jab the button, but a uniformed operator blocked it. Why was he here? Like everything else in her life, there was always some glorified minion to do her bidding, making things more cumbersome. She hated it. She hated their dependency on her for their livelihood. She envied their freedom to go someplace else.

The door finally closed. Nola watched the maddeningly slow climb of the floor numbers. While Wade fitted the key in the lock, she shifted from one foot to another. As soon as the door opened, she tore toward her bedroom, through the wardrobe room where the maid was seated with two other women, sewing beads onto a dress. By the time they jumped to their feet, she was at the door to the next room where Lulu's crib had been.

Lulu was not there.

Chapter 15

(1984 - 1986)

Nola held on to Jenna's hand, and the two of them skipped along the path to the old man's house. Nola looked down at her little sister and her heart contracted with the old pain. When she had been five, she still had parents.

For two years now, Nola had lived with Jenna at Miss Helga's, but when she went to the big house for her piano lessons, she brought Jenna along to play. Mini-Nazi always interfered for no reason other than she hated it when kids had fun. If they didn't mess up their clothes, they wore out the rugs, or laughed too loud, or dirtied their hands. *Schmutz*, dirt, was Miss Helga's favorite word. She was obsessed with washing everything: the stone path, curtains, children. After taking a shower, Nola had to submit to ear-rubbing that left her ears red and sore.

Jenna skipped over the gravel, laughing and chattering, never letting go of Nola's hand.

"Why can't you be like this at Miss Helga's so you don't get punished so much?" Nola asked. It often seemed as if Jenna purposely invited Mini-Nazi's brand of discipline that included smearing mustard on Jenna's insolent tongue or locking her up in a closet to contemplate her disobedience.

"Don't you hate how she checks our poo-poo?" Jenna asked, a mischievous look in her eyes. "And then she makes me eat that gross stuff."

"Castor oil and prunes." Nola giggled. "It almost made me 'poo-poo' from my mouth." After one spoon of Miss Helga's concoction, Nola started lying about her poo-poo's color and consistency. "That's what people in Germany do," she added.

"I'm never going to Germany. I don't want people checking my poo-poo. It's the same way they look at my face."

"Nothing's wrong with your face." Nola crouched in front of her. "You're beautiful. Like Mommy was. If I didn't know it, I wouldn't notice any scars."

"People look and say that I'm an orphan."

Nola gasped. "Orphan is not a bad word, and you can't tell by a person's face." Yet, around Nola, the birch, elm, oak and maple suddenly looked like a giant hall of mirrors. There was no way out, except that music awaited her at the mansion. She searched for words." You'll have cookies while I have my lesson, okay?"

"I want to play with the cat," Jenna chanted, and skipped over a tree root. The speed in which the moment was forgotten left Nola reeling. She would forever be "an orphan," even if no one said they could read it on her face.

At bedtime, Jenna wrapped her arms around Nola's neck, and when Nola tried to rise, the small body clung to her, lifting out of the bed. "Tell me a story."

"Ten more weeks to Christmas," Nola whispered. "Ms. Cutter will have presents for us under her tree. We'll sleep over."

In the dim light, a smile crawled on Jenna's sleepy features. "I want a doll with a red dress," she said.

"I'll tell Santa." Nola had saved the allowance the old man gave her to have her ears pierced with gold studs, but that could wait. Did Mom have pierced ears? She couldn't remember. It was worse that there was no one to ask. "Sleepy time."

Mini-Nazi appeared in the doorway. "Good night!" She flipped the light switch and it was as if the ceiling had dropped. In the sudden darkness, Jenna began to whimper. Nola wished Miss Helga would come over and kiss her sister so that there would be one more person in the world to love Jenna, but Miss Helga had said she was paid to care for the child, not to kiss her. "Out. You're wasting electricity in the dining room," she bellowed at Nola, and Nola slunk back to her books. If it weren't for Jenna, she would have lived with Ms. Cutter. But who was she to complain after the horrible things she had caused?

At eleven, Jenna woke up crying. Nola gathered her books off the section of the dining table she was allowed to use, turned off the lights, and rushed into their bedroom. She sat on Jenna's bed and comforted her in hushed tones so that Miss Helga wouldn't wake up and growl about how difficult it was to have children around.

"Tell me again about Mommy and Daddy," Jenna begged.

"Mommy was a singer and Daddy was a musician. A lead guitarist, which is very special." Nola tucked Jenna back under the covers.

"Do I look like Mommy?" Jenna asked.

"Sure. You have her hair and her eyes."

"Did she love me?"

"You were her precious little baby." Nola pointed into the darkened corner. "She used to sit in this beanbag and hold you and sing you songs."

The worst part of inventing lies was that the real memories were crumbling fast. Sometimes, when Nola squinted, the lights shone with star-like spikes like the tiny mirrors on the Indian pillows, and Nola would think of the long, lazy days with her mother, and cry. But hard as she tried, her mother's face showed as if through holes in a slice of Swiss cheese. Nola could see the hair with the headband, or the dreamy green eyes, but the details always floated among blank spaces.

"Show me the photos again."

"You saw them yesterday, and the day before and the day before." Nola sighed, turned on the bedside lamp, and brought over from her night-stand the two framed photographs. One was of the four of them, on Jenna's first birthday, before her accident. They had been a normal family, all living together. "You see the big bow Mommy made for you?"

Nola propped up Dad's black-and-white publicity photo. It was like cheating because in her mind's eye she couldn't see his face. She remembered his smell, ripe and mixed with lemon-scented aftershave. She remembered the feel of his chest hair when she furrowed her finger to check how deep it would go. And she remembered the sound of his voice when they jammed together. Jenna would never know any of it; Dad had never recorded these sessions, which was another monumental loss. Nola would have listened to these recording every day for the rest of her life.

She had moved to her bed and curled under the blankets when Jenna asked, "Did Santa come to me when Mommy and Daddy were alive?"

"Mommy and Daddy didn't have Christmas."

"Why?"

"Because they were Jewish."

"What's Jewish?"

"I don't know. Like Kosher," she mumbled, freefalling into slumber. She hugged one of the Indian pillows she kept in her bed even though the embroidery itched. "Go to sleep or I'll never tell you another story."

At the funeral, a rabbi had prayed in a funny language, and someone explained to Nola that her mother had converted from being Jewish to something whose name she forgot. It was supposed to be about everyone loving everyone else. Except that Mom hadn't loved Jenna, so what good did it do to always talk about loving everyone else in the world? Nola shoved away the thought. She'd never think anything bad about her mother because she now knew that bad was "not good" only until worse things happened.

Beverly Cutter lived on a quiet block off of Main Street, in a house filled with tasseled fabrics, walls of photographs, and knickknacks on every surface. After Nola's parents' death, Ms. Cutter had searched the cottage for letters or documents that mentioned any kin other than the great-great-uncle. When she found none, and Jenna remained in the custody of the state, Ms. Cutter became Nola's legal guardian, which was like a godmother, and Nola could now call her Beverly. On Christmas Eve, when Beverly's daughter was visiting from college and was playing with Jenna and the dog in the kitchen, Nola sunk in an upholstered chair by the fireplace.

Beverly put a glass of eggnog in her hand. "I have wonderful news," she said. "I went to see your great-uncle, and he's agreed to pay for voice lessons in New York City."

Nola gulped.

"Look, you have a gift." Beverly put her arms around Nola's shoulders. "Two gifts, really. One is your voice, the other is your energy. Most people absorb energy from others; only a few blessed ones exude it. That's what gives you stage presence. Don't waste it. Learn how to use it."

"New York City? How will I get there?"

"Fourteen is old enough to take the train into the city by yourself. And it will be worth it. Trust me on this one."

"It costs ten dollars for a round trip alone," Nola said.

"It's been taken care of."

Nola's allowance had been barely enough to purchase tampons and shampoos. Certainly not a pair of Jordache jeans, which she was dying for. She had wanted so much to take an after-school job to earn more. Now there would be no free time.

She couldn't let Beverly think she wasn't grateful. "Okay," she said in a small voice. "But it's so far."

"Two hours each way. You'll make better use of the trip by adding on a ballet class at one of the schools near Lincoln Center." To Nola's unasked question she added, "The dance classes at school are not professional enough for you."

When Nola took Jenna to visit the old man the next day, she thanked him, and he made his funny grunts because he still couldn't speak. There had been absolutely no change in his condition for years, which made Nola hopeful that he'd live for a long time. She liked him a lot now, and was not disgusted to have Christmas dinner with him in the huge dining room where he sat at the other end of a very long table. He had a bicycle for Jenna and a small drum set for Nola. While Jenna rode around, Nola just talked and talked. About dance that was a feeling of strings pulled separately and together, or maybe like a clock with many parts gliding in and out of invisible notches. She told him about the school play in which she starred and about the songs she was writing. In the large room with its high ceiling, she raised her voice so it echoed when it bounced off the dark paneled walls.

Later, the old man's four children came by. They were much older than Dad had been, and their kids had already finished college. As always, they ignored Nola and Jenna, so she took Jenna to the orangerie and played on the Steinway to show them that she was a good girl. No one paid attention until she started to sing. One peeked in, then stayed, then another drifted in, and finally they all stood in a circle around the piano. They clapped when she was done, and two granddaughters said she was amazing.

One day, this house would belong to them and she wouldn't be able to visit. If it were hers, she would turn it into a home for good children who had no parents. She'd also invite kids whose families couldn't take care of them, like when Jenna had needed all that medical attention. One thing for sure, though: In her special home, she would hire only nice people, not nurses like Miss Helga.

The following fall, Jenna started school but quickly grew unhappy. She was mean to the children who tried to play with her. She bit or hit them and then threw herself on the floor in temper tantrums. By the end of the semester, the teachers recommended she be sent to a special school, for her behavior robbed others of their learning and play time.

Mini-Nazi, too, didn't know what to do with this ungrateful child who would not be restrained. Once, Nola called their caseworker to complain that again Miss Helga had locked Jenna in the hall closet. But a new caseworker had been assigned to Jenna, a huge, bearded Mexican man with scary black eyes who spoke weird English, and when he questioned Miss Helga, she told him that she'd rather go back to emptying bedpans at Smithtown Hospital. No one could pay her enough to have this disturbed girl in her house.

The man decided to send Jenna to a group home in another town.

It was a good thing that ninth graders couldn't die of a heart attack, because Nola was sure she would get one, and Jenna would be left all alone at this scary caseworker's mercy. "Don't separate us!" Nola begged of him. So much for her opening her mouth. Had she forgotten that things could only get worse, never better? "Jenna needs me. Isn't there a law about keeping siblings together?"

"Si. A law that says every child needs proper education. Your sister needs a structured environment in order to learn."

"Give her time to adjust to school. She doesn't have a mother and a father. It's really tough on her. I'll help Miss Helga more. I'll drop Drama Club. I'll only leave Jenna when I go to the city once a week."

He gave Nola one more year. Mini-Nazi said Jenna should have been put up for adoption years before, right after her accident. Now it was too late; no one would want to deal with her.

Every day Nola came straight home from school. She taught Jenna to tie her shoelaces, count to one hundred, and play on the toy xylophone, the only musical instrument Miss Helga allowed, because it wasn't too noisy. But Nola couldn't teach Jenna to play with other children. She couldn't teach other children to have patience with Jenna.

Sometimes she would bring Jenna into her bed, feel her breath on her cheek as she contoured her body around Jenna's warmth and anticipated each of her turns as if they were one body. Nola imagined that there was a hollow space inside her, full of muck. Sticking to her schedule for the next two years made it less perceptible. Singing was freedom, like the feeling in her cave, except that she learned about muscles she hadn't known existed in her diaphragm, throat and mouth. Her Russian voice teacher sometimes made her practice her voice while lying down and projecting onto the ceiling. And in ballet class she learned how to control her body from within and then move on different planes in the air around her. Singing and dancing defined her. Otherwise, all that was left would be the name "orphan." When she danced and sang, she felt enveloped by affection that was strangely more inside than outside. Her parents were surely watching and loving her.

Yet, Thursdays, when Nola left to take the train to Manhattan, Jenna would clutch at her and scream. Her face red and bloated, she would still be sobbing in hiccups when Nola returned seven hours later. Mini-Nazi said she'd never heard of a child behaving like that, that Jenna was a great performing artist. Nola understood the grief. She felt like crying for her parents the same way, every day, for hours, until she would melt away. Later, in her bed, she did.

"My voice teacher has met an artist-and-repertoire man from Musix Records," Nola told Beverly. She halted. This was crazy.

"That's a good label, Musix—"

"Forget it," Nola said. That man from the record company, Wade Dalton, had told the voice teacher that he didn't mind hauling himself all the way out to Smithtown on his way to a weekend in the Hamptons, but he had little faith that anything would come out of listening to some sixteen-year-old sing the national anthem at a high school football game.

Chapter 16

"Where is she?" Nola screamed at the maid.

Seeing Nola's face, the woman began to tremble, and her chin lowered so low it touched her breastbone.

"She was here!" Nola yelled, knowing the maid didn't understand. "With you!"

Wade came out of the bathroom to investigate the ruckus. Dental floss was wound on his finger. He took one look at Nola's face, murmured, "I'll get an interpreter," and dashed out.

The hotel manager promptly appeared. He spoke with the shaken maid, then said, "Two men come take baby. Say you send them, so she think okay."

"Two men? Oh, God—" Nola's legs turned to liquid, and she collapsed onto the chair. "Oh, God—Lulu's been kidnapped!"

A horrible groan reverberated in the room, a croaking like a wounded animal's cry, and Nola realized it came from the depths of her throat. She clamped her hands over her face. "Call the police. Please, find her. Oh, God—"

"Were the men Chinese or Western?" Wade asked, but the hotel manager had already hurried out.

No. Please, God. Nola could not feel her legs. She bent to touch them as if she were unsure to whom they belonged. Stay calm, she ordered herself. She must keep her wits about her. Her fingers shook as she grabbed the phone, "What's Ashford's number?"

Wade's arms wrapped around her. "My vulnerable bird," he murmured into her hair, gathering her even closer. "Everything'll be all right."

She struggled to free herself from his hug. "How?" She gasped for air. "You're not saying that you'll find Lulu." Time was rushing by while powerful forces were conspiring to destroy her baby. She gasped again. Every minute counted—

"Slow down, Hon. Take big, deep breaths. Think of your voice training," Wade said. He disengaged her fingers from the receiver.

"Call the ambassador," she cried out. The air was thin. Should she have told Wade about her visit to Ashford's office? It wasn't important. Not now. Lulu. Her brain clouded. Too late to think about shoulds and should nots.

She pushed her legs to stand up, to obey her. Could Lulu be stashed away somewhere in the suite? Nola rifled the triple rows of clothing racks, pulling at the hangers, then turned over cartons and spilled dozens of shoes on the floor. She tore behind sofas and under beds. In the bathroom, she rooted in the cabinet under the sink. Another bathroom, more cabinets. Lulu could fit into a drawer. The kitchen. The living room with its curios and buffet. In the second bedroom kitchenette, she crouched in front of the small refrigerator and fumbled with its key. Lulu. Lulu.

A strong hand pulled her up, and she glanced up to see pity written on Yoram's face. He was capable of human emotions after all. The suite was filling up with people. Wade's business staff streamed up from the downstairs suites. Chinese men and women flowed in from the corridor. Were they hotel staff? Leslie's helpers? The Israeli and an interpreter stationed themselves on either side of her. Who were *they* to her? All strangers. What did anyone know about her, about her bond with this baby?

"What was she wearing?" Nola yelled to the interpreter, and dashed back to the wardrobe room. "Ask the maid what Lulu was wearing!"

"Pink pajamas with a butterfly print," the interpreter told her.

Wade was on the phone, but at the sound of her wild voice, his arm stretched toward her, inviting. She fled to her bedroom and slammed the door. Let Ashford tell him that he had no hand in Lulu's disappearance.

She punched the phone speaker button. "The ambassador's on the phone with President Corwith and can't be interrupted," she heard Christopher tell Wade.

Her eyes remained glued to the empty stroller in the corner. What did this young Christopher know about life? She cried out into the impersonal black box, "My baby, Lulu. She's disappeared, and somebody knows something about it. Is she there? Did you hear anything? I must find her."

"Of course she isn't here, Ms. Sands. Is Lulu her official name?" Christopher's perfunctory voice brought Nola back to earth.

She shook her head and sniffled. "You know I have no idea what it is— if she has a name. She was wearing pink pajamas with a butterfly print—" Nola collapsed on the bed, wrapped her arms over her chest, her nails digging at her neck. She called out into the speaker phone, "How can I find her? Please. Please put me through to the ambassador."

"I'm so sorry about all this, Ms. Sands. The ambassador must leave for the opera shortly. He can't be late. I'm sure he'll see you there."

Wade disconnected the line and opened the door to the bedroom just as Roberta burst in. "In the meantime, let's get another one," she said.

"Another what?" Nola asked.

"Another baby. We were on a roll with this story. But then, in three days, poof!"

"Get out!" Nola shouted. "Just get the fuck out!"

Puffing, Big Mouth marched out.

"Don't alienate her," Wade said. "The last thing we need is Roberta as your enemy."

"Better than you as a friend." Violently, Nola pulled on walking shoes. "I'll go look for her."

"Where? In the streets of Beijing?"

She was by the door. "How can I stay here when God-knows-what is happening to her?" Her hand on the door handle dropped. Searching the streets of this city of twelve million was indeed insanity.

Wade's tone was placating. "Hon, for all you know, the same woman who dropped this baby in your arms has had her ancestors show up in her dreams. She changed her mind and sent two goons for the baby." He caught up with Nola and handed her a tissue. "Fans can be dangerous. Celebrities are subject to the weirdest things. You know better than to fall for it."

"It wasn't the mother; I just know it in my guts. More likely Ashford's contacts who wanted Lulu returned. But he said they'd coordinate with me. Oh, God—"

"I shouldn't have allowed you to get involved in the first place."

"You didn't." She raised her voice. "You're happy, isn't that the truth? Isn't this what you hoped for?"

Wade stepped to the bathroom and brought back a glass of water and a Valium. "It will help you cope," he said.

She accepted the pill and swallowed it. "Now leave me alone."

Leslie, who had traveled back in the trailer with her day's wardrobe, rushed in. "I've just heard! How horrible—" He stood on Nola's other side and removed a strand of hair stuck on her wet cheek. "Listen. Remember your idea earlier, about your going to the opera and talking to Kong Ruiji? If anyone can help, he's our man."

A groan spurted out of her, and she clamped her mouth to stop the ugly sound. She must pull herself together. She must be strong, just as she had been for Jenna's sake after their parents' death.

The opera building was located inside the Forbidden City. Lines of painted lanterns lit the way from the gate through moss-covered rock gardens, and open-sided, red-and-gold temples with upturned can- tilevered roofs. Chinese naval cadets in crisp white created two parallel reception lines that flanked the red carpet leading to a grand staircase carved of milky marble. At the top, two giant brass urns flared with scented mist.

In spite of the Valium, all Nola wanted to do was cry. But the press waited in front of the eighty-foot-high gilded columns, and cameras were ready to record every detail of her appearance. Her Badgley Mischka dress, a strapless stretch crepe in teal blue, flowed around her ankles, its ice-blue embroidery of seed pearls and rhinestones hugging her thighs and hips. In deference to Chinese modesty and the cool temperatures, a matching shawl covered Nola's shoulders. It felt as heavy as a lead cape.

"I'm with you," Wade whispered. "Remember that you still have me."

Her heart wouldn't stop its erratic fluttering. In a few moments, she would be speaking to Kong Ruiji. The floodlights, bright eyes in excited faces, and television cameras trained on her nudged Nola back from her state of shock. She squared her shoulders and strode up the steps. All these people with their ready adoration had the power to help. She turned and addressed the reporters closest to her.

"My baby—the one handed to me three nights ago—was kidnapped this afternoon." Ignoring Wade's sudden squeeze on the inside of her elbow, she projected her voice without the aid of a microphone. "If you know anything about Lulu's whereabouts, or why she was taken—anything at all—please get in touch with me."

Some reporters asked about a reward. "Yes," she said, "there will be a reward. And yes, you can send messages to my website." For the life of her she didn't know how to access it. But Wade had the staff to handle all that. "How much of a reward? I don't know. Whatever's fair and more."

Behind her, she heard Roberta saying to the *Vanity Fair* reporter, "And they call me Big Mouth."

At Wade's directive, Nola posed for a photographer who shot a quick series of photos of the necklace at Nola's throat for a Tiffany ad. The piece's South Sea twin gray pearls created a butterfly encased in gold, its magnificent wings fringed in aquamarine. Nola's fingers fluttered near the necklace for effect, but she could not bring herself to smile.

Finally, she moved into the Great Hall toward a set of ornate, two-story-high double doors that led into an interior hall. Searching for Kong Ruiji's stocky figure, she spotted him in a cluster of people inside the hall. Tonight he was dressed in a long fitted brocade robe embroidered in gold. Nola smiled, gathered the hem of her dress, and crossed the threshold.

Ambassador Ashford detached himself from the group, blocking the prime minister from her view. He shook hands with Wade and kissed Nola on the cheek. His pronounced girth touched her, and she recoiled.

"I got your message," he said quietly while steering her back to the doors. "Please don't bring it up here and now."

"This is a crisis. Surely, the prime minister will be able to help." She craned her neck. Her gaze darted between Ashford and the Chinese leader who was moving with his entourage deeper into the vast room. Her head buzzed. "Was this part of your deal? To spirit Lulu away like this?"

"Of course not. I would do nothing of the sort. The double mystery of this baby's appearance and disappearance baffles us. It has nothing to do with my talks with my Chinese counterparts."

"Then bring the CIA into the case. Her life is in danger. I'm certain of it."

"It's like searching for a needle in a haystack," Wade interjected, "except that it's a billion times worse."

"My baby's been kidnapped," she called out. "Why? Who would take her?"

"Your baby?" The wattles under Ashford's chin trembled. "Be careful—very careful—how you talk about this matter—" He put his hand on hers. "Listen to me carefully. I'm on your side. Mrs. Ashford and I should have adopted years ago. I feel your pain." His back was to the hall and its dignitaries, and his face close to hers. His breath reeked of pipe smoke. "But I beg of you—please don't forget your role as goodwill ambassador. You are not a free agent. President Corwith himself selected you, when he could have chosen Barbra Streisand."

"Barbra? She hates performing." Nola sensed Wade gloating over the comparison. "And none of that is relevant to finding a baby before she's killed because of some esoteric political considerations."

"You keep assuming that the Chinese government is behind this. I wouldn't make that accusation in the absence of facts." His words seemed to crawl out of his fleshy lips and drop around Nola. "But even if that were the case, look at this incident from their perspective: it's a Chinese baby on Chinese soil, and it's up to them to decide if you can keep it or not. Hey, we have the same policy back home. A Native American tribe has a right to babies born to its women—even if the mothers don't live on the reservations. The tribe's rights transcend the rights of adoptive parents."

The red, gold and green dragons supporting the vaulted ceiling mocked her. The monkeys and lions on the columns grimaced in the light of hundreds of lanterns.

"President Corwith himself told me our government aggressively pursues a pro-human-rights policy in China," she said. "Isn't the murdering of a baby a human-rights violation?"

"We can't just burst in and dictate—and to a totalitarian government

at that—how to handle its internal affairs. We can cajole, suggest, criticize, even protest at times, but it must be done in the right amounts, at
the right times, the bee sting delivered with a dash of honey."

"Very well. I'll do it with honey." She started to walk around him.

"A bad idea." His voice stopped her. It wasn't loud, but only now she
noticed how polite the crowd was, speaking in hushed tones. Ashford
continued, "The Chinese are extremely sensitive to criticism. Since you
are our goodwill ambassador, they have interpreted your public remarks
as part of a larger U.S. agenda meant to humiliate them." His hand
motioned toward the reception hall behind him. "We are about to enter
a private hall—a sanctuary, if you will, of their tradition—for a toast to
you. If you confront Kong Ruiji over this, you will not only show disre-
spect to the place and abuse his hospitality by cornering him in public
about a private matter, but you'll reinforce his belief in our hostile agenda. To top it off, you'll further insult him with your implication that he
has knowledge of this baby's kidnapping. Do you think this protocol will
help your cause?"

The air was filled with sweet incense, but it tasted metallic in Nola's
mouth. Ashford looked at her with a penetrating gaze. At her left shoulder she heard Wade grumble. She felt like a child being called to the principal's office, horrified to discover that a minor infraction had brought a
suspension. She kept her eyes locked on Ashford's. The enormity of her
loss washed over her anew. Pink pajamas with a butterfly print.

"Don't expect me to give up on her. I won't—" she said.

"A scorched-earth tactic will destroy any chance I might have through
unofficial back-channels to find out what has happened to her."

"*Knowing* what has happened would do Lulu little good if she's dead.
I want her *found* alive."

"Trust me. I've dealt with more than one crisis in my career."

"What will you do? Who are the people you'll be talking to?"

"Do I take your microphone and try to sing in front of thousands? Do
I presume to know what it takes to perform the way you do?" His hand
reached to her shoulder, but again she recoiled.

"Let the ambassador handle it as he sees fit," Wade said.

She clutched at her shawl and drew it closer. How she hated their condescending tones. But unofficial channels were open to Ambassador
Ashford; he understood the Chinese nuances so utterly foreign to her.

When she did not reply, he asked, "Do you want to leave it to me, or
do you insist on taking matters into your own hands?"

"Give me a time limit."

"You'll hear from me first thing in the morning." With a smile, he looped his arm through hers and squeezed her fingers with his other hand. "We have an understanding, then."

With Wade on her other side, the ambassador led them into the banquet hall, where a group of Chinese dignitaries parted for her. Ashford bowed his head to Kong Ruiji. "Mr. prime minister. Your guest of honor, Miss Nola Sands."

Her tongue felt thick. "Thank you for your hospitality," she said to the prime minister, with a slight tilt of her head. The rehearsed words must have come out of someone else's throat. "I'm honored that you dedicated the evening to me."

The prime minister kissed the back of her hand. He said something, but she saw his lips moving as though through a glass wall. Only his ensuing laughter told her he had made a joke. This was the man who could find Lulu—if only she could ask for his help.

Fighting the loud thumping of her heart, Nola forced a smile. He said something else. She was searching her mind for another appropriate response when two CEOs she had met at the embassy gala stopped at a respectful distance. The prime minister invited them to join his circle, but Nola had nothing to contribute, and the three men slipped into a chat about a golf game they had played on some private Pacific island. She waited until it was polite to move on, bowed her head in a show of respect, and glided away.

How could she get through the evening? The opera would be a four-hour ordeal! Just then George Mauriello arrived. With his salt-and-pepper hair slicked back from his V-shaped hairline and his athletic build in an Armani tux, Mauriello presented an impressive figure. Yet he looked too full of himself to be trusted. Nola was certain that his good looks, projected on election posters and in television commercials, accounted for his being elected twice to the U.S. Senate. Since his divorce soon after leaving office, she had seen photographs of him with a succession of leggy models. His access to screen tests at StarVision and auditions at Phonomania Records no doubt contributed to his charm.

"Sorry things didn't pan out." He caught Nola's hand and pressed it against his chest in a gesture more intimate than their relationship warranted. "The show must go on. Don't let me down."

Her brain was melted lava. "Let you down? How?" She remembered having toyed with the idea of pitching BRW a corporate sponsorship of new, decent orphanages.

He caressed her cheek with the back of his fingers in a gesture so condescending she wanted to bite them. So much for Wade's claim that Mauriello wouldn't interfere with the inner workings of his business units. She had never missed Keith Schwartz more. Keith had been without guile; he had been a friend.

Thirty minutes later, after Ashford and Kong Ruiji had exchanged toasts, a bare-chested man hit a giant gong with a mallet. Nola spotted Daniel as she and Wade settled down in the theater between the Ashfords and the Chinese prime minister and his diminutive wife. The second Valium had fully kicked in, and Nola felt herself floating outside her skin.

"Chinese opera is a centuries-old art form. It is not affected by winds of change or passing fads," Kong Ruiji said. His hands demonstrated an undulating expressive dance. "The mimes lull you with their magic until you forget all your worries and focus only on the tragedy of others. You realize that other people's lives are more complex than yours, you sympathize, then go back home to your own troubles much happier."

Nola sucked in air. This, then, was his answer to the question she hadn't even uttered. He knew Lulu had disappeared. His people had committed the atrocious act. A chill traversed her body. She accepted a cup of green tea from a willowy teenager in an embroidered kimono, and wrapped both hands around its warmth. But when she sipped some, the tea tasted like grass clippings, and the frozen center inside her could not be thawed.

She was caught in a diplomatic dance, and she had to learn its steps— fast. If only she could talk to Daniel. She turned to scan the crowd and found him seated a few rows behind, but he only nodded toward her with the hint of a smile. She couldn't just get up, pull him away, and find a corner to talk. She smiled back. She couldn't decide if either of the two Western women flanking him was his date for the evening or belonged to the men seated next to them. She wondered whether he had friends. Whom, besides his parents, had he leaned on during his worst hours?

As the evening wore on, the high-pitched voices, the foreign musical notes, so odd and quaint yet obeying their own internal logic, pooled in Nola's brain and heart, bringing her their odd tranquility. The brocade and silk costumes, in bright primary colors rich with designs, were complemented by facial expressions painted in black and red on the actors' chalk-white faces. There was no doubt about good and evil, or pride or humility. All emotions were out in the open, exaggerated, accompanied by mime that, while complex in its artistry, left little for interpretation. Taking in as much as her fogged brain could absorb, Nola studied the unfamiliar string, wind and percussion instruments and admired the singers' high-resonant voices. After a while, her spirits were lightened somewhat. To a small degree, Kong Ruiji was right. The tragedies of others were no less monumental.

If only she knew for sure that right that moment Lulu was safe.

During a set change, her host remained seated and she beside him, listening to his rich English as he went on explaining the opera. Lust, jealousy, love, sacrifice and greed. All so universal, yet transformed by artistic expression. Nola waited for him to mention parental love, the strongest of universal emotions. Instead, he stressed filial responsibility.

"It's a Chinese traditional value that supersedes all others," he explained. "The young owes the old, not the other way around as the West believes."

The hushed babble of the crowd thundered in her head. Time was passing. How many hours had it been since Lulu was taken? Nola wanted to get up, to flee. Kong Ruiji went on chatting, but she was in a pressure cooker of time. If she didn't speak now, she would forever regret it.

Yet, as much as she hated it, she must let the Ambassador use his diplomatic skills.

She'd let him handle the matter, even if her gut feeling was telling her that what was best for her and Lulu might not necessarily be best for Ambassador Ashford, or for U.S.-China relations. Except that her Valium-soaked brain couldn't tell her why.

Chapter 17

A swishing sound hurled Nola up to the surface of sleep. In her dream, Lulu had been with Jenna, both lost in shifting clusters of runaway youth with vacant eyes. As she had done years before, Nola was again searching in back-alley basement apartments and deserted farmhouses.

Scars of old wounds burst open. Nola's breathing came in gasps. Where was her sunny little baby?

In the gauzy shadows of the room, Leslie wheeled in the silver room-service tray. Nola flung back the covers and threw her legs off the bed. Her ice-blue gown of the night before had been tossed across the chair. Wade had locked her jewelry in the vault.

Her voice quaked over the lump in her windpipe. "I should have said something to Kong Ruiji. He could have found Lulu."

"Shhhhhh." Leslie put a finger to her lips. "Warm up your vocal cords. It'll take your mind off things."

"It won't close the hole in my heart." She dropped her face into her hands. "If I don't find her, I'll be worried about her every day of my life."

"Does your pain have anything to do with your sister?"

"Jenna?"

"Whatever happened there, you're still carrying garbage." Leslie halted. He had never brought up this topic unless she initiated the conversation. "And your parents' death."

"What's this got to do with anything?"

"These are unresolved losses." Leslie examined her face as though searching for a blemish. "With my parents, I get things out of my system and out of the way. Even if they disagree, there's always tomorrow to make up. When a person dies, there's no one to argue with."

"For that matter, so are things as far as Jenna's concerned. It's as if the last events were captured on film and I can never change that one last frame. There's so much I could tell her if she weren't hiding—" Nola reached for a tissue. "She's an emancipated adult, even if she likes me enough to accept the yearly stipend Wade deposits in her account."

"For all you know, she's writing The Great American Novel and will show up when she needs it published."

Nola sniffled. "Please call New York and tell them to add a 'Where's Lulu?' option on my website. Many Chinese are connected to the Internet and might have information."

She got up and walked to the stroller. Lulu's toys were piled in it. She flung them on the floor. Dingggg. Plingggg. Klingggg. The clattering reverberated in the room. She dropped to her knees and shoved the toys about, as though Lulu were ready to be plopped down in their midst. She hit the blue key and the head of a dog popped up. Lulu had begun to say "dog."

Nola was surprised when her security man informed her that Daniel Chen was waiting in the living room. Wade was keeping to himself in his office suite downstairs. She had dressed in a leotard, and her hair was pinned up. Now Leslie made her change to a miniskirt, a sweater and sandals, and wouldn't let her leave her room without first touching up her face "no matter how unimportant the guest is." Sometimes she felt she was Leslie's dressed-up doll, as Jenna had been hers when they had staged shows for their father.

She stepped to the bathroom for mouthwash. There, she picked up Daniel's snuff bottle from the silver tray and examined it again. The magnificent bird in a cage. The brush strokes by an artist whose vision of each detail of the final product was so clear that he started by marking them first. What attracted Daniel, who had selected the present before having met her, to this particular picture?

When Nola entered the living room, Daniel was scanning her publicity photo album, a glossy chronicle of her career that, in its Chinese version, was selling by the thousands. He was dressed in a light tweed jacket, chinos and brown leather loafers. Upon her entrance he turned, and both her mind and body registered the handsomeness of his chiseled cheeks and easy, yet controlled, posture. She almost chuckled, remembering Leslie picking on Daniel's "flat feet." For a split second she wondered whether to give Daniel her hand to shake or offer her cheek for a kiss. She opted for a smile.

"I'm sorry not to have had the chance to tell you how terrible I feel about the baby," he said. "How are you faring?"

"Devastated," she whispered. "No one understands how much I love her."

"Adoptive parents often speak of love at first sight. And she's special—"

"You're the only one who doesn't refer to her in the past tense."

"I should tell you that I'm here on Ashford's behalf," he said. There was a deprecating note in his voice. "Or rather our government."

She looked at him. Again that strength, that center within him that she wanted to reach. "I hope it has something to do with Lulu."

He nodded. "The official version?"

"God," she murmured. "Go ahead."

"The baby's mother has been found."

Nola's breathing stopped. "What?"

"According to the Chinese." The intimacy of their phone conversation was gone from his voice. "They've produced some peasant woman. With urban migration increasing, millions of homeless peasants are living in train stations. They don't receive *hukou*, the registration status that entitles them to benefits in the city—"

Nola interrupted him. "The mother? She didn't want her baby; she gave her to me instead of throwing her into a garbage can. Did they find Lulu?"

He shook his head. "Nope."

"The mother alone is of no use to anyone, right? No one's looking for the mothers of babies found under bushes. You're not telling me yet that Lulu is alive! Is she?"

He went to the CD player, rummaged through the stack of CDs next to it, and a minute later, the soft notes of Berlioz' *King Lear* overture came through. She smiled with recognition. He turned up the volume.

"Sorry," he said below the level of the music, but loud enough for her to hear. "I've delivered the official version. I don't believe it matters except for one reason."

She looked at him.

"I was made to understand that they would like to see mother and baby reunited."

"Hold it. In order to reunite them, they must have Lulu," she said. "And how can that be unless they are behind her kidnapping?"

"I see a subtext, and that is their efforts to placate you."

"There's a simple way to placate me and they know what it is." She dropped onto the couch and cocked her head at him. "Sit down. I can't talk to you like this."

He chose the upholstered chair. His knees touched the coffee table. His wrists dangled past his knees. The fingers were long and flexible.

"I'm sorry," she said. "I don't let you speak. I'm so miserable. It's been eighteen hours."

"I understand."

She began again. "The subtext you were mentioning..."

"Everyone's heavily invested in you. Your public image is bigger than you, and it has a life of its own."

She leaned forward and pulled down the edge of her skirt to cover her thighs. "Meaning what?"

"They're looking for ways to involve you in quieting down the storm," Daniel said from his seat behind her. "They need you for it, which gives you leverage. They are worried about other global negotiations that are at stake."

"No problem. In the interest of international harmony, why not just let me have my baby?"

"It is not so much about you as it is about China. This incident reflects poorly on the Chinese's efforts to control population. They're in fact conforming to the international pressure that recommended population control in the first place."

"I've heard all about that from Ashford. China has prevented the potential birth of three hundred million more people, more than the entire U.S. population." She wanted to scream over the loud music. "I'm not against voluntary planned parenthood. I am not even against abortion, within limits. I am against infanticide, which is quite a different matter. Am I supposed to agree that under the 'population control' strategy it is the local government's prerogative to kill Lulu?"

She rose and stepped to the window. The same buildings under construction, the same thousands of people in the main thoroughfare, the same market she had shown Lulu. The spice merchant exchanged animated comments with his wife, and while she pulled out straw baskets filled with herbs, he tied a bright blue tarp as an awning over open sacks of colorful spices.

Nola's cheek pressed against the cold glass. The image of a patch of pink with a butterfly print flashed in front of her eyes.

After a few minutes, Daniel asked, "Are you all right?"

She turned fully toward him." Why are you here? You've told me that you don't do anything just because it's expected of you."

"I'm assuming that you'd want to hear it from someone who can level with you." His voice had the same rich quality she had noticed the first time she heard him speak.

She bit her lip. The hour at the Dying Rooms would be their shared experience forever. And his confession about Kate. Another song percolated in her. "Through Your Eyes I'm a Better Person." She was beginning to see her old capable self through Daniel's eyes.

"How would they want to involve me in quieting down the storm?" she asked.

"There's a whole dog-and-pony show they will ask you to go through. Uniting Lulu with her mother, etcetera." He rose and moved closer, but stopped three feet away. "I don't believe they have the mother. For all I know, they'd produce any poor peasant woman who'll make remorseful statements. Ditto for the baby. They'll put her and the presumed mother on television."

"But I do believe they've got Lulu," Nola said. "Who else would kidnap her? And there are too many of her pictures circulating the globe. They can't easily substitute her."

"To much of the world, Chinese babies all look alike."

"How gullible I was to think that all I had to do was run to the U.S. Embassy and have them save the day. The truth is that if Lulu is with her so-called mother, Ashford's problems are over. He's no longer under pressure to help me adopt this one particular baby. But he is under pressure from both governments to get me to play a friendship farce." She chortled. "Friendship indeed. The Chinese and U.S. governments are in cahoots to destroy a seven-month-old baby."

At least Lulu was alive. They would need her healthy and smiling for their propaganda. She was out there, although Nola might never see her again. "I'll ask Kong Ruiji to tell me this to my face. I'll call him—"

"It's my hunch that he won't take your phone call right now," Daniel said. "But I also heard that he's willing to reward you for your cooperation."

"Reward me? But not by giving me Lulu back? How?"

He shook his head. "Some offer will come directly from Kong Ruiji's office."

She sucked in her breath. In her mind's eye she bent and kissed Lulu's little head. The tuft of dark hair was soft as silk. From now on, she might speak to every influential TV host, or use every stage to sing about the injustice of Lulu's fate, but she had lost the battle. She had failed her as she had Jenna. Tears filled her eyes.

"I'm so sorry," Daniel said. "I'll follow the news and keep you posted."

Nausea churned Nola's stomach. The truth dawned on her. Neither government had understood the depth of her bond with Lulu. They hadn't expected her to put up a fight. A fawn lost in the woods of political intrigue, last night she had gone along with the ambassador's delaying tactics.

"The Chinese and Ashford are right about one thing," she said. "I do have a price. Lulu. But what they're wrong about is that they can silence me." She walked to the door. "Please tell Ashford that if he wants to shut me up, he'll have to kill me."

Just as she turned to the corridor, she thought she glimpsed Daniel nod in appreciation.

Before going downstairs for her rehearsal, she picked up the snuff bottle again. Had Daniel seen the caged bird? Her brain quivered at the enormity of staring down the wills of the world's two superpowers.

Wade's quick steps brought her back. "What did Daniel have to say?" he asked.

"Whatever. But I invited two governments to kill me." She could smell the oxygen-sucking odor of defeat. "Do you know of an offer the Chinese want to make me?"

"Actually, I do," he replied. "Some movie deal."

"After all your talk about a script for me, the one that pops up is from the Chinese government?" She raised her fist in mock triumph. "A new central casting: Ashford and Kong Ruiji."

"We'll talk about it when you're in a better mood."

"Stop treating me like I'm a blabbering fool." She sat on an ottoman to put on her dance shoes. "Shoot."

The pull of distaste at his bottom lip told her how difficult he found her to be.

"Here's the deal," he said. "The Chinese are hoping to make a big-budget *Schindler's List*-type movie to dramatize the horrific Nanjing massacre by the Japanese in 1937. A German civilian saved thousands of Chinese refugees from rapes and murders. There's a Caucasian female role that Kong Ruiji believes you can play. You'll show your compassion toward the Chinese people and at the same time work with their government in its efforts to garner sympathy—"

"If sympathy is what they're after, they could find it without my help if they stopped rolling over protesters with tanks and killing babies in orphanages." She yanked at the dance shoes. Lulu would be a poster child. What would happen to her once the media diverted its attention to the next sensation? "I hope you've told him to do you-know-what."

"You're missing the point. They're trying to make you happy. The Double Happiness tour has encountered some glitches and it is important that we smooth things out."

"Please don't insult me like I'm a kid with a scraped knee. Of all people, you should know that I can't be compensated for my loss of Lulu with a movie offer. A *movie* offer!"

He drummed his fingers on the dresser. "What do you want me to do?"

"I assume that you've done as much as you can in this matter." She rose to her feet, feeling the ache of their estrangement. But the certainty that she would never see Lulu again broke her inner self into a million pieces. Lulu, her flower. All that remained to fill the vacuum would be the song that would create awareness of China's infanticide.

The fourth stanza for "Flower Babies" popped up inside her.

"Flower babies, forever in our hearts you'll glow,/ Each little silenced flower now a star.//

You shine down on a world you'll never know,/ Your wails strum the strings of my guitar.//"

Chapter 18

Nola bounded into the hotel's grand ballroom.

Jean-Claude's nervous fingers were rifling through the music pages strewn around him. "Let's go over tomorrow's program," he said. "We've broken up your performance into two parts, before and after that mega-Las-Vegas-type show by the Australian dancers. They're already practicing in Shanghai. More feathers and glitz than China has ever seen."

"They're supposed to warm up the audience for me, not the other way around." But she liked the idea of splitting her performance. She was exhausted.

Jean-Claude bent over a list on which he marked the audience responses to various songs at the Forbidden City concert. "We received huge applause for 'A String of Magical Moments,' and 'Superstitions.' We can add another love song. How about 'Don't Wait for Life to Begin?' An oldie but goodie—"

That magical night only four days earlier—the peak of her career—seemed to have taken place in another era. That night, all that was elusive was her relationship with Jenna. Wade had still been her devoted, if overly demanding, hero and husband. Within hours, nothing mattered. One baby changed her in ways she hadn't imagined possible.

"I've finished 'Flower Babies,'" she said.

He grinned. "Let's hear it."

"*Lost in the cold of the night,/ In a place with no heat or light.//Flower babies die unloved,/ Reach heaven on the wings of doves.//*"

He took over, and the half-notes, climbing to the higher end of the scale, twisted and turned on themselves, as in Chinese music. "How about a single flute for the repeat theme?" he asked, and called over the flutist to demonstrate.

The clear, clean high notes wove an oral vine over the gravestone of her bond with Lulu. "*Fantastique*," she said, "It sounds like the song of a nightingale."

She felt feverish with the prospect of making this song happen. How many women here had suffered the separation of babies snatched from their arms to be murdered? This would be the song not only of those babies, but also of their tormented mothers. Jean-Claude and she repeated "Flower Babies" several times. Occasionally, he brought in instruments and made corrections to the music. "It's a great song," he concluded, "Let it simmer. In the meantime, let's go back to finalizing our program for tomorrow."

" 'Flower Babies' is ready," she said.

"No time for a full orchestra rehearsal. You can't take the chance of bombing."

It would be an explosion, all right. Flashes of the protest rallies from her parents' years came to mind. She remembered being awed as the huge crowd was riled up by songs of protest. The message of "Flower Babies" must reverberate around the globe, too.

"Don't have a heart attack," she said. "But I want to sing it in Shanghai tomorrow night."

Bruuummmmm. Jean-Claude pounded his palm on the piano keys, and Nola jumped. The blare of notes rolled around the hall.

"Don't you get it?" he shouted. "Our song list had to be approved by a bunch of slant-eyed bureaucrats. Last year, after inviting the Lincoln Center Festival, the Chinese withdrew their invitation because they didn't like one piece. One piece! This is China, for Christ's sake! We'll be thrown into prison the moment we break regulations. And not one phone call to a lawyer, either!" He wiped the saliva at the edge of his mouth. "Shanghai is even worse than Beijing. It's more commie, with more bureaucrats. I've told you before: I don't want to get butt-fucked by some meddling government official with a political hard-on!"

The musicians and dancers pretended to be practicing. "You've made your point," Nola said calmly, "but it's my name on the marquee."

"No, it's not. We're married by music, remember? No sex, only music marriage." He ran through a few scales on the piano. Then he turned to the triple keyboard and pounded a series of angry notes. He dropped his hands on his lap and hung his chin on his chest.

In the silence, she heard the lingering argument.

She was almost relieved to see Roberta sailing into the ballroom, her nose upturned like a dog scenting food. Roberta's finger on her mouth shushed the five reporters following her for a peek at rehearsal.

Nola crossed the vast floor toward them. *Vanity Fair* had a three-months lead time for publication. Supermarket tabloids were weeklies, but didn't indulge in serious journalism. Broadcast was the fastest, but the morning shows with their snippets of information wouldn't do. For the kind of investigative reporting she needed, she should talk to Don Hewitt from *60 Minutes* or Stone Phillips from *Dateline*. Their programs, though, had very long lead times. If she could get hold of a journalist from a daily like *The New York Times* or *The Washington Post*, she'd give them the story.

"Hi. What's the word on the street about my baby?" she asked, scanning the reporters' I.D. tags.

An older man whose I.D. identified him as working for *The Star* said, "The Russians have kidnapped her to cause a rift between the U.S. and China."

The *Vanity Fair* reporter shook her head. "Lulu was an 'out-of-quota' baby. Her mother wanted her to receive your blessing so she won't be exterminated."

But the young MTV host threw his bleached head back in exaggerated hilarity. "Isn't it a publicity stunt coming out of your own camp?"

"You don't believe that, do you?"

"How come the cultural attaché who objects to your concert tour is the one in charge of it?"

"What? Daniel Chen?" Nola asked.

"Politics," Roberta cut in. "We've lived through enough misquotes and survived them."

Nola half-turned to Roberta. "Get me all the clippings and videos covering Lulu, will you, please?"

"Pronto," Roberta replied, her tone sarcastic.

Nola took in the five reporters and smiled. They weren't her first or second choice, but they were the only ones present. "Here's a statement. Neither government is cooperating. They hope I'll forget about my baby. But I won't—and neither should you. Stay tuned. I'll deliver a message at my concert in Shanghai tomorrow night."

Roberta called to the reporters, "Let's hold off on this statement, okay? Off the record for now, please?" To Nola she hissed, "You're a loose cannon."

"My name is 'Bashful Fire,' remember? It was your idea, with emphasis on 'Fire,' until I get Lulu back." Nola left. She must get hold of some phone numbers, but there was no point in asking Roberta for them.

Twenty minutes later, working with Leslie, she pushed aside all thoughts. Using a sketch of the Shanghai stage, Leslie marked the dimensions on the floor with yellow tape. For the next hour, they practiced her dance routines with the musicians. But the heaviness in her heart traveled to her legs, and her series of quick turns failed as she kept tripping.

"I'll truly break a leg," she said, massaging her hamstring.

"Look, misery is an equal-opportunity employer. It just recruits the older faster than the young." Leslie's tone was sympathetic. "You can't give up the dancing. If you do, you'll lose the newest MTV generation. You keep up with the music, but you must dance better than any newcomer. And they pop up fast." He handed her a concoction of juices. "We'll take a break and continue after lunch. How about an Oriental salad?"

All she could think of was that to sing "Flower Babies" she needed no dancing, but rather to see Lulu's face on the projection screen of her eyes and let her mind roam through the rows of cribs of the Dying Rooms.

It occurred to her that she could be there right now, comforting the babies who had no one to love them. "Tell you what," she told Leslie. "Bring that salad along. I want to show you a place that will change your life. Get the driver."

Leslie placed a silver tray on the teakwood table in the center of the limousine. He unwrapped two bone-china salad bowls, ivory chopsticks and cloth napkins folded in the shapes of tulips. Yoram sat in front by the driver, munching on something from a brown paper bag.

Nola leaned her back against the door and put her feet up on the seat. Her gaze fell on a folded piece of paper tucked in the door pocket. She pulled it out.

"What's that?" Leslie asked.

"Oh, Daniel's article I got at the embassy a couple of days ago."

Leslie held his creamy-white chopsticks to the light and admired their inner glow. "I've unveiled a mystery that will interest you."

"Oh?"

"Daniel Chen's tragic love story."

She twisted her head and stared out the window. "I've heard it."

"You have? Well, there's something positive to draw out of this story."

She unfolded the photocopied article. "I can't imagine what that would be."

"A man capable of deep love can love again."

If only she could frame her emotions and their disjointed logic. The breakup with Wade wasn't helping her fight the attraction to Daniel.

"Well," Leslie said, "Are you going to read us the article?"

She held up the article and stared at a highlighted blurb in the center. *"The Chinese, chuckling behind their bamboo screens, act too polite to refuse the gesture, which they regard as an asinine, disingenuous Western notion of friendship...."*

The blood slammed into her temples. She scanned the previous column. *"...with the U.S. and China's mutual enemy—the Soviet regime— out of the race, these two leading global powers are jostling for supremacy, a struggle in which there can only be one winner...."*

"My God. It's the same article from Wade's file! Daniel wrote this."

She now understood the MTV host's question. *"The White House should wake up from its euphoric ignorance to smell the tea. Instead, it has mustered its most formidable weapon: a cultural dose of pop music! Send Nola Sands and let this China doll reset the buttons on the control boards of history."*

She crumpled the paper, not looking in Leslie's direction. Oh, no! Daniel had indeed objected to her goodwill tour; he had publicized the ridicule with which the Chinese had accepted her. Never mind his cynical view on the state of the U.S.-China relationship. It was his dismal, unflattering, deflating view of her mission that belittled her.

"What was that about?" Leslie asked.

She punched her fist on her thigh. "You know what's the absolute worst part about being a celebrity? I have no true friends. I can't trust anyone—"

"I'll follow you through flood and fire."

"Thanks." She touched his arm. No point mentioning that he had no tolerance for things that didn't fit his agenda. She would never know which way he would have gone on the issue of Lulu.

Nola instructed the driver to stop at the Western drugstore, where they emptied the shelves of baby powder, ointments, wipes, pacifiers, disposable diapers, light blankets, cold medicine, small toys and some clothes.

Not knowing which side street led to the Dying Rooms alley, Nola ordered the driver to park a few feet past the American Embassy, and retraced the route by entering the Silk Market on foot.

Their arms full, Nola, Leslie, Yoram and the driver wove their way down the busy alley. All around them, shops and stalls burst with shirts, ties, jackets, backpacks and umbrellas in solid or printed bright colors— all made of silk and smelling of biting chemical dyes. Leslie spotted American designers' labels, surplus from local manufacturers, but Nola did not let him stop.

"I remember vaguely my promise to follow you through flood or fire," he said, "Which one is this?"

"An earthquake."

The street was filled with shoppers, tourists and merchants, and Nola had to slow her pace to keep the purchases in her arms from being knocked off. She was carrying so many items that she could barely see over her burden.

The overflowing stalls from the main alley ran halfway down the block leading to the orphanage, and Nola almost missed the turn. After a moment's confusion, she stood in front of the building with the "Happy Door" calligraphy. Nola tried the handle.

The door was unlocked, and again there was no one in the foyer or in the first floor loft. But the building was filled with sounds of activity: furniture being moved, footsteps on the stairs, hammering, television and babies' cries.

She stepped into the loft, the others behind her. The driver set down his boxes and hurried out to bring the car around.

"Gosh. This place stinks." Leslie pinched his nostrils, but his expression soon changed. "God Almighty," he said at the sight of the seventy-foot-long double rows of cribs. He dropped his packages on the floor and took Nola's from her.

She shivered in the chill of the room. In the milky light that streamed through the unwashed windows, babies were awake, crying, babbling. Some rocked or thrashed about weakly. Only a few sat up.

An abject yearning for Lulu's two small arms around her neck rose in Nola. "Make yourself useful," she told Leslie and Yoram. "Open the toys and distribute them. These babies get no sensory stimulation."

"Miss Nola, Miss Nola, I don't know nothin' 'bout no babies," Leslie whined. But when she glanced at him, she saw a cast of gray under his eyes.

"Weren't you the one to say that babies were a wonderful way to start people?" she asked. "Well, take a look at these—"

At the far end, in an open area, two dozen babies, all girls wearing only short, loose shirts, were sitting splay-legged on bamboo benches underneath which chamber pots had been placed. The chest-high tray of each bench was fixed over two vertical bars and locked the girls' torsos and open thighs. The girls looked at Nola with hollow, dark eyes. Nola crouched in front of them and little white buttocks like pale, unripe peaches peeked at her below the holes cut into the benches.

Yoram rattled a trinket in front of a baby who did not try to reach for it. "I did shifts at the kibbutz nursery, but I've never seen anything like these babies. They're zombies."

Leslie touched one little head after another as though counting them—or perhaps transferring positive energy onto them. "Nola, this is not my idea of a lunch break," he said after a while. "We must go back and rehearse. We're in the midst of a concert tour."

Nola surveyed the floor under the cribs for a scurrying rat. From above, the sound of rhythmic banging, accompanied by a choir of cries, echoed down. "I'm going to check things on the next two floors." She dashed out and took the steps two at a time.

The first thing she noticed was the banging sound of babies who rocked and hit their heads against the slats of their cribs. Some accompanied their violent rocking with percussion-like chants, "Aha-a, aha-a, aha-a."

A woman walked among the cribs in the middle row, carrying a bucketful of baby bottles. She turned over the babies who were on their stomachs. A second woman rolled rags to prop up the bottles and then stuck them in the babies' mouths. When a baby's feeble shriek protested the loss of the bottle, she shoved it back in. Other infants lost their bottles and simply closed their eyes.

The women gestured for Nola to leave.

Her fists clenched, she stood still. There were thousands of orphanages like this one all over China. She could sink all her money into them, but it would be sucked into a black hole. There must be a better way. A grassroots swell of public outrage would translate into collective power. Drops of water could come together to create a great river. A large enough flow of water could wear down a stone, Daniel had said. If ferocious enough, water could move boulders, break dams. It could force the Chinese government to right this wrong.

From the bottom of the stairwell, Leslie called to Nola, then bounded up the steps. Thirty feet away, the women's hand motions, shooing Nola away, were clear. She remained standing, taking the strangeness in the room, some imbalance she couldn't pinpoint. Then she knew. The babies in the wake of feeding were asleep, or nearly so. Their sluggishness was not the contentment of feeding, but the stupor of drugs.

She tried to convince herself that Lulu was not being intoxicated in one of these institutions, but the notion failed to find a corner of comfort within her. Her gaze traveled up and down the aisles.

One of the women reached her. As if pulled by a magnet, Nola stepped around her. The woman yanked at her arm, but Leslie shoved the woman away, urging Nola to leave, but she kept on moving, her eyes searching each of the cribs.

Her blood slammed in her ears a split second before the information registered in her brain. There were the pink pajamas with the butterfly print.

Chapter 19

(1986)

At the Seven Stars Diner, plates clattered and waitresses called orders into the kitchen, children ran around, and everything was normal, except that in the booth seat across from Nola was Mr. Wade Dalton. From Musix! He had taken her to the diner after the school football game and ordered her a hamburger. Since she didn't know what else to do, she ate. Anything tasted better than Miss Helga's cooking. The woman's chicken was so overdone she might as well have laundered it in the washing machine.

Mr. D. said, "This has been quite a surprise. What a voice! What projection!"

Nola smiled, but when his pale blue eyes kept studying her, she worried that he was counting the pimples that resisted any of the dozen creams she had tried. But he went on to say how impressed he was with the ladylike way she cut up her hamburger with a knife and used her fork to pick up the French fries. She wasn't about to tell him that never touching her food with her fingers was a survival skill at Mini-Nazi's home.

In the booth behind her, the jukebox changed from "Broken Wings" to "When the Going Gets Tough, the Tough Get Going." She tapped her foot to the music and felt the dangling ribbons in her barrette swinging. Mr. D. ordered her a second hamburger and said that he liked people who ate with zest. "Hunger for life, enjoyment of simple pleasures, tell me about an artist's innate enthusiasm," he explained. "No star can fake it for a lifetime."

Something giggled inside Nola at the word "star." He spoke as if she could become one, and it amazed, thrilled and frightened her.

He was really nice, though, and big brotherly. He was strongly built, though not tall, and had a commanding presence even in the confines of their booth. Each feature on his face was right, yet the combination was merely pleasant, and in their animation, the features moved in and out of position. The only oddity about him was the port-wine stain that bled from his shirt collar to his jaw. She liked this. The old man's deformities and Jenna's reconstructions made people with imperfections easier to trust. But what Nola liked the most about Mr. D. was his laughter, like coins tossed in the air and then tumbling all around her.

"I can't get over what you looked like on that huge football field with the microphone in your hand. You were this waif, but then a miracle happened. A transformation." He laughed again, then shook his head as if the wonder of what he had heard still rang in his ears. "I can't get over your command of your audience. Few seasoned artists possess such a gift."

Nola's feet tingled. She wanted to jump and dance in the aisle or something. Here she was, filled with music that shaped her days and at night flooded her with dreams of Sting, George Michael and David Bowie. She would die now if she got another chance to meet Bono; at ten, she had been too stupid to appreciate his kiss. And now, Mr. D., who knew everything about the entertainment world, was praising her!

"Thanks," she said quietly, and he commented on her poise. "It's extraordinary for a sixteen-year-old. Is your mother like this, too?"

"She's dead." Nola looked at her plate. Her voice teacher hadn't warned Mr. D. that she was a walking disaster. Mr. D. would change his mind once he knew.

His lips gathered in a show of sympathy. "Sorry. How tough. You must miss her a lot."

"My father's dead too. The same accident." She raised her gaze. Suddenly it was easy to talk. He was so worldly and solid, as if the ground held to his feet for support. "She was a singer. He played lead guitar for several bands. They met at Woodstock." A smile crept into her voice. "When I was ten, they put me on stage at an anti-nukes rally. I also got to hear U2 playing on their first American tour."

"I'm surprised no one signed you then." He ordered her a huge dish of ice cream, with oodles of whipped cream dotted with strawberries like roses cast on snow by a good fairy. She offered to split it with him but he said he would live vicariously through her because he was on a perpetual diet. Again he let out a laugh full of gaiety. Only someone who grew up with loving parents could laugh like this, she thought.

Mr. D's hands made motions in the air. "I want you to picture what I saw when you sang the anthem. Everyone froze. No one scratched, drank Coke, roamed up and down the bleachers, or did any of the things people do when they're itchy for a game to begin." He pushed his plate away and placed his elbows on the table. "I'm telling you all this not because I want to fill your head with illusions of grandeur, but because I want you to know your strengths as I see them."

The coolness of the ice cream hurt her sinuses. She sat on her hands to stop their shaking.

He continued, "I want to make sure you understand that it nevertheless takes a miracle to turn talent into success. Fabulous voices are a dime a dozen. I'm on the lookout for star material: charisma with the right mix of temperament, style, discipline and motivation." He leaned forward as if to tell her a secret. His aftershave smelled of leather and wood. "Talent alone can be more a curse than a gift. It gives many performers just enough hope to waste money and years getting nowhere."

Nola brought her hands out of their hiding and poked at the melting ice cream. What about looks? She was no Olivia Newton-John. Mr. D. was speaking to the wrong person. She touched her nose. Its tip was still bulbous. Her fingers brushed over her cheek. It was as flat and hollow as always. The glimpse of her dull brown hair that fell on her chest told her the crimp had gone limp.

Mr. D. leaned back again. He looked as though he were smiling even when he wasn't. "Tell me about school. What are your favorite subjects?"

"Geography. I like to know about people from other places. What they eat, how they dress, what kinds of houses they live in, what music they listen to." She looked up at the wall at the picture of a Greek port framed by olive trees. "D'you think that landscape makes them who they are? You know, ocean people are different from mountain people, different from jungle people, different from desert people? I think they make music to fit their lives. One day I'd like to see singers from every place come together—like in 'We Are The World.'"

He made a goofy face. "For once, these guys were able to leave their egos at the door and do something good together." He signaled the waitress for the check, and kept on talking. "I like you. You're witty, which is handy for the stage and interviews, and intelligent, which is critical both for discipline and for maintaining an artist's cool." He crossed his arms on the table and looked into her eyes. "And don't underestimate the pressure, even the pressure of fame. When the glow of stardom is reflected back by millions of admirers, it is magnified enough to burn— as it has many an experienced artist." These last words were said with theatrical flair as he slapped his credit card on the table. "Drugs. The bane of our business. Do you do any?"

She shook her head. Never again would she want those dreams before sleep. "I'm squeaky clean."

"Good. I want you to audition at our studios, then we'll take it from there."

The word "audition" grew in front of Nola's eyes into a giant multi-armed creature. For two days she didn't wash her hair, stayed in bed, and refused to eat. She stared at the window until the brightness outside blinded her, yet she would not avert her gaze. A full orchestra played in her head and she dreamed that her voice had turned into a howl.

Beverly Cutter blasted in, all bouncing curls, her legs scissoring a long, full black skirt. "What's the matter?" She put her hand on Nola's forehead. "Why haven't you been in school?"

"I don't want to audition. I don't want any change in my life. Didn't you want me to go to Yale? Tell Mr. D. that's what I'm planning to do. Please? It was your idea all along."

"I think I know what this is about." Beverly closed the door and sat at the edge of the bed.

"No you don't." Nola crossed her arms over her chest.

"You think you don't deserve a break." Beverly stroked Nola's arm. "Let me tell you something. You blame yourself for your parents' death. But I was the adult in charge that day." Her voice was low as she went on, "Their death was caused by alcohol and drugs, not by a couple of shrubs that had been moved."

"It was my arrow that sent them over the cliff."

"They couldn't even see the sign in the dark." Beverly wiped a tear that ran down Nola's cheek. "It hurts just the same."

For a while, neither spoke. In the yard, Mini-Nazi was beating a rug; she distrusted vacuum cleaners. Nola's fingers poked at a buttonhole in the blanket cover. "Aren't singers first supposed to do gigs in nightclubs or weddings? At least it would be a preparation."

"Most make a career of it and never get to cut an album." Beverly continued stroking Nola's arm. There was a smile in her voice as she added, "Here's a secret: Someone is keeping score. In that ledger, your bad luck has earned you a shortcut."

"I can't move away! Jenna is worse than ever." Nola shut her eyes, blocking tears. Every day, there was another fuss over small or imagined hurts. Jenna believed that even her dolls hated her. "What will happen to her?"

"It's only a test recording," Beverly said.

"It's just a test recording," Wade said. He had told Beverly that since he was only twenty-six, they should call him by his first name.

He telephoned Nola again just to chat, asking what book she was reading, and telling her about the Broadway shows he'd seen. Wearing her favorite shirt, burgundy-colored with a keyboard design running down the left sleeve, Nola sat on the stool in Mini-Nazi's corridor that smelled of disinfectants and clutched the phone to her ear. Wade laughed and talked about the music world. He was excited that long after the Beatles' breakup, American artists were taking the world lead, with U2 just an exception. America also had technology on its side. The easy-to-break-and-scratch vinyl records were being replaced by the transportable cassettes. And digital technology was making new music in diverse ways that still weren't obvious to many industry insiders. And then there was visual music. It was a line-extension that would be equally profitable as records. "With your first album, Musix will release a music video," he said.

Nola gulped. Wade's talk reminded her of her father bringing home the sounds of new groups, telling her who was producing what music. But Wade moved among people who had the power to create and spread music. With his laughter and talk and promises, echoes of the big world streamed toward her, tantalizing, awesome, frightening.

She dared not confide her fears in him lest he never call again.

For the scheduled day of the audition, he mailed her and Beverly a pair of tickets to the American Ballet Theater for later that evening.

He told Nola to trust Beverly, and Beverly told her to trust Wade.

Two days later, he called to say he was authorized to sign her, in spite of her young age. Musix had great hopes for her future.

Nola cried and decided to never speak to Wade Dalton again. She went to a friend's to watch MTV because Mini-Nazi didn't allow it, and looked with renewed awe as Madonna shimmied her boobs and gyrated her hips. No way could Nola be like her, to have that presence and be so sure-footed even while floating on the screen in a cloud of mist. She was so homely.

It took Beverly days to come up with the clinching argument to convince Nola to speak with the lawyer Wade had recommended to represent her interests. "Do it for Jenna's future, too," Beverly said.

The night before the contract-signing, Nola was at Beverly's, when Wade called to say the meeting had been canceled.

"What do you mean 'canceled?' " Nola asked Beverly. "They hate me after all?"

"Canceled, but Wade says he has a better deal. A surprise."

"I told you!" Nola sunk to her knees and leaned her head against the wall mirror. "It's not going to happen."

"He's driving out here to take us to dinner. He wants me to pick the best French restaurant in town. That doesn't sound like someone who's giving up on you."

A couple of hours later, at the restaurant, Nola sat dressed in a light blue suit with zippers all over it, anticipating more bad news, while Wade gossiped about singers and bands and rattled off names of composers and heads of labels. Nola pulled at each of the zippers, listening to their music. Wade's conversation had nothing to do with her; she was never going to break into that world.

He asked her to predict who would top the charts. "Anything Billy Joel," she replied.

Wade's light-colored eyebrows shot up in surprise. "Anything?"

She shrugged. "Since his marriage to Christie Brinkley, millions of men believe they stand a chance with a beautiful woman."

Wade and Beverly burst out laughing. Letting go of a zipper, Nola gave a wan smile. "Also Madonna. Boys like her, girls like her. Totally."

"Madonna," Wade repeated, mauling the name. "The little virgin has become quite the little fornicator. She'll either fall flat or make it big."

"Some call a music channel devoted entirely to teens depravity," Beverly said.

"I think it's progress," Nola said. "Someone's paying attention to what we like."

Only when the main course arrived did Wade get to the point.

"I did something I regret. It's part of my job, but it is also the part I dislike the most. I referred you to a good-for-nothing lawyer, then stuck this lousy contract under his nose. I was ready to screw you." He stopped to let the words sink in. "Sorry. That's the way a bottom-line corporation takes advantage of artists."

Beverly put down her wine glass. "My, my."

"I apologize. Really." Wade's eyebrows drooped to show his sincere regret. "If Nola signed this contract, she'd be tied up as the lowest-paid singer in Musix' stable for just about forever—and I would get a fat bonus check."

Nola pressed against the back of her chair. The slats pushed into her ribs. His words were far, yet near. She had trusted him so, yet he had been conning her all along! No, he had given her a break, yet.... Now he was honest.

"I'm really sorry I couldn't be more up front with you," he told her. "It was my job. But I can't do it to you."

Beverly asked. "So that's it? End of story?"

"Just the beginning. I have a better idea." Wade's smile was directed toward Beverly, but he spoke to Nola. "I want to resign from Musix and become your personal manager. Instead of helping a label exploit you, I'll protect your interests. You're extremely talented, but you need the attention of a professional if you're going to make it in this cutthroat world. And I'm talking about making it big. A star. Not just another artist."

"Well, well, well," Beverly mumbled. "How do we know that this time you're being straight with us?"

"Look, I'm taking more of a risk than you are," Wade went on speaking to Nola. "I'll quit a good-paying job, a promising corporate career. I'll be investing in you all of my time, my money, my knowledge and my connections. I will only succeed if you succeed. I'm betting my career on you."

Nola stared at him. She didn't know what to think. She hadn't yet left Smithtown but was already out of her element.

Chapter 20

In a blur of shouts and sights, Nola clutched the inert bundle in her arms. Leslie slapped a wad of yuan into a caretaker's palm. Yoram's long arms created a protective shield around Nola and Lulu as he whisked them out.

"Everything'll be all right. Hang in there, Lulu, my baby. You're strong. Be strong a little longer until we get a doctor for you," Nola panted the words. What doctor? Where could she find one who would not take Lulu away again? Nola slid onto the car's back seat.

"I'll call Daniel and see if he knows one," Leslie said.

She was about to object. Daniel wasn't a friend. "Do it," she murmured.

Lulu's breathing was shallow, the intake of air quick, its expulsion long. Her hair was caked with dried vomit, and her odor suggested she was soiled. How much of the drugs had she ingested? Was there a way to undo it? Oh, God. "Is there an emergency room? No, that's a bad idea." Nola patted and bounced the little body, but it remained as rubbery and inert as a giant marshmallow. The lightweight pink pajamas were insufficient for the chill of the day. Nola took off her sweatshirt and covered her. Her baby. She couldn't bear it if she died. Not another loss.

Leslie reached Daniel, gave him a brief explanation, and asked that he locate a doctor ASAP. "I'll leave word with security at the hotel to let you in without delay."

Nola tickled the soles of Lulu's feet, trilled her fingers on the damp cheek, and massaged the small ribs in an effort to wake her up. But Lulu lay listless in her arms. *Oh, God. Please.* Nola's chest burned with corrosive despair. "My little dumpling. I'll never let you down again."

She broke into *Bridge Over Troubled Water*. It was either sing or have her fear drag her down like an undertow. She went on singing, tears streaming down her face.

The limousine pulled through a side entrance into the garage. Upstairs moments later, Nola passed through the foyer of her suite, her eyes never leaving Lulu as though they had the power to penetrate the shield of sleep. She was vaguely aware of Wade conducting his phone business behind the living room's closed doors. With Leslie at her side, she headed straight into her bedroom and lay Lulu down on the bed.

"I mustn't lose her." The bile taste of horror had lodged in Nola's mouth as she stripped and cleaned the little body with a wet, warm washcloth, all the while massaging the limbs, the back, the chest. Lulu remained unresponsive.

Leslie put his head to Lulu's chest. "She's breathing fine. Her color's returned." He walked to the far corner of the room, lit incense, and settled on the carpet Indian-style. He began to chant. "Hawoooooo—"

"What are you doing?" Nola asked.

"I'm bringing Hawaiian spirits so that divine sparks will leap from your fingers onto our little Lulu. Ha-woooooooo—"

"*Baruch atta Adonai*," Nola murmured, the only words she remembered from her Judaic studies, then added, *God, please be good to her—to us. Rescue us—* She massaged the sluggish body some more, and, when Lulu's eyelids fluttered, put her head to the little chest. The skin had warmed.

"The prayers are working," she whispered to Leslie, and kept at them. Anything to fill the slow-dripping minutes of waiting until the doctor arrived. She hated waiting for Daniel. He could go to hell. "It's been thirty minutes since we found her," she said.

Without using his hands, Leslie uncoiled his legs into a standing position. "You're the one who needs reviving now. Take in a cleansing breath." While she took in a lungful of air, then another, he poured green tea into two cups.

She sipped, but tension strained her nerves, as tight as guitar strings. She covered Lulu's naked body with a blanket, but the palm of her hand kept tracing circles on it. "Wait for the doctor, little dumpling. Please?"

The rapid movement of Lulu's ribs slowed to a normal rhythm. She would be all right. She must be. It had all been ordained. In the book of rights and wrongs someone was keeping, it said that Nola had paid her dues; she had been paroled.

Sounds from the foyer made Leslie sprint out.

Daniel appeared at the door. With him was a miniature Chinese woman in a long white coat and blue cotton pants, with a stethoscope around her neck and large, dark-framed glasses covering a third of her face. She was holding a physician's satchel.

The woman walked briskly while inserting her stethoscope earpieces. She adjusted her glasses on the flat arch of her nose. Without a word, she proceeded to the bed, checked Lulu's pulse, and with a small flashlight examined the pupils, ears, nose and throat. She tickled Lulu's feet and listened to her heart and lungs. Her hands glided over the scalp, spine, ribs, abdomen and limbs, her movements concise and assured.

"Bring bowl of warm water."

Nola sprinted to the kitchen, almost colliding with Leslie.

"I pump baby stomach. Maybe not much drug left. Most absorbed in system." The physician's English had a strong accent, but the words shot out of her with confidence. She tucked her short hair behind her ears. Her face was so young she looked like a child playing doctor.

"Hold baby, face down, head a bit lower than body," she instructed, adjusting Lulu's position in Nola's arms. "Not swallow when vomit, okay?" Nola winced and nodded. At least by helping she was doing something. She found herself breathing easier.

The physician inserted a rubber tube in Lulu's throat and pumped water into it. The little body in Nola's arms heaved and retched, and whitish water poured out.

"She be okay," the doctor said after a couple of ministrations. "Stop now. Lot of strain not good. She sleep off rest of drug what's left."

Nola could barely utter the words. "Any chance of permanent damage?" she asked while diapering and dressing Lulu.

"I don't think, but I check tomorrow when drug out of system."

"I don't know how to thank you."

"I thank you. You helping stop baby killed."

Daniel, who had been standing by the window since entering the room, stepped forward. "Dr. Ming-Ji Liang is a college friend of mine."

"From Georgetown University?" Nola asked, not looking at him.

"Johns Hopkins." Dr. Liang raised her diminutive fist. "And fellow human-rights fighter." Solemnly, she extended her other hand to Nola and shook it. "I help you any way I can, but my work not public. I am no good in jail." On the back of a business card, she scribbled a number. "Cell phone. Call me this evening, and we set time you bring baby for checkup."

Nola put her arms around the small woman, but a tensing of the shoulders indicated the doctor was not given to physical demonstration.

Leslie had wheeled the crib back into the room. Nola placed Lulu in it, covered her, and kissed her on the head. She wound up a mobile, and "Twinkle, Twinkle Little Star" chimed. Leslie remained standing by the crib, and the tender expression on his face was unlike any Nola had ever seen on him.

"I'm sorry," Nola whispered to him. "I've been too wretched to consider the effect this ordeal has had on you."

He shrugged, but remained at his post by the crib. She saw Daniel and Dr. Liang out to the foyer. She was eager to get rid of this man who thought her mission to help bridge the cultural differences across the ocean was a fool's errand on a colossal scale. But Dr. Liang's cell phone rang and she unhooked it from her belt to answer.

"I'm glad Lulu's back," Daniel said to Nola. "Are you all right?"

He was just a man doing his diplomatic job; she should have read it all along, Nola thought. Kindness carried no promise, and personal losses didn't make one a kindred spirit. She had read somewhere that suffering was a traveling migrant worker settling down for the season; it didn't bond its dispersed employers.

She dared to look up at Daniel's face.

From the domed skylight, a ray of sun made his eyes shine a deeper green. Nola's mind searched for something witty to say, as though to prove to him that there was more to her than fame, glamour and success. That she wasn't just a China doll. Nothing came to mind.

"Thanks," she said. "I must get back to Lulu."

Dr. Liang flipped her cell phone shut, and Yoram's deputy escorted them to the elevator.

Exhaustion from four sleepless nights was knitted into Nola's limbs, and her eyelids were grainy. She paced the room, stopping at the crib to watch the full lips as they fluttered with each deep breath. She picked up Lulu and walked to the window to look at the flow of life outside. Although it was only early afternoon and some stubborn rays of sun in the west slashed through the clouds, the east was darkening. In the market across the street, shoppers moved faster before getting caught in rain. The world was oblivious to the drama taking place in her life. How many other dramas—and human tragedies—were happening right now behind thousands of darkened windows, in back alleys, or inside the tiny, bereft stores that looked from Nola's angle like mouse holes?

She turned to see Wade standing at the door, surprise lifting his brows. For a moment, the two of them locked eyes. As his gaze traveled down to the baby in her arms, his stubbornness closed in on Nola. Yet it could not dampen the serenity that went so deep and fanned her smoldering ember of hope.

"You got another baby?"

"It's Lulu." With a shift of her elbow, Nola tilted the baby so he could see the sleeping face. "The Chinese left her at an orphanage, but I found her in time."

"They drugged her, but she'll be all right." Lulu's hair still smelled sour, but the damp washcloth had removed the stickiness. Nola laid her back on their bed, sneaked a finger between the pajama leg snaps to check the skin temperature. Satisfied, she covered Lulu and reclined beside her.

Wade walked to the window. Not long ago she could have seen his jaw working. Now the muscles had slackened.

Nola wished she had put on a classical CD to thaw the icy silence. She spoke. "You know I'm keeping her."

Wade's figure in front of the window rocked from toe to heel, heel to toe. "Ashford thought things were calming down."

"The Chinese lied to him. They were not going to unite her with her mother; they were just going to kill her." Maybe the Chinese had told Ambassador Ashford the truth, but he had been the one who had lied. She might never know. "Anyway, what he thinks is a moot point now."

From her spot on the bed, she could see only the sky. The lip of afternoon brightness had narrowed. The east was now cloud-laden, offering no comfort. Then a steady patter on the huge glass blotted out the world.

"We're in this marriage for the long haul," Wade finally said, his tone that of a survivor of marital strife. "I'm not going anywhere without you—or you without me."

He hadn't said that he loved her, she noticed, or that he would adopt Lulu. But recollections of his past kindness, of the way he had propped up her orphan psyche, of his patience with Jenna, ran through her head. He would soften.

When she didn't reply, he said, "We can pretend this is another baby. Who will know the difference?"

We. Yes! He was already figuring out a way to make it possible. He had been reluctant and afraid of babies, but so were many men. She remembered the recent moments of fear when she was certain she'd have to tackle life on her own. That was over. Wade would continue to be her protector. She curled up next to Lulu, resting her head in the crook of her own elbow.

"You look pale. Have some fruit." Wade peeled the top half of a banana and handed it to Nola. To her surprise, he passed his hand over Lulu's chest. "She's tiny."

Nola sat up and fluffed two pillows to support her back and ate the banana while giving herself to the moment. They could be a family if she allowed it.

Wade sat down on the bed. "We're going through a rough time. A marriage is like a river. When the water is low, you can see the debris at the bottom. Let the water rise again, okay? I'll do my best, too."

"May I use these lines?" She was no longer angry with him, only very tired.

"They're yours, with all my love."

"From now on, I want you to run everything by me."

"Everything?" His breath smelled of mint. "I haven't kept anything secret from you, but I always shielded you from the tension. There're so many details that can drive you bonkers: a major record distributor goes bust and we lose millions in money owed us, or a silly staffer lets herself be seduced by a bodyguard, then slaps him and us with a sexual harassment suit. I never bother you with any of it. Why would I? So you, too, can get aggravated and dissipate that God-given gift of yours?"

"I don't want to be treated like a child."

"There is only one of you, and you can only do what you do best when you stay focused. I concentrate on what I do best and protect your energy. We've both been equally proficient in this partnership."

"Maybe not all details are in the no-need-to-know category." His tone was soft. "I've made countless deals these past fifteen years. That's what good managers do; they're the bad cops so clients can be the good guys."

Marriages were made-to-order, she thought, yet they came with too many options and no manual. She slid down again and punched the pillow into a neck roll. She touched Lulu's cheek, then closed her eyes.

Contentment at having her baby back overtook her, erasing the highs and lows of other emotions—ambition, lust, guilt, doubt, emptiness, desire. She wanted to trust Wade again, to resume the old, familiar comfort, not to face the unthinkable.

As she lay curled around Lulu, the feel of the little body infused her with utter bliss. "Thanks," she whispered to Wade through closed lids.

She felt his kiss on her forehead, then heard the soft click of the door as it closed behind him.

She was still asleep, unaware of the mental process that kept working, like a night press churning out a newspaper, when the gears came to a screeching halt. Her eyes flew open.

The room was quiet, but the rumble went on in her head. She rose and gently put Lulu in her crib. When she opened the bedroom door a crack, she could hear Wade in the living room behind the closed door. Not on the phone. He was arguing with another man, an American. The voice was familiar. Oratorical, haughty, it projected from the far end of the living room. The cadence of someone used to an audience.

The sound of fine leather shoes on the parquet floor became distinct as the speaker approached the door. She overheard him say, "I was to deliver Nola. You were to deliver Nola. She fucked up and I'm holding you responsible."

Her hand flew to her mouth an instant before she knew who it was. George Mauriello.

"We still have the Shanghai concert and half a dozen other events to undo the damage," Wade replied, his tone uncharacteristically pleading.

"And she will be there without the baby. I guarantee you. And in four weeks tops, she will have forgotten all about it."

What!? Her hand still covering her mouth to keep from screaming, Nola fled back to her bedroom.

Wade had joined her enemies. There was no turning back from this. Ever.

Chapter 21

Out. Uproot. She was a wild woman with wind driving her wings. Clutching Lulu to her chest with one arm, Nola stuffed diapers, baby clothes, and some of her own things into a duffel bag. The floor shook as she ran through the bathroom and swept a toothbrush and the hotel soaps and shampoos into a bag, then raced through the kitchen, where she threw the refrigerator door open and collected Lulu's prepared bottles and a sealed bowl full of mashed broccoli and carrots.

Wade followed her, imploring that she hear him out, but his pleas echoed and looped on themselves. When he tried to touch her, she recoiled. Her eyes must have reflected the madness that had seized her because he took a step back.

With her free hand, she grabbed her coat and a baby blanket and, as she rushed out, snatched a shawl thrown over a chair. All she wanted was to get lost, to be free of the tears and emotions of the recent days. "Don't follow me," she barked at the black deputy bodyguard on duty, who sent Wade a confused look. If Wade had so instructed, the man could have restrained her, but she suspected Wade was already plotting a better way. *The enemy.*

"Where will you go?" he asked from the door while she jabbed at the elevator button. The blinking lights above both elevators did not indicate whether her escape was near. "At least wait until Leslie returns."

If she responded, she would scream, but that would give him an excuse to act concerned about her state of mind. "Get out of my life," she grumbled instead, and was relieved when the first elevator arrived.

As the doors closed, she heard the ring and swish of the second elevator and saw Wade gesturing to the bodyguard to follow her.

"Lobby," she told the operator, and leaned her burning forehead against the mirror. The cold touch offered an infinitesimal refuge, enough to clear her head. Where was she going now? Where was she going with her life? Think. The ballroom floor. Its wide double staircase, used only for banquet guests, led out to a side street. Nola reached around the operator and punched the button marked "mezzanine."

Clumsily, using one raised knee to support Lulu, she fashioned a sling out of the shawl and tucked the baby into it. The elevator stopped. Nola hoisted the bag on her other shoulder and stepped out. Indeed, the spacious air-conditioned banquet foyer was deserted at this mid-afternoon hour, as were the hotel shops surrounding it. Their display windows, with their array of jade, cloisonné and embroidered silk, looked like an orchestra playing to an empty theater. The artifacts reminded her of Daniel's snuff bottle. In her hurry, she had swept it into her bag along with the toiletries, but there had been no time to fish it out.

Only then did she remember the detection device the insurance company insisted on installing in all her street shoes. She looked down. Luckily, she had slipped on her rubber-soled exercise shoes.

A bored doorman manned the side exit. Probably uninformed of her escape, he held the door for her. "Taxi?"

She shook her head and marched out.

Half a block away, she looked back, but the one-way street was empty. She had outsmarted Wade and Yoram's men! She turned into another street, and from there, she became lost in a series of alleys. For once, she welcomed the anonymity of this city of twelve million. An unfamiliar sense of freedom made her feet lighter even as she darted past the back doors of foul-smelling fish stores, her shoes sloshing through puddles of rotting fish heads and entrails. It felt good not to have someone hovering about her, even Leslie with his good intentions. She only served as the conduit for his many talents.

A Chinese couple accosted her to examine her curly red hair. With the naiveté of children, they reached to explore its texture. Submitting to their curiosity gave Nola a sense of human contact in this foreign land. But after the encounter, she twisted her hair up and stuffed it under a baseball cap she found in her bag, then put on sunglasses. She hurried on.

The alley joined a street of dilapidated residential buildings. The two- and three-story houses of bare concrete or peeling plaster looked drunk, leaning on their neighbors for support. Yet, in a startling contrast to the poverty, the children who chased each other in a schoolyard were beautifully dressed, the girls in frilly dresses and the boys in sailor suits. In the briefing the team had attended upon arrival, the guide called these kids "Little Emperors." The second generation of the single-child policy, each was the only child in his or her family, pampered by six adults—mother, father and two sets of grandparents. None had aunts, uncles, nor cousins.

She pushed on, thoughts crisscrossing her mind. She was alone in a vast country whose language and customs were incomprehensible to her. Since she had moved out of Miss Helga's, she hadn't had the responsibility of caring for anyone.

Lulu's head nestled between Nola's breasts, their two hearts beating together. Nola lowered her head closer to the black crown. "I love you like I've never loved before," she whispered. "Just wake up. Let me see that you're still yourself, that they haven't damaged you."

A public urinal's stench made Nola pinch her nose and cross to the other side of the street. There, a fearless flock of geese came chasing after her, nipping at her calves. She broke into a trot. The geese pursued her. She had never imagined these creatures could be so nasty. "Get away," she shouted, and kicked at their insolent chests. At the traffic light, they retreated.

Lulu was warm and quiet at her bosom. Nola kept speaking to her as she reached a main thoroughfare and pressed her way through the thicket of people, through block after block bustling with activity. Perhaps the creaking of pushcarts, the trilling of bicycle bells and the blasts of broken tailpipes would wake up her baby.

A blister formed on her foot, and the straps of the travel bag and the weight of the sling cut into her shoulders. Nola stopped to catch her breath. She massaged her trapezius muscles. How long had she been wandering like this? An hour? Two? Her bladder was full, and the stench of another public facility announced its proximity. She wavered, not wishing to expose herself or Lulu to the noxious odor, but there was no choice. Entering a hotel where she might encounter Westerners and journalists was not an option.

She examined the hunkered-down lavatory, unable to decide which side to enter, until a woman emerged from the right. Breathing through her mouth, Nola rounded the partition wall, and stopped at the sight.

In a room tiled from floor to ceiling, about ten women crouched one behind the other over a one-foot wide trench. While each benefited from a full view of the output excreted by the woman in front of her, a thin stream of water from a faucet at the start of the trench slowly carried the materials beneath their spread legs toward the other end, where it was collected in an open drainage basket.

Gagging, Nola made a turn to leave, but the urgency of her need made her accept the attendant's signal to step to an available spot. Get over it, she told herself. Lulu must be used to these conditions, and this was how most of humanity lived. A wad of cut-up newspaper hung from twine on the wall. She ripped off a piece. This was a new life; no more Wade to fold and hand her soft toilet tissue. Tightening one arm around Lulu's sling, Nola fumbled with her own clothes, silently thanking Leslie for her Amazonian thigh muscles that enabled her the whole feat without slipping on the soiled tiles.

When she came out a few minutes later, the low sun was still pushing the margins of the encroaching night. Nola fanned the air in front of

Lulu's face, hoping that the stench had awakened her. But there was no change in the shallow, even breathing, and the skin was warm with an almost-healthy tint.

From somewhere in the distance, she heard '40s Big Band music. The strangeness of it, the improbability of hearing "Always True to You in My Fashion" in this place, drew her to the sound. Anything to jog her brain back to action. Anything to chase away the urinal's rankness that stuck in her nostrils, and, she was certain, had penetrated her pores and hair.

Around the corner, a chiseled-stone plaza occupied the center of a long block. A rose garden at the back was fringed with Japanese maple, cedar and poplar trees. In the plaza, music pumped out of loudspeakers hanging from the surrounding trees. About fifty couples—all middle-aged Chinese in their work clothes and flat cotton shoes—danced ballroom dances.

There was solemnity on their faces and earnestness in the way the partners held one another. Intent on the steps, the rhythm, the pace, they moved to the music. Their expressions showed concentration rather than joy. No one smiled, nor was there eye contact between partners.

Nola tucked errant hair tresses under the baseball cap and took a deep breath. Along with the scent of the roses and car fumes, she detected a different sweet smell. Only after she glimpsed an old man behind a tree sucking on a pipe did she identify the scent as opium. The man cleared his throat, brought up phlegm, and spat.

She averted her eyes. "We'll find a small hotel," she told Lulu. "Okay?" With a start, she realized that she had neither money nor credit cards—not even a passport. Leslie or Wade had always been at her elbow with her documents and a wallet full of bills. But even if she had those, the moment she checked into a hotel, Chinese officials would descend upon her. She had escaped, all right, but she was like a driver who had set out on a moonless night. She knew her final destination, but could only see as far as the headlights.

How ironic. She owned a ranch in the Colorado mountains, a villa on her private Azure Island in the Caribbean, and a twenty-four-room Manhattan penthouse overlooking Central Park. Each was stuffed with furniture, draperies, rugs, planters, gilded mirrors and original art. She hated minimalism in interior design. No understatement for her. "Less is more," the decorator had tried to convince her, but she had been raised in a home with too much "less," and it had never become "more."

She must switch gears. This path of thinking might only send her over the precipice of despair. Nola made her way to the back of the plaza and sat down on a stone bench beside a patch of roses. What next? She untied the sling, and for the first time since finding Lulu in the orphanage four hours earlier, the baby stirred.

Nola tickled her cheek. "Wake up, Dumpling. Time to eat. Your tummy must be starving." She massaged the little body through the clothing. The round belly of two days earlier had flattened.

Lulu opened her eyes. Her gaze was unfocused, then her lids dropped again. A surge of protectiveness ballooned in Nola, a force so large that it could not be crammed into the simple word, "love."

"Wake up!" she urged. "C'mon, you can do it. You're a resilient girl. Open your eyes and look at the world. Mommy's here, waiting for you." She propped Lulu against her shoulder and tapped on her back. The small body moved, then the little head lifted and twisted around to look at her.

Nola felt her mouth crinkle with a cry of happiness. She planted kisses on Lulu's head. "I'm here, Dumpling. Yes, it's me."

The music changed to *The Blue Danube Waltz*, and the couples, unsmiling, their backs rigid, waltzed past her in a large circle, their coordinated feet chasing one another, intent on perfecting the task.

Lulu began to fuss and whimper. Nola brought out a bottle, and at the sight of it, Lulu clasped her fingers around it and closed her mouth on the nipple. Nola cradled her in her lap, but a few minutes later, Lulu's arms became heavy, and Nola took over holding the bottle.

On the bench next to her, a fat green caterpillar gathered itself, then stretched, gathered itself again, then stretched once more. Its stunted limbs, dark protrusions against the bright green of the body, seemed useless, yet this low life-form moved with purpose. In a short while, it had covered the width of the bench, then halted, half its body poised in the air. Swaying to and fro, unseeing, it searched for a foothold. Its limbs found the curve in the stone, and the body contoured around it, then rolled into a ball. A second later, it exuded some goo and hung itself on a strand that became longer as the caterpillar lowered itself down. Once on the ground, it wriggled, straightened and continued on its way.

Nola watched it disappear in a rose bush. A diminutive, blind, limbless and mindless creature had conquered life's tribulations. "We can do it too," she said to Lulu, then on second thought, added, "We have done it."

Yet how had she gotten to this low point? Which fork in the road had she missed? Or hadn't she? She had been depressed and had given up on passionate love by the time Wade had made his amorous overture. She had been fearful of losing him when all she had was wrapped around him. She should have taken her time. No matter. The next decision had been about Lulu, and from the first moment, it had felt right as though predetermined.

Lulu's lids drooped, then closed. Only her mouth kept working with vigor, when a gnat landed on her cheek, then another and another. In an instant, a cloud encircled Nola and Lulu. Nola swatted them away, but in the waning light another cloud of gnats hovered above as though planning their next attack. They moved in unison, like an army of skydivers, and descended. Again they levitated to evaluate their next target. Soon the dancing couples lost their composure and were swatting at the gnats.

Whipping a washcloth in the air around Lulu's head, Nola jumped to her feet and retied her sling, but even after she marched away from the plaza, the cloud of gnats refused to let go. Undeterred by Nola's wild swinging, mocking her, they dive-bombed onto Lulu's face, neck and hair, feeding on dried lactose. Tiny red dots appeared on the porcelain skin.

Escape. Flee from it all. How could she shield her baby from two governments if she couldn't even defend her from gnats? Nola waved the washcloth as she marched into the crowd of thousands of Chinese heading home at the end of the day.

A hundred feet later, hiding in a building doorway, she scanned the waning pinkish light. The cloud of gnats was gone, as though the plunging darkness were a clock striking midnight. She reached into the side pocket of her bag for a baby wipe, and her hand jiggled coins. She was certain they weren't yuan, and sure enough, when she scooped out the contents of the pocket, she also found a few dollar bills. Still, she couldn't buy herself a drink. Exchanging dollars, forbidden to common Chinese, might get her arrested.

Streetlights came on, casting yellow circles. Lulu was fussing, probably needing a diaper change.

The name of the only person in this city who could help her had been flickering in Nola's mind for the past hour. But Daniel was no friend either. Although his and Ashford's views were opposed, they stemmed from the same perception: she was just a fool, a China doll.

And given Daniel's grim view of the tense relationship between the two nations already heading toward an open conflict, why would he help her to further botch it?

Darkness shrouded the world. The streets emptied fast. Nola stopped under a lamppost, a refugee with an abandoned baby lost in China. Fifteen years after starting as an orphan, having traveled farther than most people ever dared dream, she had nowhere to go.

Chapter 22

The pay phone was a bright orange box mounted on the side of a news-paper kiosk, where tabloids featuring scantily clad Asian women hung from lines like laundry. A large tree, bent with age, stood behind, its saucer-sized, waxy leaves a protective enclave. Nola eyed the phone. A bulky receiver rested on top, and on the post behind it, a plastic panel depicted dialing instructions.

Through the kiosk's open side, Nola glimpsed the display on the inside wall. There was her own over-sized promotion album. Two teenagers with identical shiny black braids asked to see it and flipped through the glossy pages. For a wild instant she considered stepping forward and ask-ing for their help. She watched them pay. Giggling, they departed with the book, never aware how close they had been to having it autographed.

She fished for her American coins. Lifting the receiver, she dropped in a penny. It tumbled somewhere with a clicking sound. The echo told her it accomplished nothing. She tried a dime, but it, too, made a series of metallic jiggles before coming to a stop in the belly of the box. The quar-ter was too big for the slot. She dipped her hand into her side pocket and found two more coins, one of them a nickel. She dropped it in the slot. A shrill dial tone almost pierced her eardrums. She brushed away the tiny stab of concern that she had just committed a crime, pulled out the busi-ness card she had kept in her pocket since early afternoon, and dialed the number scribbled on the back.

The ring was more like a series of bleats, but after five of them, her call was answered. She heard static and background chatter and clanging dishes.

"Dr. Liang? This is Nola Sands." The words shaped themselves into tri-angles with sharp edges. "I need your help."

"What is it? The baby all right?"

"I— I—" Nola felt embarrassed and humiliated. "I— I—" she said again. Finally she blurted out her predicament.

"Where are you?"

"I can't read the street signs—wait. There was a plaza and a rose gar-den two blocks away." She scanned the street. "There's a department store diagonally across the street from me. I am next to a newspaper kiosk. This place looks like Chicago. There's a computer store with a big neon sign for Microsoft—and Kentucky Fried Chicken!" How she would have loved to bite into a piece of chicken. The sign alone already made her feel like she was home. She couldn't help smiling as she added, "But they made the Colonel Chinese."

"Gi'me ten minutes."

"Thank you, Dr. Liang."

"Ming-Ji. I come only if you call me Ming-Ji."

"Thank you, Ming-Ji." But the phone was already dead.

She surveyed the crowd for Ming-Ji's diminutive figure, for the quick steps of a no-nonsense woman in a white coat whose child's face was hidden behind large, dark-framed glasses and therefore failed to notice the black Mercedes that sidled up next to her until it came to a stop. Nola's breath caught at the sight of the diplomatic license plates. The tinted windows hid the car's occupants. It was too late to flee.

Nola clutched Lulu and sprinted back to the shadows of the tree. Jerked out of her slumber, Lulu let out a shriek and struggled to free herself from the confines of the sling.

A hot iron burned in Nola's chest. What did they do to goodwill ambassadors who turned into badwill ambassadors? Images from spy movies flashed in her head. Black-suited men with expressionless faces behind dark sunglasses would force her into their car and deliver her to Ambassador Ashford, Mauriello, and Wade to fulfill their geo-political agendas. They would take Lulu from her and make sure this time she would never be found. Governments did that, even democratic ones.

"Shhhhhh," she whispered to Lulu, but she knew that they had spotted her. She was a worm wiggling from a bird's beak.

Inside the limousine, someone on the passenger side struggled with the door, while on the driver's side, the door opened. A head emerged above the car roofline. To Nola's consternation, she recognized Daniel.

He straightened. His slim figure rounded the car as he moved to assist the other person. Nola pressed against the tree trunk. Daniel moved with his now familiar, disarming ease. His head was trained in her direction, but with the streetlights playing on his face, she was unable to see his eyes. He was no friend, but was he a foe? Would he be the next one to betray her?

The passenger door finally opened, and out popped Dr. Ming-Ji Liang.

With a mixture of relief and disbelief, Nola looked from one to the other. "What's he doing here?" she asked Ming-Ji.

"We have dinner when you call," the woman replied, pointing to the cell phone hooked onto the belt of her cotton pants. She bent to the whimpering, struggling Lulu and untied the sling. "You up little one? Not sleeping no more?"

Released, Lulu calmed down. "Lulululululululu," she said.

Daniel clucked, and Lulu clucked in return. He turned to Nola. "Come on. You must be tired." He reached his hand out to her. It was warm and strong and reassuring, and she felt it scorching hers with its newness. It was the first time their skins had touched. But this man had mocked her mission to this country; he had called her "China doll." He worked for the embassy, and his job was to see that she fulfill her temporary diplomatic mission.

She released his hand, fighting the urge to press it to her cheek. "Where are we going?"

"We must get you settled somewhere." He opened the back door.

All she wanted was to hide from the hostile world, but she made no move. "Where?"

"Get in." Ming-Ji slid into the back with Lulu in her arms and removed her glasses to salvage them from the curious little fingers. "Not Hotel Intercontinental, but comfortable for tonight."

Nola shouldered her bag and followed. Lulu babbled while the doctor's hands checked the reflexes of her legs, toes, knees and elbows, then pressed on her stomach and took her pulse.

"Is she okay?" Nola asked. "Any side effects?"

"Healthy." Ming-Ji spoke into Lulu's palm as the baby grabbed her mouth.

Daniel put the car into gear. Nola leaned forward in her seat and said to him, "If you'll lend me money, I can check into a hotel, but not a Western one where I'll be recognized."

He shook his head. "A hotel can't offer political asylum; it is subject to local regulations. I wouldn't leave you at the mercy of the Chinese. Any official might flog you for insubordination-"

"They'd beat me? I have not committed a crime."

"It's enough that others—your husband or your government—are searching for you. We've heard of your clever escape." He chuckled, and Nola's scalp contracted. She hadn't told Ming-Ji the details of her flight. His tone turned serious again. "Bosses, factory supervisors, and government officials use corporal punishment."

"With heavy sticks. They break many bones." Ming-Ji's head bobbed up and down in agreement.

"Even a foreigner?" Would they flog a superstar?

"Not much beating in big cities lately," Ming-Ji added.

The exchange sounded like a comedy routine except that it was real. Nola dropped back into her seat. Telling Ashford that they would have to kill her before they silenced her had been only a figure of speech. She had never considered physical danger as part of this ordeal.

"We have a place for you," Ming-Ji said.

For how long? Separate fears—Nola could no longer tell them apart—welded into one. "I'm afraid to resurface. I want to hide, but I've never missed a performance. I'm supposed to fly to Shanghai for tomorrow's concert."

"I know," Daniel said. "I'm scheduled to accompany you on your Gulfstream."

Self-conscious about her wealth, Nola listened for cynicism in his remark, but could detect none. Right now, all her money and influence amounted to nothing. Once more she was powerless and dependent on a man she wasn't sure she should trust. But at least, unlike Wade, *the enemy*, Daniel had proven that he cared for Lulu's physical safety.

Nola slouched in her seat and closed her eyes. Her sense of equilibrium was missing. Her perspective was off, as though some parts of her had broken down and the others functioned on life support. What was the point of her escape from the hostile world? Sooner or later she would have to face her entourage and Lulu's pursuers.

For the next twenty minutes, the only sounds in the car were Lulu's clucks, answered by Daniel and Ming-Ji. Nola placed her finger in Lulu's fist, and the plump touch gave her comfort.

Chapter 23

(1986)

In her room—Wade's childhood room at his parents' home in Little Italy in lower Manhattan—Nola slouched on the beanbag she had brought with her. Wade was pinning up a motivational poster. *"Remember what you wanted to be when you were ten. Just follow that path."* Like when she was at that No-Nukes rally, getting her first taste of stardom and wanting it more than anything. Now, for her and Jenna's sake, she must become a star, so she could get her sister out of Mini-Nazi's house. The bright eight-year old was composing stories that Beverly had submitted to *Newsday*'s Kids section. Nevertheless, Jenna's temper tantrums—at Mini-Nazi's, at school, on the street—were controlled only by medication.

"How long will it take?" Heat climbed up Nola's cheeks. "I mean, for success?"

Wade laughed. "What's your timetable?"

"Two years." Her voice was barely audible. She was being ridiculous; she wasn't even pretty enough. "When I'm eighteen, I want to prove to the courts that I can make a home for me and Jenna."

He crouched in front of her. "As good a motivation as any. Now that you are close by, we'll get working on making you a star."

Nola nodded. She couldn't envision it.

He lifted up another poster that read, *"We get a fresh start every morning."* Hanging it, he said over his shoulder, "Jenna, too. Even at eight she makes choices every day. Don't let her choices be yours."

Wade Dalton, Nola had learned, was the name Waldo Didonato had given himself while working with a voice coach to acquire his private-school diction. He now lived on the Upper East Side, his shirts were handmade in Hong Kong, and he dressed in Brooks Brothers suits despite the implied insult to his tailor father.

"Repackaging myself is the first step to opening doors," he explained. "Self-improvement means 'you,' only better. If we didn't perfect our-selves, we'd still be living in caves." Wade did stay true to himself, she noticed, even if he had changed his name. He made no secret of his immigrant-family background. He was a master of networking and col-lected acquaintances like some people collected stamps. "I have circles of friends from high school and college. I keep up with former colleagues and clients as they move up the corporate ladder," he explained. Meticulous, driven, he added them all to his Rolodex, which he showed

Nola. "Keep a clean record, work hard, be honest and don't ever renege on a promise. Even those who don't love me respect me."

He was terribly proud of his girlfriend, Deanna, a colleague from Musix. A Southern heiress, she was tall and fair and had been educated in Europe. He showed Nola a copy of *Town & Country*, featuring Deanna's large family in front of their Virginia mansion. When Deanna joined Wade and Nola for a late-night bite, he gazed at her with unabashed awe while, in between nuzzles to his neck, Deanna inquired about Nola's progress and made suggestions. Wade and Deanna's affection and harmony in shared interests excited Nola. She had never been this close to a couple in love.

But if she had anticipated that life in the city would be glamorous, she saw none of it. "Hectic" was more like it. Wade selected a jazz dance school for her. With years of ballet behind her, the transition between disciplines was easy. Six times a week she moved across the floor of the Upper West Side studio in fast, complicated step combinations, her body falling into the new movements as into ready grooves.

The new downtown high school was less welcoming.

When Wade accompanied her on the first day of school, she felt like a kid starting first grade. Everything was new and strange. She wished she could hold Wade's hand.

"You'd do better at a private school, I know, but they won't allow you to cram two years into one." Wade pointed at the concrete schoolyard, where a crowd of youngsters with tattoos and peacock-colored hair carried more boom boxes than book bags. "Treat this place as your chance to meet your future audience. Get to know the lives of teenagers in every city across the country."

It was too late to break into the cliques of mostly minority students, many of whom had been born to single welfare mothers. To fit in, Nola left her hair uncombed in the morning and made up her eyes with Kohl. But her suburban speech, combined with the refined manners drilled into her at Mini-Nazi's, set her apart more than her fair skin alone did. Once more, she was the oddity in a sea of "normal" kids. But she was worse off than they; at least they had a mother.

She understood why Jenna hated school.

At home, Nola teetered on her high heels because Wade had said it showed when a woman was unaccustomed to them, while Wade's Mama hovered around her with tenderness the likes of which Nola had never known.

Late at night Mama pushed aside Nola's books. "You get blind doing homework so late." She placed a glass of milk and a slice of cake on her desk. "Eat. You lose weight since you come live here, and you are too skinny to begin with."

"Your son makes sure I burn all the calories you're feeding me." Nola squeezed Mama's hand. It was plump and warm. Mama wasn't "Mommy," but felt like one, and Nola yearned for Jenna to experience this, too. The tiny apartment on a crowded street—where during the day uncollected garbage baked in the sun and at night prostitutes greeted her at building entrances while police sirens and drunken neighbors' fighting conspired to deprive her of sleep—was the best, most loving home she had ever had.

In the days and weeks that followed, Wade courted writers of chart-toppers to sell him something for his new protégé's first single. Indefatigable, he also shopped around for the best home for her talent. Within a month of becoming her agent, he made a deal with Keith Schwartz, a visionary, hands-on president of a hip, up-and-coming label. Keith gambled on her, cut her first single, "Superstitions," and mar-shaled his clout for buzz and the widest possible distribution.

But there were no public appearances. Not yet. "Right now, your 'thing' is your mystery. Not a single photograph of you is to be released until we take care of your appearance. Give you a make-over," Wade said.

As the months wore on, Nola wished the year until graduation would never end, so she could stay with the Didonatos and hang out with her dancer friends. For the first time, she had a close girlfriend from her jazz school, Gabby, a long-legged Brazilian with whom she traded clothes and second-rate secrets. Nola never spoke of the circumstances of Jenna's accident or of her parents' death.

She and Gabby traveled in a mixed-nationality group of cool teenage hopefuls dedicated to maintaining their taut bodies, who took acting classes and voice lessons, auditioned for off-off-Broadway musicals, vied for gigs at private parties, searched *Variety* for leads to summer stock— and waited tables for money. On weekends they all went out to the movies, attended experimental theater readings at student rates, listened to music in one of their shared studios, or explored the restored alleys of Tribeca and SoHo, crowded with boutiques, galleries and tattoo parlors.

Wade was away for weeks at a stretch, journeying from city to city, from radio station to radio station, to hound disc jockeys and force them to listen to his one single from this teenager. He called Nola often. "I'm running 'Superstitions' contests on every campus, and the DJs play your single, and everybody loves it," he reported. "The posters with the lyrics are popular at the Student Unions. They disappear within the hour."

She giggled. "Thanks. I want to perform it live—"

"Everything in due time." There was warmth in his voice. And certainty. "You already have fans dying to meet the mysterious Nola."

Back in New York City, he wined and dined network executives, sent out letters with clips of reviews to broadcasters and newspaper editors at his next stops, and used that single to persuade Carole King, Leonard Cohen and Burt Bacharach to write for his hidden protégé's full-length album.

Within a few months, Nola's single made it to the top of both the teen and pop charts, surprising everyone but Wade.

Days after Nola graduated from high school at seventeen, he applied the proceeds from her first single toward a stay at a discreet East Side townhouse, where a world-renowned plastic surgeon's patients could enter and leave unobserved.

Nola arrived with a small bag, apprehension and excitement filling her. In three weeks, she will inhabit a new shell. She had pored with the surgeon over her photographs, and although she had approved each detail of the upcoming change, she couldn't picture what it would feel like to be pretty.

Her green eyes, which had been indistinct, came to life once the surgeon deepened the folds above them. He trimmed her nose, tucked back her ears, reshaped her chin, and embedded cheek-bones where none had existed. He filled up her lower lip to a sexy pout, and implanted gelatinous pouches in her tiny breasts. He liposuctioned fat Nola hadn't known existed from beside her gluteal muscles, defining her buttocks.

Sedated and blinded underneath the bandages, Nola stayed in the townhouse for two days, then was taken back to Mama, who clucked over her bandaged head and body with the worry of a mother hen. From under the bandages, the closed door, and the fog of pain relievers, Nola thought of what Jenna had endured as a baby. How frightened she must have been.

Ten days later, most of the swelling had subsided, and even Mama exclaimed, "So beautiful! *Principessa*!" Dozens of times a day Nola returned to the mirror to study the face of the beautiful creature that couldn't possibly be her, yet was. She touched the tip of the nose, searching for the missing bulbous cartilage.

Could a person remain the same after their face had changed? Nola did feel different. New. With her new face and body came a chance for a new identity, one that didn't have to remember her childhood pain in every pore. One that could be a star if she wanted to.

She waltzed naked in front of the mirror, examining her new contours still covered by deep purple bruises. She cupped her breasts, now full. Perfect for her slim frame. *It's me, Nola*, she whispered to herself. *Believe it. It's me.* That's what she would tell Jenna next week. It's me, Nola. And I'm doing it all for both of us, so I can make money and we can be together.

John Sahag was persuaded to squeeze Nola into Goldie Hawn's canceled hair appointment. After Nola's hair was woven with locks grown elsewhere and treated to seven shades of highlights, she was a beauty her mother wouldn't have recognized.

Saturday, following her double morning jazz class, Nola took the train to Smithtown, using the two-hour ride to catch up on her sleep. No matter what happened with her life, Jenna, troubled and difficult, unloving and unlovable by anyone else, was still a part of her, never to be excised like the cartilage from the tip of her nose.

Chapter 24

Nola followed Ming-Ji into a building with buckled walls and crumbling yellow plaster. Daniel brought up the rear as they clambered up three flights of steps and entered a tiny apartment with furniture that seemed to have endured more than the Cultural Revolution. But the walls of the small living room had been recently whitewashed, and new bamboo blinds gave the modest space a clean, albeit unlived in, feeling. A paper scroll with red Chinese calligraphy hung on one wall.

"Here we meet sometimes," Ming-Ji said.

Nola guessed that the "we" referred to whoever worked with them on their human-rights issues, and that they couldn't risk gathering in someone's apartment.

Lulu was quiet and content in a sleepy way. Nola eased her onto the low couch. Daniel stood watching the baby for a moment, his gaze tender.

"She needs a bath," Nola said.

"Water good to stimulate her," Ming-Ji said. "There aluminum tub in kitchen." She turned to leave.

"Let me." Nola rushed after her. "You've had a full day of work."

Ming-Ji replied with a dismissive wave of her small hand.

"I'll get you something to eat." Daniel stepped to the front door. "Any requests?"

She glowered at him.

He walked back. "Are you cross with me?"

"Does it show?" She let out a chortle. "*That Washington Post* op-ed piece of yours. I had thought you were a friend until I realized that all along you objected to my coming here."

He stood still. The comment snaked on the floor between them, writhing and curling around their feet. From the kitchen came the sound of an aluminum pail scraping a surface. In the street below, a merchant chanted an announcement of his wares.

The seconds stretched and Nola's brain registered that she had never seen Daniel touch his head, scratch his chin, or fidget.

"My objection is to the U.S. *strategy* of appeasement toward China. That doesn't preclude the fact that meeting you has been a pleasure," he finally said.

She let out a wry laugh. "A serendipitous one, no doubt."

"My writing reflects my political views." His voice was soft. "You, the icon—not the person—are part of a political strategy."

"There's only one Nola Sands," she said, knowing that he was right, and the only Nola that counted to anyone was the icon Nola.

"I disagree where any public figures are concerned," he said. "But could this wait until I bring you some food?"

She lowered her tone. "I've been caught in some global political intrigue. How do I fit—or not—into the scheme of things?"

He stepped back and sat down on the couch. Nola sat at the other end. Her tailbone registered the hardness of upholstered foam rubber on a board. She placed Lulu between her and Daniel and let Lulu clutch her finger.

"There are two schools of thought about the strategies the U.S. must deploy toward China," Daniel said. "'Engagement' holds that the more channels of communication are open between the two nations, the more it is inevitable that China will transform from a totalitarian state to a democracy. 'Containment' maintains that China is a dangerous, ambitious nation that must be isolated. This is not just an academic debate; behind these philosophies lie forces that shape people's lives."

"I take it that my concert tour is part of 'engagement.'"

"The icon you." He nodded. "Engagement is the U.S.'s official policy. Sixty thousand Chinese students in U.S. universities learn firsthand about freedom and democracy. High-tech factories here are built and managed by Western firms. And yes, China's cultural wall is being cracked by Western pop culture—be it jeans or music."

Lulu made little sucking pops as she chomped a pacifier. "That's more or less what Ashford says," Nola said.

"He would." Daniel's hand stroked Lulu's leg. It dawned on Nola that had Daniel's fiancée lived, their baby would have been only a couple of months older than Lulu.

She swallowed. She wished he didn't captivate her so easily. "Go on. I can't believe how obtuse I've been."

"The engagement idea is to help build China's economy because when we look around the globe, we see that strong economies are democratic in nature, and democracies are less likely to declare wars on other countries." He smiled. "Now that I've convinced you of this view, let me tell you that I do not share it."

"I figured that much from your article," she said. Touching Daniel's soul meant she must grasp the essence of his political work. New lyrics flickered in her head. *Let me touch the places where you hurt, and I'll be the woman that you need me to be.*

"China sees democracy as a weak form of government," he went on.

"Their astounding success in influencing top U.S. politicians—including financing the re-election of a president—and the ease with which they have infiltrated both open American scientific institutes and closed military installations are proof that democracy is a failure."

She imagined him at a lecture hall, his tone easy, his explanation simple. Even the wisps of straight black hair dropping on his forehead were under his control. Stroking Lulu, her fingers accidentally brushed against his. She withdrew her hand as though from a hot stove.

He continued to speak as though he had not been scorched by the same fire. "As China bides its time, it aids countries hostile to the U.S. but uses the U.S.'s willingness to share its top secrets to arm what is soon to become the strongest military power in the world. In my opinion, China and the U.S. are on a collision course in their struggle for world dominance. Yet U.S. corporations and their senators dismiss the warning to stay guarded. They're willing to sacrifice global security and human rights—present and future—for greater profits."

"I always thought that I wasn't a political animal," she said. "I believed that art could cut across all our differences. That it could bridge borders."

"It often does. Your song 'We All Share The Feeling of Love' is an example. But I wish music were the answer to all conflicts." He got up. "By the way, now that I've read some of your lyrics, I wouldn't concur with your view of yourself as being apolitical. You do have definite views about the world."

She felt heat rise up to her face.

He continued, "Please accept that my objection to your tour as part of the engagement strategy was not personal."

She rose to her feet also. "Let's get personal, then. Didn't you take me to the Dying Rooms so that I, a celebrity, would take up your cause?"

The green in his eyes darkened. "Sharing the things I care about was not a premeditated agenda."

"I surprised your camp when I took your cause further than you had expected."

"Please don't," he said quietly. "Don't do that."

She examined her fingers. "I'm a pawn in a game played among more players than I can count."

"I'm not one of them."

She raised her eyes. "What am I to you, then?"

"An exceptional woman who's coming into herself."

A rush went through her. His words, and their subtext, turned up the flame.

He moved toward the door. "How about Chinese take-out?"

After he left, Nola stood looking at the closed door until Lulu tried to roll over in her sleep. Nola moved her down to the mat on the floor and walked to the kitchen while a theme for another song bubbled in her. *Gifts aren't promises, touches aren't contracts.* She should remember to jot it down. Daniel's attractiveness—and elusiveness—were generating a flood of new ideas. How much could his love bring out? Wade had been right about one thing—passion fed the creation of her music.

Ming-Ji had set a laundry tub on the kitchen table and was using a pot to fill it with water from the sink. A block of oatmeal soap floated in the water.

"It's my turn," Nola said. "You've been much too good to me."

"Bring baby."

Lulu met the feel of the warm water with awe. Her little foot swayed in the water, then the other, tentatively, like two puppies poking out their noses to explore unfamiliar territory. A moment later, the expression on her face changed to one of delight. Then there were legs kicking and water splashing, and Nola's face getting wet and her shirt becoming soaked with water; and Nola's laugh rolling away from her, and more of Lulu's legs pumping, and Nola's grabbing the little foot with her mouth, prompting a cascade of baby laughter; and more spraying in Nola's face, and Lulu's boundless belly gurgle; and there was so much happiness Nola didn't know how to contain it, until she felt the wetness on her face that was soapy but also salty from her own tears.

Ming-Ji introduced plastic cups and tin spoons, moving them in and out of Lulu's vision in a game of hide-and-seek. "Baby clean," she finally said. "Eight hours since you find her? Feed her, then she sleep the drug off."

In the only bedroom in the apartment, Nola laid Lulu on one of the two cots and surrounded her with her bag and pillows. She chanted good night, ending it with the puckering of her mouth in a show of a kiss. Lulu's cupid lips mimicked the gesture. She accepted the pacifier, the corners of her lips extended in a quick smile, and closed her eyes.

Ming-Ji, who stood watching, followed Nola back to the living room. "You got outstanding baby."

Nola could not contain the wide smile. "Yup."

"Mentally, she many months ahead of age group," Ming-Ji continued. "Very much rare for seven-month baby to speak. She know Chinese sounds."

"She speaks?" Nola felt a little pang of regret about being unable to ever fill that cultural void even if she hired a tutor. "Maybe she's older."

"Eye-hand coordination good, too, but not exceptional like speech. Her size, teeth and motor skills—try sit by herself—consistent with seven-month-old, not much older."

"She loves music."

"I don't surprise if she imitate rhythm. Try banging with spoon." Ming-Ji demonstrated two, then three consecutive taps in varying rhythms. "She also have instinctive counting ability. I test her when I put three items in tub. When I hide one, she look for it. I try four items, too, and she look for one I hide. This baby off charts."

"A genius." Nola laughed. She didn't say what was surely on Ming-Ji's mind, too. Recognizing her daughter's brilliance, Lulu's mother had sought to give her more than just life. The alternative for this sunny and gifted baby was unbearable to fathom.

"What made you return from America?" Nola asked.

Ming-Ji shook her head sadly. "My mother, she sick. Very sick and alone. No one take care of her, and government don't let me bring her to Johns Hopkins. So I come back." Suddenly remembering her glasses, she retrieved them from her pants pocket.

"What a remarkable person you are," Nola said. At twelve, she would have given anything to have her mother back. But at this age she wouldn't have sacrificed her freedom for the dysfunctional mother of her childhood. "I envy the love you and you mother must share," Nola added.

"In China, we honor our parents. Confucius said, if we honor parents, we honor other parents, and all older people, and then our country." Ming-Ji paused. "Also the babies here. I also come back for sick ones. Government not want to make them better, just let them die."

Using his key, Daniel opened the door and walked in, carrying a set of baskets that nested one on top of the other and were held together by a bamboo handle. "Room service," he announced. "Dim sum."

It was the birdcage in his other hand that caught Nola's attention. She sent him a questioning look.

"My canary." He put the food basket down on the low table, then held the birdcage up for Nola's examination. "Meet Harry Wu. Harry Wu, meet Miss Nola Sands."

"Harry Wu? Like the dissident?"

Daniel wiggled his finger between the cage bars. "Proud to be a troublemaker. A thrice-over jailbird." He tickled the bird's neck. "He'll keep you company tonight. It's past his bedtime, but in the morning you'll appreciate the way he carries a tune."

The man in the room was so unlike the Daniel she had known, she was amused. "Together our singing can bring down the house."

"I wish I had taken you to visit the bird market."

"You were busy showing me other places." She thought of the old men she had seen in the garden enjoying their birds' singing, more beautiful than boom boxes.

Ming-Ji was at the door. "I leave for rounds at hospital."

"I'm sorry to say good-bye before we've had a chance to get to know each other better," Nola said. No words could describe her crocus-budding-in-the-snow feeling that she was no longer alone in this city.

"I'm honor that you called me," Ming-Ji said.

"Tell me what you need for your hospital—or for your cause. I'll see to it that you get it once I'm back home."

Ming-Ji nodded. "Maybe we meet again. Soon."

After she left, Nola said, "All too often, on my travels, people enter my life only to leave much too soon. One day, I'll settle down and have time for lasting friendships." She caught herself and glanced at Daniel.

He didn't seem to hear, or perhaps decided to ignore the implication. He covered the birdcage with a towel, turned on the TV, and watched the Chinese news.

"Still no mention of Lulu or her presumed mother," he reported after a while. "There has been nothing from the Xinhua News Agency."

"They must know I've found her. I've called their bluff."

Throwing away her diet considerations, she ate. She was hungry, and every morsel of food was delicious. "Would you like green tea?" She poured some for both of them. She needed a shower and sleep, but there was too much she wanted to discuss.

Daniel turned off the TV. "Wade called me shortly after you ran off."

Nola splattered her tea. "What? You knew about this before I called Ming-Ji?"

"There's a Chinese saying, 'The go-between needs a hundred pairs of sandals.' Wade asked me to negotiate a truce. Shall I put on my first pair of sandals?"

Her jaws clenched at Wade's assumption that she had run to Daniel. "I wouldn't be talking to you now if it weren't for Ming-Ji. What made you so cocksure that you would say 'yes' to Wade?"

"I hoped you'd call me. I'm sorry that you didn't trust me."

"It's that article. It has changed things." Her finger traced the smooth edges of the ceramic tea mug. Under the towel covering his cage, Harry Wu flapped his wings to adjust his position. Neither she nor Daniel spoke until she finally said, "I don't see how I'll get Lulu out of China and into the U.S. over both governments' objections. Wade is the master of making the impossible possible. He could have made it happen. Instead, he sold her out." She sipped her tea to wash away the taste of bile. The disgust she felt toward Wade's ruthlessness had a kinetic power that bored its way down from her skull to her bowels. "Our marriage is over."

"You may consider retaining the business partnership." Daniel raised his hand. "You don't need to make that decision now. Or share it with me."

"Our personal and professional lives were okay until I allowed it to get all twisted up in a knot. Marrying him ruined everything."

"Isn't it interesting how both the strengths and weaknesses in a relationship spring from the same fountain?"

"You sound like a fortune cookie." She looked at her fingers. "What I discovered today absolves me from a lifetime of debt." Her voice dropped. "But it's so sad."

"Endings always are," Daniel said.

"Had he not cultivated my career, I might have been a cabaret singer, with only dreams of international stardom." She wanted to cry, but didn't know exactly why. "I've met talented performers—I've lost competitions to better singers—who had mediocre managers and unmemorable songs, who fumbled around and amounted to nothing."

Slowly, she rose to her feet. "I'd like to shower. Will you wait?"

In the bedroom, she breathed in Lulu's scent, now mixed with the smell of oatmeal soap. Only when she searched her bag did she realize that her only change of clothing was an oversized T-shirt and panties. She brought them with her to the bathroom.

She had discovered earlier that the toilet was a hole in the floor with twin footsteps marking where she should position her legs. However, she hadn't expected the same hole to serve as the drain for the handheld showerhead. She lost her small hotel soap before she was careful with the sliver of oatmeal soap left from Lulu's bath.

After the shower, she rifled through her bag of toiletries. Daniel's snuff bottle was among them. She traced the miniature details of the phoenix. In his way, possibly without intending to, Daniel had helped set her free from her gilded cage.

But she had entered it freely. She regretted none of it—until Wade had locked her cage and thrown away the key. A wave of anger filled her.

She brushed her wet hair and clipped it up. She lifted her blush brush when a glance in the mirror made her stop. She liked the clean feeling. No pretense. Tugging on the hem of her long T-shirt to cover another inch of her thighs, she was ready to step barefoot into the living room when, self-conscious, she reconsidered and put on her jeans.

Daniel stood by the window, his hands in his pockets. The light from the paper lantern behind him threw a circle of yellow light that reached his feet, but did not travel up, leaving his upper body in the shadows. He turned and took a step forward, partially entering the light until his mouth was illuminated, carved and strong. His eyes remained in the shadows.

"You look lovely," he said.

Sexual excitement bloomed inside her, spreading, making her limbs heavy with anticipation. The seconds ticked in her veins, and nothing happened. She wanted to reach her hand inside him and twist and pluck that control board, yank loose the internal springs, computer chips and gears.

She sat down while digesting his first compliment. Having seen her in full makeup and evening gowns, he chose to praise the soap-and-water look. She refilled their ceramic mugs with tea, aware that Daniel didn't rush to take over that task. No one in her entourage ever let her pour tea for herself, let alone for someone else.

For the next hour, they discussed her predicament. All too cognizant of Daniel's presence in the small room—and under her skin—she filled him in on the details and listened to his explanations.

"Whichever way I look at it, I feel like a sparrow caught in a hurricane," she concluded. Her hands gripped the ceramic cup. "Since hopping on my jet is out of the question, is there any way for me to leave China with Lulu?"

He took her hand and examined her palm for a long time. Did he see the losses? Nola's heart thumped as he turned her hand over and ran his index finger over the bluish veins. His touch left tingles of electric shocks in its wake. Then he brought her hand to his lips and kept it there, his eyes closed. Nola caught her breath, wanting to bring her face closer, restraining herself.

He lowered her hand, but kept it on the couch between them, staring at their joined fingers as though imprinting their touching in his memory. When he finally raised his gaze, she saw a depth of untold sadness. And she understood. Kate. He wasn't ready. Not yet. Some day, perhaps, after he'd healed—perhaps even cleansed himself of the hatred he must feel toward the butchers of his dreams. But not now.

And she would not take a place in line after a dead woman who was still alive in his heart. Nola slid her hand from under his.

Finally he spoke. "I can't get you and Lulu out without great risks. There's nothing that's safer than staying put—albeit in daily danger— and trying to get things straightened out legally."

In her mind's eye, Nola saw herself trekking for weeks through the

Himalayas, drinking goat's milk, and fighting bandits with dark, hungry eyes who brandished machetes—only to find herself arriving in an arid part of Pakistan or India, or whatever it was that lay beyond Tibet.... It wasn't worth even consulting a map. It was no less dangerous than the former Soviet state where Daniel's fiancée and their unborn baby had been murdered.

"Even if I can't escape now, I wish I could cancel this tour and hide. But the show must go on. The show must go on. It's been drilled into me for as long as I can remember."

She bit her lip. A new game plan had been forced on her. What were her options if she couldn't sing and couldn't escape? She imagined weeks and months in China's countryside. She saw herself moving from one small town to another, picking food in fields, washing her own clothes in the river, and caring for Lulu while trying to avoid detection. She'd cut her hair, color it black, and iron it straight, as her mother used to do in the seventies.

Nola rose and paced around the room. "I won't even leave this apartment. If Ming-Ji agrees, that is. I'll coop up with Lulu in this place for as long as it takes."

Chapter 25

Words had been left unspoken, touches unexpressed. After Daniel left, Nola checked the pillows around Lulu, then curled up in the other cot under a cotton quilt that smelled a bit musty. She listened to her baby's lip smackings and fell asleep with a new sense of peace.

Sometime during the night, heavy rain pelted the glass windows, clothesline wheels squeaked, and a shutter banged against the wall. The sounds became mixed in Nola's dream into an erotic scene in which Daniel's body pounded into hers. She climaxed, and then, still wrapped in sleep, puzzled at her crossing of this sexual Rubicon.

When Lulu woke before dawn, Nola changed her, gave her the last prepared bottle of milk, and then said, "Let's get more sleep. Please?"

"Eezzz." Lulu was fully awake, ready for play, and engaged Nola for an hour before laying her head on the pillow. For long minutes, the two of them looked into each other's eyes. Then Lulu cuddled like a puppy, and Nola fell asleep again, enjoying the tender kick of the small feet. Was this what it felt like to be pregnant? Soon, Lulu wriggled out from under the quilt, climbed onto Nola's stomach, and brought herself up to a sitting position. Through cobwebs of sleep, Nola held the little waist before she became fully conscious of the new development.

She woke up. "You're sitting all by yourself!"

"Ba-ba-uuu-efff." Lulu began to whimper, and her cry turned into the inconsolable wail of the previous nights.

It was still dark outside. Nola paced the apartment with her. "You'll wake up Mr. Wu," she whispered and lifted the towel off the birdcage. "You see?" But neither the bird nor the baby seemed impressed. The bird slept on, its head buried in its chest, and Lulu went on screaming.

Nola sang one song after another, her heart breaking at Lulu's pain. "I know what you feel," she whispered, "You've lost your first mommy. I'm your next mommy. We'll stay in this place and no bad people will ever take you again. No one. Okay?"

A few hours later, Nola was awakened by the lovely melodious notes of a songbird. Her head swimming, it took her a few seconds to get her bearings. The strange room, the cot, Lulu sleeping at her side. Daniel's canary singing in the living room. What had happened to her life?

There was a tap on the open bedroom door. Daniel stood there, dressed in a dark suit and a striped red tie. "I'm sorry to wake you. You didn't hear my knock. I let myself in before drawing the neighbors' attention."

"It's okay. What time is it? Never mind. Give me a few minutes." She passed her tongue over felted teeth, and her hand went to brush her hair into submission. She must look like hell.

"There's green tea and a sweet cake in the kitchen," he said. In the morning light she noticed the first crinkling of crow's feet at the corner of his eyes, like hesitant sketch marks before the tackling of a painting. She averted her gaze. This was not to be.

Harry Wu's melodious chirping filled the air. Whistling in response, Nola went about washing up, sipping tea and biting into the sticky cake, which tasted like unflavored, uncooked dough. She set a pot of water on the burner to boil Lulu's empty bottles. Following her request last night, Daniel had bought fresh milk, powdered rice and a soft banana. Only in the States, Ming-Ji had told Nola, could she get formula, disposable bottles and ready-to-eat baby meals. For now, Nola found an unexpected pleasure in preparing Lulu's food herself.

Back in the bedroom, she dressed in her jeans and sweater and peeked out the window. This was her neighborhood for as long as she was in hiding. Boxes, ladders, washing basins and furniture were stacked high on the balconies across the street. Laundry lines filled every free space. After the night's rain, puddles of reddish clay, like Darjeeling tea, blocked most of the narrow street. A teenage girl supported an old woman wobbling on tiny, four-inch feet.

Lulu was still sleeping. Nola walked to the living room, feeling a lift of spirits from exercising her power. Daniel was sitting on the couch, his eyes on a Chinese newspaper.

"Morning again," she said.

He folded the paper, not bothering with the crease lines. She had expected him to be meticulous about everything, and liked this casualness about him.

"Wade called me this morning," he said.

She suppressed a flare of anger at the mention of his name. If a loving husband believed his wife had a lover, shouldn't he be jealous? "Your wearing the go-between sandals is not a good idea," she told Daniel. "Take them off. I don't want Wade speaking to you when he can't speak to me."

"Okay."

"Tell me what's happening otherwise," she said. "Are they all frantic?"

"Your inside circle is withholding confirmation of your absence, but the media is on to it." He laughed softly. "Wade is upset that you might not show up for the concert—as are other people on the Chinese side."

"Such as?"

"The Minister of Culture, for one. He'll be held responsible."

A slight pang of guilt dissipated as quickly as it came. There was nothing she could do about the Chinese's convoluted ways. "Are you sure you weren't followed?"

He nodded. "We're fine for now."

We. He approved of her decision. In a way, she wished he didn't, so he could point out the foolishness of her decision and she could argue and defend it. "I need to call Barbara Walters or Larry King," she said, "Can you get me their phone numbers?"

"We'll need to find access to international dialing," he replied. "In the meantime, you should know that Mauriello says he's come up with a solution."

"Mauriello? What kind of a solution?"

"He insists on telling you in person at the airport, where your plane is ready to take off to Shanghai."

"Which means that he first wants to flush me out."

"According to Wade, Mauriello's proposal has already been accepted by the Chinese."

Ribbons of fire burned inside her. "How lovely. Mauriello's discussed with everyone but me the solution to my problem. I trust neither Mauriello nor Wade. Wade couldn't give me what I wanted because it was no longer his to give. In the final deal of our life together, he's sold both our souls." She smacked her lips with renewed disbelief. "What new promises has he made to Mauriello now?"

Daniel said nothing. Her voice tight, she asked, "Does the deal guarantee that I can keep Lulu and take her to the United States?"

"That was my first question. Yes."

She bit her lip. "What about Ashford? Is he cool with it?"

"Ashford has his priorities. He wants to put an end to this crisis. Instead of dealing with world peace, he's mired in a conflict over a fifteen-pound baby."

Perspiration erupted on her neck and face. "Am I supposed to accept the deal with blind faith? Wade's in the service of the Chinese. And Mauriello—I'm not even sure what his agenda is. Are you?"

Daniel shook his head. "He's a player, though." Again she liked it that he delivered the facts, not directives.

"Perhaps Mauriello is in a position to negotiate among the parties," she said, weighing the words. She wished she had paid attention the night of the embassy gala, when Wade had mentioned BRW's business in

China. "Why would Ashford let him take over?"

"Your demand for Lulu has been added with great reluctance and haste to the shopping list the U.S. presents China. The list is normally negotiated and compiled by the State Department and the White House. Your crisis has been forcing a negotiations deadline for which neither side is ready."

"I don't want Ashford off the hook. I need our government in the picture as a guarantor. With his deal, Mauriello saves Ashford."

Daniel leaned forward. "It might work to your advantage to have your demand out of the competition with the many others Ashford must put on the table. From his point of view, what would the U.S. give the Chinese in exchange for Lulu? Ignore the next Los Alamos spy scandal? Grant China more one-sided import-tax concessions? Forget about Tibet?"

"Letting me keep Lulu should not have become an issue in the first place. It certainly should not have turned into an international crisis."

She walked to the window and opened it for fresh air. Her feeble attempt to escape had failed. She couldn't hide in this apartment forever, but she dreaded emerging from it to watch for real and imaginary enemies.

In a crack between the ledge of the windowsill and the cinder block next to it, a tiny daisy swayed in the wind. Nola reached to pluck it, but changed her mind. A seed had flown in the wind, had been hurled against a wall, had held on, nestled, and taken root. It had bloomed in this unlikely, inhospitable spot, its soft white and yellow bloom challenging the hopelessness of its destiny and the grimness of the place.

She spoke over her shoulder. "This could be either a trap to lure me out of my hiding, or a sign that my message has landed where I expected it to."

In the street below, the ancient woman with the bound feet was still braced by her young attendant as they headed back. It occurred to Nola that in Ashford's tally of the communists' accomplishments these past fifty years, he had failed to name the abolition of the barbaric foot-binding practice, a change that had come too late for this woman.

She didn't hear Daniel get up, but she felt his heat as he took a spot at her side by the window. She trembled, either from the chill in the air or from his nearness. For a while neither spoke. In her field of vision, she saw his long, tapered fingers rest on the windowsill, an inch from hers. The magnetic field between them hummed, and she had the urge to shift her pinky and touch his. She felt him examine her face, but she did not move. If only he parted the hair on her neck and placed his lips on her skin—

She looked up. For a long moment, their eyes locked, and an invisible string tightened as though to pull them closer. She felt his warm breath and saw his Adam's apple bob behind the knot of his tie.

But his heart still belonged to a dead woman and was buried with her in a foreign soil. Nola turned and closed the window. There were other, more urgent demons she must stare down right now. A new love—and a frustrating one at that—would be a throwback to the dependency of the past.

Yet with her first decision without Wade, she had landed in a mess. "I shouldn't have talked to the media about the Dying Rooms," she said. "It was stupid of me to charge ahead like this—"

"That was a brave act. And it was good that you did it, or you couldn't have gotten this far and still held on to Lulu," Daniel said quietly. "Do you ever regret not returning her the moment she was thrust into your arms?"

"Never."

The wild fluttering of her heart told her that being brave was as frightening as being afraid.

Daniel brought the car to a stop in front of a small park, where a group of men in traditional costumes practiced the ancient art of swordplay. Leslie waited at the curb; he had to do Nola's makeup before she arrived at the airport to face a mission of Beijing dignitaries and their long-winded farewell speeches. Lulu babbled against Nola's shoulder as she looked at the view outside. Holding her close restored something in Nola. In a paradoxical way, it assuaged her anxiety over the high stakes of showing up in public.

Nola regarded Leslie, attempting to read his body language as he lifted his bag off the ground and glided into the car. He must be cross with her.

"My, my. The prodigal daughter returns." He placed his hand over his heart. "You gave me a fright." His eyes were deep and troubled. He kissed Lulu.

"What's this on your face?" Nola asked. His upper lip was sprinkled with stubs of reddish hairs, like crystallized brown sugar. The color was different from the brown hair that grew on his head, still closely shaven. "You're growing a mustache?"

"I'll be the only young one in China wearing one. This is a nation of mustacheless men."

"I've only been gone for one night." She giggled with a minute relief. "And look at you."

"Next time take me with you." He fingered the ends of her hair.

"Everybody's hysterical. Jean-Claude is already in Shanghai, staging a grand dress rehearsal with that Australian extravaganza. Your backup singers and the musicians are there, too. And we're still here! We'll be so-o-o late for the concert, and you must warm up before dancing on stage."

How sure they had been that she would capitulate and come out of hiding. What would Mauriello's proposal be? The false ring of everything associated with him blared in her head like a foghorn. But there was no other choice. Instead of feeling triumphant for having stared them all down and won her battle to keep Lulu, she felt empty. Empty and tired. She longed to sleep for days.

"I don't know how I can get through this evening, let alone the coming week," she said.

Leslie touched her middle. "You need to unleash your spirituality right here from your gut." He called over to Daniel, "What's the Chinese name for what the Japanese call 'hara?' "

"Tan Tien?"

"Yup. That's it. *Tan Tien.*"

Nola smiled. "How does one go about acquiring it?"

"You've got plenty of it. Just release it. It's a center of energy physically located in the human body that manifests itself spiritually and psychologically. Right, Daniel?"

Daniel met Nola's eyes in the rearview mirror. "Absolutely."

"If only it were strong enough to suck me out of here." She sighed, then smiled at Leslie. "What happened to all the gods you've been collecting?"

"It all comes to the same thing. They all reside inside you, in your *Tan Tien.*"

"Leslie, it's called 'the human spirit,' and the Jews have had it since the beginning of time." She paused. "At the end of the day, all we have to rely upon is ourselves."

All through their drive to the airport, in the confines of the backseat of the Mercedes, Leslie balanced his brushes on his knees while maneuvering to keep them out of Lulu's reach. He clucked over Nola's skin. "Ach, Darling. What have you done, walked through the Gobi desert? You know you must properly nourish your skin for the makeup or it will reflect flashbulbs like a witch's face."

Self-conscious of putting on a mask to re-enter her stage life role, she avoided meeting Daniel's eyes in the mirror. But she had *Tan Tien*, and she would use it for all its worth. Jolted from her fifteen-year hibernation, the capable, self-reliant child who had braved a stormy young life had reawakened.

Chapter 26

Daniel drove to the gated noncommercial airport terminal, designated for dignitaries and party officials.

"So perfectly egalitarian," Leslie remarked. "So Commie."

"Pull up to the curb here," Nola instructed Daniel, pointing to the gathering of photographers and reporters. Roberta was nowhere in sight. "I'll stay in front of the international media at all times. It will make it hard on the Chinese to renege on their agreement." She halted. "I need them in case Mauriello's deal is unacceptable, or even a trap."

And it would make it harder for Wade to get Lulu, she thought as she saw him push through with the bodyguards. The dark circles under his eyes, treated by a cosmetic surgeon not long before, had reappeared. The enemy.

"Honey," he said. As though nothing had transpired between them, he tried to plant a kiss on her cheek. She shrank back, aware that cameras chronicled her reaction. How would she get through five more concerts—or bear his presence for one minute?

"Will you sing tonight?" "Did you have a nervous breakdown?" "Will you go on with the tour?" The reporters' questions hit her like darts. So much for keeping them in the dark.

"We'll have the best concert ever tonight." Wade's teeth sparkled, and he waved like a politician. "Everything's fine. Hope to see you all there."

Nola lifted Lulu to the cameras. Lulu squinted at the popping flashlights and gurgled at the faces in front of her. Nola's eyes darted about as she surveyed her surroundings, uncertain of what to expect. Yoram's face was grim. His security personnel failed to make her feel safe.

Inside the terminal, Nola stopped before the massive teak-and-bamboo door to the VIP room. She steeled herself to meet Mauriello.

Someone held the door for her. Greeting her on the wall was a two-headed dragon. Its face was painted in cheerful vermilion and yellow, its twin lolling tongues in striped green. Under it stood the Chinese minister of culture. The night at the opera, where she had last seen him two days before, seemed eons away. He bowed from the waist.

"Pleasure to see you again. Did you enjoy the rest of your stay in Beijing?" He enunciated the words as though he had learned them by rote. "I hope you find our hospitality to your liking."

A rush of air caused the two-headed dragon's tongues to sway. Rocking

Lulu against her shoulder, Nola reminded herself to be polite. She'd charm the pockmarked skin off this minister's face. Breathlessly, her voice as sweet as plum wine, she said, "China's everything I had hoped for and more. Oh! I particularly liked the street performances and the group exercises in the parks."

"I'm glad you got the chance to witness our people's contentment." He handed her a flat wrapped package. It was too light to be a book. "A token of our esteem." He bowed his head. "Please open."

She feigned a giggle of delight, made a show of appreciating the fine rice paper wrapping, then handed Lulu to Leslie. In slow, deliberate movements, she untied the gold satin ribbon, and uncovered a picture made of exquisite silk embroidery stretched over a polished mahogany frame. Millions of tiny stitches, made with the finest of threads, created a scene of a tiger eyeing a songbird on a tree branch.

White, hot anger burned in Nola's skull. "Beautiful. I would like to learn more about this form of stitchery. A helpless bird and a vicious tiger. Is there a folk tale behind it?"

Then she thought of her *Tan Tien*. It would not tolerate the minister's insult. Aware of the handpicked group of reporters representing *Vanity Fair, In Style, Entertainment, People, Billboard*, HBO, MTV and VH1, she smiled openly into his face. She refolded the picture in its wrapping, returned the package, and said sweetly, "I'm so sorry I cannot accept this wonderful gift."

She thought she heard Wade's groan. At least Roberta wasn't around to interfere.

The minister's face reddened. "It made by our women artisans. Best in world!" He bowed again. "Since it my honor to accompany you to Shanghai, I make sure you see special atelier where we make this—and also learn more about our way of life."

The instruction would probably cover the sacrifice of the individual for the good of the many. "I'm always interested in learning more of the Chinese ways." She flipped her hair away from her face, and, feline-like, turned her back to him. As her new chaperone, he would see more of that part of her than he cared to.

She opened the stroller Leslie had brought and motioned to him to put Lulu in it. Before she straightened, she heard the squeak of leather shoes and George Mauriello's voice. She shielded Lulu as though his mere presence had the power to corrupt her. At least dealing directly with him eliminated Wade. She would give the CEO of BRW what he wanted, and obtain in exchange the one thing she needed from him. Finally, everything would be set right.

"Here you are." He handed her a bouquet of almond blossoms. "Feeling better?"

She buried her nose in the sweet-smelling white and pink flowers. "About what, exactly?" Her eyes took in Mauriello's magnificently fitted Armani suit, his small-print silk tie, and that full head of slicked-back, salt-and-pepper hair. The inveterate charmer's charisma had hardened into cold granite.

In his other hand he held a large stuffed panda. He bent toward Lulu, who, in turn, closed her mouth over the bear's shiny nose. He laughed. Nola gently pulled the bear away.

Mauriello looked at Nola as though she were the focus of the universe, then, as he had done before, skipped several stages of acquaintanceship and looped her hand through the crook of his elbow, closing his fingers on it in a gesture of intimacy. He steered her away from the crowd toward a set of two love seats.

Still holding her hand, he gazed into her eyes. "I've neglected you this past year, and I apologize. I hope you and Wade will be able to join me in Morocco to celebrate New Year's, then a few days in the Mediterranean on my yacht with some friends? I'd like you to be my very special guest of honor."

"My, thanks," she purred. If she wanted to spend time at sea, she would have accepted Keith Schwartz's invitation.

She used the business of sitting down to disengage her arm while keeping an amiable expression. Mauriello had set the rules for this game and she was going along; afterwards she would owe him nothing. "You have some good news for me, I hear?" she asked.

"I sure do." Again that sparkle in his eyes. She felt herself being carried away on a rising spiral of hope before she remembered that this was the same voice that had demanded that Wade "deliver" her. Mauriello patted her knee. "Panda bears and Lulu."

"Panda bears?"

"The National Zoo in Washington, D.C., has been trying to replace the old pair given to them when Nixon first came to China in 1972. Hsing-Hsing has joined his mate in Panda Heaven, or wherever it is that giant pandas go. With all the animosity between our countries, the Chinese were reluctant to offer another pair. Now they will, and they are allowing Lulu to accompany the pandas with fanfare."

"Is this a joke?" Nola blurted. No, it wasn't. Everything in this saga had become so bizarre that nothing was improbable.

"Doesn't Uncle George deserve a big hug? I gave you the baby to keep and saved the concert tour for you."

"What an ingenious plan." She forced a smile. "For the first time, someone is saying I can keep Lulu. But the details are fuzzy. What's the time frame for this exchange?"

"Not an 'exchange.' The pandas and Lulu will be traveling together."

"And where will I be? In first class with the baby or in the cage with the pandas?"

He laughed, but did not reply.

"For all I know, things can 'accidentally' go wrong just as she and I are ready to leave the country," Nola said. "Did you see the gift the Minister of Culture tried to give me? They are on the warpath with me."

"Who cares?" Mauriello wiggled his finger at her. "You'll have to trust me on this one."

"Sorry. I want a foolproof plan. What if the Chinese break the deal after my last concert?"

"What do you suggest?"

She had never thought she would say this. "I want Lulu in the States within twenty-four hours. Someone from my staff will fly home with her while I finish my tour."

She had no clue who, in an entourage of more than a hundred, would take a bullet for her and Lulu. All were Wade's stooges.

Mauriello raised a magnificent arched eyebrow. "The baby may be ready for the trip, but the pandas are not. Prepping them and making the physical transport arrangements takes time. We don't want them dying in transit."

"No deal, then." Her plan would mean six days without her baby, but that was the best she could think of. Ten feet away, Leslie was playing peek-a-boo with Lulu. Both were laughing.

"I've just explained about the transportation problem," Mauriello said.

She got up. "So Lulu and the pandas won't make the same flight. You can still keep all the fanfare."

He sighed. "Make it forty-eight hours, then. Anything to make our diva happy."

"One last question: What have you offered in return?"

His smile was a crocodile's. "That, my dear, as they say, is none of your business."

If there were such a thing as blood curdling, that was what Nola felt happening in her veins. A corporation owned her, and Mauriello was collecting his fee.

Her hand on the doorknob of the middle school principal's office, Nola swallowed a glob of saliva. As a student here, her dealings with the principal had been limited to her singing Christmas carols over the PA system. Now, even as she took in the familiar, comforting odors of sweaty socks, stale cafeteria food, and linoleum polish, she dreaded hearing about yet another Jenna problem.

Nevertheless, she hadn't anticipated that they would expel Jenna, which was what the principal demanded as soon as Nola sat down. "Just give me a few weeks until the custody hearing," Nola said. "Then she'll come live with me—"

The woman shook the mass of gray hair. "Every day there's a problem. Yesterday, during recess, some girls were giggling—you know how twelve-year-old girls are. Full of secrets. Jenna thought they were ridiculing her. She flew into a rage, charged into them and hit and bit them. She left teeth marks! This morning I got calls from parents. Not for the first time, nor the tenth. They want her removed—and so do I."

Nola bit her lip. "I'm sorry. I'll speak to the doctor about her medication. Please help me find a way to keep her here without creating another interruption in her life."

The principal looked at her for a long time.

Nola couldn't even come up with a good argument to convince her. "Please," she said. "Just a few more weeks."

The woman nodded pensively. "I'll try because it's you. I respect how well you've done under the tragic circumstances." She summoned one of the girls working in the office and introduced her as the captain of the high school cheerleading team. "Lauren is also a finalist in the New York State Spelling Bee." She turned to the girl. "Would you keep an eye on Jenna? She's excellent in English. Train her to become the next Spelling Bee Queen in her division."

"Cool." The girl's awestruck gaze fixed on Nola. "I'll hang around with her at recess. After school I can take her out for ice cream."

Nola let out a sigh of relief. "Thank you so much. I really appreciate it. I'll pay, of course, for your time."

Jenna stormed into the office but stopped short when she saw Nola. Her features squeezed together into the center of her face like a string purse. "What are you doing here?"

"I've come to pick you up. Remember? We had a date for a picnic at the estate—"

"I mean here, in this room." Jenna stomped her foot.

"Jenna, honey." Nola rose to put her arm around her, but Jenna pushed her away. Nola avoided meeting the principal's eyes. "Lauren will help you practice for the Spelling Bee. Everyone thinks you have a chance at winning the championship."

Jenna turned to the girl. "You'll mock me with your popularity and perfect looks, and I'll throw acid in your face."

The old man no longer recognized anyone. His breathing was labored. A machine at his feet bumped and jolted his legs to keep the circulation going. Nola sat by the bed and held her great-great-uncle's convulsing hand, singing softly. The room smelled of his sour flesh and acrid medicines. A cat that had replaced the one who had long since died purred at his other side.

Nola's finger traced the blue veins running down the old man's temples. Broken capillaries criss-crossed his cheeks and liver spots covered the top of his bald head. In all the years she had known him, he always wore fresh, clean clothes as he sat downstairs by the window overlooking the Sound. He had retained his dignity in his solitary existence while his personality—of which she knew only the kindness and now understood the determination—had been trapped in a body that had long ago said its good-bye. And all along he must have loved her, the little girl who came by for food, who sang through her days, who later filled his home with music and chatter.

Maybe even now he could hear her.

"I'm working on a new album," she began to speak, as she had during their dinners at his long table. "Wade wants me to stay ahead of the curve, but he says I can straddle the sentimental and the personal growth I'm experiencing. The new album will be all love songs. No, actually, it's about my breaking up with Troy. You've never met him, but he was special."

The old man's breathing was unchanged. The tremor in his left hand had nothing to do with anything.

She went on. "Troy's a good musician who needs to find his own groove." The memory of Troy's tanned, muscular body and intense, dark eyes hovered nearby. She missed his musical humor, his touches. "Maybe 'Letting Go' should be the title for the album. It's the story of so many women who can't let go of a guy who's wrong for them. They'll understand."

Nola squeezed the old man's hand lightly. "Or, 'Bad For Me.' I can see thousands of women dancing in front of the stage to the beat. *Bad for me. You are bad for me. Yeah, Yeah. Bad for me, bad for me. You are bad for me.*" Nola giggled. "Or maybe, 'Not Intimacy, But Fusion.' Fusion is a good word. Not yet used anywhere, but it rhymes well. Fusion, con-fusion, illusion."

The only response was the rhythmic croaking of the foot-stimulating machine. Jenna's footsteps bounding up the stairs announced her arrival before she burst into the room. "You coming or not?"

The cat vaulted off the bed with a screech.

Nola rose and looked down at the only family member who had cared. She bent to kiss the parched skin on the forehead. "Thank you for sav-ing me," she whispered, thinking of her Steinway, of the music lessons, of the food in his refrigerator, of his continuous presence. "I love you." Tears streamed down her cheeks. "What would have happened to me if you weren't here?"

The left eye blinked.

The woods stood leafless, brown and desolate. Nola didn't cross them to her former home, but laid out their picnic lunch on a blanket twenty feet away from the cliff. She fed Jenna's imagination with her own memories of laughter and music and guests who loved to stay forever. And some fabri-cations. "Mommy and Daddy used to picnic with us out here," she said.

The early winter day was warm enough for them to sit outside with their jackets zipped up. Patches of snow clung to shaded spots by the trees. The Sound was quiet, its gray-blue surface shimmering like an oil spill. Swans curled into themselves, and gulls squawked from above. Jenna read a new story she had written, in which, as always, her charac-ters suffered macabre deaths.

"Let's act it," she said when she finished reading.

Nola went along with the game. "How about if instead of falling into a well, the princess finds a bird with a broken wing and nurses it back to health?"

"Yeah! Turns out the bird is a cursed prince, and he turns back into his princely form and they fall in love," Jenna said, delight in her voice. She proceeded to act it out.

Nola clapped. "Keep thinking of good endings. Happy endings." She inserted a cassette into the portable recorder she had bought Jenna. "Want to hear The New Kids on the Block?"

The two of them sang along with the tape. Once Jenna lived with her, Nola thought, she could always be this happy child.

In Nola's limousine on the way to Mini-Nazi's house, Jenna began to whimper. By the time they arrived, her crying had turned to screaming. In the front yard, she threw herself on the ground, thrashing and kicking. "I hate you! Don't leave! I hate you!"

"I'll be back." Nola tried to gather Jenna's flailing limbs. Her mouth was parched and her brain felt as if it were stuffed with cotton. "I'll be back next week."

Jenna bawled and kicked and pummeled Nola's chest. "Don't leave me!" she cried. "Please, please, please."

"Shhhhhhhh," Nola whispered. "Remember to tell yourself that I love you. After the hearing you'll live with me. Forever. I promise."

The following week, though, while Nola was rehearsing in Cleveland, the principal called. Jenna had been caught with a cigarette lighter in the cafeteria line, attempting to set a girl's hair on fire.

"I'm expelling her," the principal said. "Sorry. Ms. Cutter will tutor Jenna at home until a suitable placement can be found."

Nola returned home the next day, drove out and packed Jenna's things. The four-year wait for the court hearing was over. Her sister belonged with her, in her apartment. Let Social Services fight her to take Jenna away. She doubted they would, given their workload.

Nola lay in the dark of her bedroom, Jenna next to her, flailing her limbs in her sleep. Nola's eyes were wide open, and she curled away from Jenna's kicking. Her mind free-associated. One day—not yet—she would write a song about the "one moment." The one moment of Jenna's accident that froze in time, that she never stopped wishing to turn back, replay and fix, to make right. Then the second "one moment," in which both their lives had been hurled into orbit. By then, though, Jenna had already been an orphan in practice, if not in fact.

In the gap between the tall Manhattan buildings, a friendly moon hovered low in the sky, large and full, as puckered and uneven as the face of the old man who had died last week. The last of her adult family was gone. The moon sent translucent caresses through the slats of the Venetian blinds, as if the old man were still around, his silence reassuring. Jenna kicked. Nola rose out of bed, went to the next room that served as her study and sat on the window bench, her knees under her chin, rocking herself. Poor, poor Jenna. What could she say to a girl who only wanted to show her ugly side? At the movie that afternoon, when a five-year-old in the next row talked too loud, Jenna had poured her Coke over his head. The theater manager had insisted they leave.

For three weeks now they were living in the spacious apartment Nola had prepared with the hope of satisfying the caseworkers. Their life together, which she had visualized for so long—laughter-filled meals at their kitchen table, Sundays in Central Park—was coming together. For so long she had fantasized about the richness of a mother's love that she was now filled with knowledge. She acted it out as she tried to infuse Jenna with that kind of caring. At Nola's former city school, many deprived children had coped well. They had played. They had laughed. They had made friends.

Not Jenna. Wade had pulled strings to enroll her in a private school, jumping years ahead on the waiting list. Samples of Jenna's writings had helped convince the principal. But at the gate on the first day, Jenna broke into one of her temper tantrums.

"My scars make me the ugliest thing alive, and everybody will hate me," she screamed, attracting the attention she claimed to dread.

"C'mon. You can hardly see them." Nola fanned Jenna's hair. It was thick and golden. "You look like Mom and you're as beautiful as she was. And you're so inventive and fun. You make up great games. Use that great smile of yours, and in a couple of days you'll make new friends."

"I'll hate them. They'll be snotty and mean."

"One day you'll be a famous writer, and they'll all come back to ask you to autograph your book. I'll be known as 'the sister of that great author, Jenna Sands.' " Nola halted. "Until then, always remind yourself that you're the only little sister I have and I love you very, very much. Okay?"

Since Jenna wouldn't even walk to the principal's office, he rescinded her acceptance at the gate.

Since then, Jenna wouldn't hear of visiting another school. She accompanied Nola everywhere, slept in her bed and, although as tall as Nola, tried to sit in her lap, even in restaurants. Distrustful of her ability to cope, Nola hired a therapist, who was to move in with them Monday. Nola believed that Jenna's clinging would stop once she was certain she could stay. All Jenna needed was time and lots of love.

Nola tightened her arms around her knees and rested her head on them. She had been wrong in her speculation that Social Services would just move on to the next case. Her taking possession of her sister had jump-started them, and the hearing date was set. It was her celebrity status, the lawyer explained, that had made them take notice. And Jenna *was* a disturbed girl.

"A disturbed girl." The words almost choked Nola, but there was no escaping the truth. It was as if Jenna carried the double burden of their orphanhood, or something more: Nola suspected that whatever had caused their mother's ills—that had made her not leave the house for months, prompted her crying spells, and caused her inability to care for her children—had been passed on to Jenna.

Nola shook her head at the moon. No more sorrows. To shove away her fears, she should focus on her blessings. On the shelf were the dozen trophies she had accumulated from local arts and folk festivals, topped by Teens' Choice and MTV New Artist awards. On the wall, next to her three gold albums, hung framed posters of the concerts she had headlined and copies of articles in *Seventeen* and *People*, highlighted by the *Rolling Stone* cover which dubbed her, "The Divine Songbird." Good, but not a Grammy nomination. She was still very far from the top.

"Your Honor," Nola said at the hearing, hoping the spirit of the deceased old man was intervening on her behalf. "I'm a very mature twenty year old. I have a career and the financial means to support us both. I've hired a trained counselor to live with us; she'll supervise Jenna when I work." Tears streamed down Nola's cheeks. "Please. I beg you to understand that I'm her only family. Isn't that what everyone agrees disturbed kids need most?"

"Yes, she's disturbed, all right." Mini-Nazi seconded the caseworker's opinion that only an institution could give Jenna the professional care she required. Nola's consternation grew as the Suffolk County judge grilled her about the dangers of living in Manhattan and her social milieu of entertainment people. In preparation for the hearing, Wade had cut overnight travel by rescheduling Nola's upcoming months with only day-long recordings, mall appearances and local TV shows. The judge tossed the document aside and probed Nola about her previous frequent, lengthy tours. He was puzzled by her failure to send Jenna to school.

"Can't you take a secretarial job around here?" he asked her.

"I'm a singer. I make money so the two of us could have our own home. No other twenty-year-old can maintain a home and pay for therapy on a secretary's wages."

"An adult may see to it that the child attends school."

An hour after Nola had entered the courtroom, the judge ruled that she was unable to provide her sister with the stability a suburban group home would offer.

Chapter 28

On her way to the Shanghai arena, Nola stared through the rain-streaked limousine window, intent on blocking out Wade on the seat across from hers. Whenever he caught her eye, he had the imploring look of a neglected puppy.

The enemy. At least during the short flight from Beijing, she had locked herself with Lulu in her sleeping cabin, and when they arrived at the hotel she had insisted he get a separate suite. But now he faced her, his tuxedo pants rucked up around his calves with static cling. A rare Scotch sat on the teak side table, a wet circle spreading under the glass.

His nearness in the confines of the small space drained Nola's ability to focus on her upcoming concert. She had never been late for a performance, nor had she ever failed to practice. Her critics were right: she wasn't giving her work her all. The slack, though, was not caused by the demands of a baby but by the storm others created about her.

The limousine waited for the light to change, and Nola looked at a small shrine whose red pagoda roofline with yellow corners cried thin rivulets of rainwater. The green paint on the heavy double doors had chipped, yet the temple stood solemn and proud, tucked as it was between '70s-style concrete-and-steel commercial buildings. Nola wished to pray to any gods who would hear her. *Baruch atta Adonai*— If only she could remember the words....

She put her hand on the sleeping Lulu, snuggled in a blanket against her thigh, and closed her eyes to psyche herself up for the show. She envisioned the beauty of the stage, the glory and glitter, and the rapture that would ignite all her nerve endings. After a while, anticipation trembled inside her. A part of her would never stop looking forward to exciting her audience. Only another artist could understand the elation of being the recipient of the love the fans reflected back.

Nola opened her eyes a crack. The rain had stopped. She hoped Lulu would wake up soon; it would give her something with which to occupy herself. It would give Lulu, a baby who had already suffered one stupendous loss, another thread to hold onto during the weeklong separation.

"I want my passport. And a credit card and money. Lots of cash," Nola told Wade.

His movements were short and furious as he unlocked his briefcase and fished in its pockets. He tossed what she'd asked for onto the seat beside her. Without looking in his direction, Nola tucked the passport and the wad of hundred-dollar bills into Lulu's diaper bag.

She wished Leslie were there to buffer the thick tension that hung in the air like a foul odor. But he had left earlier to prepare for tonight's show.

Lulu stirred. Nola rolled down the window to let in some chilly air. She shouldn't think about being bound to Wade in the coming week. Only about the next three hours. If only his betrayal didn't pulsate in her temples.

He sighed and pressed the button to close her window. "Your hair frizzes." When instead of a response she smiled at Lulu, who had awakened, he leaned over and tried to take Nola's hand. "Look, I'm sorry for being such an ass about it—"

"Don't touch me." She yanked her fingers away. "Ever."

"If only I could turn back the clock. You, of all people, know what it means to make a huge mistake. I hadn't had enough time to digest the idea when the baby was dropped from the sky, but I'm ready now."

"Thanks for a below-the-belt comparison. How kind of you."

He sat back, then popped a mint into his mouth.

Nothing mattered any more, she told herself. Nothing mattered except getting Lulu out of this cursed country. She dangled a cloth ball. Dling, dling, tinkled the bell inside the ball. Lulu let out gurgles of delight. Then, looking at Wade, she said, "Da-da-da-"

"Is she saying 'Daddy?' " he asked. "Isn't she a bit young for that?"

"Too young to know her friends from her enemies."

"I'm sorry. I really am," he repeated. "I love you. I'll take care of everything. Adoption, passport, visas, whatever."

"My stop was three stations back, before I found out you tried to have this baby, whose name you still can't utter, killed."

"I did no such thing!" His hand banged on the table. The contents of his drink splashed on the floor, the ice cubes skittering.

She moved her foot from the puddle of ice and liquor. "Rather than having a tantrum, how about if you explain what you were doing by promising Mauriello that you'd 'deliver' me, that Lulu would soon be gone, and that I would forget about her?"

"You're becoming paranoid."

"No wonder the reporters asked about my 'nervous breakdown.' Is that the new image you're developing, in case I don't go along with your plans? And where's Roberta to develop this new twist on my state of mind?"

"I wondered how long it would take for you to notice that she's up and left."

"The *Titanic* has sailed. Hurrah."

"We're in the midst of a concert tour, for Heaven's sake, and she's defected! Her CNB contract allowed her to stay the week. You did a magnificent job of botching her work."

"Oh, I should have let you hand Lulu to those murderers in order to make Roberta happy?" Nola shook her head. "Don't bother. But I do want an answer to my first question."

He sighed. "When the Chinese agree to do business with an American corporation, they demand that the corporation obtain privileges in the U.S. that the Chinese on their own can't make happen. BurgerRanch didn't simply get their foot in the door here because Chinese people prefer Bao-Ji-La hamburgers to McDonald's, but because a former senator like Mauriello has delivered other perks. To the Chinese, the public hoopla in the U.S. over your tour is more important than great publicity here. It's American public opinion they seek—not their own. That is why so many American news services have been allowed in. When Americans know that those slant-eyes on the other side of the globe share their love for an American star, they are less likely to regard them as alien and an enemy."

"And will be more predisposed to handing them more favors? I'm getting it." Nola seethed with anger. "So it's not my message of friendship that counts? I was giving my Chinese fans my all, but that never mattered to their government?"

"That's the way of big business," he said.

She cringed, then bent to nuzzle Lulu. That made the world recede back to its comfort zone. Wade had still not explained his promises to Mauriello, but his failure to do so had lost its magnitude. He had exhausted her.

Backstage, the screeching of dollies, the off-key sounds of instruments being tuned, the rip of duct tape as cables were rolled and secured, and the fresh aroma of pinewood being cut and hammered had the calming effect of the familiar.

Pushing Lulu's stroller, Nola introduced her to the roadies. She didn't know the many Chinese who swarmed backstage; only a fraction of them wore the black T-shirts with the gold Double Happiness calligraphy. Which of the others were local union representatives, carpenters and electricians—and which were government agents out to get her baby?

"When I'm on stage, you are not to allow anyone to touch Lulu for whatever reason, except me, Leslie or Daniel," she told Yoram. "She goes—I disappear. You let no one get near her—not Wade, not anyone.

The password is 'Mommy.' "

She pushed the stroller back to her dressing room. Teams of stylists, makeup artists and assistants bustled about. Wade was waiting. "Twenty minutes to curtain and you haven't even started to get dressed!" he called out.

"Out!" She pointed to the door. "Get out of my room—and out of my life!"

"Watch your vocal cords—" he began, but Leslie glided in between them. Wade clammed up and left.

In the hush that settled after his departure, Nola eyed the front of the rack. Her first gown was made of pale yellow viscose with a chiffon overlay of the palest orange. It streamed in long, animated strips with tentacles of beads slithering up from the hem to the bodice, where they sparkled over the chest. When Nola had first tried on the dress, her body had giggled with excitement. Now she sought that elation. Soon, the ecstasy would turn into a love affair between her and her audience. It was all so elusive, residing in another sphere.

"Let's do some yoga to get you focused." On the carpet, Leslie folded his legs in a lotus position and tapped on the spot beside him. "Breathe in and out. Breathing is God's gift to us."

"You don't say." But as the assistants tiptoed out, she settled next to him, her legs crossed.

"Say a mantra. Ohooooooom—"

She gave over herself to emptying her head, to psyching herself, to be the best she could be. Ohooooooom—" Fans counted on her, looked forward to basking in her music. She loved each of them. Ohooooooom—"

"Oooo." Lulu grinned at them. "Oooo."

"Breathe in and out," Leslie repeated.

Soon, serenity lifted Nola's spirits. That was it. She couldn't wait for the concert to begin, for the music to sweep her, for the fans to shout her name with love. To hell with their government.

A light knock on the door caused her to open her eyes. The willowy figure of her stage interpreter stood by the door.

The girl with eyes full of adulation was a promising singer from the Beijing Music Conservatory. She had done a fine job at the Forbidden City concert translating Nola's transitional patter as well as the key lyrics. She now held the song list approved by the minister of culture, along with a brief synopsis of Nola's introduction for each song. "I'm ready when you are," she said.

Meeting this Chinese artist was a customary courtesy, but this time

Nola gauged her with a different eye. This singer must enjoy the support of her government to be singled out for such a plum assignment. Her future surely depended upon her acquiescence. What if they had asked her to kidnap Lulu?

From the arena came the steady clapping of an impatient crowd. At the same time, shouts broke through the exposed cinder block walls. Nola tightened her robe around her. "What's that?" she asked the interpreter.

The young woman lowered her gaze to the tips of her shoes.

Just then, Yoram, by the door, muttered into his sleeve. The shouts outside grew louder, rhythmic, chanting, "Ya-Ke-Go-Ho."

"What's going on?" Nola asked, but Yoram, still speaking into his sleeve, strode out.

"Ya-Ke-Go-Ho. Ya-Ke-Go-Ho."

Nola climbed on a chair to peek through the small window. Her dressing room was set against the outside wall of the giant arena, and she was startled to see, cordoned off by police, a mob carrying placards. Most of the protesters were very young—not the mixed-age crowd that had attended her Forbidden City concert. She blinked, once, twice as she recognized the Chinese character of her name, Bashful Fire. At the same time she spotted a sign painted in crude English letters, the words stumbling drunkenly across it.

"Yankee Go Home."

The ramifications of this demonstration spread through her like an ink stain. She jumped down from the chair and yanked out the oversized rollers Leslie kept in her hair until the last moment. "That's it. I've had it with these games!"

She picked up Leslie's cell phone and retrieved Daniel's number. When Daniel answered, she asked, "Nothing here is done without a government directive. What's this protest about?"

"They've bussed in students and incited them with inflammatory comments about your remarks. The leaflets say that you're an actress in the service of the CIA."

She flipped shut the phone. The hostile shouts from outside hit her like hundreds of darts.

Someone must have summoned the minister of culture, for he strode in while Nola was zipping up her pants.

"I'm out of here," Nola told him. "Send your friends my love."

"Ovvvvvv," Lulu said.

The minister bowed. His smile seemed to lie outside his pitted, saucer-like face. "I'm sorry you not feeling well."

Nola felt her eyes zapping fire. "I was feeling perfectly fine until you pulled this garbage on me. Twice." She stepped behind the partition, where she threw away the kimono and pulled on her sweater. But before she finished straightening it, she went back to pick up Lulu off the floor. Sweat dripped down the sides of her cheeks. "Ready, Dumpling?"

Wade squeezed in past Leslie. "I see we have a syndrome here."

"Plea-ease!" Leslie said, gesturing for him to leave.

"Millions of tickets have been sold—and posters, CDs, T-shirts, baseball caps—what have you," Wade told Nola. "You can't quit—"

She frantically gathered toys. "Try me."

From the arena came the sounds of the Chinese anthem. The demonstrators' shouts suddenly stopped. But their echoes, demanding, infuriating, loitered in Nola's head like witnesses to a brawl waiting for the drawing of a knife.

"Please, madam." The minister put his hands together in supplication. "Everything under control. I deeply embarrassed. This not proper hospitality. I assure you unruly people being sent away."

"Are you crushing them with tanks?"

His face reddened. "Please, madam."

"I don't have to be where I'm not wanted."

"Only one thousand demonstrators," he said. There was puzzlement in his voice as though it were self-evident. "But almost a hundred thousand people in our biggest stadium waiting to hear your nightingale voice."

"Oh? A hundred-to-one ratio to make sure I don't forget what you guys can do? Is this your idea of enforcing an agreement?" She sucked in her breath. "I'm sick of all this."

He shook his head. "We've given you best hospitality. Gala parties, best places for concerts—and our prime minister personally sponsored the evening at the opera."

"So what's a bit of hostility to even things out? Keep me in my place, right? Well, guess what?" She pointed at her throat and croaked, "I've just lost my voice. Can't sing."

Chapter 29

"Get Yoram," Nola told one of his men who stood outside her dressing room door. So much for leaving the concert stadium. With so many Chinese officials around, she wasn't about to venture out alone with Lulu.

The baby in her arms was pulling on her hair while Nola craned her neck in anticipation of Yoram's lanky figure. She was startled to see instead Ambassador Ashford. His face was ruddy and his jowls flopped to catch up with the rest of his face as he hurried. No one had told her he would be in Shanghai.

"Can we discuss this in private?" he asked as he neared, glanced at the guards, and ushered her back in, where he motioned everyone to leave. He closed the door and leaned his back against it, but the creaking sound made him ease off. The air came out of his lungs with a whistle. "Let's calm down first, both of us."

She had already decided that she would act more dignified than at their previous meeting, when he must have seen her as a capricious, curl-tossing, foot-stamping, nostril-flaring Scarlett O'Hara.

He waved a finger at her. "I have no idea what you want now. Mauriello has pulled off the agreement. You got the baby. There will be no second chance."

"I don't trust the Chinese to keep their end of the bargain. A demonstration against me? What's this muscle show for?"

Ashford shook his head. "They have their ways of doing things. It doesn't matter. What's important is that you be a good girl and stop causing trouble. Too many people are pissed off at you. There isn't much sympathy you can draw on—"

"I have public opinion on my side," she said calmly. "All over the world. You've said so yourself."

His voice was steely as he said, "If I were you, I'd lower my confidence level a couple of notches. Public opinion is a matter of manipulation—as you should know. It may sway drastically in the other direction once certain facts about your past come out—"

"My past? How dare you?"

"All gloves off in a war you've started." His hand patted the pocket of his jacket as though searching for his pipe. "Didn't you burn your baby sister? And then there was your parents' *accidental* death—was it something to do with a gardening project you were in charge of? The FBI has all the information."

The blood drained from the roots of Nola's hair as a wave of incredulity filled her. To mask her emotions, she bent to place Lulu on the carpet and handed her oversized plastic keys to chomp on. How easy it was to twist the facts. It had been a struggle to forgive herself. The world would be far harsher. She and Wade had long debated opening the subject to public scrutiny, and realized that the questions would never be put to rest, regardless of her explanations. Interrogation would mark every interview. Even the silence-accusing, denouncing—would haunt her with every retelling. She could already imagine the article a *Globe* reporter would pen after speaking with Jenna: "My Big-Star Sis Burned My Face."

So much for staying at the top. This China tour would be her short sojourn to the top rung before dropping off the edge.

"I can't believe that my government is threatening my career," Nola said. "An orchestrated leak of vicious rumors generated by the beacon of democracy? At least the Chinese don't pretend."

From the stadium, the rhythmic clapping of the audience waiting to hear her went on, uninterrupted, patient, as though they understood that a diva was entitled to be delayed. They loved her. They belonged to a different species than the demonstrators. She knew them; she connected with them through her *Tan Tien*. But what if they knew the "truth" about her family's accidents? How quickly they would become her judge, jury and executioner.

"Mauriello's bailed you out," Ashford said. "You can pull yourself out of this mess and get on with the tour even if some aspects are not to your primadonna liking, or you can walk off and leave the baby behind. No one I know will help you. Least of all me, Mauriello, or even Wade."

He turned, yanked at the door handle, and left.

Rage coursed through Nola's veins. Her enemies had her. Her rebellion had come to naught, no more effective than an infant flailing its arms. There was little to gain by refusing to sing, but plenty to lose. She must sing to save Lulu—and herself.

Her fists punched her own thighs. "I've never felt so humiliated," she told Leslie, who had walked in.

"Come with me," he said. Carrying Lulu, he led Nola to the side of the stage behind a curtained panel. "Look."

The crowd was there. Thousands of people were waiting in their seats for her. For her music. The stadium was the largest in which she had ever performed, not as an opening act for another headliner.

She swallowed hard. "You're right," she whispered. "My war is not with the Chinese people—only with their government."

Back in her dressing room, Leslie crouched in front of her and held both her hands. "It won't be as bad as you think. Focus solely on your performance. Psych yourself. And there will be the love of your fans. It's yours alone."

She smiled weakly at him. "Mine. Mine alone. I won't let anyone wrench it away."

The countdown. Excitement, like heady wine, spread throughout Nola's limbs. She put out the flickers of disgust, disappointment, and defeat as soon as they flared up. Not now. From behind the silk partition she scanned everyone's position. Wade, out of her way, was busy at the opposite end of the stage, gesticulating and touching as he talked with the tour producer. A few steps from Nola, Yoram stood beside Leslie, who kept Lulu in her stroller. Behind them, security men fanned out in a semicircle, facing out to guard the rear. They all seemed to be doing their duty for her and Lulu. Daniel was planted fifteen feet away, his body strong and solid. A smile played in his eyes, but his scar seemed to have deepened.

"Got the pacifier?" Nola asked Leslie. She kicked her leg in a *grand battement*. Front, side, back. Then the other leg. "Even if Lulu frets, don't take her away, or I'll walk right off the stage and come looking for her."

Her backup singers clustered like a twittering bunch of teenagers. Dozens of dancers in sequins, fishnet stockings and ostrich feathers pranced about. Readying for the special glitzy numbers, they flexed, stretched, bent and twisted.

The musicians had taken their seats. The huge multilevel set was a masterpiece of ramps and raised platforms bordered with imitations of the Forbidden City marble balustrades. The faux marble, strategically illuminated by moonlike light, glistened in white, as in contrast, section by section, yellow and red beams of light burst upward from the floor.

A set of drums glimmered at the right side of the stage, while to the left Jean-Claude perched on a stool in front of a triple-tiered keyboard, perpendicular to a single-tiered one. On the raised platforms, a full orchestra of musicians had taken their places. They tuned their instruments, sounding like amplified crickets, but the noise charged every cell in Nola's body, readying her once again to become a conduit for the music. She bent her knees, rose on her toes, twisted her hips. Mauriello could broker for her ten more deals, she thought as a flash flood of exaltation filled her, as long as she could continue to sing. She smiled at the sight of the battery of cameramen whose equipment sported the logos of HBO, MTV, CNN and others she didn't recognize. In addition to the tens of thousands of fans in the stadium, millions would see her performing live tonight, and many millions more would watch her later on video. And they would see Lulu.

Nola felt the radiating warmth of another, unfamiliar internal glow. Motherhood. Mommy. Her new password to life.

Roosted on his bridge high above the stage, the light engineer gave her the thumbs-up. Nola's hand swept the dazzling stage and she mouthed, "Magnificent," then smiled at his Chinese assistants. Stone-faced, they stared back.

"Ready?" the stage director asked her.

Still hiding behind the panel, she borrowed his binoculars to scan the aisles and the viewing boxes at the periphery of the stadium. Uniformed Chinese were all over, but far enough away so as not to distract her. To hell with them all. Lulu would be all right. Nola bounced in place. In her head she heard the rumble of her internal engine revving up.

"Go spread your plumage," Leslie said. He had changed to a satin shirt in bright green with its hem above his navel. His upward palm went up and down his chest in a gesture indicating she should take a cleansing breath. She sucked in a giant breath, then slowly let it all out. Time to make love to her audience.

"Prum-pum-pum, prum-pum-pun," Leslie chanted. "Go for it."

"Prum-pum-pum, prum-pum-pun," she snapped her fingers, every muscle taut. In her mind's eye, her body was a NASA rocket ready for launch. The jets of fire whirled under her feet. Ten-nine-eight-a series of blasts in her ears kept in tempo with her *Prum-pum-pums*. Five-four-heat enveloped her, radiated from her. Her fingers kept snapping to the rhythm of the band's opening notes as she hopped in place and her body swung. The roar of the crowd was the ignition she needed. Two-one! She sprinted onto the stage.

Moments later, all else was forgotten. It was only she and these people whose hearts she filled with rapture. The stage was her natural habitat. Moving about, the microphone an organic part of her, her dress sensuous around her back and thighs, she felt like an exotic bird hopping from treetop to treetop in the forest canopy.

The crowd cheered, clapped and rose to its feet when she sang "We All Share The Feeling Of Love." She twisted, twirled, tapped her feet, and flipped her head from side to side.

"We are tall, we are short, we are black or white,
We are blessed or are cursed by fate or birthright.

But if our beliefs are different, our opinions don't mesh,
We still feel the same, on the inside or in flesh.
Because the world over, peace is the color of dove,
And we all share the feeling of love."

Through her ecstasy, she glanced to the right of the stage at Lulu, and the brightness illuminated all corners of her being. Whether or not her parents were watching from above no longer mattered; the bewilderment of the orphan had vanished. Nola's chest broadened. She loved life, she loved her audience, and she loved Lulu.

She rested while the dance troupe dazzled the crowd with its brilliant costumes and its play of limbs, jewels and lights. She took her time changing into a red bodysuit, shiny and smooth as a car hood. The outfit hid as much as it revealed. Over it, Leslie tied a sequined black-lace sleeveless tunic with ankle-long tails. She launched the second act with "Superstitions" to pull the audience back into the rhythm of her performance. She had reached the song's finale when she saw them.

Three soldiers in fatigues conferred with Wade on the far side of the stage, gesticulating. Fatigues? Nola had seen plenty of uniforms this past week, but none right out of a war zone.

Yoram argued with four other Chinese.

The audience's clapping blasted in Nola's head. Her fear reached a new pitch. She signaled to the band to wait a moment longer before breaking into the opening notes of "A String of Magical Moments." The song after this one was "A Day Like Any Other," but both were wrong. She would have loved to sing "Plant My Own Garden," a song about the freedom of the spirit, but it had been banned by the minister of culture. It was now perfectly ironic in a place where soldiers in fatigues intimidated performing artists.

Her hands resting on her hips, she scanned the area to her right again. Daniel, his face somber, had joined Yoram and was talking to the soldiers. Suddenly, the indignation that had seethed in Nola earlier mixed with a new fear. It took possession of her. If these men took Lulu, there was no way she could snatch her back!

As though moving on rollers, Nola glided to the silk partition and unstrapped Lulu from her stroller. As she carried her back to the center of the stage, she motioned to Jean-Claude to wait. His forehead crinkled, questioning, but she would not tell him her choice for the next song. He'd get it soon enough.

At the sight of Lulu in her arms, the applause subsided.

"You must be good now, Lulu," Nola whispered to the baby, who examined her with wise, serious eyes.

"Lululululululululu," Lulu said. Her mouth was near Nola's body mike, and her trill reverberated, bringing a burst of laughter from around the stadium. Startled, Lulu's lips curved downwards, as though ready to cry.

"Quiet, now," Nola whispered, caressing her belly. "Don't cry." Or perhaps her cry would be the perfect accompaniment for this song. Nola indicated to the interpreter to stand next to her. In a solemn voice, she began, "We know that in China there are one hundred and seventeen boys for every one hundred girls. That means that one million or more girls disappear each year. Vanish."

The interpreter stopped translating.

"Go on," Nola said. "I'm quoting official government statistics."

The young woman sent her a beseeching look, then completed the sentence.

"I've visited an orphanage where the death rate is eighty percent. It's called the Dying Rooms," Nola went on. "But many other infants are killed at birth or shortly after. To all these murdered babies, doomed before they had a chance in life, I dedicate this song."

The interpreter's lips trembled, and she shook her head.

"Please. This is important," Nola whispered.

But the young woman bowed and walked off the stage.

A murmur went through the audience.

Nola felt lost for a split second, when Daniel stepped forward.

He stood at the side microphone, and, in a clear voice, repeated her statement in Chinese.

People shifted in their seats. The TV cameramen jostled for new positions.

Without waiting, Nola began to sing. *Grave.* Slowly, solemnly, she directed herself. The sad melody tore out from deep inside her, but the pain suddenly dissolved in a sea of calm.

"There is a place where babies live,
With no hope for tomorrow.
A place where flower babies die,
Filled with only grief and sorrow."

And then she heard the flute. Under the circumstances, she hadn't expected her flutist to join. She turned to nod her thanks, and realized it was not her regular American flutist but one of the locally hired musicians who had trained with Jean-Claude.

"Flower babies bloom unseen,
Flower babies die unloved.
Flower babies, petals plucked, the color's gone

Morning dew has dried before the day's begun."

Her heart strumming with the enormity of the moment, Nola played the visuals for their dramatic impact. The single beam of muted light on her face poured down her upper body, where she held Lulu. With an outer eye she saw her own silhouette against the red glow from behind. The Chinese flutist—brave and unflinching—stood several feet back, awash in a ray of light projecting from below. Daniel remained half-hidden in the dark.

In the red shadows behind her, she heard the soft whisking of a drummer's brush. Another Chinese musician who risked more than she did.

"Would you translate the lyrics?" she asked Daniel while she conducted the flutist, gesturing to him to keep on with his accompaniment. *Grazioso*, gracefully. *Obbligato*.

Daniel stepped into her coin of light. There was not a rustle or cough from the audience. Lulu seemed shocked into silence as her dark eyes observed everything.

"Lost in the cold of the night,
In a place with no heat or light.
Flower babies die unloved
Reach heaven on the wings of doves."

With the flute mellifluently carrying the melody in the background, Daniel spoke the words of the refrain, a bit awkwardly. Before he retreated, Nola handed Lulu to him, then picked up the song where she had left it. She tilted her head upward as though in a prayer. Unencumbered by the concern of frightening Lulu with the volume of her projection, she gave the music her all.

"Flower babies, forever in our hearts you'll glow,
You shine down on a world you'll never know.
Each little dead flower now a star,
Your wails strum the strings of my guitar."

Her voice soared as she sang her *fortissimo* finale. The world would finally hear of the Dying Rooms. The truth about millions of murdered babies would never again be silenced.

She bowed. No more intimidation. No separation from Lulu.

A long hush. Absolute stillness. Her second—and now last—concert in China had just ended, and the rest of her life had begun.

From the bridge where the lighting engineer had stood came a scuffle and angry commands. The klieg lights were killed. The shrieking, flat siren of the microphone, like a patient's heart monitor announcing death, filled the air, then was cut.

A murmur passed through the crowd, now lit by the dim stadium lights. Nola's eyes, no longer blinded by the brilliant stage lights, took in the thousands of solemn, shocked people as they remained seated. Then one pair of hands clapped. It was joined by another, then another. The lonely, scattered applause came from separate areas of the stadium.

In the flash of light that flooded the arena, Nola saw it was women who applauded. Brave, lonely women who must have suffered the coercive loss of a child. They did not stop, even under the exposing glare. A moment later, they were joined by several men, who put their hands together in tentative applause. Within seconds, hundreds of policemen materialized and shoved their way down the aisles and into the audience.

Simultaneously, the squad of soldiers created a half circle behind Nola on stage, and she glimpsed George Mauriello's somber face and Ambassador Ashford's ruby one as they approached. Wade's frantic hand gestured "cut," and his facial features stretched as he urged Nola to get off the stage. Eclipsing it all, Nola was cognizant of the charged bubble in which she and Daniel stood alone with Lulu.

"I'll be forced to leave," he whispered. "Contact Ming-Ji. Tonight. She'll help you get out."

"Da-da-da-" Lulu said, and clutched the lapel of his tuxedo.

He disengaged her little hand, and with his eyes locked into Nola's, brought Lulu's fingers to his lips tenderly. He turned and left.

Nola knew this kiss was meant for her.

PART THREE

The Dragon Lantern

When the boat reaches midstream,
it is too late to stop the leak.
—A Chinese proverb

Chapter 30

Later, when Nola tried to reconstruct the chain of events, they blurred into one another, like a LeRoy Neiman montage chronicling historical occasions, except that the closing of her concert celebrated no obvious triumph. Ashford had relayed the message that the rest of her tour was canceled, and the Shanghai gala party for the local dignitaries, foreign diplomats and American industry giants was called off. She was whisked, with Lulu, into her limousine with six armed Chinese—and no Wade or Leslie—and deposited back at her hotel. From then on, she was under house arrest, although no one quite said that she was.

Uniformed police hovered about, turning each of her bags upside down and inside out, fingering the seams of the clothes, and rifling through her books and magazines. Worst of all, two policemen sandwiched her, their arms touching hers. They moved with her like a double shadow. They refused to let her go to the bathroom unchaperoned. When she sat down on the bed they simply sat beside her, their thighs against hers. To her horror, when she tried to lie down, they stretched out beside her, so she jumped back to her feet. She had to think, but her mind was paralyzed by their nearness.

Wade entered, also squeezed between two uniformed Chinese, who forced a sidelong entry. It would have looked comical, except that nothing could make Nola laugh.

Fury broke out in beads of sweat on Wade's high brow. "Ashford is seeing to it that this farce ends. The Gulfstream is ready for departure as soon as the Chinese give him the green light." He spat out the words. "Are there any more surprises you'd like to pull?"

She managed a saccharine smile. "Just make sure he includes Lulu on the list of those authorized to get on the plane."

He glowered at her and turned to leave, his human bookends moving with him.

"You know I won't leave without her!" she called to his departing back, certain she heard the gnashing of his teeth.

The breath of her jailers was foul. This was a Chinese torture she had never heard of, but she would take it more stoically than Wade did. The thought energized her enough to go about the tasks of changing Lulu's diaper and giving her a bottle while keeping her elbows tight so as not to jab the men's ribs. Being flogged was no longer a ludicrous possibility.

By midnight, Ambassador Ashford had pulled strings and made the men leave her side, her bedroom, and finally, the suite. Nola let out air that had been trapped in her lungs for the past three hours and ran to the bathroom. She must plan. If she waited for the last moment, just before boarding the plane, Chinese soldiers might snatch Lulu out of her arms.

Yoram and one of his men were still in the corridor outside the suite, although a Chinese squad had taken over their guard duty. More soldiers must be swarming through the hotel corridors and lobby. Below, a dozen armored vehicles lined the circular hotel driveway like a set of rotting teeth. She had become an enemy of the state.

The city lights flickered as they stretched away before her. What had happened to the flutist and the drummer who had accompanied her singing? She might never know. Had she done the right thing? An image of the soldiers who had closed in on Lulu during the concert gave her the answer. Men in fatigues didn't just gang up on a baby.

She checked her travel bag, which contained Lulu's things, and squeezed some of her own clothes—khaki pants, a sweatshirt, panties, T-shirts and socks—into its corners. She placed the pouch with cash and her passport in a side pocket. As an afterthought, she added toilet paper, bottled water and personal items, and after a glance around, wrapped Daniel's snuff bottle in tissues and rolled a face towel around it. She was ready to escape. But how? To where? The Chinese had downgraded her assigned penthouse to a suite on a third floor. Had they chosen this room because it was bugged? Goosebumps rose on Nola's skin. The odor of the men who had flanked her sides and the feel of their coarse uniforms against her exposed arms returned. She couldn't risk giving the Chinese an excuse to separate her from Lulu, to jail her, or worse—to shoot them both while escaping.

The only one with any experience in crossing enemy lines was Yoram, but his sole interest was to keep her body and limbs whole.

Daniel's last words echoed in her head. "Contact Ming-Ji." What if the phone were tapped? There was no choice, and Ming-Ji was a pediatrician who could believably be paged for the baby. Nola fished out the business card she had never believed she would use again until after she returned home, when she would send a donation to Ming-Ji's clinic.

An unfamiliar female voice answered the doctor's line and informed Nola, "Doctor go check baby. Come soon."

What did that mean? Nola scanned the driveway outside. The armored cars were still there, and soldiers carrying machine guns paced back and forth.

Only when she sat down on the bed did she realize how exhausted she was. A week of fatigue, emotional upheavals, adrenaline surges, sleepless nights, and the demands of a baby—on top of the usual rigors of touring—had taken their toll. She must sleep or she would get sick. Then there would be no one to save Lulu.

She lay down in the dark, Lulu curled up next to her like a kitten. Lights from passing cars flickered across the walls and furniture as erratic thoughts stumbled through Nola's tired head. She stared at the dark ceiling for so long that it seemed to move away from her, and she was falling, except that she was falling upward, toward infinity. Nauseous, she sat up to see the dark skies tinged with an orangy glaze from the city lights. She willed the morning to come, yet dreading it all the same.

A tug on her toes jolted her awake. With fright she sensed someone in the room. The shadow turned on the bedside lamp. It was Ming-Ji.

Nola bolted upright. "How did you get in? What time is it?"

"Shshsh." Ming-Ji pointed at Lulu. "We don't want to wake her up. If you want to leave China with baby, we must go now."

Nola's hands flew to her chest. She glanced at the bedside clock. Four o'clock. She swung her feet off the bed. "Okay."

"Difficult trip. Rough couple of days."

Nola nodded. Somehow, Ming-Ji had gotten in through the guarded corridors. She'd know how to get her out.

"Do you have money?" Ming-Ji asked. "You need lots."

"Will two thousand dollars be enough?"

A movement at the door leading to the connecting room made her catch her breath. Leslie in his plaid, ankle-length nightshirt glanced suspiciously at Ming-Ji before he recognized her. "Dr. Liang!" he whispered.

Nola's heart skipped a beat. Leslie wouldn't let her leave. This would be the moment he would revert to his old self, entrenched in his artistic visions, of which she was the center.

She kept her voice low. "I'm getting out of here."

His mouth opened as though he were about to say something, then closed.

"Please bring me whatever jewelry and yuans you can lay your hands on," she said, observing him.

"You can't do that." He grabbed her hands. "You're like a declawed kitten; you can't go out alone. You haven't bought a cup of coffee on your own in years." His eyes glistened. "I'm coming with you."

Ming-Ji shook her head. "No place for another person." She turned Lulu onto her stomach. Her hand, holding something, went inside the diaper.

Nola rushed to her. "What are you doing?"

"Suppository. For sleep. Mild."

Nola swallowed. "Just tell me first next time, okay?"

"Like American. Don't trust doctor?" Ming-Ji smiled. "Good mother."

Nola turned to Leslie. "The money and jewelry, please? And a credit card." The expensive pieces were locked in Wade's vault, but Leslie kept her gold watch and several bracelets, rings and earrings in small Ziploc bags in the bottom drawer of his makeup valise, as though they were merely costume baubles.

"Are you going to cross the Tibet mountains on foot?" Leslie asked Ming-Ji.

"Too difficult. Too much time."

Leslie shook his head toward Nola. "I can't let you do this—"

Nola shivered. "Please don't try to stop me for my own protection." Her tone pleading, she said, "Leslie, you'd donate a kidney for me if I needed one. Please let me leave. I have to."

He gazed at her for a moment, his deep-set eyes examining her. Then, with his face raised to the ceiling in a silent prayer, he walked out.

What if he woke up Wade? Nola rushed to the door and put her ear to it. She heard nothing until Leslie returned a moment later and handed her a pouch. He pointed at the bottoms of a pair of her sneakers. The security tags had been removed.

"Thanks," she said, in the absence of better words.

Ming-Ji requested five hundred dollars, and when Nola gave her the bills, Ming-Ji rolled them up and placed them in the pocket of her cotton pants. The doctor's brow and upper lip glistened even though the room was cool. A new swell of adrenaline pumped into Nola's veins. Ming-Ji was risking far more than she was.

Nola gulped down a glass of water, put on a sweatsuit and the sneakers, and gathered her hair under a baseball cap. She grabbed a heavy jacket and a thick baby blanket. Two days? Did Ming-Ji mean two days and one night, or two days and three nights? *Don't think. Just do it. Get out of here.* There was no other way. "Let's go," she whispered. For the second time in forty-eight hours, she had become a fugitive.

Leslie hugged her. With an edge of hysteria in his voice, he said, "Remember to use only disposable chopsticks."

His hug felt foreign. Through his exercise regime and beauty care he had come to know her body, but physical affection between them wasn't in their repertoire. Her life had always been the focus of their universe, while his remained closed to her. Mistress and servant, tied together in a symbiotic existence.

"You're my best friend," she said. "Go back to bed. You've heard nothing, you've seen nothing. Don't get into trouble. We have many years ahead."

Chapter 31

Nola sneaked with Ming-Ji out of the suite kitchenette and along a stark service corridor, surprisingly empty of sentries. With years of Leslie's arduous training, Nola had thought she was strong. But with the heavy travel bag on her shoulder and clutching Lulu to her chest, she realized that covering a great distance would not be simple. She let Ming-Ji carry a second bag of diapers and bottles. Good thing they weren't crossing the Tibet mountains.

A Chinese officer stepped forward from the dark. Nola gave a yelp of fright.

"It's okay," Ming-Ji murmured. Without stopping, she entered a freight elevator that smelled of fried foods. The officer regarded Nola, but his eyes were kind. A moment later, he led them to the huge hotel kitchen, silent and dimly lit. They skulked along the line of pantries against the wall, until they reached a double metal door.

Two peasants in Mao quilted jackets waited behind the garbage dumpster by the hotel's loading dock. The officer coughed into his coned palm, and Ming-Ji handed him the five hundred dollars in rolled bills and bowed deeply. He bowed in response. Before taking his leave, he brought up phlegm and spit. At five hundred dollars a pop, Nola wondered, how long would it be before her money ran out?

The two peasants, who looked like father and son, silently opened the door of an ancient pickup truck. Even in the dark she could see the dented, rusty sides and the caved-in ceiling of the cab. After she climbed in, the younger man settled in the truck bed among some bulbous vegetables Nola couldn't name. His face was glued to the cab's back window, examining her with open curiosity. There was something wild in his eyes, the kind of intensity she had seen in some male fans.

"First thing, we leave Shanghai," Ming-Ji said.

Nola, squeezed between her and the old man, surveyed the deserted alley. "Let's go."

The driver covered his mouth with his hand and giggled, that odd gesture of embarrassment. He adjusted his cap, grasped the gearshift, and, against screeching protests, sent the truck jerking forward.

A yelp escaped Nola's throat as she was thrown out of her seat, barely protecting Lulu's head from banging against the dashboard. To stop her fall, she jammed her hand against the windshield. Pain shot up her wrist. Lulu slept on as Nola pressed herself back onto the bench and searched for a seat belt, but found none. On her right, Ming-Ji fiddled with her glasses, which had slid down her nose, and wiped her brow with a cotton handkerchief. Her stare was fixed straight ahead.

The truck rattled and squeaked its way out of the city. A Mao pendant hanging from the rearview mirror bounced wildly. Two more days—or two more days and two nights, if this night didn't count.

It seemed like an hour before Ming-Ji spoke. "They made Daniel leave. The Chinese government never like him; he's a pest. Not kind of person they want, you know. They like journalists and academics who write about good Chinese government."

Nola turned to check the expanding pink line that marked the end of the inky night behind them. They were heading west.

Ming-Ji went on, "Two officials glued to him. Their method, yes? Can be much worse. They can say he's Chinese—because of ancestors, you know—and put him in jail for life. Better they throw him out." She touched Nola's hand. "He told me to say Chinese proverb: 'One's acquaintances may fill the empire, but one's real friends can be but few.'"

"How true." Nola reflected on the words. "I can't get over how he came on stage to translate the song. Because of me, he'll never be welcomed here again."

"He don't do it for you. He do it for himself. We all do what we do for ourselves. For what make us happy. I help babies not for babies, but because it make me happy to help babies."

Nola smiled. "What an interesting take."

"He ask me to recite you poem he translate from Chinese. The most famous poem by Li T'ai-Po, who live twelve centuries ago. But I don't remember all English words."

"Try," Nola said.

"*A pot of wine among flowers.*
I alone, drinking, without companion….
… I dance, and my shadow shatters and becomes confused.
In my waking moments, we are happily blended."

Ming-Ji paused, collecting the words like butterflies in a net. "This is important," she said.

"*… For a long time I shall be obliged to wander without intention. But we will keep our appointment by the far-off Cloudy River.*"

The portentous words left Nola breathless. Her nerve endings jingled with Daniel's message of promise. "Thank you. It's beautiful," she managed to say. Oh, yesss. They'd keep their appointment by the river. Cloudy or not, she'd be at the Potomac.

The truck grazed a sharp turn, and Nola was thrown into Ming-Ji's lap. In her arms, Lulu stirred, then kicked a leg out from under the blanket.

"It okay; wake up," Nola said. She tickled the little cheek. "Mommy's here."

Ming-Ji rummaged in her satchel and took out two soda-sized cans of baby formula. "I bring this for her. Use them only when we have no milk."

"Thank you. Thank you so much. I couldn't get baby formula even in the Western drugstore. It must cost a fortune on the black market—"

Her words were cut by the sight of an oncoming eight-wheeler that filled the width of the road as a curve was rushing toward them. On the left, a cliff towered. On the right, the gaping blackness could only be a sheer drop. "Watch out!" she yelled as she braced her legs and tightened her arms around Lulu.

The old man hit the brakes and the truck swerved, dipped to the side, and almost turned over before he yanked hard on the steering wheel and, tipping to the other side, got them back on the road. "Hee-hee-hee," he laughed. The eight-wheeler was now behind them. Lulu cried at Nola's sudden squeeze.

"It's all right," Nola cooed. "We're going home." Home. She tried to calm herself with mental images of her Colorado ranch, where in years to come Lulu would learn to ski and ride horses. She would play with Gabby's children.

"Where are we going?" she asked Ming-Ji.

"South. But very far."

"What will happen once we're south?"

"Leave China. Safe for baby."

Nola tried to reconstruct the map of China. To the south, the vast South China Sea opened to the Pacific Ocean.

The driver pulled out a basket from under their bench and, taking his eyes off the road, gestured for Nola to put Lulu in it. The padding in the basket was tattered. She placed Lulu's blanket on it, stifling her apprehension; the basket might be infested with lice, and the stale, hot air must be worse at the bottom of the cab, but at least on the floor Lulu would not risk crashing into the dashboard or flying through the windshield.

She handed Lulu the bottle. "Bottle," she said. "Bottle."

"Boddy," Lulu repeated.

Nola smiled at Ming-Ji with pride. "You're right about her speech."

As the truck chugged on, Nola dozed while her body jerked in concert with the mountainous, rutted roads. Several times, her head hit the ceiling and she woke up.

The morning brought a breathtaking panorama of hills, serene in their undulating, lush green. Rows of tea plants stretched like corduroy as far as the eye could see. But the picture-perfect scenery was marred by unbearable heat. Nothing was as good as it looked, Nola thought, as she took in the view beyond the crushed insects dappling the windshield. She asked Ming-Ji to roll down the window to let in fresh air, but insects that had escaped the fate of their kin flew right in along with the dust that billowed about the car.

"They don't know you are a famous singer," Ming-Ji said.

"Who?" Nola asked.

"The insects. Have no respect for American star."

Nola laughed.

The truck left the hills and descended into a valley slashed by a river. The green of the rice plants shimmered in the pearl-gray water until it was hard to tell where the rice paddies ended and the river began. Terraced fields on the far bank of the river climbed the mountain ridge, dotted by tiny figures in straw hats. Closer to the road, laborers shucked dry corn and bundled it into sheaves. They never looked up from their tasks.

The road cut through a series of industrial towns where huge factories with grime-covered windows ran for long blocks, almost touching one another, as though fighting for a scarce foothold in this vast land. Debris filled the streets. An occasional tree struggled for existence. At the edge of each town, the factories were replaced by multifamily prefabricated housing with thousands of small windows. Beyond them stretched rows of four-story concrete buildings with washed-out fronts and tiny verandas that exposed underbellies of rusted, twisted metal. Like ducks, unkempt children squatted at buildings' entrances or scampered about in trash-filled lots.

Nola thought of Ambassador Ashford's lecture that China managed to feed its people. At the time, she had resented the purpose of his talk. "This country is immense," she remarked to Ming-Ji. "I'm beginning to appreciate the task you face."

Ming-Ji crinkled her nose. "Smell this? Chemical factories. Many cancer."

Nola held her breath, wishing that Lulu, too, could stop breathing for a few minutes.

On the outskirts of one town, a pickup truck like theirs had flipped off the road. It lay belly up, its wheels splayed like the limbs of some roadkill. Next to it crouched family members, crying. Two bodies covered with blood lay in the midst of strewn vegetables.

"Lot of accidents in China. Bad roads, bad drivers," Ming-Ji said, and Nola thought that there but for the grace of God were she and Lulu. And their trip had barely begun.

Ming-Ji said something to the old driver, and he slowed down but did not stop while she viewed the scene. In the wide field beside the accident, men and women, young and old, all in the bluish or gray Mao work clothes, cut sugarcane. They loaded wooden wheelbarrows or handcarts. No one came to check on the victims.

Nola glanced at Ming-Ji.

"Get you and others out more important," Ming-Ji answered her unspoken question. "We stop, and everyone run to see you, then tell police about foreigner. And my friends are waiting in train station."

What others was Ming-Ji saving? Nola glanced at the physician's profile. It was hard to fathom the kind of harsh medical choices this intrepid woman faced every day.

When the sun was high in the sky, the truck stopped at a village with small huts and sparse tiny gardens beside a canal only ten feet wide. Only the glimpse of an occasional lantern or embroidered red curtain hinted at things Chinese.

Nola pressed money on Ming-Ji and the two men, and the three set out to buy food. She stayed in the cab of the pickup, bending down to avoid detection. She perched a coolie hat on top of her baseball cap and peeked at the bare-bottomed children who jumped in and out of wooden dinghies tied to the dock. Ducks and pigs splashed in the mud. Ravens soared, shrieked and dove into a garbage pile. The air was putrid.

Ming-Ji and the men brought back woven steam baskets. They drove out of the village and stopped by a shed made of vine trellises. This late in the season, the vines had lost most of their leaves, except for a few that still clung along with clusters of shrunken grape buds that had never blossomed. Bees buzzed about as the three Chinese, chattering excitedly, laid out a feast of pickled eggplant, salted eggs, sticky cakes stuffed with bean paste, cabbage cooked with scallion, small fried fish with their heads and tails, and hot tea in a large thermos. They shared the screwon cap of the thermos as their collective cup. Nola asked to have her water bottle refilled, but Ming-Ji wouldn't permit her to drink unboiled well water.

The young man kept staring at Nola. Finally, Ming-Ji spoke to him in a harsh tone, and the old man slapped him on the head. Nola lowered her gaze.

Ming-Ji pounded steamed rice into a small ball and gave it to Lulu. "Next couple days maybe you won't find boiled milk," she told Nola. "Feed her everything. Chew meat first."

Where would Ming-Ji be? Nola pushed away her sudden sense of abandonment. "Can she digest it?" she asked.

"Here babies eat everything adults do. Just more mush." Ming-Ji went on to instruct Nola on how to expand the use of the canned formula by diluting it with mashed fruit or pounded noodles.

When they finished their meal, the men belched. Ming-Ji followed. Smiling, Nola joined them.

The three Chinese laughed. "Good food, eh?" Ming-Ji asked. "The men say 'the best.' Usually eat only noodles, not get vegetable dishes like Chinese food in America."

"This was excellent." Nola tapped her own belly. "I never eat so much either." The entire meal, she calculated after Ming-Ji had given her back the change in yuan, had cost only three dollars.

She walked a bit, anticipating having to sit again on the bruises caused by the broken seat springs. A lone, leafless tree stood in the distance, out of place in the grazed field, looking like a lost child waiting in vain for its mother's return. She headed back to Lulu.

Ready to set off again, Nola pointed at the young man as he climbed to the truck bed. "He must be very uncomfortable."

"He guards us." Ming-Ji's hand pointed toward the hills. "Many bandits come down."

"Bandits? As in 'robbers?' "

"They stop cars and rob people, then run hide in mountains."

Nola's stomach tightened. "How can one unarmed man protect us from a sweeping band of outlaws?"

Ming-Ji shrugged. "He got many knives."

The truck bumped along beside a riverbank that occasionally disappeared behind a high levee. The smell in the cab became foul. Three times Nola checked Lulu's diaper but found nothing. Figuring it had to be the old driver's indigestion, she breathed through her mouth. Only when they stopped again at a desolate area, where she and Ming-Ji crouched by the side of the truck, did Nola realize the pungent odor became stronger.

"What's that smell?" she asked.

Ming-Ji giggled. "The farmers collect human excrement. Mix with lime to fertilize fields. It okay until epidemic of a sickness."

Nola stretched her limbs. She was tired, her body ached, and her sticky skin needed a shower. Fleeting images of her moment of glory on the stage at the Forbidden City floated through her mind. Her songs. The excited audience. Her glimmering dress that had opened like a butterfly. The applause. Her life before Lulu. And here she was, breathing air steeped with the stench of excrement, sharing her drinking cup with men whose diseased gums made her gag, fearful of bandits hiding in the mountains, afraid the truck might turn over at the next curve, worried people might detect her and tell the police, and knowing there would not be enough milk for Lulu. Even with all these separate fears, she was more scared of the unknown. Still, instead of feeling diminished, she felt enriched.

She looked into the cab, where Lulu, freed to use the length of the bench to crawl, tried to bring herself to a sitting position. The driver watched her, munching on a foot-long unlit pipe. Standing outside, Nola wanted to steal more minutes of freedom for Lulu's exercise. She put her arm in to prevent her from falling backward and gushed words of encouragement. Too soon, though, an attack of flies with glistening blue bellies sent her and Ming-Ji back inside.

"Do you miss America?" Nola asked Ming-Ji once they resumed their trip.

"Banana split. I miss Baskin Robbins ice cream with cherry syrup and pecans." Ming-Ji brought her bunched fingertips to her lips and kissed them. "The best."

Nola laughed. "I could gobble one down right now."

"I miss husband."

Nola stopped laughing. "You have a husband in the United States?"

Ming-Ji nodded gravely. "Not want to come back for my mother."

"When was the last time you saw him?"

Ming-Ji's glasses misted. "He have new wife."

Oh. "I'm so sorry," Nola said. "It's so sad."

"Love is to want the same things."

"Love is to want the same things," Nola repeated. "You're a brave woman, Ming-Ji. You've left your husband, whom you still miss, to be with your mother."

"And with babies who need me. They need good doctor."

Nola envied her convictions. "Love is to want the same things," she said again. She'd remember that every time the dissolution of her marriage sent her into a state of gloom. *Love is to want the same things.* What a wonderful theme for a song. "I admire you. I'd like to be your friend."

Ming-Ji giggled. "Don't be polite. You *are* my friend."

In the mid afternoon, Lulu whimpered and squirmed, and then her restlessness turned into a demanding, persistent wail. When Nola freed her from the confines of the basket, Lulu kicked and struggled to get out of her hold. Each new introduction of a toy distracted her for only a minute before she became bored and resumed her crying. She threw up, and the sour smell of vomit hung in the cab. Nola would have asked to sit in the truck bed if it hadn't been for the dust, the stench from the fields, the blue-bellied flies, and her fear of being thrown out into the gorge from the violent bouncing as the truck climbed yet another mountain ridge.

She was relieved when they descended again into a valley and drove into a sprawling village that had a train station. The sky had opened in a downpour, and when the truck stopped, Nola put her hands outside the window and gathered the water in her cupped palms. Water had never tasted so good. She splashed it on her face and neck. Again she filled her palms but stopped at the approach of a Chinese man and a woman jointly holding a plastic canopy over their heads. Water streamed down in sheets as they stopped beside the truck to greet them.

"Friends come to say good-bye." Ming-Ji said. "They make travel arrangements."

The two looked alike, a picture of unison that filled Nola with a sudden longing. These were two people who wanted the same things. No one partner diminished the other.

The woman bent into the cabin, stared into Nola's eyes, and said something. They all giggled.

"Husband say you eat grass for such color eyes," Ming-Ji explained, "but wife say you have lanterns in your eyes."

Nola smiled. "What would they say about Daniel's eyes?"

"He have three-dimension face, too." In response to Nola's puzzled expression, Ming-Ji added, "That's what we call Western faces. Not flat like ours, two-dimension."

Nola bade the truck driver and his son good-bye and gave them one of her bracelets. Glad to not have the son's eyes pierce her neck through the cab's back window, she squeezed under the plastic sheet with the couple and Ming-Ji holding Lulu. The Chinese woman produced a large square red kerchief and dropped it over Nola's head and face.

"Now people think you are Chinese bride," Ming-Ji said.

Her view blocked by the cloth that reached down to her shoulders, Nola stumbled on the way to the station, seeing only the rivulets of water under her feet. Sheltered in the building, she heard the rain pounding on the galvanized roof and saw patches of puddles on the cement floor.

Ming-Ji passed Nola's money to the husband-and-wife team. For only a few dollars, they bought tickets, baskets of food, and, at Nola's request, two candles. They paid the female conductor for boiled water, a fresh supply of linens, and for clearing a compartment of its occupants with their straw baskets heaped with produce and live chickens. After Nola was seated with Ming-Ji, they assured her that the conductor would make sure she would not be observed for the next day and a half. Whenever she needed to use the toilet, the woman would carry her chamber pot away.

"Custom. No one allowed to see bride on way to groom's village," Ming-Ji said, and hugged Lulu. "People think she my baby."

Nola thanked the couple with exaggerated head nods. She couldn't help but think about Wade, stretched out in comfort in their private jet. By now, he was no doubt in New York, while she was venturing deeper and deeper into China.

Chapter 32

(1995-1996)

Nola met Eddie Silver at a SoHo party. After talking all evening, the two of them walked the seventy blocks uptown. By the time they said good-bye at Nola's building lobby, the sun was almost up, and she had fallen in love with the bespectacled accountant who had a boyish face, ran marathons, and played the piano.

The next evening, she accompanied him to the opera, and the following Sunday, she drove up with him to visit his parents' in Westchester County. His Jewish family, and its host of aunts, uncles and cousins who gathered on weekends and holidays, was the kind she had spent a life-time pressing her nose against the window to watch. A cousin's birthday was celebrated that afternoon with a table laden with food and drink—and more important, with storytelling and practical jokes. As she and Eddie shared the piano bench to everyone's delight, she dreamed of becoming a part of that inner circle.

The following week, Nola took Eddie to meet Jenna at the group home, but Jenna refused to come out. When, a few days later, Wade sent a lim-ousine to pick Jenna up for Nola's new album release party, she refused to come.

The party took place at a terraced loft overlooking the Hudson River, from where the guests could watch the fireworks' display. Phonomania enticed their other performers to pay tribute to their rising star. Each guest left with a small potted plant and instructions on how to "plant your own garden," Nola's theme for the album.

The next day, before Nola was to leave on her five-week tour, she flew by helicopter to visit Jenna. She found her sister crouched under a tree, and it took her a few moments to realize that her sister was cutting the skin of her arm with nail scissors. Nola struggled to restrain her, but Jenna was strong. She snaked out a clawed fist and scratched her own face. Nola's shouts brought the caretaker to help. Jenna was sent to a psychiatric hospital.

Nola sat on a hard bench at the West Side Synagogue. The dusty leather scent of old books enveloped her as the rabbi instructed the small group in the Jewish tradition of doing good. *Mitzvah*. Share your plenty with others. And when you don't have much—if you have only one coat—give it to someone who has none. The concept appealed to Nola, although she doubted its practical application. Could she give her only coat? Should she have given her last to Jenna? She hadn't. For all her promises, she hadn't sacrificed her career for her sister. She might have begun that career to help the two of them, but when Jenna's problems grew beyond her ability to solve them, she had continued to sail on her own.

Her hand caressed the Bible's embossed antique leather cover as she imagined the many others who had touched it before, who had leafed through the pages in their quest for wisdom. Most members of Eddie's family had not gone through this formal learning; they'd grown up with the knowledge. It had seeped into them through osmosis as they'd observed their traditions.

She wanted so much to fit in with them. The eagerness with which she and Eddie savored the texture of their love was met with less than enthusiasm by the Silvers. In a household that cherished family ties, Nola's orphan status was a drawback. Among people who guarded against impostors, her untraceable Jewish roots were distrusted. In a family whose graduate degrees provided the backdrop for a Nobel Prize laureate, her high-school education stood out like a broken front tooth. And her profession—regardless of her immense success at twenty-five—was the last thing they wanted in a future daughter-in-law.

But she loved Eddie. Edward Silver. The name had music to it. The gleam of morning dew quivering on a leaf, tempting Nola to drink it. His family's subtle disapproval churned in her as a reminder of the girls who wouldn't invite her to their homes. She had hated being different then, and she hated it now.

The rabbi was speaking about one's relationship with the Divine, with fellow human beings, and with oneself. All three were equally important. Together they defined "love," Nola thought. She put her hand on the left side of her chest. Love must reside there, because she could feel its untapped surge pulsating.

When Wade came to pick her up, she was at the synagogue gift counter, buying a crystal clock whose face showed the hours in the Hebrew alphabet.

He wrinkled his nose as he paid. "I hope that's not for me."

"For Keith." She tucked the wrapped gift into her bag, along with her books and notes. Playbill had reported that Phonomania had tripled its list of artists, and she needed to find out where she stood in a pyramid chart Keith Schwartz kept on his wall. "I need to buy more presents. And a printed shirt for Jenna."

She would visit her sister day after tomorrow. Not tomorrow, the Jewish

New Year's Eve, which Nola would spend at the Silvers' synagogue, show-ing off her newly acquired knowledge of the prayers. Afterwards, they would have a holiday dinner at their home. Eat apple with honey, the rabbi had said, to bless the coming year with sweetness.

An hour later, Wade swung the bag containing some of the Silvers' gifts, a gold-leaf picture frame for Eddie's mother, a crystal decanter for Eddie's father, an onyx tiepin for Eddie. "You're spending too much ener-gy on these people."

"No less than you have on Deanna's family."

"They have important contacts—" The ringing of Wade's phone stopped him.

Nola stood in front of Tiffany's, examining a Fabergé egg. The diamonds and semi-precious stones sparkled in the red enamel as she took in the details. For Eddie?

When touring, she would often find Eddie in her hotel bed on Saturday nights, or she would fly to see him on Mondays. She demanded that Wade schedule no travel or media appearances on the Jewish holidays; she was doing well enough to make time for herself. Last year, her fifth record had made the top ten on the pop charts for her first platinum, and DJs kept "scratching" her tracks, pumping up sales. She had won the American Music Award for Favorite Vocalist, and "Plant My Own Garden" won the Grammy's Song of The Year for its lyrics, bringing her up on the stage for the first time. However, Best Female Vocal Performance in Pop still went to another, as did Album of The Year.

A "Damn!" from Wade made her turn from the store window.

His face contorted. "It's Jenna. She's run away."

Nola dropped her bag. "Maybe she's heading here?"

"It's been a week."

The blood drained from her head. "What??"

Wade shook his fist in anger. "I wonder when they would have told us if you hadn't been planning to visit."

Nola collapsed against his chest. "Oh, God! She's never been on her own!"

Wade disengaged her hold and called a detective, a former school-mate, and asked him to meet them within the hour.

Wearing jeans and sneakers, Nola stepped out of the car and sloshed through mud, clutching two supermarket bags. Beside her, Gabby carried a pile of folded blankets. Nola's heart pounded. This could be the day. In just a few minutes she would finally see Jenna. The door to what had once been a farmhouse hung on a single hinge, squeaking in the wind that swept across the open fields. The window frames were gone. Some openings were blocked with cardboard.

"Iowa sure is flat," Gabby said, scanning the horizon.

Nola peeked inside. The interior walls were evidenced only by an occasional two-by-four. A dozen youngsters huddled on mattresses in the back of the hollowed-out space, some smoking. At the sight of her, someone asked, "What d'you want?"

"We've brought food and blankets," she called back. "May we come in?"

There was a gruff "Um-hum." Nola exchanged a glance with Gabby and stepped in. There was no table to lay anything down on. On the one lopsided chair was an empty pizza box filled with crushed beer cans. A puddle on the floor matched the gaping hole in the ceiling.

"You must be cold," Nola said, and put her bags down. "Here are some blankets."

A boy with a fuzz of a mustache reached to accept a blanket.

"Can we talk?" Nola directed her question to the group.

"About what?" asked a girl with vacant eyes. One of her front teeth was broken.

Nola handed her a hamburger. "Oh, about things. Music, maybe?"

The wind got stronger, blowing through the house. Nola zipped up her jacket. The youngsters wrapped themselves in the blankets. After a while, Gabby produced a photograph. "We're looking for my friend's sister. Jenna. Have you seen her?"

"Sure." Her mouth still full, the girl kept chomping on the hamburger. "She went off with some guy with a car. He said he was going to New Orleans."

"She's right there," said the boy with the lip fuzz. "This is the one you mean." He pointed behind him to a girl who was sleeping, curled up against the wall.

The strands of long hair were matted, but there was no mistaking its honey color. Nola's heart leaped. The detective had been right! Jenna was here!

Nola crouched down and touched the thin shoulder. "Jenna?" she asked.

When the figure didn't respond, Nola bent closer, sensing Gabby leaning forward behind her. "Jenna?" She lifted the hair off the side of the face.

The girl turned, her eyes still closed. It wasn't Jenna.

"She's stoned," someone said, and Nola forced herself to stand back up, never taking her eyes off the girl, willing her to be Jenna.

Gabby put her arm around Nola's shoulders.

"I'll be fine," Nola steadied her voice. She should have been in Europe, on her now-cancelled tour. Addressing the vacant-eyed girl, she pointed to the photograph and asked, "Jenna has some scars. Is she the one you saw, who went to New Orleans?"

The girl nodded, her mouth full.

"Give her another burger," the boy interjected, "and she'll tell you she saw Elvis dancing with the Virgin Mary."

But the girl shook her head. "I saw her. I did."

The others ripped through the food bags and began eating. "Are you some kind of social worker?" one asked, "Because if you are, get lost."

"I'm looking for my sister," Nola replied. She searched the girl's face. "Someone may be looking for you, too."

The girl let out a bitter laugh. "Yeah. My Dad's looking for me, all right."

"Maybe he's waiting for your call," Nola said and pointed to her cell phone. "Can I call him for you?"

"Don't!" the girl screamed. "So he can come fuck me?"

"Shut up," one of the boys told her. "Ladies, just leave. Leave us alone."

Gabby took out the car keys and motioned toward the gathering clouds outside. "May I drive anyone to town?"

"There's a church where you could stay. At least it's warm in there," Nola said, scanning the faces in front of her. They were so young, yet disillusioned.

A couple of the youngsters shook their heads. The others didn't bother to respond.

Nola handed a Coke to the boy with the fuzzy lip. "Winter's coming. At the church they'll help you get a job, you know. You can learn things."

He turned his back to her. Dejected, Nola followed Gabby outside.

Only when back in New York with Eddie that night did Nola break down. He held her and when she woke up in the middle of the night, he read her poetry.

Cherry trees were blooming pink in Central Park when Wade took Nola for a walk. He ambled along with his hands clasped behind his back, his head tilted, as he spoke to her. He looked comfortable in his chinos, Izod shirt and leather loafers.

"You've set your career back at least a year, plus you've acquired a reputation for being unreliable since canceling the European tour. Venue owners say they can't count on you. Now we're looking at a new season. I say Europe is lo-oong overdue."

"Sorry," she mumbled. "I know this is difficult for you. But I can't—I won't—leave the States. I must keep looking for her."

"For how long?"

"For as long as I know that she wants me to come and get her." Nola shrugged. "She's testing my love."

"C'mon. It's you she's hiding from. We don't know why, but for that matter, we've never known why she does anything."

The following week, Eddie asked Nola to marry him. She hesitated, sadness and happiness playing within her like two actors on a stage. The Silvers, sympathetic when it came to filial devotion, had placed her scrapbook in their library. They were proud of her. She belonged. "How can I be happy when Jenna is out there, lost and lonely?" Nola pressed against Eddie. "But I love you so much!"

"Well, keep this." He put a three-karat diamond on her finger and bought a new Steinway for his apartment overlooking the East River. Nola kept her place, but rarely went back there. The highs and lows of her life were out of sync. She felt like a pianist reversing hands, playing the bass notes with the right hand. The only new song she wrote was "The Runaway Kid." Keith released it as a single and it quickly went gold.

"Did they do their best, but their best wasn't enough?
Are they searching for you, with their last shred of love?
It may not be ideal, it may not be what you want.
But it is better than this, being under the gun,
Oh, runaway kid, come back, please don't run."

Maybe Jenna, somewhere, would hear it and come back to her.

Chapter 33

The long train ride was a faint reminder of Nola's early years on the road with her band, except that instead of the exhilaration of those times, filled with music and laughter, this trip dragged on for hours of sheer boredom. The sights outside speed-blurred, offering the eyes nothing to land on. Nola lit two candles, explaining to Ming-Ji that it was Friday, and although she rarely practiced this Jewish symbol of welcoming the Sabbath, she felt the urge to recite whatever prayers she remembered. Afterwards, she stared for a long time at the flickering flames.

For the rest of the trip, Ming-Ji studied her medical journals and spoke little. When Lulu slept, Nola stretched in the small space, but was unable to practice her voice. She wished she had brought a book with her; for once, there was enough time to read. The food consisted of sweet potatoes with pieces of pork, cabbage fritters, and the usual pale, sticky pastries. When they were served bowls of noodles in broth, Ming-Ji slurped hers. Feeling playful, Nola joined her in noisily sucking down the soup.

At dusk the next evening, they sneaked off the train and climbed into another rickety truck, almost identical to the one that had smuggled them out of Shanghai. The arid terrain of the high plains, though, was more desolate than the countryside of their first day. Nola almost welcomed the sight of the mammoth factories, with chimneys burping curls of dark smoke that canopied the city. Miles of windowless warehouses rolled on without a green break to soothe the eyes.

They'd been traveling for more than two days and were only moving farther away from civilization. As the truck sped along, the mismatched tires thumped in rhythm. *Cheer up, cheer up, cheer up.*

Nola turned to Ming-Ji. "Will you teach me a Chinese nursery rhyme I can sing to Lulu?"

Ming-Ji had a gentle, clear singing voice, different from her low, authoritative speaking voice. *"Yi er san si wu liu qi, wo de peng-you zai na li? Wo de peng-you zai zhe li."* The musical half-notes of the song were strange and beautiful, monotonous even as they climbed to the higher end of the scale. Nola caught onto the music, but her pronunciation caused Ming-Ji fits of laughter.

"What does the song mean?" Nola asked.

"'One, two, three, four, five, six, seven, where is my friend? My friend is here.'"

My friend is here. Nola held Lulu close, singing her newly acquired song, and Lulu, perhaps familiar with it, rested her head in the crook of Nola's neck. The truck's clanging and clunking became white noise as a burst of happiness radiated through Nola's body. For that instant, she knew what rapture was.

She kept holding Lulu, humming the strange words, savoring the feel of this borrowed love, until half an hour later, as night fell, a series of hills squeezed the road into sharp turns, each threatening to overturn the truck. She placed Lulu back in her basket.

Unlike the ride out of Shanghai, this one took place in the dark, the mountains were higher, and the road more pitted. One headlight beamed too high, the other too low, neither illuminating the road ahead. With each new gaping gorge, the road curved sharply and the truck swerved with such force that its body creaked and tilted, ready to tip over.

This was a roller coaster without the benefit of tracks, Nola thought. Time and again, her breath got trapped in her lungs while her body lurched forward into the windshield or sideways onto the driver or Ming-Ji. Tied in her basket, Lulu shrieked, oblivious to Nola's attempts to coo words of comfort. This was suicide. In the panic that seized Nola, the blood hammered in her ears, and her throat was parched. By the time the truck began a downhill glide on a steep, curving road, she found herself hyperventilating. Ming-Ji suggested she close her eyes, as she herself did. Nola imitated her, powerless against Lulu's cries and the groans of the truck's rusty parts.

Her body was too battered and her spirit too depleted to register at first that the road straightened. A familiar, pleasantly salty odor brought her back to reality.

"I think I smell the ocean." Nola rubbed her sticky arms and licked her dry lips, then mumbled, "I've been exposed to more smells in China than in any other country."

"We almost there," Ming-Ji said, and Nola let go of some tension. She was not relaxed, but the balloon of terror was shrinking. She calmed Lulu with a bottle, and then asked Ming-Ji to roll down the window. She leaned over and filled her lungs with fresh air.

The full moon, huge and radiant, transformed the world to charred black and translucent white. A world of two colors. Like hers. Make it out safely or fail.

The stench of canneries told Nola they had entered a fishing village, where the rising corners of the tiled roofs suggested Chinese architecture. The truck rolled down a silent street until it came to a stop at the docks. Dozens of small ships and boats were moored, and to the far right, fishnets stretched across a field of bamboo poles, all bathed in moonlight.

"We here," Ming-Ji said. She and the driver got out and disappeared in the darkness.

Where was "here?" The only sounds were the lapping of waves at the dock, the creaking of rusted hinges, the soft bumping of boats against each other, and the flapping of loose canvas sails.

Headaches occupied the places behind Nola's eyes, her temples and the base of her skull. She needed to move her legs to get the circulation going again. She kissed the sleeping Lulu, put on her wool-lined jacket, and scrambled down from the truck. Her feet sank into mud. Her arms stretched out like a tightrope walker, she sloshed her way onto a broken piece of wood, conscious of staying within hearing range of Lulu. The rolling mist carried the tartness of seaweed and rotting clams, biting but not unpleasant. Nola filled her lungs, and it soothed her headache some-what.

A jerking of light startled her, but it was next to Ming-Ji, who reap-peared with a man. A lantern dangling from his outstretched arm illumi-nated a path of flat stones, which enabled Nola to find steadier footing.

Ming-Ji told her to leave her bags but to bring Lulu, and they followed the lantern-bearer into a two-story warehouse with rusted galvanized tin sidings. They plodded up a dark, wobbly staircase that smelled of mildew and stopped at a bathroom. The man flipped on the light switch then left, his straw flip-flops slapping the creaking stairs on his way down.

Nola crouched over the hole in a small stall, then walked over to the sink.

"Don't let water in your eyes and mouth," Ming-Ji said. "Your body not immune to bacteria here."

Nola splashed water on the back of her neck and dabbed some on her cheeks and forehead. In spite of the chill, she still felt hot. "What are we doing here?" she whispered, although the building seemed deserted.

"Getting documents."

Back in the stairwell, something swished by Nola's face, then another. She yelped and waved her arms above Ming-Ji's head to scare the bats away. By then Ming-Ji had pushed open a door.

They entered a bare loft that seemed to stretch the entire length of the warehouse. An occasional exposed lightbulb hung from the ceiling. Behind a massive desk sat a uniformed Chinese, his eyes bulging between tired lids, his square shoulders diminished by the huge picture of Mao that hung on the wall. Upon their entry, the man yawned, rubbed the sparse stubble on his flat cheeks, and put on his hardedged hat that bore an emblem above the visor.

Ming-Ji stood in front of his desk and clasped her hands in supplication. She spoke in low tones, her voice pleading. He said something in a belligerent tone, then, with slow, deliberate movements, opened the center desk drawer and ceremoniously brought out a red inkpad and a chop stamp. With the same lumbering deliberation, he took out a few forms from another drawer and handed them to Ming-Ji.

At a chest-high table, Ming-Ji wove quick, tiny strokes into Chinese characters. Once in a while she asked Nola a question—her date of birth, address, health status, names of people in her neighborhood who would vouch for her sincerity and good character. She instructed Nola to sign each page.

All the while the man's bulging eyes were trained on Nola like a frog appraising a fly. His hand stroked his chin as though he were reconsidering the transaction. He rose and examined the sleeping baby in the basket and said something to Ming-Ji in his quarrelsome tone. Nola experienced a moment of panic. Whatever this official was supposed to authorize, he wasn't satisfied—or fooled enough—to do it.

Ming-Ji lowered her head, mumbling something. Again he studied her, Nola and Lulu. Ming-Ji spoke modestly, and, apparently pacified, he pivoted and paced the length of the loft while she completed her paperwork.

She placed the documents on his desk and stood still, her head bowed, until he completed another round, returned to his seat, and rustled through the papers. He weighed each on his palm as though Ming-Ji's writing had added to their weight. Finally, again pondering the importance of the act, he lifted his chop, ground it into the inkpad once, twice, and, puffing his chest, landed the chop with a thud on the top document. He repeated the slow process with each page.

He took an abacus out of another drawer. His fingers flew over the beads. He announced something, then at Ming-Ji's gesture, Nola handed him five hundred dollars.

Each holding a handle of Lulu's basket, Nola and Ming-Ji rushed out.

"What was that about?" Nola asked when they were outside.

"You can't get papers for Lulu in Beijing or Shanghai, but China has many other cities, yes? This place too far for Beijing to supervise, so local officials decide everything. Especially if get money." After a pause, Ming-Ji added, "People adopt in many places."

Nola's heart leaped with joy. "You mean I've adopted Lulu legally?"

"You got official seal. If Beijing government want to, it can revoke. You win trial, but they don't even give you chance for trial. These papers okay for America; legal Chinese documents. Exit visa, too, legal."

Nola looked up at the sky. It was clear and high and dotted with millions of shiny stars. This was the moment she would remember forever, when Lulu legally became her daughter. No champagne toast, only the Milky Way, distinct with its arching clusters of stars. If it weren't for the basket, she would have jumped for sheer joy.

"Thank you," she said, directing the words both to Ming-Ji and to all the powers that had brought her here.

Silhouettes materialized from one of the boats. From another direction came three uniformed men. Beside her, she heard Ming-Ji's quick intake of breath. Nola took a step backward, and again her foot sank in mud. The silhouettes from the boats scattered.

"What's the matter?" Nola whispered.

"Problem."

Nola dared not pull her foot out of the mud as a policeman beamed a flashlight into her and Ming-Ji's faces, then locked it on hers.

Ming-Ji pulled up all four feet, ten inches of herself and spoke quickly. She elbowed Nola, who stood still, the cold mud seeping over the rim of her right sneaker and the light beam piercing straight into her skull. "Money," Ming-Ji told her when Nola seemed too dense to respond.

Should she put her hand in her pocket? The men might think she was about to draw a gun. But when Ming-Ji elbowed her again, Nola pulled out three hundred-dollar bills. Ming-Ji's imperceptible nod told her that was enough. She handed a bill to each man, and they turned and disappeared behind a mess of fishnets.

Ming-Ji helped her back onto the flat stone and sneered in the direction the men had gone. "Corrupt cops. They come, always, ask for money. First one cop, then two, now three cops. Next time four cops come."

"How often do you make this bone-breaking trip?" Nola shook her sneaker and scraped its sides against the stone to remove the mud.

Ming-Ji tucked her hair behind her ears and tied a scarf over her head. She buttoned the top of her cotton jacket, and went on muttering. "This town too far for the law. Like in many Chinese villages, people buy public positions because they get private profits. Capitalism as old as China, but it show in ways the West won't tolerate."

"So much for totalitarian government control except when it comes to one baby."

"I sorry it cost you more money," Ming-Ji added.

"I'm enormously grateful to you for coming up to Shanghai, then making this long trip down here—and for everything else."

"Daniel wanted to save you. Not like what happened to his other wife. You are good woman, even if you are very famous."

His other wife, Kate. What kind of a person had she been? What had she liked and disliked? What was the sound of her laughter? What had Daniel felt when he made love to her?

Fog rolled in from the ocean. Nola guessed the time was about two o'clock in the morning. The fishermen came out of the shadows and handed Ming-Ji a lantern. She directed them to get Nola's bags and gave them a basket with the dim sum, steamed rice, strips of dried fish, and sticky cakes they had bought before leaving the train station. For Lulu, Ming-Ji had bought a banana, litchi fruits and an open tin can with a creamy substance.

"Cheese?" Nola asked.

"No cheese in China. Tofu."

Nola scanned the deserted port, but could see nothing in the thickening fog. The enormity of what was happening hit her again. "What now?"

"My job finished. I say good-bye." Ming-Ji cocked her chin in the direction of the boat. "You go with fishermen."

To be left in the care of strange men? The sky had lowered, and the cloud of fog kept drifting in. The scent of the ocean carried biting memories of Nola's childhood fear of her feet being entangled in a fishing net, of pending doom. "Where am I going?"

Ming-Ji's hand waved toward the water. "First, there an island and jail for political prisoners. Not important prisoners; not ones you read in papers. You can buy some freedoms. Maybe four allowed out in small plane. You take prisoners with you."

"In a plane? Where will we be flying to?"

"Taiwan, then—"

How could she haggle for prisoners—and with whom would she negotiate? Take a boat, then a plane…. Nola felt dizzy with trepidation. This trip was supposed to be over by now, yet it hadn't begun. That night at the apartment, when she had asked Daniel about an escape, he had replied that there was no safe way. She now understood.

"Taiwan? Isn't it still China?" she asked.

"It have democracy with elected president. But he careful to avoid confrontation with China, who claim Taiwan under its rule. President Corwith push democracy for China, but keep quiet about independence for Taiwan that is already democratic. Anyway, from Taiwan you go to Philippines. Daniel say go to embassy in Manila. After that you go to

America." Ming-Ji turned her head toward the water. Her flat, bland face was in the shadows. "You pay four hundred dollars for each prisoner. Expensive. Roll money. You see how many men they release, pay them. Very simple, as they say in America."

Very simple? Nola wanted to cry.

"You've risked so much for me," she said and looked at the inky water where trash floated.

Ming-Ji shrugged and gave her a small packet. "A suppository for Lulu when you get to island."

"She's had so many sleeping drugs—" Nola stopped and smiled. "Sorry. I sound like an American, questioning a doctor's order."

"It's mild. Dangerous to let Lulu cry. No way." Ming-Ji extended her hand. "Good-bye."

"That's it?" This was sheer lunacy. Nola wanted to run, but there was nowhere else to go. She had reached the end of the continent, was about to fall off the edge of the world. Once again, she had become an orphan.

"You be all right," Ming-Ji said. "Tomorrow Philippines."

"Thank you very much, my very good friend." Nola restrained herself from forcing a hug on Ming-Ji. Her hands trembling, she gave her money to cover her expenses for the trip back and rolled four wads into her own pouch. She would buy the lives of four men. Let this ordeal be over.

A new fear slammed in her head. The fishermen could rob her, kill her, and throw her body into the South China Sea, and no one would ever know.

Chapter 34

Somewhere in the fog, but very near, a boat engine coughed and revved. A cloud of smoke steeped with gasoline burned Nola's nostrils. She clutched Lulu's basket and shuffled her feet on the stepping-stones toward the noise until a hand grabbed her elbow. In the dark, Lulu's basket was lifted. A hand guided Nola into the flat, narrow boat that rocked wildly as she searched for a footing between her bags.

Six black cormorants perched on a ten-foot bamboo pole that stretched across the front of the boat, awaiting their masters like family pets. They seemed unaffected by the din of the engine other than occasionally adjusting their grip on the poles. Nola too, curled into herself, one hand tucked inside the sleeping baby's blanket to feel her warmth.

A couple of hours later, when a ribbon of pink showed at the underbelly of the sky, the boat neared the island. The men killed the motor. In the sudden silence, the roar droned on in Nola's head. She hadn't expected the boat ride to be so long, yet it made sense: A jail on an isolated island ought to be too far for prisoners to swim ashore.

The boat bobbed on the surface of the water while the men waited. Both held long-stemmed pipes between their teeth, but did not light them. One of the cormorants dove into the water and brought up a fish. As a ring around its neck prevented it from swallowing, the fisherman removed the fish from the bird's beak and rewarded the bird with tiny pieces it could swallow. Satisfied, the cormorant returned to its hunched position.

The men had their backs toward Nola. When one turned to lift a rope, she smiled, but it was too dark for him to notice. She kept still, attempting to decipher the night sounds for a clue as to what they were waiting for. The sloshing lapping of the waves at the sides of the boat and the caress of the wind on the water, caused small ripples. A gull shrieked, then another. The fog had lifted, and the moon hung low, no longer bright, more like a painting of a pockmarked, flat, whitish disk. Emboldened by the moon's weakness, the stars repeated themselves on the surface of the water. Nola touched the spot where the reflection of lights broke. An image of her father floated by, then vanished, then returned. He had been unable to protect her even when she was a child. He had died at thirty-four. She was now merely three years younger than he had been then, and she missed him. Her stomach tightened with pain.

Time. Flight. Cormorants and sea gulls. The end of the world. She had been sucked up by a cyclone and dropped from the sky into a fishing boat in the South China Sea. Who was she? The woman whose Chinese name, Bashful Fire, had been splashed all over Beijing and Shanghai must have been someone else, someone she barely knew.

Lulu's little moan gave her a partial answer. Lulu's mom. But there was more. Forever she would be that child in her cave by the Long Island Sound. Losses and separations were the material that made her. She could never twist away from that pain. Loss was the most profound human experience. Our greatest feeling we shared wasn't love after all.

A gull's shrill call sounded again. The fishermen put away their pipes. The shore was a distance away, yet they gestured to Nola to get up. She fumbled with Lulu's clothing, reached under the diaper and gently inserted the suppository. She tried to stand up, but her body ached from hours of brutal travel conditions and her mind was hazy from a missed night of sleep. Her stomach cramped. Her legs wobbled with the boat, and she plopped back down, falling sideways as she managed to miss Lulu.

One of the men grabbed her arm to help her up, while his friend stood knee-deep in the water. Only then did she understand that he meant to carry her on his back.

At what point would she regret this hasty trip? Carefully, she lifted Lulu's basket. The man heaved it on his back and looped his arms in its handles. She lowered herself onto the other man's back and straddled him, feeling the strain of his muscles and smelling his unwashed, sour sweat as he trudged through the water to the island.

The fishermen made another trip to bring her things, then motioned her to follow. Her sneakers crunched seashells, then stepped over mounds of seaweed as she plodded up the beach.

Past the stretch of wet, packed sand, her feet felt the scrunch of the coarse dune. She climbed up the rise and lifted her gaze to locate the moon, the last familiar piece of her life. A few remaining stars still struggled to hold onto the night. She had read somewhere that stars twinkled red while receding, and blue when approaching. She located a red one, the star moving away. Wade. Another one, blue, was moving toward her.

"*... we are divided from one another and scattered. For a long time I shall be obliged to wander without intention. But we will keep our appointment by the far-off Cloudy River.*"

Dawn broke on the horizon. The ocean behind Nola was a distant echo when she stopped at the sight of an ancient single-propeller airplane strapped together by leather bands. Even in the context of the surreal recent events, she took in this new menace with disbelief. It was hard to imagine this airplane had flown since the Korean War.

The pilot looked at her with an open curiosity that made Nola recoil. He brought a stepping stool for her to climb up, but she remained frozen. Had the death-defying truck rides been merely a prelude to the real danger? She and Lulu might not come out of this alive.

She touched the surface of the oversized grasshopper, the metal cold, chipped and brittle. The seams that had held her determination and emotions together unraveled. She glanced behind her at the oily pink and orange smear that crawled along the horizon, spilling onto the skin of the water. This was it. There was no return.

Or was there? She sent a last beseeching look at the world—not even one she had ever known—and only then noticed that the scattered boulders to the west were a cluster of buildings with flat roofs washed in the dawn's pink. Tall bamboo poles and barbed wire surrounded a wall with pagoda-like towers on each corner.

Nola's stomach tightened again. If she could only escape this madness. That evening in the apartment, Daniel had asked her if she would have done anything differently. If only he asked her now. She'd click her heels, and she and Toto—Lulu—would be back home, or even back at the hotel in Shanghai. Yet there were no ruby slippers, no witches and no wizard. Only she alone in muddy sneakers with Lulu.

Ming-Ji had paid the fishermen in advance, but Nola gave them one of her rings. She rose to her tiptoes, slid Lulu's basket onto the plane's floor, and climbed in. In the dark cavity, two benches ran along each of the unfinished walls. The ceiling, curved downward, forced her to lean forward as she sat down. Tattered khaki straps served as seat belts, but she had to glide along the bench in search of one with a belt-like buckle. She tucked Lulu's basket next to her duffel bag under the bench, hoping it would protect the baby against the jolts. Lulu slept on.

While waiting, Nola rotated her joints and listened to her growling intestines. The cramps intensified. Her teeth rattled with a sudden shiver. Was this the onset of hysteria? That or something else; she felt sick. She unbuckled her seatbelt and peeked outside. Only one of the fishermen stood there, smoking, while the pilot, carrying a gasoline can, moved about, then adjusted wedges under the wheels. He scratched his crotch as he surveyed the sky. *Let's go!* Nola wanted to call out. She found her vial of Tylenol, and swallowed two tablets with tea from the thermos. She tightened her jacket around her body and stretched out on the bench.

Ten minutes later, she heard noises outside. She bolted up, hitting her head against the low ceiling, as three men in threadbare clothes climbed into the plane. In her basket, Lulu moaned in her sleep.

Nola smiled at the men to let them know she was a friendly stranger. But they lowered their heads and settled on the bench across from her, as immobile as sleeping pelicans. Her prisoners. Her free men, their freedom bought with the proceeds of the Double Happiness tour.

Their body odor in the closed space was pungent. Even in the dim light she could see that they had been beaten. Gashes cut across their faces, on their shaved heads, necks and knuckles. The slashes in their clothes exposed raw skin with parallel slices.

Tears formed in Nola's eyes. Would this have been Daniel's fate had he not been thrown out of the country? Human cruelty was hard to comprehend.

Or, if caught, this could be her fate.

She handed the men Ming-Ji's baskets of food, and they scooped the rice with bare hands, stuffed their mouths, and chewed hungrily on dried fish.

Nola slipped off her seat and scrambled out of the plane. "There are only three men. I want four." She raised four fingers and pointed at the plane. The fisherman shrugged. The pilot shook his head and clucked something. "Four?" She waved four fingers, but he motioned in dismissal for her to get back into the plane.

Inside, she sat near the door, still open, for fresh air. The pilot took his place in the cockpit, but his window remained open. As in an old movie, someone outside gave the propeller a shove, then another. The third hurl kicked the motor to life with a succession of blasts. Lulu woke up with a scream and struggled to free herself from her basket as though fleeing fire. Nola released her and tried to calm her, but her words of comfort drowned in the ear-piercing thunder.

The pilot sat unmoving, his eyes fixed on the prison buildings.

"Let's go," Nola called out, knowing that even if he heard, he didn't understand.

The roar of the engine went on with an occasional cough that made the pilot glance at his instrument board. He stepped out to rummage beneath the plane, and his banging in the belly of the machine, right under Nola, felt as though he was hitting the bottom of her sneakers.

The motor's din reverberated in the tin drum that her head had become. Nola was uncertain which of her fears overwhelmed the others—of unbribed guards initiating a chase and shoot-out, or of flying in a plane that should have been retired when the wooden nickel was removed from circulation. When had the plane last been serviced? The spasm in her stomach urged her to banish all such questions.

Lulu's wail kept up unabated. Nola rocked her and tried to give her the pacifier while the noise hammered in her head. The stench of the men's unwashed bodies, infected gums and untended wounds made the air too thick to breathe. For a split second, she swooned, then came to, disbelieving that she passed out while sitting up.

A uniformed man poked his head in the door. His epaulets glistened in the light behind him. He pushed in a clean, white Styrofoam container with a red top, fastened by twin stainless steel clasps.

"Let's go," Nola called out again.

"Dollar?" The officer extended his hand and rubbed a thumb and a finger. The watch gleaming from under his shirt looked like a gold Rolex.

Nola's brain swam in confusion until she remembered to pay for her fellow passengers. She withdrew three of the four-hundred-dollar rolls from her pocket and handed them to him. The remaining money roll for the fourth prisoner burned her with sorrow.

Throughout the exchange, the ex-prisoners did not raise their heads.

"Go now." The officer gestured frantically with his hand and said, "Go quick. Kidneys get bad."

Nola thought she had misunderstood his English. Her questioning eyes probably told him so.

He pointed toward the cooler. "Kidneys, yeah? Hearts, yeah?" He pointed to his eyes. "Eyes?"

The blood drained from Nola's scalp.

Chapter 35

The prisoners had long ago devoured the rest of the food in the basket. With the closing of the door and the pilot's window, the engine's deafening noise had decreased, or perhaps, her eardrums had been punctured, Nola could no longer tell. The pumping of oxygen to her brain must have been blocked, for slices of time lapsed. Her nodding off wasn't sleep, she realized, but sickness. Even though she hadn't eaten since the previous evening, her intestines heaved with a force that threatened to burst the veins in her temples. Bitter fluids filled her throat, but when she tried to wash them down with tea, her hands trembled so much that she was unable to hold the cup. The shaking of her body was independent of the wild jolts of the plane as it struggled through erratic air pressures.

The men had been afraid to look at her but glanced at the baby. Once Lulu was back in her basket, one of them smiled at her.

Nola was cold, and her teeth rattled. Things disappeared from her view, then returned, like a chopped-up film. Then the film burned, leaving holes. Ming-Ji had warned her about introducing foreign bacteria into her body. It had happened in spite of her caution, Nola realized. It had been in the food or in the water. Another stomach cramp seized her, bore down, stabbing her insides, until she doubled over in agony.

In the two hours that followed, the prisoners took turns playing with Lulu. They made Chinese sounds to which the baby responded with delight. But whatever Nola saw or heard was through a befuddlement of odd sensations. She drowned in warm goo. She swam in a swamp, hacking her way through reeds and undergrowth.

Questions of how long the prisoners had been away from babies became mixed with visions of Wade, who took on the face of her father. For so many years it had been her mother's features that rippled and echoed in her memory, but now Nola looked at her father's young face. She had loved to burrow her index finger in his chest hair…. Suddenly, she was the one on the motorcycle, flying through the air, plunging off that cliff. The breath was knocked out of her, her bones crushed. Who was slicing her intestines with knives? The pilot didn't make money from freeing prisoners; he had been scheduled to transfer body organs! He traveled a regular route, with specific orders. Get me two hearts, three kidneys, a couple of livers, some retinas, too. Patients draped in white sheets waited in operating rooms at the other end. Profit from the living prisoners had been a bonus. No one but Nola bought live people only to set them free. Another plunge off the cliff. The motorcycle's handlebar got jumbled in her guts, spilled her insides. Save the flying organs! White hot scalpel. Ice packs. Once they got her innards, she'd be out of the way, and they'd get Lulu. Another disposable baby. Her organs and Lulu's would fetch a good price. Did Daniel know that someone was trying to kill them?

If only the horrible noise would stop. Nola lifted her head. No one was killed. There were only three Chinese men with ancient, parched skins and toothless mouths. Like the old man had been, except that these men were tanned from hard labor. They had scars, scabs and scratches. But at least they were alive. Her free men. Sam, Max and Zach. Good, solid names she'd named them, to give them life. She wanted to laugh. It was hilarious how she'd tricked the authorities. These three had been sold to her whole, unlike their friends who had been sold piecemeal, one organ at a time.

A huge plunge of the plane jerked Nola back to consciousness and she found herself curled up aft, her head on her travel bag, a blanket smelling of urine and horses covering her. It took her a moment to realize that the box behind her back, preventing her from rolling into the wall, was the cooler with human organs. She remembered being lowered onto the floor a long time ago. Before she swam in a warm swamp. Before all these happenings turned to squatters in her head.

The pain intensified. She wished she could die. No more music, no more fame, no more love. Death would be better than this fire that flamed in her stomach. But what about Lulu? There was nothing she could do for this baby. She had failed her, too. If only Jenna were a friend, a sister who could help. So neither one of them would be alone.

Invisible ropes tightened inside her. There was the blue star, the one moving toward her. Daniel. He was still too far. He had recognized the piece of her that could be teased back to bloom, that could grow from the precocious child she had once been. He had no interest in the world-famous woman whose beauty had been carved by a surgeon's knife. This time he wielded the knife. Grow up. Uncover your other self. The last details were being etched over, not with a delicate artist's brush, but with a machete.

Another air pocket. They plunged, then steadied. The flat, clean cold against her spine. She recoiled, but there was no room to move. The cooler! The air dive that had awakened her seconds before had thrown two of the unbuckled men off the bench, and they had fallen into a heap. One of them folded himself into a tent over Lulu, protecting her with his body. Sam. That was his name. As the other shook himself free, Sam remained on the floor and gestured to Nola to stay put until the strongest turbulence eased.

She slithered on the floor and extended her hand to touch Lulu. "Mommy's here," she whispered, and sank back into her fever.

There was nothing to indicate that the airstrip was in Taiwan. Two small military planes were parked at the edge of the field, but otherwise there was no one in sight. After the plane had landed, an ambulance driver took the cooler and drove away with tires screeching. The pilot supported Nola's head as he made her drink a whole glass of clear, red liquid like diluted beet juice. The bitter, medicinal taste made her gag. There was a terrible stench in the air, like that public toilet in Beijing. And she felt sticky all over. Excrement. It was she! Stinky Nola. And where was Lulu? "Lulu!" The pilot made Nola sip more of the red liquid, and when she shook her head, he pressed on her shoulder blades, until, after her retching, she finished the last drop. He left her lying on the plane's floor, her face toward the open door. The red, bitter drink spilled into the crevices of pain, which began to ebb.

Outside, beyond Nola's field of vision, she heard Lulu's gurgles and babbles and the men's chuckles. Nola tried to get up, but her muscles had turned to jelly. She had no energy even to think.

The pilot returned and helped her get up. There was no one else to trust, and she was too sick to resist. Her own stench was undignified, revolting. The horror of having soiled herself traveled down her spine. With the pilot propping her up, she staggered, and he led her around the hangar to a lean-to that served as an outdoor shower. From outside, she could see a square solar panel atop a water tank and a showerhead contraption. Behind her trailed the three freed prisoners, carrying her luggage and Lulu. Sam, Max and Zach. Her friendly angels.

The outdoor stall doubled as an open storage area, large enough for her to bring in her bag and place Lulu's basket in a dry section. Nola shucked her clothes, rolled them into a ball and placed them in a debris-filled barrel, then turned on the water. Her legs buckled and her head felt light. She pulled over a fruit crate, turned it upside down, and sat on it, letting the water cleanse her.

Her bones jutted out in unexpected places, her muscles felt like mush, and her stomach was concave. And she had thought she couldn't lose any more weight. Leslie and Wade should see her now. No, not Wade.

The sun shone on her as she shampooed her hair and rinsed away the last remains of her previous life. If she'd had scissors, she would have chopped off all that hair, mostly others' tresses woven into hers.

When she was clean, she stripped Lulu, held her on her knees, and bathed her. The feel of their wet skins touching was delicious. "Get a taste of this first class," Nola cooed, proud that in nine days she had become adept at handling the slippery body. "Stick with me, kiddo."

She dried them both with the face towel as best as she could, but remained seated in the stall for a little longer, feeling her strength return. She was grateful for the morning sun on her face and back. She was grateful for the steady ground under her feet. She was grateful to Sam, Max and Zach, who had helped her with Lulu through the tough hours, and who were now guarding her privacy outside. There were many other things she ought to be grateful for—for Daniel, and Leslie, and Ming-Ji, who had given her knowledge, friendship and a passage for freedom, for Beverly, whom she missed so much. But right now she was unable to summon the brainpower to list everything.

Half an hour later, dressed in her khaki pants, a T-shirt and a sweatshirt, Nola lay on the grass under a sycamore tree behind an unkempt hibiscus hedge, while Lulu played. Once, Nola caught sight of two passing mechanics in military uniforms. The pilot returned with one of Lulu's bottles refilled with milk and another glass of the red liquid for Nola. Whatever this concoction was—probably minerals—it flowed through her veins, pumping her body back to life. Nevertheless, shivers still ran through her. She curled up in her heavy jacket.

The prisoners, showered and dressed in clean cotton overalls, dipped chopsticks into the bowl of sticky rice the pilot brought, and Lulu, cradled between Nola's knees, tried scooping it with pudgy fingers in her eagerness to imitate the men's frenzied eating. Nola hoped Ming-Ji was right, that the baby's body was safe from the local germs.

Nola watched the men eat. Even though her stomach still felt tender, she stabbed her chopsticks into the communal rice bowl. It felt good to sit among the men, bound together by the experience of the night. Forever they would share their rebirths. She hoped they would be able to unite with their loved ones.

She pointed at her watch to the pilot and raised her eyes in question. He gestured toward the sky, one way, then the other. Nola failed to understand him. Were they waiting for a change in wind direction? For dusk? For another plane? Only one plane had landed, a military one. The pilot looked at the equipment on top of a tower. Radar? Had their plane flown below the radar detection level? Were they waiting for the flight operators to change shifts?

Sam, stronger and younger looking than the other two, paced around in growing concentric circles. After a while, gathering confidence, he threw his arms in the air and jumped. "Oooooh!" he cried in delight, "Oooooh!" He broke off a stick, threw it as far as he could, and then chased after it, as though disbelieving his right to move at will. When he picked it up, he laughed. "Heeeeee, Heeeeee." The other men teased him, but he kept cackling, running, throwing, like a puppy at play. Nola tossed him Lulu's ball, and he threw it at his friends, enticing them to play, but they giggled and remained seated on their haunches.

Zach, a stooped man with a grizzly face, lowered his jumper top to soak in the sun. His back was criss-crossed with flogging scars in various degrees of healing. The horror of it made the fuzz on Nola's skin rise. Max filled a tin bucket from the storage area with warm water and brought it over. Zach rolled up the bottom of his pants to reveal a blue-and-purple ankle the size of a small tree trunk. He submerged it in the water and, with his back toward the sun, closed his eyes.

Sam returned from his circles and handed Nola a lemon. Twin leaves were still attached to it. She smiled her thanks, brought the fruit to her nose, and smelled. If she weren't still on the run, with one of the men needing hospitalization, and this weren't a military airstrip in Taiwan, the morning would seem like a picnic. She put the lemon under Lulu's nose. "Lemon."

"Mun," Lulu said.

"Lemon," Nola repeated.

"Emun." Lulu stuck out her tongue and licked its surface. Her mouth pursed in a cute scrunch. Nola laughed, squeezed her in delight. She lay still, sensing the fever-fighting, invigorating effects of the red drink in her bones. She looked up as the wind caressed and separated the sycamore leaves.

Nola noticed the figures, and at first thought they were mechanics, but startled, she sat up before the full impact of the knowledge hit her. More soldiers rounded the corner of the building. One minute there was no one but herself and the three ex-prisoners, the next moment there were shouts as the soldiers grabbed Sam, targeting him first.

Nola sprinted to her feet. "Stop it!" she shouted and ran over. The world tilted, and before she knew it, she was splayed on the ground. Hands grabbed her arms and legs, lifting her. As she was carried away she heard Lulu's shriek. Nola tried to look toward the sound, but her head dangled backwards, and her ponytail brushed the dust.

"Put me down," she yelled and kicked. "Put me down!" With her feet gripped, her kicking jerked her joints until she heard them pop. This was a terrible mistake. Had the pilot saved them only to sell them here? Was he collecting on both ends?

She was thrown into the back of a Jeep, and the impact bruised her right knee. Her neck felt as though an ice pick had been inserted in it, and her skin was scraped hot and raw. Lulu was dropped on top of her, and Nola was relieved that her own body had cushioned the fall.

Her pulse leaped in fits and starts. She clutched Lulu. "Mommy's here. Everything will be fine," she whispered, surprised at her ability to fake bravery.

Chapter 36

(1997)

Fifteen months after vanishing, Jenna called Wade at his office from the Port Authority bus terminal. He reached Nola at the studio and she, too, rushed to Forty-second Street and Eighth Avenue.

Nola barely recognized the emaciated seventeen-year old. Jenna's exposed arms and neck were covered with fresh scars Nola guessed were self-inflicted. Jenna's body odor was strong. Nola hugged her and touched the matted hair. Jenna disengaged herself from the hug and glared at her. "I'm so glad you're back," Nola said. "I've missed you so!"

"Bug off," Jenna said. "Don't start with me."

"I'll call a doctor to meet us at home," Wade said quickly. "Let's go."

"No doctor!" Jenna yelled. "No doctor!"

In the limousine, Nola tried to hold Jenna's hand, but Jenna pulled it away and stared out the window. Suddenly she said, "I had a baby. A boy. A beautiful boy."

Nola gulped. "Where is he?"

Jenna shrugged. "I gave him up for adoption."

Cold sweat erupted on Nola's skin.

"Everything'll be okay," Wade told Jenna. "We're glad you're back."

When they entered Eddie's apartment, Nola said to her, "I'll fix you something to eat," but Wade suggested he'd take over the task while Nola drew Jenna a bath.

Jenna's bones protruded everywhere. With the scars from skin grafts on the abdomen, Nola couldn't detect any stretch marks. To her surprise, Jenna leaned back in the tub and let her bathe her. Nola curbed her desire to ask questions and instead worked the lather all over the long, thin body.

There was a knock on the door. Wade handed Nola a tray with a large sandwich and fresh lemonade. He then produced a bottle of LiceCide. "She needs it," he whispered.

In between water sprays as Nola shampooed Jenna's hair three times, Jenna took an occasional bite. They didn't speak, but Nola was euphoric. Except for the baby, whom Wade would surely locate, everything was coming together. She had a loving fiancé and would soon have a family that had already added her birthday to their list of celebrations. Jenna was back, alive. There could now be no question about establishing a home for the two of them—a home they had never had. Nola rinsed Jenna's hair once more, using the hand-held showerhead.

Afterward, Jenna slept for twenty hours.

At breakfast three days later, Jenna was slouching at the table in fresh jeans and a T-shirt, her expression bored. Her magnificent hair was gathered up. The scars on her jaw and the side of her cheek looked like red lint.

"Is there anything you want to do?" Nola asked.

"Where will *he* go?" Jenna's head gestured toward Eddie.

"Go? This is his apartment." Nola swallowed. "But if it's really important to you, I have kept my place. It's not great." She hadn't anticipated that the old hostility would pop up against Eddie. In her mind's eye, she suddenly saw the three of them moving into two adjacent apartments, keeping Jenna and Eddie apart, yet near her. Anything to make it work. She went on, "Once we find your baby, we'll raise him together."

Jenna, with the tone of someone discussing the breakfast menu, replied, "Right. Like I'd ever leave him with you."

Eddie's eyes opened wide. "How can you speak to your sister that way? Do you have any idea how worried she's been?"

Jenna's arm brushed the dishes off the table. Eddie's expensive china shattered on the floor. "She owes me!"

By the week's end, Eddie's reluctance to live with Jenna hardened into an outright refusal. "She's nuts, she's cruel to you, and she's stoned out of her mind."

"She's had an unhappy life. She swore to me she's clean. Give her time. Please. She needs a home and our understanding."

Nola was about to leave for a week in Texas, taking Jenna along, when Eddie called her into the kitchen. He held a garbage bag and pointed to needles sticking out at the sides. He opened the bag and, rummaging with a wooden spoon, found empty vials.

"Jenna belongs in a rehabilitation center, not be loose in New York City with drugs available on every street corner," he said quietly as he tied the flaps of the plastic bag.

"You were looking for it! You wanted to find proof so you could get rid of her!"

"I can't empty my pocket change without it disappearing to feed her drug habit," he said. "She must be checked into a facility—"

Nola could hardly believe they were fighting. "I can't lock her up." She broke into a sob. "I won't put her with strangers ever again."

Eddie took her in his arms. "Sweetheart, this is not how I've envisioned my life—our life. We can't live with a junkie. We'll take care of her. I'll help you. But not here."

Wade agreed with Eddie. Jenna needed rehab. To solve the crisis, he parked Jenna for a week in his apartment, and for the first time, sent Nola and her entourage on tour without him while he kept an eye on Jenna. He was the only person she would listen to.

The week of touring without Wade was fraught with difficulties. His assistants handled the administrative details, going through the motions like soldiers lost without their general. The worst was Leslie with his intransigent opinions. With his theatrical flair, he had already managed to become Nola's fashion advisor, but he continued to push the buttons of the set designer, makeup artist and hair stylist. He was even critical of the chef regarding Nola's nutrition. Everyone around Nola was fighting while she worried about Jenna. Her sister was disturbed, she told herself, but it was the lack of nurturing that had pushed her to drugs. If she could only give Jenna more moments of caring, like that time in the bath, her sister would heal.

And if only Eddie would be patient.

Upon her return home the following week, the choice between him and Jenna was difficult, but clear.

Wade attempted to talk her out of her decision, which he considered an open-and-shut case. "Jenna's too far gone for us to help her. Choose a normal life. You're going places few people ever venture. Eddie is a wonderful asset on this trip."

When Nola wouldn't budge, Wade enlisted Beverly, who took the train in to meet them. Beverly had attended all of Nola's record launch parties and supervised Nola's foundation work for children's services, but now she looked thin and ashen, and her hair had grayed. Menopause, she told Nola, and she was working with an Indian homeopath on regaining her hormonal balance.

"You're swimming in a sea of denial," Beverly said to Nola. "You love Jenna, but the only method proven effective with drug addicts is *tough love*."

"She's had all 'tough' and no love. I promised her a home. It's been nine years—instead of the two I vowed when I signed up with Wade."

"You're twisting things to suit your guilt," Beverly said. "You did try for custody. You spent all your free time visiting her. You did everything to find her when she ran away—"

"If I desert her again, she will never trust me again. I can't—I won't—do that."

She gave Eddie back his ring and let Leslie pack her things.

Leaving Eddie—her hope, his promise, their dreams—brought to the surface the old crushing sense of loss. The loneliness was so all-consuming, the bass strings growling so loud in Nola's head, that her vocal cords hardened.

"I've set up an appointment with a psychotherapist," Wade told her.

"I have that psychiatric nurse for Jenna. *I don't* need a shrink."

"Your heart—and your body—are crying for one. You might as well listen."

Within a week, Nola bought a ten-room apartment in a building with a health club and a swimming pool, and assigned Jenna the task of working with a decorator to make it a home. Under the decorator's guidance, Jenna played with textures and colors. Her room was filled with decorating magazines and fabric swatches. Her vocabulary became one of jewel-colored silks, flowered chintz and damask tassels. She spoke of rugs: Killim, Bukhara and Berber.

At a lunch at Lutéce, Wade said, "Judging by the decorator's bills pouring in, you guys are in full swing."

Nola smiled. "Jenna must have inherited her artistic talent from our mother. She's loving every moment of it. She also writes a lot."

"I still want her out of your hair. We have work to do." He pulled out of his briefcase a list and placed it in front of Nola. "What do you think?"

She stared at a list of names of young male celebrities. For publicity purposes, before Eddie, Wade had arranged the occasional date for Nola through agents of baseball players and heartthrobs. The dates provided mutually beneficial photographs and mentions in gossip columns. Nola had smiled, chatted, posed for the cameras, and even accepted romantic dinners at chic spots, compliments of restaurateurs seeking the attention.

She pushed the list away. "Thanks, but no."

"It will be good for you to get out," he said. "Get back on the horse, so to speak."

"What about Jenna's baby?" Nola asked. "Any leads?"

"There was never any baby."

"What d'you mean?"

He pulled out another folded paper. "Read the doctor's report. Your sister's pulling your chain." There was a sadness in his voice. "She'll destroy you if you give her the chance."

"Whatever the difficulties, I'll prove to her that my love is unconditional," Nola said. "Like the parent she's never had. It's a long, slow and painful process for both of us."

"I'm sure your shrink has told you that the more famous you become, the more Jenna enjoys bringing you down to your knees."

"My shrink is busy analyzing my early childhood," Nola replied in a light tone. No need to report that her therapist, too, had suggested that she was obsessed over a promise she could not have delivered and which had become moot since.

Wade looked at her. "How are you feeling otherwise?"

"I'm miserable over Eddie." Nola's eyes welled up. Years ago, she had learned about the trade-offs, only she had forgotten the lesson. "And I'm writing stupid, unhappy songs."

"Get well and we'll reschedule your European debut," he said, his tone soft. "They're waiting for you. Don't let your fans down."

"If Jenna comes along. Will Deanna join us?"

He shook his head. His eyes clouded over.

"What's the matter? Oh, Wade. I'm so sorry."

"We've drifted apart. Just as I've made it, I've failed. I can't give my wife what she needs from me."

"It's so sad." Nola guessed it was the constant travel. No way to raise babies. She was therefore startled when Wade added, "She's jealous of you."

"Of me? I am 'work!' "

"My only client for nine years. The woman with whom I spend all my waking hours. A woman the world looks up to. She can't walk down the street without seeing your face on the side of a bus, or open a magazine without you jumping out at her with your beauty and charm and accolades for your extraordinary talent. She can't get into a taxi or a store without your voice pouring out at her from the radio."

Nola sat back in the chair, looking at the open face she was so used to but hadn't really seen in a while, the pale blue of the kind eyes so devoted to her that she had long taken it all for granted.

Neither one spoke. The waiter came, removed the dishes, and set down a thimble of sorbet.

A couple of weeks later, Jenna showed Nola a sketch of the living room she planned: it would be decorated in a harem-like tent with thick Oriental carpets and dozens of embroidered pillows in lieu of couches.

The plan stunned Nola. It was a glorified version of their parents' living room, which Jenna couldn't possibly remember. "All my life I wanted to own real furniture," Nola said. "It means chairs and couches people can sit on. Pillows on floors don't count."

"You've told me I'm in charge. You lied, like you always do—"

"Decorating our home means a style that would appeal to both of us," Nola said. "C'mon. You're so creative. Come up with something great that would include furniture."

Jenna threw the plans on the floor and trampled them. "I'm through with it!"

Wade's accountant, who paid the decorator's bills, noticed multiple invoices. Three microwave ovens? Six clock radios?

Nola refused to believe Jenna was converting them into cash until Leslie's friend discovered several of her costumes at a SoHo vintage clothing store. Each gown, costing ten thousand dollars or more, was priced at only a couple of hundred.

Leslie broke the news to Nola. "We'll need to put locks on your closets," he said, and Nola only bit her lip.

She would not let her bodyguard enter the apartment with her because Jenna hated her staff's coming and going. In the foyer, Nola halted at the sound of laughter from the living room, which still had no furniture. Nervous laughter. A man hooting. More voices. It was not the nurse.

She walked into the living room and stopped.

Jenna and three men were half-naked on what seemed like a pile of all the bedding in the apartment. Giggling, Jenna traced a razor along the skin grafts on her stomach while the men laughed and licked her blood.

Frantic, screaming, Nola struggled to grab the razor out of Jenna's hand, cutting herself in the process. Hearing the commotion, her bodyguard entered and threw the men out.

Nola called an ambulance, her psychotherapist, Gabby and Wade.

That evening, dizzy with the finality of it, her slashed palm throbbing under a bandage, she signed the papers, admitting Jenna to an institution that combined psychiatric treatment with drug rehabilitation.

One week later, five months after she had moved out of Eddie's apartment, Nola called him.

"I will always have a corner in my heart for you," he said.

She was certain he was crying on the other end. She clutched the phone, longing to be there with him, to smell his scent, to trace the line of his nose down to his lips, to kiss him. "Please come over," she whispered.

His voice was hoarse when he said, "I'm sorry. I'm getting on with my life."

Chapter 37

Nola raised her head above the uncovered Jeep's tailgate to peek out, careful not to hit her face against the metal as the car bounced on the washboard-like road. The engine exhaust curled out the tailpipe, back onto itself and into her lungs. Lulu's crying tore at her. Her mouth was dusty from the road, and her knee throbbed. Fear of being flogged hammered in her chest. Or, she might get gang-raped.

They drove to a village and jerked to a stop, tires spitting pebbles and dirt. Nola was yanked out and shoved toward a mud hut with barred windows and an insignia above the door. The rotting clams and fish smell told her this was a fishing village like the one she had left back on the Chinese mainland. Chicken clucked about the street. There was no sign of Sam, Max, or Zach.

Be strong, she told herself, but she had barely eaten, and her joints were raw. What if she disappeared? No one would come forward to claim she had arrived at that God forsaken Taiwanese airstrip. This was a scene from a horror movie, except that it was real, and she might not come out of it alive. There was no safety net to stop her freefall.

In her arms, Lulu pitched herself sideways, screaming, her little arms pushing Nola's shoulders away, her feet kicking. Nola held the flailing limbs. Someone shoved her, and she stumbled on the threshold to the police station, but a soldier gripped her elbow. Lulu arched her back and threw her weight backwards and almost slid out of Nola's grasp.

"Shshshsh," Nola cried, her fear mounting. She couldn't handle this. Her illness had weakened every sinew and muscle in her body, and the force of the struggling baby brought her to the breaking point. Any minute, one of the men would find a more efficient way to silence an infant. Nola's eyes darted around the small room with the low ceiling.

A soldier stood by the window, holding up a transistor radio. He tilted it this way and that in search of a clear radio station, but the signal broke into static, a sound like crushed cellophane. A burst of song made him stop turning the dial, and Nola was unprepared for the voice that poured out. Her own "We All Share The Feeling Of Love" crackled.

A short officer stood ramrod straight, his hand poised on the butt of his service revolver. Lulu's struggle had weakened but she kept screaming. "Please stop," Nola begged.

She wiped her face with the back of her one free hand, and wrenched out her ponytail band. She fanned her mane, glad she hadn't cut it, and tapped on her own solar plexus. "Nola. That's me."

Behind her she thought she heard the word "America" spoken with awe. She took in a deep breath. Her stomach and her lungs ached, but she had to convince them she was a celebrity not to be harmed. With Lulu still crying, but not fighting, Nola began to sing along with the radio. Singing for her life.

"We are tall, we are short, we're black or we're white,
We are blessed or are cursed by fate or birthright—"

How pathetic the effort was, how pitiable she must look with tear streaks on her dusty cheeks. At the sound of Nola's voice, Lulu was momentarily shocked into silence. The men laughed in quick gulps of air that sounded like reverse flatulence. The officer slapped his knees and guffawed in a series of hee-haws. More soldiers entered. Their body odor, mixed with the stench of gun oil and cow manure, stuffed the room like cotton. The ceiling fan spun and whined on rusted hinges. Nola's head felt light; the air was too thick for her to sing. But it was now or never. Lulu resumed her crying, but Nola grabbed a breath in a way that would have made Jean-Claude twitch, expanded her diaphragm, and put more force into her song, as she followed the scratchy soundtrack.

In her mind's eye, these were not snickering Taiwanese. They were a part of a crowd, up on their feet, hands swaying in the air, a mass of underwater weeds moving with the current.

"Because the world over peace is the color of dove,
And we all share the feeling of love."

The men stopped their sniggering. Someone brought in a magazine printed on cheap pulp paper and opened it to a spread showing her face and the Bashful Fire character. The article was four pages long and used poorly reproduced photos from *In Style* magazine.

As the men consulted the picture, a policeman pulled a chair toward Nola and she collapsed onto it before ending the second refrain. Lulu's basket was carried in, and someone handed Nola a cup of tea. She sipped it while rocking the basket. Where was that damned pacifier?

The officer asked her to autograph the magazine pages. Then he made a phone call.

It was late at night, and Nola fought sleep. Earlier, two policemen had served her some spicy, watery vegetable soup and a bowl of rice, which she forced herself to eat. They had also given her a tin basin with warm water to wash herself. Local people came in and gazed at her in her cell. They pointed, giggled and clucked. One boy probed her with a long bamboo stick. Hours after nightfall, their curiosity finally satisfied, they left. She lay on her cot, her cheek resting against the silky crown of Lulu's head. In the distance, the ocean was stormy, angry, like a pack of wild dogs. A lightning flash strobed through the small, shutterless window, leaving the air smelling of ozone.

At the slam of a door, Nola peeked through narrowed eyes and the bars of her cell. A man entered. Keeping still, Nola took in the decorated chest, the rimless glasses, the steeled Asian face. There was a snap to his razor-pressed uniform. But it was the hair—not a crew cut but worn long and jelled back—which unsettled her. This man had achieved individuality within the system and the uniform. The idiosyncratic type could also be an egomaniac.

He stopped outside her cell. Two soldiers stood at attention behind him. "I'd like to have a chat," he said in accent-free English, but his exaggerated inflections suggested a James Bond complex.

A siren blared in Nola's head. Her fate was in this man's hands, and hope was as elusive as catching a falling meteor. She rose from her cot, and for a moment, the bare walls swam.

She hesitated before lowering Lulu into the basket—she hated to disturb the baby's sleep—but then carried her out, limping.

"Your name," the man stated, not asked. The expression on his knotted brow was of someone ready to sink an armada.

If she allowed her weakness to show, he'd pounce on it. Without asking for his permission, she took the only chair by the desk. "Nola Sands."

"Are you the famous singer?"

She nodded.

"What were you doing spying here?"

"I was escaping China, not spying." She heard her voice, charged with tears, flip into a bravery she didn't feel. "You've read the papers."

"Looks like you cut a deal with the Chinese. They've sent you here."

"To spy at a godforsaken airstrip? A nuclear plant would be a better destination."

"The airstrip could have been just your first stop."

"I'm traveling with a baby, for Heaven's sake."

"Who's helped you?"

She smiled. "Your English is excellent."

"We have ways to get information out of you," he said.

Her insides rumbled. She touched her throbbing knee; it must be tended to soon.

"How did you get to that airport?" he asked.

The question confused her. "How does anyone get to an airport?"

"Our Coast Guard didn't spot your boat."

Nola swallowed. Who would have believed she had flown in on that ancient plane? Even this man thought she had arrived by sea. "I'd like you to help me get to the Philippines," she said.

"That's out of the question. We'll have to send you back."

"Back?"

"To China. You're their guest, not ours."

Her brain saw colors, not thoughts.

He tapped his pen on the desk. It occurred to Nola that he enjoyed this exchange in the quiet hours of the night. Perhaps he liked showing off his English—and his power—to a celebrity.

Outside, the night air was filled with the honking of geese, croaking of frogs, and trilling of cicadas. The room was hot, and the mud walls smelled of earth. The humidity drenched her clothes. Back to China. To Lulu's certain death. Nola passed her tongue over dry lips. Decisions had been made behind closed doors. This officer was here only to deliver them, not to negotiate them. Back to China.

Her voice pulled from the pool of dread. "I must be quite a trophy."

"We have enough troubles with China."

"The cat bringing the bird for the tiger?" She regarded him. He had been schooled in the States and was probably more than a military man; maybe he had some important foreign-ministry position. If her brain could only break out of its stupefaction, she could think.

She must be quite a sight with her messy hair and dirty clothes. Not the image of dignity and authority. "May I have some fresh tea?" she asked.

He shouted an order over his shoulder, and a moment later the soldier by the door brought a ceramic pot and two cups. The officer poured one for her.

"Thanks," she said. "What school did you go to?"

"I'm the one asking questions here."

The hysteria she was holding in check crept up her throat. Back to China. She must give him instead something to bring to his bosses, an accomplishment to show off.

Her mouth strung disjointed words together as she summoned every iota of her conversations with Daniel and Ming-Ji. "On one hand, Taiwan is fighting the 'One China' concept," she said. "On the other hand, you're willing to ship me back to the mainland as if you're no more than its colony, subject to its whims?"

"This is our problem, not yours." But she thought she saw a flicker in his eyes. Doubt or interest, she couldn't decide.

"Somehow, my baby and I are involved in this too. You'll extradite me, and in one dramatic feat you'll make a mockery of your claims of independence. Worse, you'll raise public outrage in the West at a time you're seeking its support. I can see thousands of my fans picketing in front of the U.S. Congress when it votes on Taiwan-related issues. Can't you?"

He looked at her, spinning his pen like a miniature baton.

She spoke in her lower range. "However, if you get me safely to the Philippines, I propose my silence. I will not reveal my visit here."

"Our reports indicate that even the United States is not enamored of your recent antics."

"I guarantee you that my own government wouldn't want to see me sent back to China. Why don't you check with the White House?"

He shook his head. "I'm sorry, but we can't take chances upsetting our neighbor. You seem to make a poor partner when it comes to agreements with a government. Too fickle for our liking."

"You might appease your one neighbor—albeit a powerful one—and lose the world's sympathy. If Taiwan wants to prove that it condemns human-rights violations, sending this baby to her death is a huge error. You will negate thousands of statements you may yell from the rooftop."

His pen stopped twirling. "You haven't told me how you plan to guarantee your silence."

"I must protect friends who helped me out of China. I can't reveal that my route passed through Taiwan."

He examined her.

"Look," she said. "Taiwan gets out of it clean. I get to go home with my baby. It won't even serve me to inform the State Department of this episode. It's a win-win solution."

He rose to his feet and, to her surprise, offered his hand. "You got a deal. You've never set foot in Taiwan."

She did not take his hand. "What time is it?"

"One thirty. Why?"

"What time can I be in the Philippines?"

"In two hours we can drop you off at one of the Philippines' hundreds of small islands. It will take you some time to get to Manila."

"I need you to bring me safely to the U.S. Embassy in Manila. Door to door."

"I'll see to it." He pointed at her knee. "I'm sorry about this. I hope you heal soon."

"One more thing. The three Chinese men arrested with me. I want them." She thought of the gangrene eating up Zach's leg.

"*Three* Chinese men?"

She gulped. "The men captured at the airport the same time I was. I want them to accompany me to Manila."

The officer consulted with the local commander who sent a soldier out. The soldier returned minutes later.

"There are only two of them," the officer told Nola.

Chapter 38

The bed was the most comfortable one Nola could remember. After four sleepless nights, the dead weight of sound sleep refreshed her, although her rest lasted only as long as Lulu's afternoon nap. The baby now stirred in her crib, let out a sweet moan, and would soon be up.

The windows in the American embassy guest cottage were open, and a soft, warm breeze billowed the printed curtains into the room, carrying a scent of orange. The late-afternoon Manila air was clear, though humid, and the ceiling fan hummed. A lark sang outside, provoking a chorus of other chirps and warbles. Nola lay back and listened to the jumbled, broken-chord music with its varied ranges and tempos. She raised her head to sip the fresh mango and guava juice and to swallow the pills the embassy physician had prescribed, and caught sight of spacious tropical gardens that stretched up to the main building. Drooping elms, clusters of banana trees, and other exotic trees flowering in purple, red and pink dotted the landscape. A forest of eucalyptus trees whose tops sparkled silvery green blocked the horizon.

She placed the juice glass on the bedside table. Daniel's miniature snuff bottle lay where she had unwrapped it. Her feverish memory of the plane ride resurfaced. The symbolism of the art form hadn't been just the caged phoenix, or the power of the dowager queen, but more so the reverse painting, directed from the outside in, the last detail drawn first. It was so clear, Nola was amazed it had eluded her before. Having pictured the final product, Wade had worked backwards. Willingly, delighted at being the one chosen, she had gone along. Wade hadn't deceived her; he had used the terms "product" and "brand image" all along with his vision. But he had failed to predict that one day she might grow to have a will of her own that would not conform to his design.

She held the bottle against her cheek, savoring its cool feel. From the time Daniel had met her, had witnessed the way she interacted with a foreign audience, he had seen right through to that core that needed awakening. "A woman coming into herself," he had remarked after she had embarked on her journey.

Her knee throbbed. She tried to stretch it. Whether the movement was confined by swelling or by the ice pack, she couldn't tell. She'd exercise it soon. Even Leslie would have agreed it was okay to rest for once. She was worried about him, though. "One's acquaintances may fill an empire, but one's real friends can be but few," Daniel's message had said. Leslie had passed the test. Now he was probably back in New York, upset, sleepless, pacing her apartment and rearranging the furniture and knickknacks in his newly acquired feng-shui spirit. He might believe that she or Lulu—or both—were dead. She would call him soon.

What if she knew Jenna's phone number? Forget it. Wherever she was, Jenna had probably shut off the TV at the first mention of her sister's China tour.

Nola sat up. It was pre-dawn on the East Coast of America. Within an hour the trees would blaze with late fall yellows and reds. She imagined Daniel up early, strolling in the woods along the Potomac, stopping at the riverbank to practice Tai Chi. He'd remove his tweed jacket. Were the elbows patched in leather? His arms, legs and sinewy back must be moving in fluid movements, celebrating the rising sun, life, humanity, and perhaps the conquering of his grief and his readiness for a new beginning.

She smiled, no longer fighting her longing for this man who was stable, rooted to one spot, even when traveling across the globe. She was the one who had been lost and found.

In the crib at the far end of the large room, Lulu rolled over. She raised her head, caught sight of Nola, and sent her a toothless smile. "Ta-ta-bi-bi-bi-bu-upup." The willowy Filipina helper tiptoed in and, following the doctor's order to keep Nola in bed, brought Lulu over.

"We've made it out of China safely." Nola ticked each word on Lulu's toes. They were warm and slightly damp with milk-scented perspiration. "The worst is over; the bureaucratic procedures should be easy to handle."

"Add—lala."

"Yup. Time to heal," Nola went on. "Tomorrow, the ambassador will return from wherever. She's a woman. Don't you love that? She'll get you a visa. Anyway, unlike Ashford, she has no political interest in the outcome of your adoption. Right?"

"A—at."

Nola's arms felt heavy; she was weaker than she had imagined. She instructed the Filipina on feeding Lulu, and repeated her stipulation that the baby must remain in her presence at all times. Propped up by a pillow on the carpet, Lulu sucked on her bottle while making little content-ed sounds of pleasure. Nola ignored the flutter of envy at the sight of the helper with Lulu. There would be time; they had the rest of their lives. For now, she must get well for both their sakes. She swallowed two Tylenol tablets and dozed off, in awe of that other sense that had been added to her original five, allowing her to listen to Lulu while floating in the twilight of consciousness.

In the continuous low rumble of repose, she thought of Sam and Max, who had accompanied her in the speedboat until they reached the first Philippine Island. Sam's face and the top of Max's shaved head showed new bruises. Nola had raised three fingers in question about Zach. In response, Sam's eyes became damp. Once on Philippine shores, she gave them most of the money she had left, hoping it would help them connect with their families back in China. They left to melt into the rural landscape.

Nola opened her eyes. Her temples still pounded and her knee throbbed. She was definitely not herself yet. "Can you crawl here?" she called over to Lulu. "Come to Mommy."

"Momm-mom."

She'd remember this moment for the rest of her life. Momm-mom. This was it. The voluminous emotion that filled all of her crowded out the pain and the struggle. It made everything worthwhile.

Lulu threw her almost-empty bottle, pitched her little body toward Nola, and wriggled on her stomach, like a swimmer. But her movements were futile, leading her nowhere.

"Crawl," Nola reminded her. "You can crawl."

"Kaw?" Lulu's lips remained pursed around the word as she brought herself up on all fours, straightening her legs and toes. Her limbs would not coordinate and they tripped her. Undaunted, she tried again, throwing herself forward. Nola urged her on until Lulu tired. The helper picked her up and placed her in Nola's lap.

Nola sang her the Chinese song Ming-Ji had taught her, then chanted, "It's time I wrote a song for you, Dumpling." She bounced her. "Let's sing about going home. Home, home."

"Ommm, Ommm." Lulu grabbed her own toes and brought them into her mouth.

"*East or west, home is best,*" Nola chanted. "*When you reach a fork, you go to New York.*" She laughed and nuzzled her way into Lulu's middle and trumpeted, "East or west, home is best" into the rounded bundle. Lulu yanked at her curls and squealed in delight.

Later, when screens had been pulled across the windows to keep away night insects, and the evening filled with their buzzing and trilling, Nola calculated that it was now morning on the East Coast of the United States.

In her borrowed stroller, Lulu pressed the cloth diaper to her face and closed her eyes. Outside, six-foot torches with open flames lit a paved path flanked by a magnificent display of birds of paradise, ginger and dragon flowers blooming in fiery reds and smelling tangy-sweet. Nola took a shortcut through a fragrant orange orchard and stepped into the press secretary's office through the side door.

The radio was on, and an enthusiastic male voice-over announced ticket sales for *The Lion King*. Two women sat at their desks, keeping to their Washington colleagues' schedules.

"Hi, Sharon," Nola said to the press secretary's assistant whom she had met earlier, a young woman with a bobbed haircut and a long nose that fit her lanky figure. "Thanks for sending over all these toys." Sharon's boss had been less welcoming when Nola had first arrived, as though her presence there were a liability.

Sharon pointed to the radio. "You should hear this."

"What?" Nola cocked her ear to *The Lion King* commercial.

"Big-Mouth Roberta. We get all the American stations. It's morning rush hour in New York. Roberta started her CNB program the day before yesterday, and you are all she's been blabbering about." Sharon laughed. "Thousands of people are e-mailing her or logging on to CNB's site. She's just asked everyone to stop before the website crashes."

The commercial ended, and Roberta's voice boomed.

"She's been missing for four days! Can you believe it? A woman whose face and voice are recognizable the world over, with two governments searching for her, and poof! Vanished into thin air. Now what do you think this means? Is she on a honeymoon with that baby on some snowy mountaintop, an honored guest of the Chinese? Let's call the White House. President Corwith himself sent Nola as our *Friendship* Ambassador. You should have been at that party. I was there. But did Core ask me to dance? No, sir. He had eyes for our gorgeous Nola. And let me tell you, she has grace, our Nola—"

"Whoops! It's ring-ing-ing-ing! May I speak to President Corwith please? This is Roberta Fisher, and I've got ten million listeners—your basic American commuters, your beloved constituency—holding their collective morning breaths. Thank God they are all in the enclosed privacy of their cars, or the ozone layer would be like Swiss cheese."

Nola laughed softly. "She has guts."

"How come the president hasn't issued a statement yet?" Roberta demanded of the White House spokesman. "Isn't he a bit concerned? Nola might be dead!"

"We're sure she's fine—"

"Look. The Los Alamos spying scandal breaks amid a flurry of prior accusations of China stealing military secrets. Kong Ruiji comes here to clinch China's entry into the World Trade Organization. He agrees to all the concessions requested of China—and it costs him oodles at home—but what does America do? We bomb the Chinese Embassy in Belgrade—"

"Ms. Fisher— Roberta—" the spokesman tried to break in, but she gushed on.

"A tragic mistake, but that's not how our Asian friends see it. Anyway, as they get over the shock, Taiwan makes noises about independence. So what do we do? Send our Navy to meddle in what China sees as an internal affair. This fracas is not yet over when we down their plane at their own coast. We proceed to protest their sales of missiles to hostile nations, when China accuses Nola of sticking a dagger into its collective pride." Roberta paused. "And you want to tell me you're sure they didn't *kill* her?"

On the wall, a world map sported three clocks set to Manila, London and Washington, D.C. time. "May I use your phone?" Nola asked Sharon. She must get to Roberta before her hour was up.

She hadn't noticed that the press secretary, Trentafillos, had entered the room, but at the sound of his cough she turned around. She flashed a smile. "Thanks for sending the doctor," she mouthed. In the background, Roberta's voice droned.

Trentafillos motioned toward the phone Nola was holding. "You haven't talked to the ambassador yet." There was an edge in his voice, an accusation.

"I will. Just as soon as she's back," Nola replied sweetly. "I expect to be on a plane by tomorrow afternoon."

"It would be wise if you checked with her before you called anyone."

The word "wise" pushed Nola's button. "Why? Are my whereabouts a national secret?" she asked. There was no longer a need for hiding, and calling Roberta would be her smoke signal to Leslie and Daniel.

"That's not it." He shook his head, but his eyes remained fixed on Nola. "I wasn't going to mention it—it's the ambassador's place to discuss this with you—but your being here puts us in, uh, a bit of a pickle. Politically. We need to strategize—Uh—"

Nola shot him a sharp glance and, with the receiver in her hand, rifled through the nearest Rolodex. "Hold on," she told the operator who had come on. Her fingers stopped at CNB. "Please connect me to this number." As she read it aloud, her gaze was hooked onto Trentafillos'.

"Miss Sands—" he began again.

"Please make sure the line is not disconnected 'by mistake.'" Her voice was steel. She clutched the phone.

Trentafillos exited, while Sharon kept busy aligning stacked documents at right angles. Within moments Nola was connected to Roberta's studio.

"News flash!" Roberta announced over the airwaves, and Nola turned down the dial on the radio to cut the echo. "We have Nola on the line! She's alive! She's back from the end of the earth! I can't believe it! Hallelujah! Nola! My Ginger Goddess! Is that really you? How are you?"

"I'm fine. Happy to hear your voice again." Her Ginger Goddess indeed. Nola could smell Roberta's sweat, rising with excitement over a good story.

"Now, guys, you heard it here first. On CNB's *Big Mouth's Morning Hour*! Didn't I promise I'd deliver the goods? Nola! Where are you? Have you heard the callers? We've all been praying for Lulu and you. Right, everybody? Honk your horns if you, too, are happy to hear this wonderful news. Honk. Honk! Guys, I'm listening up here on the twelfth floor at West Fifty-Seventh Street in Manhattan and I don't hear enough honking. Honk! That's it. Nola, can you hear all this honking?"

Nola chuckled. "I'm not that near."

"Where have you been? Where are you now? How is our precious little baby?"

"I've played Marco Polo. Like you say, I almost stepped over the edge of the earth, but I'm all right now. Lulu's well, too. Please tell all your listeners how much we appreciate their concern, support and prayers."

"You're telling them yourself. Thank the master of the universe!" Roberta hollered. "We all love you. I love you. My bosom buddy, my sister. Tell us about Lulu. Such an adorable little thing."

"She's a wonderful baby. At seven months, she's already beginning to speak. This past week, she learned a few English words."

"A genius! And that's the baby the Chinese wanted to kill?"

"That's all behind us now."

"Fabulous. Superb. Really. Now, Nola, everyone is talking about your 'Flower Babies' song. When can we expect it in the stores?"

"As soon as things are settled, I'm sure." She hoped that Phonomania's new management would release a single instead of an album that would take months to produce. "It's a great song, and I can't wait to share it with you all."

"HBO got the footage of your famous Shanghai concert but won't share it. And the Chinese confiscated all the other videos. There's a black market for copies of it. A listener has sent one, but our lawyers have put the *kibosh* on playing it."

"If I knew how to upload and distribute a song over the Internet, I would have done so," Nola said. But perhaps giving the song away was not the best option for raising awareness of the crimes committed against babies in China. After all, Elton John hadn't given away his adapted "Candle in the Wind." He had sold it to raise millions for Princess Di's causes.

Nola passed her hand over her abdomen muscles. They felt slack. She needed another day or two to recuperate. "Would you like me to sing it now?" she asked.

"What a fabulous idea!"

For a split second Nola regretted her impetuousness. The crackling phone lines would not do the song justice. And that flutist and drummer had added a wonderful touch. Behind her, she heard Sharon instruct the operator to hold all calls and keep the line open. Standing next to a shredding machine bin filled with the discards of a workday, Nola held the phone receiver like a microphone and let the song happen. Wherever they were, Jean-Claude was having another fit and Wade was counting on his gloved fingers all the copyrights she was risking.

When she was done, she thanked the listeners with all the warmth she felt. "Bye. I love you all."

Trentafillos re-entered. There was a scowl on his forehead. "I'll drive you back to your cottage," he said. "If you have any special requests, we'll try to honor them. Please page me." That belligerent tone again, regardless of the content.

"Isn't there a deputy ambassador?" Nola asked.

"He's away on an assignment."

"What if there's a diplomatic crisis? Who issues visas around here?"

"We have staff for routine processing."

"Well, then, can you issue a visa for Lulu? What am I waiting here for?"

"I assume you're not her official legal guardian."

"Actually, I've adopted her," she said, regretting that she might not be able to keep the location of Ming-Ji's operation secret.

"Is that so? Can you prove it?"

She took the rolled documents out of a plastic bag. "They're in Chinese."

"That's all right."

He glanced at them and was about to place them in a folder, when Nola said, "I'm sorry. I must hold on to them. You may make a copy or review them in my presence."

He handed them back to her. "Regardless, I'm afraid you'll have to wait until the ambassador's return."

She forced her tone a couple of notches below his. "I need to make another phone call."

"I'd rather you waited—" He coned his palm and coughed into it.

Heat filled Nola's head. "Am I missing something? Am I under house arrest?"

"Of course not." He coughed again.

"Would you please leave the room?" She reached for the phone, doubting the line was secure from his eavesdropping. "It's private."

After he left, Sharon lingered a moment, sending glances at the door. "I've compiled a report for the ambassador," she whispered. "These past four days you have become the single most beloved Westerner in China—in spite of the Chinese government's propaganda against you. Your music has become so big, Beijing has given up on trying to block it. It recognizes that it has been losing credibility with its people by depicting you as a CIA spy. The people saw with their own eyes, heard with their own ears."

"Cool. Thanks for telling me," Nola said.

"I'm your fan, and I believe in what you've done. About Lulu, I mean, and the song." Sharon's lips curved up in a shy smile and she glided out.

Nola asked the operator to locate Daniel Chen's number in D.C. and connect her.

He picked up on the first ring. "I thought you'd be out doing your Tai Chi," she said.

"Not till I heard from you."

"Have you been listening to Big Mouth?"

"Yes." He laughed softly. "I was so relieved to hear you're all right. Are you?"

"A bit rattled." In her mind's eye once again, she saw Daniel standing, brave and solid, in the coin of light on the stage. "How was your trip out of China?" she asked.

"That will have to wait for another time."

"I want to tell you where I am, but not how I got here," she said. "That, too, will have to wait for a more opportune moment."

"Looks like there's a lot we want to say that must wait."

"Yes," she whispered. She felt tingling in the hand clutching the phone and excitement spreading down her spine. "I'm at the embassy in Manila. And as if getting here has been easy, I may run into a snag of sorts. I wanted you to know where I am, just in case…." The notion that she was unsafe at an American embassy was preposterous. "Stay tuned."

"I'm sorry. You must have been through a lot," he said. "Come home."

Come home. For a while, the silence that stretched over the thousands of miles was alive.

"My pearl," he finally said.

She wouldn't bring up "China doll." She was certain he no longer thought of her in those terms. "Until very recently I was a phoenix in a reverse painting," she whispered.

Again that soft laughter that wrapped around her. "Now you're a pearl, formed in the soft tissues of an oyster, hardened by the roughness of the sand."

There was so much promise in his voice, that Nola felt her soul lying bare before him, his fingerprints all over it. She could count the places on her body he would touch.

Chapter 39

On Nola's second day at the embassy, Trentafillos told her, "Madame Ambassador has been detained on important business and won't return until tomorrow."

Perhaps it was a good sign that her escape from China had ceased to be headline news, Nola decided. It was no longer a pressing issue to hasten the ambassador's return. She'd have a rare vacation day, a break before facing whatever awaited her. And she could use unpressured time with Lulu. There was nothing like filling her baby's tireless, sponge-like mind with new discoveries.

Nola emptied her duffel bag to take inventory of her few clothes. None was appropriate for a hot day of leisure. She removed the batik tablecloth and tied it around her hips like a sarong and pranced toward the mirror. Imagining Daniel's response to the style made a coquettish, delicious shiver run through her. After that climactic plunge on stage, they were now connected in a life-changing experience, in a pledge that was still shaping itself as it gathered force across the thousands of miles separating them.

She turned on the radio, and with Lulu in her arms, twirled around the room. "Do you like dancing? Here's a song for you."

"Yoo," Lulu said.

Nola tilted her head from right to left and to the right again. *"Look at me, here,/ Look at me, there,/ Look me right in my eyes,/ And nod your head from side to side."* She kissed the baby and waltzed some more.

She went on practicing her voice and scribbling new lyrics. There was a career she would soon return to—and a mission more worthwhile than any she had ever tackled. With Lulu as the symbol, she would use their popularity to help millions of babies. She smiled to herself, jotting down new ideas. Wade had been right to say that passion fed her creativity, but he had never imagined that the fire would come more from her being someone's mother rather than someone's lover.

In the early afternoon, the day was bright and balmy, and the leaves on the trees sparkled green as though a troop of elves had polished them all morning. Nola sat cross-legged on a blanket spread on the lawn, Lulu nested between her knees. Nola banged a rhythm on the plastic piano, hid toys in a bowl, and imitated the birds. She invented more games, thinking with pride that this baby's intellect would challenge her in years to come. Playing with Lulu made her laugh and laugh; it carried no shadows of her anxious hours with Jenna years ago. If anyone had told her how accomplished she would feel teaching musical notes to a single baby instead of singing to millions of people across the globe, she wouldn't have believed it. Yet, these past eleven days, she had been taking delight in small, private activities as she hadn't done since her childhood magical hours in her cave on the Sound.

At the chugging sound of an approaching golf cart, Nola turned her head and did a double-take. George Mauriello brought the cart to a halt at the cottage porch and, with a light step, dismounted.

Nola gathered the edges of her sarong and remained seated as he stepped toward her. "What are you doing here?" she asked. Her mouth was suddenly dry, and her brain clicked through the improbable chain of communications that had revealed her whereabouts to him.

"I was in the neighborhood." He laughed, hitched up the knees of his white cotton pants, and gracefully folded his long legs as he settled down on her blanket. Nola had never seen him in anything but a tuxedo or a dark Italian-cut suit, but now he wore no socks with his woven-raffia loafers. His pink Polo shirt exposed tanned athlete's arms.

He tickled Lulu. "Coochie-coochie-coo."

Lulu's face lit like a lantern. "Oochie," she replied.

He raised an eyebrow. "She's awfully young to be talking."

Nola brought Lulu closer, wanting to tell her not to smile at Mauriello. Suddenly, she felt less like a guest at the embassy than like a hostage.

Mauriello leaned back on his elbows, crossed his ankles, and his gaze shifted to the drooping elm that towered nearby. The lines of Mauriello's jaw were more defined than was typical for someone his age, but for that matter, there was no slack on this man.

"I just wanted to verify that you're okay," he finally said.

"Nice of you to care. I guess you came here to facilitate the paperwork." She drew out the words, weighing them. "All I need is a U.S. visa for Lulu."

He broke off a blade of grass and began to probe his teeth.

Nola caught her breath. In and out. Take it easy. "Is there a problem?"

He tossed the grass away and straightened up, his elbows resting on his knees. "Coochie-coochie-coo." He tickled Lulu's exposed toes. "Coochie-coochie."

Through the light blanket, the coarse grass irritated Nola's skin. "Can you tell me what this visit is about?"

"You understand, of course, that you've kidnapped this baby?"

"I did no such thing."

"I stand corrected. You left China with this child without obtaining official permission from her legal guardian."

Nola sprang to her feet and scooped up Lulu. "Is this a tribunal to determine the legality of my adoption?"

He patted the blanket in the spot she had vacated.

"Hear me out. We have the same interests in this."

"You'd better get to the point, then." She remained standing. His quick glance toward her thigh told her that the sarong had shifted, but she made no effort to readjust it. Let him get an eyeful of her half-a-billion dollar body.

"My, my. Haven't we become gutsy."

She turned to leave.

"Miss Sands. If you want to play with the big boys, you'd better get used to hearing what the big boys have to say."

"Well, then, do not talk to me like I'm a little girl."

"Touché." His laugh was throaty and warm, and she felt hatred climb in her throat. He went on, "I'm sorry; I didn't mean to offend you."

"Why don't you start by explaining your deals with the Chinese?" she asked. "I know that BurgerRanch hasn't simply gotten its foot in the door in China because the Chinese preferred Bao-Ji-La hamburgers to McDonald's, but because BRW Entertainment has offered more. A lot more. Even if you promised to deliver favorable PR in the U.S., that doesn't explain why you, of all people, represent the Chinese government, here, now."

He regarded her. She could almost hear the gears clicking in his head as he readjusted his perception of her. "You know those pandas I was going to ship back with this baby? If you had trusted that I'd take care of things and not provoked your hosts with that cockamamie song of yours—" When her face remained immobile, he continued, "There was some problem with the toy version of the pandas. We've produced millions in China, but Congress would not allow us to import those fuzzies to the States. All kinds of regulations and tariffs. After some negotiations, I managed to smooth the way, so to speak."

She stared at him. "You take me for a complete idiot."

"Aha!" He raised a finger in the air. "Not an idiot, but naïve in the ways of big business."

The sun had become hot. Nola was out of the shade, and she was too weak to remain standing for long with Lulu in her arms. "I can't imagine you'd be speaking to Kong Ruiji like this."

"Are you comparing yourself to the prime minister of China?"

"You seem to be mediating between us." She looked at him. "I'll say it for the last time. You've come to see me. You want me to hear you out."

"Very well." He smiled. "You see, there were some bleeding-heart lib-erals in Congress who objected to the way these toy pandas were manu-factured, saying it was against the World Trade Organization's regula-tions. Some nonsense about forced labor in Chinese prisons. When we procured U.S. import concessions and tax breaks for these furry crea-tures, we broke down the barrier for similar deals. This agreement is a landmark in relieving the Chinese of certain practices."

As he spoke, she put Lulu on the grass and propped the little back against her shins. "The 'we' being the royal you?" Nola asked.

"Your humble servant."

"I assume that the real live pandas became part of this package so the Chinese would score brownie points in the U.S. in case some human-rights group makes noises about the forced labor camps where the toy pandas were made," she said.

He smiled his assent.

"As a former senator, how can you justify using prisoners to manufac-ture goods?" she asked.

"Labor camps are operated by the Chinese military, which also hap-pens to own most of the industry in China. It's not for me—nor the U.S.—to tell a foreign nation how to manage its army, nor how to pay for its maintenance and growth. For that matter, I don't think they would listen. Would we?" He went on. "BRW is developing the stuffed animals as cartoon characters, Wei and Mei, to be sold at all our outlets—the restaurants, movie theaters and theme parks. There's a huge profit in owning beloved premium characters; it will pay hefty dividends for gen-erations to come. Our StarVision studios are working on a Wei- and Mei-animated video and TV series that will replace *Teletubbies, Dora* and *Clifford.* That's the beauty of synergy. We create a new entity—the char-acters—and, by cross-marketing, tie together all our venues into some-thing bigger than all its parts."

"Synergy. I get it. Soon I'll be asked to do a voice-over for one of these cute pandas—if not record songs for the movie soundtrack," she said.

"You wouldn't want us to ask another performer, would you?"

"As Confucius says: 'Cut to the chase.' Where do I—and Lulu—fit in?"

He plucked another blade of grass, and stroked the palm of his other hand. "In the U.S. and Europe, BRW has cornered the market on fami-lies and all their fun activities—movies, theme parks, music, TV shows, low-cost meals. We're poised to become bigger than Disney, and it's cru-cial that we break into the largest market on the globe. The toy panda deal is only half of a BRW's two-pronged campaign to help Chinese interests in the U.S. The other is to achieve a more favorable view of China in Congress and the White House. Suffice it to say that the idea of selecting you as the U.S. friendship ambassador did not germinate in Corwith's head, as he—or you—wishes to believe."

"It was your idea?" The unfolding truth made her break out in sweat. "Are you saying that I didn't 'replace' Madonna? That she had never been asked?"

Mauriello laughed. "It was Kong Ruiji's brilliant appraisal of the weight our Administration would give this gesture. They are so pathetically eager to see signs of Middle Kingdom's openness, they pounced on it."

"What a cynical view of our government and what it is trying to do in this part of the world. I wish some of your Senate friends could hear this."

He rattled one of the toys, and Lulu grabbed it and placed it in her mouth. "Among Sony, Disney and BRW, someone was going to pull it off big-time. Luckily, with the purchase of Phonomania Records, we picked the right fortune cookie. Synergy packaging at its best."

Packaging. She had been packaged one more time. The Double Happiness tour had been accompanied by the most fanfare, hurling her to the top. It hadn't been her voice or her songs after all, but the corporation. She had come along as its star. Being chosen to represent the U.S. in China was the peak of everyone's success but hers.

The perspiration on her exposed skin was sticky. In the silence, she heard the discordant screams of jays. A crow came peeling down from the skies and dove into the thick of the elm, raising shrieks of alarm from its inhabitants.

"You still haven't explained why you're here," she said.

"You and I had a deal, my dear. And you, as they say, fucked it up."

She scoured her brain to remember whether she had agreed to anything else in their meeting at the airport. "What deal?"

"Wade has made commitments on your behalf. This tour was making millions—and more is to come from the sale of CDs and pay-per-view specials. No one expected problems from you; you have a good compliance record. 'Works hard and plays well with others.' When you cut loose, it was not just the loss of profits." He stopped and looked her in the eyes. "You destroyed my credibility with the Chinese. You mocked my ability to deliver. You made my deal-making a big fat joke."

She made a show of searching the folds of her sarong. "I'd give you a quarter so you can call someone who cares." She kneeled by Lulu and gathered up her things. "I guess that sums it up, then."

"Wade assured us he was getting you back in line. He had seen to it that the baby vanished, except that she hadn't—"

Still on her knees, Nola stopped, as the words dropped like hail all around her. God. Wade—not the Chinese government—had kidnapped Lulu! The proximity of the Dying Rooms to the American Embassy in Beijing had made it easy to drop her there.

Nola controlled the shaking that choked her windpipe. "Why do you tell me this?"

Mauriello got up before she did. He towered over her, but extended his hand to help her up. "Wade failed. That's why I'm here."

She ignored his hand and rose to her feet, holding Lulu in the crook of her arm. "And you need me to salvage your reputation? Do you think I'd give up my baby for you?"

That warm, carefree laughter returned. "Relax about the baby. I have a compromise you'll like. And I can take care of my reputation myself. But if you help the Chinese save face, we can salvage this mammoth, make-it-or-break-it stacked deal with China, in which BRW stands to gain—or lose forever—a foothold in this colossal market." He stretched his arms to flex his muscles. "And don't get high and mighty on me. Success—even yours—translates into dollars, and you should be grateful the Chinese are still listening to me and did not pursue a request to extradite this baby. Not yet."

She thought of Sharon's report. The Chinese government was stuck, which gave Mauriello his last card. If Beijing ignored its people's love of her, or simply let time pass, Mauriello had nothing left. To keep his power, he must not let the episode die; he must keep her star status in China.

"Are you saying that in case of such a Chinese request, the White House would extradite Lulu unless you intercede?"

"Why are you insisting on bringing everything to a head? Quiet negotiations are far more effective—"

"In this case, let me ask you: Would you have BRW *quietly* sponsor the opening of a decent orphanage in each Chinese city in which you do business?"

He laughed. "You don't get it, do you?"

She turned her back to him, and, walking toward her cottage, said over her shoulder, "I doubt I can help you. Thanks for your visit."

"You're welcome. You are an important member of our family."

"Lulu is all the family I need." Then she added, "I'm sorry I'll miss New Year with you in Morocco. It sounded like such a great party."

He walked toward her. "I've come here with an offer, and I'd like you to listen and give it serious thought."

"Aren't you tired of this?" With Lulu straddled on her hip, Nola kept her other hand on the door handle. "Whatever your offer is, it can't possibly mesh with my plans. And just so you know, I'm planning to say a lot more about infanticide in China."

He sighed. "When the insects take over the world, I hope they'll remember with gratitude how I took them along on all my picnics." He smiled benevolently. "Only a quote."

She stared at him. In her arms, Lulu kicked as she strained to turn to look at Mauriello.

"Well, then," he went on. "Not only will no visa be issued for Lulu, but, as they say, your career is not entirely in your hands. You forget that even if you own your music masters, you don't own the rights to their recordings, and BRW has exclusive licensing to distribute your CDs. Oh, I'm forgetting about all the promotion dollars we allocate to stores and radio stations—as they say, those, too, are purely optional—"

"As they say," she repeated, "go to hell."

She watched the clock, and at eight in the evening she pushed Lulu's stroller into the press office.

Sharon turned away from a filing cabinet. "If you had called, I'd have picked you up in a golf cart," she said.

"My knee is better." Nola motioned with her chin toward the radio. Roberta was on, ranting about an earthquake in Turkey and about Hillary's performance as a New York Senator.

"Has Roberta mentioned our chat?" Nola asked.

"Not yet."

Nola tilted her head toward the radio, as though she could nudge things along. But her reappearance had already become old news; Roberta and her listeners assumed the ordeal was over. Or perhaps, true to Roberta's real-life indifference to Lulu's fate, the on-air chat had given her an hour of entertainment before the topic had run its useful course.

Nola tapped her fingers. There was little time, and until she connected with another media host who could pick up the story immediately, she must throw Roberta a curve to stir up her interest. In the end, all that counted were the ratings, and they both understood this.

"I'd like to call her again," Nola said. "Would you please have the switchboard connect me to CNB?"

Sharon's foot traced the grout in between the ceramic floor tiles.

"This is not Nazi Germany," Nola said softly. "We do what our con-science dictates."

She was on the line to Roberta again within minutes.

"My Ginger Goddess! How are you doing?" Big Mouth asked. "Do you have any idea how many requests we've received for 'Flower Babies' downloads?"

Nola spoke quickly. "I need your help. I am stuck at the embassy in Manila—in the Philippines—"

"God Almighty. And we thought you were on our shores! Listeners, are you there?"

Nola rushed on, fearing a giant hand would reach down from the sky and yank the telephone cord out of its socket. "It looks like someone in the State Department is trying to deny Lulu an entry visa into the United States—"

"Wow," Roberta said. "Wow."

"I'm hearing talk of her *extradition*. I'm afraid for Lulu's safety if we stay here much longer."

"You've called the right place. We're going to check directly with the White House—"

"She's entitled to political asylum," Nola added quickly.

"While I'm dialing," Roberta called out, "I need everybody's show of support. No, don't honk your horns, please. The police had a collective *plotz* yesterday. Instead, just fart and open your car windows. I want your protest to stink to high heaven."

Nola laughed. "No train and subway passengers are allowed to participate in this protest."

"You heard what our delicate national heroine tells you. Oh, here we are, the White House is on the line. Hello? Mr. President?"

It took a minute for the White House spokesman to promise that the president himself would look into the matter.

"Looking into it isn't enough," Roberta told him. "We want action. Now. By the time we go off the air in forty-five minutes, I and my ten million listeners want to hear it confirmed that Lulu has a *kosher* visa and she and Nola are being escorted safely to a direct flight to New York. JFK airport. Not a funny farm someplace, *Capeesh*? You need more time to go over legalities? I'll give you one. Lulu, this gorgeous baby, a genius who will one day find the cure for cancer, is being singled out for torture and murder—isn't that your legal definition of political prosecution? Well, she's seeking shelter in the United States of America, land of the free and home of the brave. Right, listeners?

"Now, to show our government how serious we are, let's make sure Corwith hears our wishes directly from his constituency. Listeners, are you there, my friends? Mr. President, can you show us what you can do for one baby? Okay, the White House's fax number is two-zero-two, five-five-five—"

Chapter 40

(1997)

Nola flew by helicopter to see Jenna. After a two-year rehabilitation, her sister was living in the converted mansion, at the group home run by a devoted couple hand-picked by Nola. No more city temptations for Jenna. Having dropped out of school in her freshman year, at twenty she was being tutored for her high-school equivalency tests.

As Nola's helicopter landed, bittersweet taste climbed in Nola's mouth. The void left by her family's demise was filled with nostalgia for the loveliness of the place.

The fall air was unusually warm, an Indian summer day, like a guest who had said his good-byes, then changed his mind and returned. The wooden stairs going down to the beach had been rebuilt so the young residents of the house could make the sand, sea and sun a part of their growing-up experience. Nola asked Jenna to join her, and Jenna, her face sour, relented.

The cave was no more. The overhang had been eroded by winds and collapsed into rubble. Only an indentation remained in the cliff. Nola sat down on the sand, hugging her knees. There was no other girl on the Connecticut side. There was no one like her in the entire world. Then as now, at twenty-eight, she was anchorless, with nothing to hold on to but herself and her music. Friends came and went and so did loves. The only constant figure in Nola's life, still the adult in their relationship, was Wade. Their careers and music occupied the same place in their respective universes. Their shared victories bound them with an invisible rubber band that stretched enough to allow each to move about their personal affairs, only to snap back and bring them together.

Jenna removed her sneakers and socks and dug her toes in the sand. She had pretty, tapered feet and long legs, like their mother's. Her high forehead, voluminous hair, and smooth jawline reminded Nola so much of their mother and her wasted beauty that it hurt. Jenna collected driftwood, and then, one by one, hurled the pieces against the rock, splintering them. Nola watched from the corner of her eye. She would have tossed the sticks toward the water, imagining where they would float.

Her sister had yet to congratulate her for her last Grammy's award. "How do you like your tutor?" Nola asked.

Jenna smashed another piece of wood. "I've written a play."

"That's great! May I see it?" Nola inched closer, but restrained herself from touching Jenna. Her sister hated physical contact.

"We're going to produce it at the high school."

"I'm so proud of you. I remember how inventive you were as a toddler. We wrote plays and performed them for Mom and Dad. Do you remember? Later, when you were only ten, you improved on plots and characters in novels." Nola laughed. "I'm sure you'll do great as a playwright."

"Yeah." Jenna uncoiled her limbs in one graceful movement and stood up, looking down at Nola with contempt. "Only if I get away from you."

Nola scrambled to her feet. She was six inches shorter than her baby sister. "What do you mean?"

"I hate being in your shadow. You're always controlling me."

"Jenna, I love you. It's not control; I'm eight years older. Without our parents around, wasn't it natural that I'd take care of you?—"

"You're such a selfish bitch. What do you mean, 'I'm so proud of you?' Who are you to patronize me? The big celebrity helicoptering down to the masses?"

"Jenna, please. You're taking it the wrong way."

"Here we go again. The Chosen One has spoken. I'm always wrong and you're right."

"Sorry. Jenna, I'm really sorry. I don't know when and how I hurt you. Now that we're both adults we should find a way to have a beautiful sisterhood—"

"Bullshit. You're so full of your own hot air, you make me puke." Jenna broke into a run. "I'm moving far away," she yelled over her shoulder. She galloped up the steps two at a time. "And don't you dare come looking for me."

Nola stood at the bottom of the stairs, the breeze blowing her hair onto her wet cheeks.

She had meant to discuss Jenna with Beverly, to ask her to intervene, maybe suggest that they seek joint counseling. Anything to get through Jenna's anger and stop her from disappearing again. But when Nola arrived at Beverly's home, she was shocked at the weakened, emaciated look of the formerly plump, vivacious woman. Beverly's gray hair had been chopped close to the scalp.

God. Oh, my God. Trembling with knowledge, Nola followed Beverly into the living room. "You're very sick," she finally managed to say. "Why didn't you tell me?"

"My leukemia has returned." Beverly let out a hoarse chuckle, then doubled over with a cough. Nola brought water from the kitchen and tapped on Beverly's back until the woman caught her breath.

"Returned? Why didn't you tell me?"

Exhausted, Beverly whispered, "For six years, those little terrorists have been blowing up bombs in my blood. They're winning."

Nola began to weep. She sat next to Beverly on the couch and they held each other as both cried. Beverly's bones were tiny, like a bird's, and she smelled sour, as if her flesh already lay underground. "I was thinking of buying an island in the Caribbean," Nola wept. "You'd have your own cabin."

Beverly smiled, and her exposed gums seemed large. She patted Nola's hand. "Do it anyway."

After a while, answering Nola's unasked questions, Beverly volunteered, "The first time it happened, I didn't want to divert your attention from your work. What would you have done, drop everything and sit with me at the hospital?" She waved away Nola's protest that she would have done just that, and went on, "These past couple of years I've been seeking non-traditional cures in India and Mexico. Nothing's worked. I've come home to die."

Later at the bar in a small SoHo bistro, Nola told Wade, "I'm losing two of the three most important people in my life." She had been crying all afternoon and evening. "The only time I could've reciprocated for everything Beverly had done for me, she went elsewhere for help. Couldn't she see that she deprived me of something important I could carry with me?" Nola sniffled. "And where did I fail with Jenna? I've had twenty years to make her love me. Instead she hates my guts."

Wade nudged the glass of brandy he had ordered for her. "Beverly is one thing. It is very sad. You'll take time off to be with her in the coming weeks. But Jenna? Maybe at some point, you should have started to expect something in return."

Nola took a sip. The liquid burned its way down, diverting the pain to a new center.

Wade went on, "I've always imagined that if I had a sibling, we'd be friends. It would be a give-and-take, learning over a lifetime to respond to the other's needs." He shrugged. "With Jenna, you've always given, never expecting it as your right to receive even words of thanks."

"She doesn't feel gratitude. She's empty inside."

"I rest my case." He picked up a napkin from a small pile and dabbed Nola's cheeks. "She's not empty. She's full of rage over things you couldn't have controlled then, and that are not yours to change now. Plus, it looks like she's inherited your mother's emotional illness."

"Jenna was sent out of the house because of an accident for which I was responsible."

"You weren't responsible. No sane adult would put a ten-year-old in charge of a sick baby who can't breathe. Don't torture yourself. You've been through this with your shrink." His tone was tender. "We've also established that your mother didn't function. A disaster was bound to happen."

"I'll never have kids."

He dabbed her eyes again.

She smiled through the tears. "How many times these past twelve years have you done this?"

"And I'll continue, for as long as you let me." To her surprise, he leaned forward, and his lips touched hers. The contact was so light that she would have missed it had she not seen his eyes twinkle.

Her hand jumped to the bottom of her throat. "Oh, my God," she said.

"Yes. Oh, my God." He put his hand on his own chest and grinned, his face still close to hers.

Nola's pulse thumped in her ears. She looked at him, at the shoulders in the printed golf shirt, at the fine fuzz on his exposed arms, at the contour of his lips. Questions buzzed in her head, but the pressure at the bottom of her stomach gave her the answer.

"What's next?" she murmured, seeing the whole picture. Yet another trade-off-all of Wade when she was losing the other two. "Where do we go from here?"

"It's up to you." His voice was hoarse, but his second kiss as light as the first. "It's been up to you for a while."

Her head jerked up. "You've been waiting all this time?" In her head she went over the dozens of futile dates he had arranged for her, all the short-lived relationships he had witnessed her trying on for size in the three years since Eddie.

"Only since my divorce. You were too young before then." He threw a couple of bills on the counter and helped her off the stool. "Let's leave."

She was unsure whether she could stand up, but she did. In the street, she laced her fingers through his and let new sensations settle into place, like a mosaic of her life that was finally completed.

Her two bodyguards flanked them.

Nola's shoulder touched Wade's, and she squeezed closer, watching herself from a distance. She was so sure that she needed to look no further that it frightened her. She glanced at the bodyguards. "Let's go to my apartment. We'll talk."

In the store window to her right, her face reflected back at her against a cloth with gold threads and tiny mirrors embroidered into it, sparkling in her own eyes and on her forehead. "I need to know the parameters. What if we ruin everything?"

"We won't."

"You're right," she said. It all fell into place. Right there, on the corner of Spring and Mercer, she was home. She put her arms around his neck and kissed him full on the lips. She didn't let go for a very long time.

Chapter 41

The voyage was over in more ways than one. At New York's JFK airport, Nola glimpsed Wade outside the open plane door at the off-limit jetway and her skin tightened into a shield. Since Mauriello's confirmation of Wade's conspiracy, she had been going over in her head her husband's encouraging gestures during the first days, his words of love after Lulu had been kidnapped, while he had been the one sending her to the Dying Rooms.

The first-class flight attendants, who had doted on her and Lulu, ushered them out before permitting the other passengers to get up and handed Nola's carry-on luggage to Wade's new security men. Wade lurched forward, his eyes shining with delight, and tried to take Nola in his arms.

"Back off," she growled. "Baby killer."

A look of incredulity crossed his face. Nola marched past him, Lulu straddled on her left hip. In the narrow confines of the platform, her body brushed his. His hand clasped her free arm.

"Don't touch me," she sneered.

"The media's waiting for you." He reached a hand to pat down her flyaway hair. "You need to fix your makeup."

She swatted his hand away when Leslie materialized between them. He raised his hands heavenward, mumbling, *"Kua-Lo-ma-lua-waia-ko-numa-ti,"* and there were tears of happiness in his eyes. His new mustache had grown into a reddish bristle. A surge of love went through Nola as her free arm gave him a hug. A moment later, he eased Lulu out of her grasp. "My baby. My baby," he cooed. "My wonderful baby."

Lulu grabbed his nose. Her face was sweetly puffed from long sleep, her straight hair, staticky from the dry air in the plane, stuck out like a daffodil's.

Nola was startled to hear Wade's whisper in her ear. "You've been through a lot. It's okay. I understand." She snapped her head around to see his expression veer into a sympathetic, forgiving smile.

She kicked his shin.

"Ouch!" he cried out, and bent to grab his leg. "You're nuts!"

"I told you to keep away." She took Lulu out of Leslie's arms and strode ahead fifty feet to the first battery of reporters. "We're home," she whispered to Lulu and lifted her for the cameras. "Say hello to our friends. Hello."

Lulu regarded them with eyes full of awe. "Lo." She smiled. "Lo."

Nola wished she could enter their apartment alone, take Lulu through the rooms, and introduce her to the pictures, sculptures, trophies and the panoramic view from her Central Park West penthouse before evening set in. Then she'd shower to rid her skin of the stale-coffee and wet-muffin odor of the airplane. And she'd have that talk with Wade and get it over with. Close another door.

Then she'd open a new one. On her second call to Daniel, she had asked him not to meet her in New York until she cleaned house. Anticipation rose in her whenever she thought of their upcoming rendezvous at the Cloudy River, the two of them alone at the Potomac.

But after the flashbulbs and the microphones at the airport, and the crowds that had filled the terminal and the road outside, carrying well-wishing placards, Nola stood in shock and delight at the sight of a party going on in her home.

Amid magnificent flower arrangements sent by radio and TV stations, concert halls and record-store chains, her staff of a hundred and fifty was supplemented by friends from the entertainment world. Nola scanned the faces of producers, directors, TV and radio hosts, songwriters, actors and singers and former executives of Phonomania Records. "It looks like a 'This Is Your Life' broadcast," she said as she walked among the people who filled her many rooms and the pool area, then poured out onto the huge wraparound terrace, except that there was no one from the first sixteen years of her life. Beverly was dead.

Roberta was there, big-mouthed and big-hipped and big-presenced, who sucked all the air out of the room as she directed cameramen and inner-circle journalists. She also was the vice-queen of the party, bowing to a standing ovation for her role in obtaining political-asylum status for Lulu. Nola made no mention of the fact that, just last week, she had detested the woman who now rode high on the wave of being her closest buddy.

Then came the phone call from Air Force One, and President Corwith asked Nola about her health and that of the baby, congratulated her on behalf of himself and Mrs. C., and told her they'd talk when she came to D.C. about doing some human-rights work. Daniel should have been there to hear this new twist. Or Mauriello, for that matter.

Gabby called, too, blabbering with excitement, crying. She would have flown to New York, but with all those babies and two mares about to give birth…. Nola promised to come out West as soon as her schedule would allow.

As the party flowed, uniformed waiters passed around drinks and finger food while the band and Nola's backup singers performed a medley of songs. Small groups bumped and grinded in a spontaneous dance.

Nola wished they would all just leave. She longed for her forced vacation on the lawn at the Manila embassy, when it was only she and Lulu imitating the birds and playing. When Wade was far away.

"I hope you got a bunch of new songs from your adventure," Jean-Claude told her. "My wonderful Ginger Goddess. I was afraid you'd miss the Grammy."

She winced at his self-centeredness, but then again, he had no more followed his inner music than she had hers. Why carry a grudge over his reluctance to support her cause? Jean-Claude's lunacy—or the pretense of it—served him well. After all, he had managed to get away from the Chinese wrath over her insubordination.

She smiled. "Got an album's worth of new lyrics. 'Gifts Aren't Promises; Touches Aren't Contracts,' and 'Love Is Wanting the Same Things.' And something that goes like 'Let me touch the places where you hurt and I'll be the woman you want me to be.'" She laughed. "And listen to this one. She began to chant. *"Oh, the places I'll go if I choose,/ Let go of the sorrows, let them run loose.* It will be an upbeat number."

"You're fantastique." He grinned and his ears poked out between strands of long hair. "We'll get to work before you lose the ideas? Tonight?"

"Not tonight." Nola motioned to the band, and the music tapered off. Murmurs summoned people to squeeze in from the other rooms. She surveyed the faces and tried to evoke the old euphoria. But the rapture had diminished; it was no longer the oxygen of her being.

Wade stood nearby, his hands clamped under his armpits. He smiled at everyone, as though redefining a new comfort zone in the bosom of friends, employees and business acquaintances.

"I'd like to thank you all for your love and support these past few days—these past many years. Without all of you, I would not have been here or become the person I have," Nola said. Holding her glass of champagne out of Lulu's reach, she raised it and toasted all of them. They were good people who wished her the best.

As she was about to take a small sip, Wade stepped over, put his arm around both her and Lulu, and bent to kiss her.

Nola's throat tightened with anger at this public display. Hadn't he heard her? Courage, she told herself. She had passed worse tests. "You asked for it," she hissed, then wriggling away, she said to the guests, "I hadn't expected this impromptu forum, but I might as well close a window of speculation. I will be filing for divorce."

He gave out a chortle, as though her statement was a silly joke. Recovering, he imitated the swing of a golf club, twisted his body, aimed and hit an imaginary ball. His Chiclets teeth shone too bright.

"No more details yet. It's been thirty hours since I left Manila. I've missed a night's sleep and my body clock is set to tomorrow morning," she explained. "Again, I love you for your support. For being a part of my world."

With Leslie carrying Lulu, Nola walked toward the sweeping, half-circle staircase that led to the top floor.

A wiry man with wavy gray hair and the rugged, tanned skin of a yachtsman stood on the first step, mapping out the party. "That was quite a bombshell," he said when Nola approached.

"Keith!" Nola squealed. "You're here!"

"You were right to bring it up. Even at sea I heard of a rift between you two."

How she had missed the quick, contagious smile that sparkled on his face and disappeared with the same ease. "The greater the trust, the greater the downfall," she said.

"If you need help, please let me know. I mean it. I'll be in New York for a while."

"Thanks." She planted a kiss on his cheek. "I'll call you for lunch as soon as I'm myself again."

She walked up to the first landing, where her skipped heartbeat made the connection before her mind did. At the door to the vast living room stood her mom, except that it was Jenna. Nola clamped a hand over her mouth, remembering on time that Jenna hated public displays.

Jenna ambled over, a reserved smile gracing her beautiful face. Her features hadn't changed much, yet they showed the maturity of twenty-three.

The band started playing again. "Jenna," Nola said, choosing her words as she stepped down again. "Wonderful to see you."

Jenna stopped walking, too far for Nola to try to hug her. "Oh, I thought I'd drop in," she said in that indifferent tone of hers, as if it hadn't been three years since they had last seen each other. She tilted her chin toward Lulu. "So I'm an aunt?"

Nola laughed. It hurt to hold back from falling into Jenna's arms. "What about you? Have you given birth to a novel?"

"A couple of full-length plays." Jenna let out a cryptic laugh.

They walked upstairs into a sitting room and sat on the couch. Nola took Jenna's hand, and Jenna let her hold it, but it was deadweight against Nola's palm. "I'm so happy to see you," Nola said again, wanting to add, "looking well," but figured that Jenna might take it as a value judgment. "Tell me more about the plays."

Jenna chatted for a while. She was living in a small writers' community upstate, she said, and hated the big city, but had to come in to see plays. She asked no questions about Nola, her life, or her singing. Not a single comment about Nola's recent China tour and ordeal. Nola's discomfort grew.

After a while Nola said, "Look, Jenna. I'm truly happy that you are back here, and I hope that you'll stay in my life. However, I'm already on edge trying to tiptoe around you. Your indifference wraps around me like it did just before you left. I'm trying to adjust to something you want, but I'm not sure what it is. What do you want? Why are you here?"

Jenna shrugged. "If it's one and the same for you, I can leave."

"That's not what I said." Nola's voice was soft. "You're still playing psychological games with me, picking up where you left off. I will not fall into this trap. That is not what I need from a sister." She looked into Jenna's eyes. That old defiance was still there, not their mother's hooded, sleepy gaze. "You've hurt me. Whether you want to admit it or not, I did an awful lot for you when there was no one else in the world. I loved you then very much. It did not make up for all your deprivations, but it has defined my life." She thought of giving up Eddie, of her searches among runaway communities, her European debut postponed for more than two years, of the ever-present worry, like an underlying chronic illness. "I made sacrifices, possibly more than many parents would do. For years, I carried the double burden of both our orphanhood. Your pain consumed me, too, while I struggled to crawl out of the hole of my own life. Even today I am still living our past. If you've come here to punish me for everything else that was missing in your life, I will not make myself available. If you've come here to share the good things we can offer each other, then I'm here for you. But you must be here for me too."

For a long stretch, all Nola could hear was their breathing and the muted sounds of the party downstairs. She noticed that Jenna did not get up and leave. A quiver traversed her sister's chin. Then Jenna began to weep quietly. "I've been through so much therapy and I'm finally learning to form relationships. I don't know how to do it, how to start—"

Nola inhaled deeply, fighting the tears springing to her eyes.

Suddenly, Jenna's face crumbled. She fell onto Nola's arms. "I missed you so much."

Leslie had stocked the upstairs kitchenette with baby formula, and Nola went to fetch a bottle. Even though Lulu had been drinking diluted fresh milk, her diapers showed signs that the frequent diet changes disagreed with her.

Nola smiled to herself. Below, a party was going on, and here she was checking a baby's stools and loving it.

"How did your talk with Jenna go?" Leslie asked.

"We're going to a play together next week. It will be nice to see the theater through her eyes." Nola looked around. "How about if we set up the nursery in Wade's study? It's the closest and it's sunny all afternoon."

"I'll have the dark paneling removed and the room redecorated in pastels."

"Only pink," Nola said.

"Pink?"

"If I could, I would have painted all of China pink." She threw herself backward onto the giant bed next to Lulu and let out a luxurious sigh. She scanned the expansive room, taking pleasure in the details of its busy yet balanced clutter, now bathed in orange and gold from the last sunrays of the day. A portable crib had been placed at the side of her bed.

"Thank you, Leslie," she said. "For everything. But mostly for being who you are."

"It's great having you back home."

"It's good to be home," she mumbled, turned and nuzzled Lulu's neck.

"Bommm," Lulu said.

Leslie sat behind Nola and massaged her shoulders and neck. "We need to give thanks to the Hawaiian spirits."

"Why them, of all gods?"

"I summoned them and pleaded for your safety. They've obviously delivered."

She laughed. "Do you really believe in all of these religions? I mean, deep down?"

He shrugged. "All roads lead to one place, and it ain't Rome." He touched the spot below his sternum. "It's right here, and it works."

"I'm not sure my God would agree with all your pagan practices." Nola halted. "It's time I resumed my Jewish studies."

"Until then, shall we use what we have?" He placed Lulu in the crib, motioned Nola to lie on her back on the carpet, and crouched next to her. Gently, he closed her lids, and soon the air swished above her as his hands made broad swimming motions.

"I'm calling to Goddess Amakuas and God Kanaloa," he chanted. By way of explanation he added, "She's the guardian god of each individual, and he's the god of healing." He made a series of hard consonant sounds while massaging Nola's neck and shoulders. His chanting turned to a quiet, long hum. After ten minutes, his palms moved on her body in sweeping outward motions. He took each of her limbs and rattled them. "To rid you of negative energy and poisons," he said.

From her portable crib, Lulu hummed, banging together two plastic teethers.

Nola remained lying on the carpet. The tranquility that settled over her was almost tangible, but it was more from Leslie's ministrations and caring than from the contents of his prayers. "Whatever works. Thanks," she whispered, and opened her eyes. Leslie was again kneeling at her side, his head tilted upward, his eyes closed. A tear rolled down his cheek and glistened in his mustache. She touched his hand. "You're incredible. What would I have done without you?"

His eyes flew open. "You'll need a barracuda of a lawyer."

She burst out laughing and sat up. "I'll make this split as friendly as possible."

"Wade won't go away peacefully. And he controls all your money."

"He can take almost anything he wants. He can't take my voice."

But there was Mauriello's last statement hanging above her head. He would drag her down with the collapse of his China scheme, and there would be no Wade to fight him. With no distribution, no co-op dollars for store advertising, no guest appearances, no promotions to radio stations, no approval for airing music videos on TV, no specials on pay-per-view, no web site and Internet links—and, mostly, no new recordings—her career would come to a screeching halt.

"Why don't you talk to Keith?" Leslie asked. "Let him help during the transition period."

"He doesn't need a job. He landed with a golden parachute when he sold Phonomania."

"At least seek his advice. He adores you."

She touched Leslie's cheek. She had never dared articulate the distrust that had crouched at the edge of her consciousness in the recent weeks of turmoil. "I was afraid someone might lure you away——maybe even extort you—"

He looked away as though listening to faraway music. "I thought that's what the new job offer might be all about."

"What job offer?"

"Oh, some hotshot position at the National Endowment for the Arts. The whole thing was too weird, and my muse told me to ignore Wade."

"Wade?"

"He urged me to consider it."

Nola's seething had the rumble of an old echo. "'Thank you' doesn't describe what I feel—"

"I'll ask Keith to come up."

"Not yet. I'll call him tomorrow."

"Cool. That will give you time to exercise. We'll start easy. Some stretches?"

"May I have a break, please? Lulu and I need a bath, and I still must speak to Wade." She watched Lulu hoisting herself to a sitting position. "Please send everybody home. And keep the staff away from this floor. I want no eavesdropping."

She decided it would be better to have the talk in Wade's suite. If an argument heated up, she'd retreat to her bedroom and lock the connecting door.

When she stepped into Wade's study, he was leaning on the fireplace mantel and poking the empty cavity with the iron. His jabbing released the smell of damp ashes. He turned, and the wild look in his eyes frightened her. "Have you lost your mind?"

"Wade, I—"

"I've made a mistake. Everyone's entitled to one in life. Lord knows you've made some very serious ones. Where are you coming from, to make a statement about a divorce? And without speaking to me first?"

"You set the tone when you forgot to consult with me about a thing or two before we left for China. And while we were there."

"Oh?"

She waved her hand in dismissal. "I have no interest in rehashing things. I'd like to end this marriage amicably."

"I'll give you 'amicably.'" He stepped toward her. In a surprisingly swift move, he got hold of her mane of hair. "Do you think your shit glows in the dark?"

She yelped. "Let go!" Her hand flailed in an attempt to catch her hair below his clutch and release it. But he yanked again, twisting it, and dragged her toward the mirror. He shoved her face sideways against it and locked her head in place. For a few seconds, she was in too much shock and pain to resist.

"Stop it!" she tried to call out, but her cries broke midway.

"You listen to me, little slut," he hissed and gave her hair another yank. "You listen to what I have to say."

She pushed the words out. "Let go, or I'll scream."

He jerked her head further to the side. "No, you won't. There's no one on the floor to hear." His face contorted with fury. She remembered the squashed mouse in the Beijing market. And how he had tried to dispose of Lulu.

"Wade!"

"You've had it too easy!" he yelled. "You have no idea the rare talent it takes to grow and ripen an artist. How many one-hit wonders have you met over the years, never to be heard of again? How many record companies lost interest in an artist—pulled the plug!—and there was no manager to prod them to keep on going? How many managers have dropped the ball on their clients!? How many artists have freaked out or gone on drugs because there was no one to prop them up through difficult times?"

The spray of his saliva hit her cheek. "Do you realize how, with a single misstep—the wrong song, the wrong venue, the wrong outfit—a manager can torpedo a client's career? I forged the way for you. You didn't have to spend years singing at bar mitzvahs or shake your tits at off-off-off Broadway musicals while waiting tables. It was I who traveled alone to godforsaken AM stations, sleeping in cockroach-infested motels and eating shit on muffins for breakfast and shit on pizza for dinner. I paved a shortcut for you directly to Heaven so you could start at the top! Do you think it was easy to get the best lyricists and composers in the country to write smash hits for an unknown teenage punk? And when you insisted on writing your own songs, it was I who pulled Jean-Claude in by his miserable ears and forced him turn your *dreck* into music. I charted your career with no margin of error for mistakes."

In his torrent of words, the grip of his hand loosened. Nola thought of Ming-Ji's words about Daniel, "He don't do it for you. He do it for himself. We all do what we do for ourselves. For what make us happy."

"Let go!" Nola glowered at Wade in the mirror.

He wrenched hard. "Go? I *own* you." His shout was raspy. "I own everything. Before you go I'll see you destroyed. Our contract gives me everything; nothing's in your name. It's all invested and you can't touch it. You'll get not a single one of *my* homes. You can go back to your house in Nissequogue with all those half-breeds and rot there!"

Red-hot iron pierced her skull with rage. "Enough!" she screamed. She twisted and shoved her knee in his groin. He released his clutch, doubled in pain, and sank to the floor.

She stood over him. "I will never lose my home again. You hear? Not my home. Never! You want war? I'll give you war."

His shoulders heaved, and a sob tore from his throat.

Nola's anger melted into pity. She bent and touched his back. Her hand flattened his errant hair. "I'm sorry," she was about to say, but checked herself. "We had a great ride. You were a wonderful partner. Now it's over."

She walked to the door, closed it behind her, and locked it. In her bedroom, she sat in the chair by the window for a long time, staring at the city's flickering lights. Home.

Chapter 42

Nola wore flat shoes, buckskin pants and a blue blazer, and a pair of diamond studs in her ears. Her hair was down, unteased, and her face clean of makeup. One look in the mirror had told her that the fever burning in her cheeks was all the blush she needed.

"*Through your eyes I'm a better person,*" she hummed to the chugged rhythm of the helicopter while she looked down at the Long Island Sound. She smiled at Lulu in her carrier buckled into the seat beside her. "How do you like this song? *I look at myself in the mirror of your eyes, and love what you see,*" she went on, testing the lyrics. "No. *The me you see....*"

"Me-see-" Lulu said.

"Thanks. 'The me you see' it will be. It's inspired by Daniel. We'll fly to see him later at the Potomac, okay?" She kissed the top of Lulu's head. "*Through your eyes I'm a better person,*" she hummed. Regardless of Wade's put-down, the song would come out in a cohesive form—the lyrics, the beat, the tempo—even before Jean-Claude arranged the music.

Wade. His behavior bristled in her, underlined by sadness and pity. It was an ending.

The helicopter landed on the west lawn overlooking the Sound. She asked the nanny Leslie had hired—a Hong Kong-born pediatric nurse with a degree in early education—to take Lulu for a stroll on the grounds of the estate, but to keep away from the cliff.

Nola stood facing the Connecticut shoreline. A quivering chevron of geese in V formation passed above, emitting garbled shrieks. Nola looked down at the beach, and her lips moved in a silent good-bye to her parents. "*Yit'gadal ve-yit'kadash sh'mey raba,*" she chanted, one of the earlier prayers she had studied, the *Kaddish* for the dead. The time had come to excise the sorrow.

Turning away, she followed the overgrown path through the woods to the spot where her family's cottage had been. In all the years she had visited the big house, she had never come here. Now only the foundation and parts of the flooring remained, a dwelling for rats. Autumn leaves had piled up around the crevices.

Nola stood in the center of the empty rectangle. A lifetime ago, the issue of money had rarely come up among aging hippies. "We're rich in love," she could hear her mother and father say, "we share love with humanity." She trembled at the absurdity of the words. Many former sixties radicals had thrown away their beads, brushed the dust off their college diplomas, and gone on to productive, stable lives, while her parents refused to grow up, to care for their children. Had her mother's Jewish parents been damaged by wars and persecution? She would never know. Losing her parents meant questions to which there would never be any answers, except that she had seen destructive fingers that had pushed through the muck of history to poke at Jenna too.

The old oak that had shaded their kitchen porch, where her mother had once worked on her shoe collages, was now enormous, and its roots bulged from the earth. Nola sat on a massive root the size of a man's thigh, breathed in the dusty smell of dry leaves, and stared at the wreckage that remained of her parents' lives.

Her feet kicked at leaves as she walked to the spot where the old barn had been. An apple tree had taken root in dry manure and grown wild. Its rotting fruit smelled too sweet, too pungent, and drew hordes of tiny flies. Nola thought of her father's unfulfilled dream of a ranch in Colorado. She heard once again the roar of his motorcycle and for a split second, she was the little girl under the covers, falling asleep at that sound of his return from a gig, secure for the last time in the knowledge that he was home.

Her hands flew up to her chest. She suddenly identified that roar as it segued into a bass string, into that dreaded tremble in her head whenever she was alone, her grottoes of loneliness.

She returned to the oak tree and pressed her forehead into the trunk. The rough bark pockmarked her skin. Her arms encircled the tree as warm, bitter tears burst through a dam.

Another flock of geese shrieked above her head. Nola released her grip on the tree, feeling cleansed and complete. No more crying. Without looking back at the remnants of her former home, she strolled toward the path leading to the big house. At its end would be Lulu.

Just before reaching the first line of trees, Nola heard the scrunching of leaves and the rustle of breaking twigs from the path she had taken from the cliff. Daniel emerged, carrying Lulu.

Nola's eyes locked with his. His eyes sparkled green, or perhaps it was a reflection of the color in his shirt. Lulu, holding a stuffed toy kitten, prattled into the furry face and tasted one ear.

The day was so bright and sunny that the red and orange of the oaks, elms and maples shimmered all around them. Nola took a step forward, and Daniel wrapped her in his free arm. For a moment, neither moved, and she savored the clean smell of his skin. Her head sang with the significance of the moment.

Lulu's fidgeting brought her back. "I was planning to meet you later at the Far-Off Cloudy River." She laughed.

"We didn't say a proper good-bye." He lowered his face to hers and kissed her. His lips were dry and warm, just as she had thought they would be. "I wanted to come get the two of you."

"Da-da," Lulu said.

His arm around Nola tightened. "If your mom will have me, that is," he said to Lulu.

Nola felt her heart beating against his. "Yes, she will." She tasted his lips again.

Lulu chose to stay in Daniel's arms as Nola took him on a tour of the big house and its facilities. She had added an indoor swimming pool on the east side to give the children year-round exercise. Two deserted rooms on the top floor had been converted into classrooms for tutoring. "My orphanage," she told Daniel. "The Beverly Cutter Home. Named after the woman who didn't let me sink."

After leaving Lulu in Leslie's and the nanny's care, she led Daniel down to the beach.

The storms had gouged a new cave several feet away from the old one. "This is the place where my story begins," she said, hearing the echo of her voice reverberating against the rock around her. "And where it ends."

"And where it begins again." He kissed her, at first tenderly, then, with her ardent response, more demanding.

There was hunger in his body, an urgency more intense than she had expected to find. When he laid her on his jacket, she looked up at his face, and for the first time it had lost its poise. Veins pulsated in his temples, but his eyes were soft as he kept them locked on her. She gasped and held on to his back, kneading the harnessed strength of his muscles and feeling the rippling skin just as she had dreamed.

He kissed her again and again, nibbling, tasting, exploring her body, and his life opened up to her with a force that left them both out of breath. All this controlled power, she thought, as she arched and bucked and lost herself, was his gift to her.

Afterward, they lay on their strewn clothes.

"I've been waiting for this since the evening in the Beijing apartment." Daniel kissed her face. "When Harry Wu kept you company for the night, I wanted it to be me."

Nola laughed into his collarbone. "A woman coming into herself, you said."

"You were a brave, beautiful human being."

"I want you to know that I've also found religion, in the sense that I plan to go back to Jewish traditions," she added.

"I understand where you're coming from." He smiled. "I've been studying *kabala*."

She giggled. "You and Madonna." Her fingers sifted the soft, cool powder. She would stay here, in this moment, forever. She had time. They had time. She thought about her quest for the spiritual nature of the universe. "Ming-Ji said that 'love is to want the same things.' "

"What do you want?" he whispered.

"Us."

"I want us to love each other. To be a family." He spoke into her lips, the rush of air tingling as he added, "To work together toward the same goals. Is that wanting the same things?"

Coming up from the beach, Nola was surprised to see Keith's lanky figure perched on the railing at the top landing. He was dressed in worn jeans, a plaid shirt and sneakers.

"What are you doing here?" she asked.

"Leslie said you'd be here." His smile instantly wrapped her in its warmth. He looked from her to Daniel and back.

"I'm sorry. I didn't expect you to come all the way out—I mean, I meant to call you later—Never mind; I'm blabbering. Thank you for coming. You shouldn't have troubled yourself—"

She introduced the two men. "I'll be with Lulu," Daniel said. He shook Keith's hand and departed.

"Don't be upset with Leslie, but last night he was worried about your 'tiff' with Wade and called me," Keith said as soon as they were alone. "I've scheduled a couple of lawyers to come here later." He unfolded a document bound in a baby-blue cover. "In the meantime, this is a request for a temporary exclusive right to your apartment. Sign here, and we'll get Wade to pack a few shirts and find a place where he can terrorize someone else."

For a moment, Nola was at a loss for words. "I want to tone things down—and get out of the marriage."

"But he wants you crushed."

She sighed.

"The courts don't look favorably on managers who take hold of their clients' portfolios, even if they happen to be married to them," Keith said. "By tomorrow, all his assets in the U.S. and abroad will be frozen. After that, he'll negotiate all right, or he won't be able to move a single stock or cash a single check—or tip the bellboy, for that matter—until the two of you have reached an agreement."

"Keith, there are no words to express how much your friendship means to me at a time like this—"

He nested her hands between his palms. His hands were big and warm. "When Wade first brought you to me and I decided to cut your first record, it was no gamble. You were fantastic. I saw in you the same things he did. You were an incredibly determined little kid, sweet, yet haunted by the need to succeed. I've watched you work hard and develop as an artist. I've lost great singers who handled the pressure by snorting or shooting up. Nothing spoiled you."

She began to stroll toward the shade of the trees. She wished she could be with Daniel. There was so much to talk about. "Why would you get involved in our divorce? It's sure to get ugly," she asked Keith.

"I like you, you need me, and now that I am big—okay, only figuratively—I have the luxury to play in whichever sandbox I want." He stopped and put both his hands on her arms. "While I have no vested interest in your finances, I know you, I know Wade, I know Mauriello, and I know the music industry. I have no hidden agenda, but with the position presumably open, I'd like to become your manager."

"But you've retired!"

"Let me tell you a secret: Retirement sucks. Sailing makes my wife seasick, and anyway, it's too much work with gizmos and ropes. I babysit for my grandchildren once a week, which is plenty. I can invest my money only in so many companies before I become mired in their corporate nonsense, but at fifty-six, I'm not prepared to start growing tomatoes instead. Working with you will be good for me, put me back in the neighborhood where I grew up."

She threw her arms around him. "I'm thrilled. Oh, Keith—I've missed you."

"I owe you. Unlike Wade, who put all his eggs into your basket, as a record company, your success helped us build a stable of great recording artists. Hey, I sold the company for a bundle!"

"I'm trying to forget the Wade of last night and think of the man who took care of me when no one else did." Nola led Keith to a bench by the trees, facing the water. "I owe it to him to be decent, even if he's not."

"That's what I meant about you. Unspoiled. Half your joint property and your *mucho* thanks. Is that your bottom line?"

The lingering delight from Daniel's lovemaking blended with a gust of sadness. "That's fair. Neither one of us could have done it without the other. But what about future income? Half the royalties of anything that's out there?"

Keith took his Palm Pilot out of the shirt pocket and entered some notes. "He'll want a bite out of *all* your future earnings. He'll claim they're generated based upon past success." He looked up. "That will entitle him to review your income sources and question every expense."

"No way." She shook her head. "I'm going on the road without him. How much will it cost to buy him out?"

"Wade has made some very shrewd investments, because he's keyed me in to some deals. Without looking at the books, I'd estimate that with your share you'll be able to buy him out."

Nola peeked at the noon sky. The blue pulsated. "I must keep my New York apartment. Calculate it within my half."

The Sound was calm, with tiny ripples of white foam, like bridal lace. On the mansion's front lawn, Lulu held court from her stroller. Daniel, Leslie, the nanny and half-a-dozen teenage residents of the house sat in a circle at her feet. Nola longed to feel Daniel's body again. She wanted to twirl around the lawn and sing, to sweep Lulu and Daniel in her dance. She felt alive.

"She's star material," Keith said about Lulu.

Nola chuckled. "It took her half a second to capture my heart." She slouched deeper on the bench, her legs stretched forward. "As soon as you can release my foundation, please find a clandestine way to transfer a million dollars to China."

He looked at her quizzically.

"There's a friend—a woman doctor—who does good work. I want to help her causes. I'll send more after we see if she can manage it without her government getting upset."

How many babies would Ming-Ji help cure with this money? How many political prisoners' lives could be bought? It occurred to Nola that the money might cause adverse results. Corrupted local officials in out-of-control provinces might arrest innocent people on trumped-up charges of insubordination, because they'd know it to be a source of easy money. She'd talk it over with Daniel.

"The problem I see now is to get you working again. And very soon," Keith said, bringing her back. "Industry rumors are that BRW—in the form of a pissed-off George Mauriello—has put a freeze on marketing your music. I've checked their website. Your name is no longer listed, and your CDs are 'out of stock' on Amazon and other music sellers."

"Maybe it's not a bad idea for me to take time off to get my personal affairs in order," she said, weighing it all as she spoke: Wade, Daniel, Lulu, against the urgency of babies dying in China right that moment.

"You've just touched the height of your career. It's not a good idea to be thrown out of circulation. Six weeks can feel like six months to the minds and ears of listeners," Keith said. "We'll hire a PR agency specializing in corporate relations to put pressure on BRW's board. The next meeting is coming up in a week. There's no reason shareholders would forgo the enormous profits you generate, especially following—or in the aftermath of—the China tour, in order to support Mauriello's little snit."

"He will convince them it's worth destroying me from a corporate synergy point of view," she said. "According to him, appeasing the Chinese will create huge marketing opportunities for other segments of the BRW empire—the fast-food chain, the theme parks and projects involving StarVision. And there are intangible political benefits—Mauriello's credibility, for one—which I have botched."

"We need a decisive end game to this drama," Keith said.

"Good," she said. "I want to become the voice of China's murdered babies. More than shareholders' board and courts, I need to marshal grassroots support. That's where my power is. There's a wave of sympathy for me and Lulu, and it can reinforce my standing against BRW—and against a government that deserts its most needy citizens." She indicated that she wanted to use his cell phone. "Let's see what Roberta can cook up this time."

"I'm in a cab and stuck in traffic next to MOMA and there's a bunch of religious fanatics blocking the street because of this art exhibition defiling Jesus," Roberta reported. Nola heard chanting and blaring horns. "What a delicious idea: to burn in hell for taking a lookie-look at a doodoo-covered Son of God."

"Listen. Phonomania will not record 'Flower Babies' any time soon—or release its license to another distributor. Something about Mauriello being pissed off at me."

Nola barely finished her sentence when a deep groan broke at the other end. For a split second she was afraid Roberta was being attacked by a zealot who recognized her, then a series of guttural sounds revealed she was having one of her fake orgasms. "An encore. Ahhhh. I'm coming. Ah, ah, ahhhhh."

Moans bred grunts and a scream. A yell from what sounded like an enraged Arab taxi driver. Roberta's hearty laughter. An exchange punctuated by a flood of curses. A door slammed.

"Roberta, are you still there? In one piece?" Next to Nola, Keith shook with laughter.

Another gutsy laugh from the other end of the line. "I was thrown out of the cab! But it was worth it. Wow again for your great new twist. What do you say we have listeners picket BRW's corporate offices?"

Nola smiled into the phone. "That's what I had in mind. Do you think a short boycotting of BurgerRanch would be overkill?" At her side, Keith gave a thumbs-up.

"As in 'wrench bench BurgerRanch?'" Roberta asked. "Juicy, juicy. Let's call Oprah, Katie Couric and Barbara Walters. We'll give the scoop to the one who gets us on her show first. You're hot. I'm sure Larry King would interview you as soon as tonight. No need to go to Washington, D.C. He can arrange a studio interview."

"Actually, I was planning on being in his neighborhood." And spending a night with Daniel. "I'll ask Keith Schwartz to arrange it; he's my manager now—"

"Schwartzie-boy! Good guy. How did you drag him out of retirement? Never mind; you'll make me jealous with all the erotic details. But you still need a good publicity agent at once. Someone of my caliber to twist Mauriello's big brass balls. Wasn't he the one who once said, 'Fools are the reason why there are smart people in the world?' "

"Sounds like something he'd say. Let him try and make you deny it."

Roberta laughed. "Hey, what happened to the Little Red Riding Hood I know?"

"I've become a she-wolf. That's what a fifteen-pound baby can do to you. You should give it a try."

"Me, it might turn me into an angel. It wouldn't work." Roberta paused. "Believe it or not, I'm comfortable in my own rolls of flesh. Only thing missing in my life is a good daily fuck, especially now that I don't have direct access to your bodyguards. Or, rather, they don't have direct access to me." She sighed. "How's that Yoram? Could go on all night—"

Keith shifted away and rolled his eyes.

"I've become a poor risk for the insurance company," Nola said. "It's okay. I'm hiring bodyguards loyal to me, not to someone else."

"'Atta girl."

For a moment, with the horns blowing and the people chanting in the background, Nola gathered her thoughts. She, too, felt great inhabiting her own vessel, filling it with her rediscovered self. Maybe now she and Roberta could become friends.

She finally spoke. "I've never thanked you properly for your help."

"Hey, it's all about ratings. Thanks for giving me the lead on another good story."

Nola hung up. She felt a wide grin stretching the sides of her mouth. "Phew! I never imagined I could manage without Wade." She rose to her feet and kissed Keith's cheek. "There's a real life I must live."

She walked away toward Lulu and Daniel.

THE END

Acknowledgments:

This book could not have been written without the advice, insight and support of many, starting with Bruce Morrow ("Cousin Brucie") for his valuable music industry information. Emily White lent her creative mind during our hikes, while Sandi Bloomberg helped write the song "Flower Babies."

My writing group offered instrumental input and focus: Judy Epstein, Linda Davies, Anna Elman, Sue Anderson, and the late Ruth Nedbor, all of whom accompanied me on this journey with their unflagging support.

I thank the fascinating, valiant Chinese women I first met during the 1995 International Women's Conference in Beijing and in the ensuing weeks of traveling the countryside. Risking their positions as university professors, industry directors, or budding entrepreneurs, they shared with me their knowledge, customs—and apprehensions—as I shared my jars of American peanut butter. Their courage inspired me to pursue this project in the succeeding years while writers Ming Mei Yip and Xuya Chen, along with their internet compatriots, answered my questions on all things Chinese.

Filmmaker Brian Woods exposed the systematic neglect of abandoned babies in Chinese state-run orphanages. His 1995 BBC documentary, "The Dying Rooms," opened my eyes to human cruelty I could never have imagined.

David S., formerly with the National Security Administration, Herbert L., US State Department, and Sheila H., FBI, gave me insiders' views into U.S.-China relations, supplemented by fellow writer Michael G. from the Foreign Service. Special acknowledgment is owed authors Richard Bernstein and Ross H. Munro for their book, "The Coming Conflict with China" (Vintage Books, 1998).

Throughout the long process of taming the many complex issues of politics, economics, human-rights and the music industry into a multi-layered work of fiction, I studied under illustrious writers who were generous with their attentions: Alice McDermott, Tony Earley and Susan Shreve.

Then came the patient readers of partial or entire drafts: Kira Becker Kay, Mary Smitham, Cheryl Carner, Barbara Hoppe, Tad Wojnicki, Jody Pryor, Dorly Weitzen and Wendy Lestina, followed by readers/editors:

Elizabeth Sacks, Sands Hall, Annie Blachley, Lou Aronica and Carol Rial (who ended adopting a Chinese baby).

Throughout the vicissitudes of birthing a novel, my agent, Elizabeth Pomada, kept her trust in me and in China Doll. Her faith has been the fuel that brought me—and you, the reader—here.

My daughter Eden Yariv-Goldberg, has been my pop music advisor, while my daughter Tomm Miller supplied pop-culture details.

And finally, as always, there is Ron, the soul of everything I do, who makes it possible for me to spread my wings and fly as far as China or nestle in a place as near as my own heart.

To read author interview, photo articles relating to China's infanticide, Q & A about China Doll, lyrics for Nola's songs, and recent book reviews, please check the author's website at
www.TaliaCarner.com

To order books at a discount for your reading group, please contact the publisher at
www.MecoxHudson.com

Reading Group Guide

1. Nola's bond with Lulu is instantaneous. What in Nola's background has set this relationship in motion? Do you have experience with forming such an immediate, unflagging parent-child bond?

2. Many performing artists are married to their managers. Bring some examples. Why might it be? What is Nola and Wade's marriage based on?

3. Discuss how Nola and Wade's relationship evolved from the time they first met until it unraveled. Where did it go wrong? Was Wade's love for Nola genuine at first? Did he still love her at the end? Could Nola have changed the course of their relationship? Could Wade? If so, how?

4. Wade is efficient, capable, and ambitious. He gets along with both staff and business contacts. When Lulu upsets his world, can you sympathize with his refusal to adopt? What, if anything, in his behavior alerted you to his dark side?

5. Discuss the extent to which everyone surrounding Nola has their own agenda. Besides Wade, what are Roberta's, Jean-Claude's, Leslie's and even Dr. Ming-Ji Liang's and Daniel's? Do any of these agendas evolve as the story develops? How?

6. Daniel is quoted as saying, "China feeds its people. With 22% percent of the planet's population and only seven percent of the arable land, this is quite a feat." Yet he and many critics consider that with its harsh policy, China creates pressure for female infanticide. How would you strike the balance?

7. Ambassador Ashford says "...we can't barge in with our Judeo-Christian mores, judge this country by our values, and meddle in their affairs." Should the United States take a stronger stand on the issue of Chinese female infanticide? If it means giving asylum to a million babies and to their coerced mothers each year would you still feel the same?

8. Nola's childhood was traumatic. To what extent do you blame her parents? To what extent were these events her fault? Discuss her reluctance to blame her parents. Do you find it surprising that she was able to let go of her anger and resentment?

9. Discuss the complex relationship between Nola and her sister Jenna over the years. Do you think Nola would have done more or less had she not felt responsible for disfiguring Jenna? Was she too patient, enabling her sister to remain disturbed or addicted?

10. Nola decides to use her celebrity status—and her voice—to tell the world about China's neglected and murdered infants. Discuss specific celebrities and how they use their fame to publicize issues close to their hearts. Do their messages really bring change in a meaningful way, or are celebrities exploiting social, environmental, religious or political issues for mere publicity? Do you think they should only put on a good show, be paid for their performance, and leave?

11. Beverly Cutter, a teacher, took Nola under her wing and gave her the security and guidance. But what if there had been no such special teacher in Nola's life? Would the mute old man have been enough had Nola been left in the care of Mini-Nazi or in a group home? Do you know a teacher who made a profound difference in a student's life?

12. Ambassador Ashford and George Mauriello attempt to thwart Nola in her mission to save Lulu. Are they heartless villains? Are they simply doing their jobs? What would you do in that position? Could either have acted differently?

13. Discuss "containment" vs. "engagement" policies. Which, do you believe, is more effective? Given what you have read here and possibly elsewhere, do you believe the U.S. and China are on a collision course?

14. "China Doll" is the name Daniel Chen refers to Nola prior to knowing her and before she evolves and learns to assert herself. What is it about him that attracts her? How does he challenge her and why he then offers only limited help along the way? How does she rise to become the kind of woman he admires?

15. Please read about The Dying Rooms controversy on the author's website and discuss whether a novel such as *China Doll* (as well as the photo articles about fatal neglect of babies) may upset the delicate diplomatic balance that adoption agencies and the US government try to maintain. Do you think that *China Doll* or other such reports and stories should not be written?